The O. Henry Prize Stories 2014

The O. Henry
Prize Stories
2014

Chosen and with an Introduction by
Laura Furman

With Essays by Jurors
Tash Aw
James Lasdun
Joan Silber
on the Stories They Admire Most

Anchor Books
A Division of Random House LLC
New York

AN ANCHOR BOOKS ORIGINAL, SEPTEMBER 2014

Anchor Books Trade Paperback ISBN: 978-0-345-80731-1
eBook ISBN: 978-0-345-80732-8

www.anchorbooks.com

Printed in the United States of America
10 9 8 7 6 5 4

To Willard Spiegelman

The staff of Anchor Books in every department is devoted to publishing excellent books and publishing them well. Their intelligence, dedication, and professional skill make it an honor to work with them. Diana Secker Tesdell shows the series editor each year how it's done.

Taylor Flory Ogletree was the editorial assistant for *The O. Henry Prize Stories 2014*. The series editor is grateful to her for her steadiness, kindness, and sharpness.

The graduate school and Department of English of the University of Texas at Austin supports *The O. Henry Prize Stories* in many ways, and the series editor expresses her gratitude.

—LF

Publisher's Note

A BRIEF HISTORY OF THE
O. HENRY PRIZE STORIES

Many readers have come to love the short story through the simple characters, easy narrative voice and humor, and compelling plotting in the work of William Sydney Porter (1862–1910), best known as O. Henry. His surprise endings entertain readers, even those back for a second, third, or fourth look. Even now one can say "Gift of the Magi" in a conversation about a love affair or marriage, and almost any literate person will know what is meant. It's hard to think of many other American writers whose work has been so incorporated into our national shorthand.

O. Henry was a newspaperman, skilled at hiding from his editors at deadline. A prolific writer, he wrote to make a living and to make sense of his life. He spent his childhood in Greensboro, North Carolina, his adolescence and young manhood in Texas, and his mature years in New York City. In between Texas and New York, he served out a prison sentence for bank fraud in

Columbus, Ohio. Accounts of the origin of his pen name vary: One story dates from his days in Austin, where he was said to call the wandering family cat "Oh! Henry!"; another states that the name was inspired by the captain of the guard at the Ohio State Penitentiary, Orrin Henry.

Porter had devoted friends, and it's not hard to see why. He was charming and had an attractively gallant attitude. He drank too much and neglected his health, which caused his friends concern. He was often short of money; in a letter to a friend asking for a loan of $15 (his banker was out of town, he wrote), Porter added a postscript: "If it isn't convenient, I'll love you just the same." His banker was unavailable most of Porter's life. His sense of humor was always with him.

Reportedly, Porter's last words were from a popular song: "Turn up the light, for I don't want to go home in the dark."

Eight years after O. Henry's death, in April 1918, the Twilight Club (founded in 1883 and later known as the Society of Arts and Letters) held a dinner in his honor at the Hotel McAlpin in New York City. His friends remembered him so enthusiastically that a group of them met at the Biltmore Hotel in December of that year to establish some kind of memorial to him. They decided to award annual prizes in his name for short-story writers and formed a committee of award to read the short stories published in a year and to pick the winners. In the words of Blanche Colton Williams (1879–1944), the first of the nine series editors, the memorial was intended to "strengthen the art of the short story and to stimulate younger authors."

Doubleday, Page & Company was chosen to publish the first volume, *O. Henry Memorial Award Prize Stories 1919*. In 1927 the society sold all rights to the annual collection to Doubleday, Doran & Company. Doubleday published *The O. Henry Prize Stories*, as it came to be known, in hardcover, and from 1984 to 1996 its subsidiary, Anchor Books, published it simultaneously in paperback. Since 1997 *The O. Henry Prize Stories* has been published as an original Anchor Books paperback.

HOW THE STORIES ARE CHOSEN

All stories originally written in the English language and published in an American or Canadian periodical are eligible for consideration. Individual stories may not be nominated; magazines must submit the year's issues in their entirety by July 1. Editors are invited to submit online fiction for consideration. Such submissions must be sent to the series editor in hard copy. (Please see pp. 357–58 for details.)

As of 2003, the series editor chooses the twenty O. Henry Prize Stories, and each year three writers distinguished for their fiction are asked to evaluate the entire collection and to write an appreciation of the story they most admire. These three writers receive the twenty prize stories in manuscript form with no identification of author or publication. They make their choices independent of one another and the series editor.

The goal of *The O. Henry Prize Stories* remains to strengthen the art of the short story.

To Alice Munro

The announcement was made on October 10, 2013: Canadian short-story writer Alice Munro was the Nobel laureate in Literature. A great many writers and readers were elated at the news, perhaps feeling that they were part of the happy moment. The glory wasn't Alice Munro's alone but that of the short story as well.

The Swedish Academy's permanent secretary, Peter Englund, said, "She has taken an art form, the short story, which has tended to come a little bit in the shadow behind the novel, and she has cultivated it almost to perfection."

Alice Munro has long contrasted the short story and the novel.

"For years and years, I thought that stories were just practice, till I got time to write a novel. Then I found that they were all I could do, and so I faced that. I suppose that my trying to get so much into stories has been a compensation."

When she was told the news of her Nobel, she said, "I would really hope this would make people see the short story as an important art, not just something you played around with until you got a novel."

In financial terms, the short story is the weak sister, more like an even less remunerative literary form, poetry, than like the novel. In the book-publishing world, the norm is that story collections get smaller advances than novels. Few magazines pay much, if anything, for a short story. Perhaps the short story's place in the novel's shadow is in part due to its lower earnings.

In the end, though, the money doesn't really count. The argument, if there is one, about which form is superior and which is inferior doesn't matter as much as the quality of the individual work.

Alice Munro's body of work is superb, and it's been the honor of *The O. Henry Prize Stories* to include her work time and again. For her readers, her Nobel Prize is a validation of the profound and vivid experience of reading her work.

Congratulations, Alice Munro. You did all you could, and we're grateful. Thank you for the stories.

Contents

Introduction

The mission since 1919 of *The O. Henry Prize Stories* has been to encourage the art of the short story. By calling attention to their gifts, we encourage short-story writers. When we put a story between book covers, we give it a longer life and a wider readership.

Because each story's crucial first publication was in a magazine (print or online), we list the magazines that have submitted their short fiction in the back of each collection (pp. 358–77). We hope that with the information provided, new readers will find and enjoy the magazines and perhaps subscribe to one or two. These days, a reader also has the opportunity to be a patron of the arts and donate to a magazine, which helps keep the little magazines alive.

Some of the listed magazines are not struggling. *The New Yorker* publishes fiction weekly and has a sterling history of cultivating and supporting writers over the long haul, as does *Harper's*. But some fit the classic notion of a little magazine: circulation well under one thousand, inventive design, eccentric and centrist fiction published side by side. *Noon,* for example, is an annual always filled with challenging fiction and always a pleasure to see and hold.

Some excellent magazines—*Granta, Tin House, Narrative,* and *The American Reader*, founded in September 2012—are brought into being by the vision and ambition of private benefactors. *Tin House* is a rare literary magazine that's a commercial success. American nonprofit magazines with 501(c)(3) status such as *A Public Space* are eligible for support from the National Endowment for the Arts, a perennial pincushion when it comes to federal funding. *The Threepenny Review* publishes consistently readable and challenging essays, poetry, and fiction with the support of "subscriber-donors," whose subscriptions make up about 35 percent of the annual budget, along with their donations (40 percent), according to editor Wendy Lesser. The rest of the broadsheet's funding comes from grants, advertising, single-copy sales, and digital sales. *Narrative* (and NarrativeMagazine.com) is the product of its two editors, Carol Edgarian and Tom Jenks, who supported it themselves at first and gradually built a board, an advisory council, and a base of donors.

Many magazines are funded by public and private academic institutions. Shrinking state budgets may put a magazine in mortal danger, as those in charge question whether a small magazine is the best use of public funding. Does it aid the institution as, say, a winning football team does? Measuring the value of art, not to mention the value of prestige, is a trickier score to keep than that of the Cotton Bowl. Still, some institutions, private and public, continue year after year to support the magazines that give established and new writers a chance. In recent years, *Ecotone* has emerged as a solidly interesting magazine. The Publishing Laboratory of the creative writing department at the University of North Carolina Wilmington founded the magazine in 2005 and also supports its small press, Lookout Books. *New England Review* was founded in 1978 at Middlebury College, a small liberal-arts school in Vermont. *New Orleans Review* (1968) is sponsored by the English Department of Loyola University, New Orleans, and *Subtropics* by the University of Florida. Since 1915, *Southwest Review* has been Southern Methodist University's pride. The exquisite *Southern Review* is supported by Louisiana State University.

Many little magazines seek help from donors, joining schools, hospitals, scientific research institutions, museums, and a myriad of organizations that do not make a profit but add immeasurably to our lives. Your subscriptions to such magazines help keep them alive. The editors and staff of little magazines don't enjoy big salaries. Some have no salaries at all. They work with such devotion because the idea of publishing new literary work is a powerful motivation, profit or no profit. The real success of a magazine lies in the quality of the work chosen and published.

This year's jurors are Tash Aw, James Lasdun, and Joan Silber, all previous O. Henry winners. Each read a blind manuscript and chose a favorite without consultation with one another or me. In the "Reading *The O. Henry Prize Stories 2014*" section (pp. 333–38), you'll find their essays.

Years ago, my family drove to Colorado for a break from the Central Texas summer. We'd brought way too much stuff, and our rented Aztek was weighed down by the extra container on its roof. On the way, I got gasoline on my favorite white shirt and parted with it. Along Highway 90, still in Texas, we slept in a dank cement-block motel with mold-filled air-conditioning. But when we reached the rented house in Gunnison, where we could finally stop traveling, instead of flinging open the car doors and escaping, we stayed in the Aztek so we could keep listening to the audio recording of Mark Haddon's novel *The Curious Incident of the Dog in the Night-Time*. Haddon's story in this collection, "The Gun," was chosen by juror Tash Aw as his favorite. One quality the story shares with the novel is Haddon's ability to involve the reader in the improbable, sometimes confounding events of his characters' lives.

The relationship between the two boys whose adventure forms the bulk of the action isn't profound. They are together and then they part, for many reasons and with some feeling, all unstated. Their nonchalant friendship leaves both boys unprepared for the arbitrary violence and emotion to come. "The Gun" is a story made up of curious incidents that, when put together with Haddon's skill, bring the characters so close that the action of the story seems to have happened to us.

The primary relationship in "Pétur" by Olivia Clare is between mother and son, in Iceland to celebrate the mother's birthday. They, and the reader, are in a realm of "unworldly weather." The story streams past unfamiliar words such as *fjalls* and *hrossagaukur*, and a weather report—"ash from Eyjafjallajökull"—before we're sure exactly who and where the characters are. Our ignorance is dispensed with abruptly:

> Adam was a data systems analyst. He was thirty-six. He lived in a one-bedroom apartment in Palo Alto, where Laura was, in a house she'd once shared with Adam's father on the other side of town. Iceland for two weeks had been her idea for her birthday. She'd just turned sixty-one, and she'd told Adam she didn't believe it, and he shouldn't, either. She'd said, You look in the mirror and acknowledge you're as old as you like. She felt nineteen, mostly. She looked fifty.

Mother and son, on vacation in a land of ash and icebabies, are introduced with quite a few numbers (thirty-six, one, two, sixty-one, nineteen, fifty). We've been given what looks like information, though the numbers urge us to pause, add, and subtract before we go on. This odd timing is a risk for the author. Short-story beginnings are crucial, and often writers take great trouble to be as clear and simple as possible to usher the reader into the story. Clare does the opposite, giving her reader firm ground to stand on and then taking it away. The passage of the mother's birthday and the spooky volcanic ash falling everywhere seem like part of the same unpredictable event. The reader is then immersed in what is most important in "Pétur": the characters' knowledge and ignorance of each other; the transformation of a woman from a mildly negligent mother into a woman either unhinged or unloosed in her own new reality. The reader watches the son as he watches his mother drift further from him than ever before.

The sisters in "Opa-locka" by Laura van den Berg are linked, like survivors of the same plane crash. (Joan Silber chose "Opa-locka" as her favorite, p. 337–38.) The sisters' closeness is their bedrock. As the story opens, they're working as private detectives, observing the movements of a possibly adulterous husband from a rooftop. They also search, perennially, for their father, who's a disappointment whether absent or present. The slow revelation of their past and future winds through "Opa-locka" while the reader waits for the solution to the story's mystery. Surely, the deep sadness that haunts the story isn't for their client, her wandering husband, or even for Mozart's Don Giovanni, who makes a surprise appearance in Van den Berg's story.

In "Nemecia" by Kirstin Valdez Quade, the narrator, Maria, tells us that her cousin Nemecia lived with her family because her own mother, Maria's aunt Benigna, "couldn't care for her. Later, when Aunt Benigna recovered . . . , Nemecia had already lived with us for so long that she stayed. This was not unusual in our New Mexico town in those years between the wars; if someone died, or came upon hard times, or simply had too many children, there were always aunts or sisters or grandmothers with room for an extra child."

Yet it isn't Nemecia who grows up as an "extra child," but Maria. The ravenous and dramatic Nemecia is the child indulged and favored by the adults. She terrifies Maria and tortures her in a variety of ways, yet when Nemecia turns sixteen and has bigger fish to fry than her little cousin, Maria finds that "instead of relief, [she feels] emptiness." For Maria, Nemecia is glamorous and tragic; Maria's envy of her cousin begins to poison her life. A family secret, distorted by Nemecia, is the basis of Maria's lifetime imprisonment in the family. Nemecia moves to California, renames herself "Norma," and lives with her mother, brother, and stepfather in a house where Spanish is never spoken. Nemecia/Norma is free to reinvent herself, while Maria is cursed by her search for the truth and by her envious need for her nemesis.

Another pair of girls, Uzoamaka, the narrator, and Eno, the daughter of a family servant, are at the center of Chinelo Okparanta's "Fairness." Both Eno and her mother have fair skin, while Uzoamaka and her school friends have skin "the color not of ripe pawpaw peels, but of its seeds." She declares, "We are thirsty for fairness." A school friend has lightened her skin with a special product, using household bleach instead of the cosmetics— Esoterica, Movate, Skin Success, Ambi—Uzoamaka's mother brings home from her trips overseas in pursuit of fairness for herself and her daughter.

But there is bleach and there is bleach, and fairness can mean justice rather than skin color. The disaster that follows is about far more than color. The problematic reality of Uzoamaka's dark skin is another hurdle to clear for her ambitious mother, who plans to send her to America and advises powder to "brighten" her up, while the lightness of the housegirl Ekaite's skin doesn't give her the power to defend herself against Uzoamaka.

Kristen Iskandrian's "The Inheritors" is an alluring story, told by a narrator whose mother has died and father absconded to a condo in Florida; she's adrift for the moment. "I like being sad," she tells us in a long passage detailing what annoyed her about her fellow employee at Second Chances, a consignment store.

I like being sad, which mystified her; I like it until I reach the nadir where sadness changes, as if chemically, to repulsion and self-loathing, making me wish that I was "capable" of "handling" things instead of turning away from them in disgust until my disgust disgusts me, and my anger at my inadequacy as a human being angers me, and all of that pure, easy, delectable sorrow gets squandered. She refused, cheerfully, to understand this, and it wasn't her refusal that was maddening but her cheer.

Their friendship develops, and the narrator's illusion of mutual understanding grows. It's a time when she's neither here nor there, and she's lonely. Her friend from work is someone who'll be there without her having to make arrangements for company, and someone about whom she's curious. The coincidence of their jobs makes their friendship prematurely comfortable.

The silent partner in their troika is the consignment shop itself—a museum of the unwanted and the relinquished—and the hidden dramas performed there each day. Each woman has strong feelings about her personal possessions. For the narrator, the most important exist in her memory. Their weight on her is as heavy and awkward as carrying ten sets of the *Encyclopaedia Britannica*. The treasures her friend has collected are a sum greater than all of her parts. Once we see them in her apartment, we believe, as the narrator does, that this is a person anchored to the spot, but we also know, even if the narrator doesn't, that here is a person who'll never be fully known. The reader's double knowledge is a tribute to Iskandrian's talent and imagination. "The Inheritors" is juror James Lasdun's favorite; his consideration of Kristen Iskandrian's story is on pp. 335–37.

A more nefarious pair opens Dylan Landis's "Trust" with an exchange of lies:

"We're just practicing," says Tina.
"We're just playing," says Rainey.
"We're just taking a walk."
"Yeah, but we're walking behind them," says Rainey.

They could just be playing. There's something sweet about two girls walking along, playing or pretending to be "robber girls," or so it seems until the story opens to reveal the darkness of sexual abuse and the presence of a gun. There's another dangerous element at work, but it's shoved to the side. When a remark of Tina's offends her friend, it might seem no more than a momentary insensitivity, easily forgiven, if Landis didn't follow her remark and immediate apology with a description of the gun.

"Inside Rainey's purse, the gun beats like a heart." The gun is alive and vaguely sexual. There's something wrong with these girls, the reader senses, a mixture of all three elements of danger: the secret of sexual abuse, the presence of the gun, and their unexplored, explosive friendship. Rainey and Tina's criminal debut isn't on the scale of Bonnie and Clyde's, but it's a devastation made vivid by Landis's writerly skill and patience.

The Canadian writer Clark Blaise theorized that short stories reverse from beginning to end; what begins with smiles will end in tears. William Trevor's story about Cecilia Normanton, "The Women," begins with a description of the 1980s as "listless," a word that also describes the obedient and ignorant heroine, about whom we learn in the same sentence that she knew "her father well, her mother not at all."

After two years, Cecilia's been told, her parents' happy marriage ended because her mother fell in love with another man. Her father grew "melancholy," which had a powerful effect on his daughter, who never dared to ask if her mother had died. Eventually, after a childhood spent with a tutor and servants who haven't the time to converse, Cecilia is sent to boarding school, which she dislikes at first but comes to enjoy. Into her new life two women enter, and all that she missed and ignored during her childhood takes center stage.

Trevor isn't a writer who pulls the rug from under his readers as a matter of course. He isn't known for plot twists but rather for slow, steady, devastating revelations of character. The unfussy precision of his language seems like the wise conclusion to a thoughtful argument. Yet more goes on than well-tempered descriptions. Behind every Trevor story—"The Women" is no different—one detects the drumbeat of reversal, the revelation of the subtle beneath the obvious, of the truth beneath the secret.

The title of Halina Duraj's "Fatherland" refers both to Poland, the birth country of the narrator's parents, and also to the country of family. What might be called the creation myths of the parents begin the story. First, the mother's life is presented with an echo of a nursery rhyme:

> *For want of a nail the shoe was lost.*
> *For want of a shoe the horse was lost.*
> *For want of a horse the rider was lost.*
> *For want of a rider the battle was lost.*
> *For want of a battle the kingdom was lost.*
> *And all for the want of a horseshoe nail.*

Each afternoon when she was a child, the narrator's mother tended four cows and made up poems to entertain herself. Praised in school, she decided to become a teacher, but without new shoes, she couldn't go to high school, so she became a nanny. "So much depends on a new pair of shoes . . ."

On goes the story until a sudden surprise. The story's tone remains the same, though the father's life is grim. He's a man who's had no luck and has been damaged terribly by the cruelty he suffered in Auschwitz and his subsequent life on the streets of West Germany, "hooliganing," as his daughter calls his time of petty crime and overwhelming deprivation.

From her parents' lives, the fatherland of the narrator's childhood is born, a place with many barriers and strange rules, a regime of fear and rage. For all the drama and complexity of the subject matter, Duraj's story maintains its simple tone, and the story becomes as powerful and haunting as one of the terrible dreams from which the father suffers nightly.

Stephen Dixon's "Talk" also depends on tone. The author uses a blended first-person and third-person narrative: "He hadn't talked to anyone today. I haven't talked to anyone today." At first the reader might find the device confusing, but it develops into a direct route into the narrator-protagonist's state of mind as he grieves. The split in narrative embodies the life of this matter-of-fact widower whose solitary existence makes him a stranger to himself, a "he" rather than an "I." Dixon's is a rare story in which form and meaning are united.

Michael Parker's "Deep Eddy" is set in a dangerous, mysterious place—water. A man and a woman, both young, have just been to the movies. They walk a path along a river, passing black fisherwomen, arriving at the place "where the river whirlpooled and the bottom dropped so wildly myth bubbled up from it." The bottom has dropped out of the girl's world; her first sexual experiences have hurt her. As for the narrator: "she liked me only in the way girls like those boys who make them forget, temporarily, some pain I hoped was only temporary. My job was to make her laugh."

And laugh they do, bobbing like the red corks the fisherwomen stare at as if divining. The couple laughs and swims, floats and talks, and then the story's knot shows itself with the word *if.* Beneath the laughter and fooling around, under the water and under the words, there's an *if* of possibility. "Everything—then and since—hinged on a single word."

In Parker's prose the reader is swept along by the language. The narrator's watery voice pulls the reader just as a current does a swimmer. In the end, when the boy might be borne to the girl, the reader understands his desire to let go and let it happen, and the danger he fears if he does.

In Allison Alsup's "Old Houses," a community of people who "understand old houses and their architecture—Tudor, Colonial, Spanish Mediterranean"—gathers for a spring party. They know how lucky they are to live in the houses they've restored with such care and devotion, buildings with a "distinct identity," "houses that know who they are." Their children will inherit the houses, the only way the offspring can afford to live in what's become valuable real estate.

Another kind of legacy comes with the proud houses: a murder was committed, and that crime links three houses. The party-goers are proud of the age of their houses, but with the columns, "mullions, muntins, French doors, glass knobs, telephone niches," they are bequeathing history to their children. What begins as a satire of middle-class self-satisfaction ends in the undertow of a nightmare.

"A Golden Light" by Rebecca Hirsch Garcia juggles metaphor and realism: A father dies, a daughter falls under a spell. Sadie cannot speak. She cannot move. She sleeps and sleeps for so long that her loving family calls her "Our Sleeping Beauty." A psychia-trist comes to visit. Her family feeds her light food, but each time they wake her she falls back to sleep. A variety of doctors, quacks and specialists, come and go. Nothing helps.

In the fairy tale, Sleeping Beauty awakens to the kiss of the prince. The sleeper in "A Golden Light" requires a more complex awakening from her grief. In the end of this lovely story, Sadie is brought back to life by a metaphor and a reality.

In Louise Erdrich's "Nero," the narrator is in exile, for she's been sent to her grandparents while her mother gives birth to her brother. She remembers with unusual clarity her experiences during her stay: "While there, I must have lived at a more intense pitch. Or perhaps the novelty of everything that happened caused each day to imprint itself deeply on my mind."

She's "seven years old, [wears] boy's clothes, and [is] often mistaken for a boy, a sickly one." Her grandfather is a German immigrant, a former wrestler, now a butcher. Her uncle Jurgen is a strong man who wrestles animals to their death. "When the animal had tired itself out and stopped kicking, he'd use a razor-sharp knife to cut its throat with a technique so precise that the blood could be collected for black sausage."

The narrator is visiting a world of physically powerful men and, we find, of other kinds of power. There's sexual power, between a man and a woman, as well as between the family guard dog, Nero, and Mitts, a local cocker spaniel. There's the power of the lovely Priscilla over her father, who's "upright as a fireplug, and his muscles [are] thick and hard." He's vowed to fight any man who wants to marry Priscilla, and she is as determined to win her independence. Nero has his own kind of brute force, when it isn't compromised by his desire for Mitts, and also there's the grandmother's powerful Polish curse, which in the family and community "always silenced the Germans."

Dominating this three-ring circus of power, community, and love is the narrator, who is making her way as best she can with the new customs she must follow. Nero, an unlovable force of nature, can't learn and can't change. That's his power and his doom. At his death, Jurgen and the narrator lower his body into the ground, into "the timeless present." As she has before, Erdrich has written a story deeply rooted in believable detail and lofty understanding. It is human memory that holds us in the timeless present.

Another story set in memory, this one told in second person, is David Bradley's gorgeous "You Remember the Pin Mill." The story is immersed in the unforgettable landscape of Pennsylvania, where patient water, one hundred million years' worth, has created gaps in the hardest rock in the world. The landscape changes, given time and persistence, but how about human beings, whose time is so much shorter?

The scared and guilty boy, the "you" of the story, escapes with his abused mother to her childhood home. There, his distinguished grandfather familiarizes him with landscape, geology, history, ancestry, gossip, and the privileged racism of a small town. The boy, during his reprieve from his feared and brutal father, learns all his grandfather has to teach him and also what his grandfather would rather he didn't know. He becomes part of the school, the football team, his family, the town, and he proves himself to be brave and true. In the end, that isn't enough, and when he's grown and telling himself to remember the pin mill, the town, his family, and the failure of love, bravery, and truth, he finds solace in memory and a chance to change himself once again.

Chanelle Benz's "West of the Known" is set in the post–Civil War Old West, and it's about widespread brutality and racism, and a numbing sexism as taken for granted as the sunrise. Narrated by the oft-victimized Lavenia, "West of the Known" is a hell-for-leather story of rescue and ruin. When we first see her, Lavenia is living with her aunt and uncle, and their son, Cy, who visits her in the night:

> What comes in the dark?
> Stars.
> Cooler air.
> Dogs' bark.
> Cy.

Lavenia fears Cy and keeps his abuse secret. When her half brother, Jackson, avenges her, he says, "'You know they knew, don't ya? Aunt Josie and Uncle Bill. . . . They knew about Cy. Now you know sumthin, too.'"

The language of the story, whether or not true to that historic time, is true for the characters. Lavenia's world is a small one, choked by her helplessness and by the weight of her abject circumstance. Lavenia remains a victim until the story's end, which leads us to wonder when she changed from victim to witness, and when she is telling the story.

Colleen Morrissey's "Good Faith" starts in 1919, when two strangers choose to travel with the Free Church of the Savior, a fundamentalist group. The father of the careful, precise narrator, Rachel, is the leader of the church. The group is traveling in Missouri, demonstrating their faith in God by snake-handling. The two men who join them are worldly and rich, different down to the fact that they're Easterners. Their presence and the attention each pays to Rachel bring about a crisis of faith. The story is exemplary for its portrait of a self-contained young woman who is tempted to trade acceptance and humility for the frightening possibility of a bigger life.

"Valentine" by Tessa Hadley is a portrait of adolescent confusion and love. The narrator, Stella, is fifteen, naïve, and quick to investigate what she doesn't know. She feels the world is waiting for her energy, intelligence, and openness. Her prince comes in the form of Valentine, quickly proclaimed "gorgeous" by Stella's friend Madeline, who also says, "But I couldn't actually fancy him, could you? There was something weird." This opinion is echoed by Stella's mother, who says, "He looks like a girl. . . . I'm not that keen."

But Stella is more than keen. His Caravaggio looks beguile her, and she is soon convinced that they are one soul separated into two bodies, an idea she recognizes when she reads Plato later. They spend a great deal of time together, causing friction with Stella's parents. The reader comes to see that her mother and Madeleine are right. There is something weird about Valentine. For much of the story the reader is occupied by the twists and turns of their young love, so occupied that the enormous blow to Stella's future, the rendering of her fate into one far more ordinary than she's envisioned, is almost as surprising to the reader as it is to Stella.

"The Right Imaginary Person," by Robert Anthony Siegel, is on one level a love story and on another a story about language. The narrator is Benjamin Nussbaum, a graduate student in Japan, whose lover, Sumiko, makes up fairy tales and laments the conventional life she's expected, as a middle-class Japanese daughter, to live. (" 'Resistance is futile in a country like this, because the thing you reject isn't just out there, it's in here.' She tapped her head. 'Obedience is encoded in us through two thousand years of inbreeding.' ")

The title comes from Sumiko's explanation that the trick to her stories is that she pretends an imaginary person is telling the tales. Later, she says it has to be "the right imaginary person."

In an affair between lovers from different cultures, there are bound to be imaginative projections. Sumiko warns him, "You speak the language, but you don't know anything about real Japanese." But the story is about more than a cross-cultural love affair. Benjamin's sister, Daisy, has died of cancer, and the story beneath the obvious one of Sumiko and Benjamin is about his willful ignoring of his grief.

The MacGuffin in "Oh Shenandoah," Maura Stanton's tale of chivalry, is a new toilet seat, a clue that the story, though set against the fabled beauty of Venice, is something else entirely. Hugo and Marie are in Venice so that she may escape the spring pollen at home. The story begins with Marie's declaration that she wasn't planning to marry her fiancé. Her first words to Hugo are " 'What did you break this time?' " He's already shattered the hair dryer and derailed the glass shower doors. "Hugo had seemed a normal-sized tall man back in the Midwest, but here in Venice he seemed like a giant." The apartment they've rented is small and the landlord punitive.

Again, we can turn to Clark Blaise's theory that a story that begins in happiness ends in sorrow. In Stanton's charming story of lovers at a loss in a city without a Home Depot, Blaise's observation holds true. "Oh Shenandoah" amuses and distracts us with the mechanics of finding the right-sized (or any) new toilet seat in Venice, and the story unwinds from its beginning of crabbiness to an ending of openheartedness.

The art of the short story is in good hands this year. As readers, we ask nothing more of the twenty writers than that they tell us another story, please.

—*Laura Furman*
West Lake Hills, Texas

The O. Henry Prize Stories 2014

Mark Haddon

The Gun

D<small>ANIEL STANDS IN THE</small> funnel, a narrow path between
two high brick walls that join the playground to the estate
proper. On windy days, the air is forced through here then spun
upward in a vortex above the square of so-called grass between
the four blocks of flats. Anything that isn't nailed down becomes
airborne. Washing, litter, dust. Grown men have been knocked
off their feet. A while back there was a story going round about
a flying cat.

Except there's no wind this morning, there hasn't been any
wind for days, just an unremitting mugginess that makes you
want to open a window until you remember that you're outside.
Mid-August. A week since the family holiday in Magaluf, where
he learned backstroke and was stung by a jellyfish, a week till
school begins again. He is ten years old. Back at home his older
sister is playing teacher and his younger brother is playing pupil
again. Helen is twelve, Paul seven. She has a blackboard and a
little box of chalks in eight colors and when Paul misbehaves she
smacks him hard on the leg. His mother is doing a big jigsaw of
Venice on the dining table while the tank heats for the weekly
wash.

He can see the white legs of a girl on the swings, appearing, disappearing, appearing, disappearing. It is 1972. "Silver Machine" and "Rocket Man." He cannot remember ever having been this bored before. He bats a wasp away from his face as a car door slams lazily in the distance, then steps into the shadow of the stairwell and starts climbing toward Sean's front door.

There will be three other extraordinary events in his life. He will sit at dusk on the terrace of a rented house near Cahors with his eight-year-old son and see a barn on the far side of the valley destroyed by lightning, the crack of white light appearing to come not from the sky but to burst from the ground beneath the building.

He will have a meeting with the manager of a bespoke ironworks near Stroud, whose factory occupies one of three units built into the side of a high railway cutting. Halfway through the meeting a cow will fall through the roof and it won't be anything near as funny as it sounds.

On the morning of his fiftieth birthday his mother will call and say that she needs to see him. She will seem calm and give no explanation and despite the fact that there is a large party planned for the afternoon he will get into the car and drive straight to Leicester only to find that the ambulance has already taken his mother's body away. Only later, talking to his father, will he realize that he received the phone call half an hour after the stroke which killed her.

Today will be different, not simply shocking but one of those moments when time itself seems to fork and fracture and you look back and realize that if things had happened only slightly differently, you would be leading one of those other ghost lives that sped away into the dark.

Sean is not a friend as such but they play together because they are in the same class at school. Sean's family lives on the top floor of Orchard Tower whereas Daniel's family lives in a semi-detached house on the approach road. Daniel's mother says that Sean's family are a bad influence but she also says that television will damage your eyes if you sit too close and that you will die if you swim in the canal, and in any case Daniel likes their volume, their expansiveness, their unpredictability, the china greyhounds on either side of the gas fire, Mr. Cobb's red BMW which he polishes and T-Cuts lovingly on Saturday mornings. Sean's older brother, Dylan, works as a plasterer and carpenter and they have a balcony which looks over the ring road to the woods and the car plant and the radio mast at Bargave, a view which excites Daniel more than anything he saw from the plane window between Luton and Palma because there is no glass and you feel a thrilling shiver in the back of your knees as you lean over and look down.

He steps out of the lift and sees Sean's mother leaving the flat, which is another thing that makes Daniel envious, because when his own mother goes to the shops he and Paul and Helen have to accompany her. *Try and keep him out of trouble.* Mrs. Cobb ruffles his hair and sweeps onward. She is lighting a cigarette as the silver doors close over her.

Sean's jumbled silhouette appears in the patterned glass of the front door and it swings open. *I've got something to show you.* *What?*

He beckons Daniel into Dylan's bedroom. *You have to keep this a total secret.*

Daniel has never been in here before. Dylan has explicitly forbidden it and Dylan can bench-press 180 pounds. He steps off the avocado lino of the hall onto the swirly red carpet. The smell of cigarettes and Brut aftershave. It feels like the bedroom of a dead person in a film, every object freighted with significance. Posters for *Monty Python* and *The French Connection.* "Jimmy Doyle Is the Toughest." A motorbike cylinder head sits on a folded copy of the *Daily Express,* the leaking oil turning the newsprint waxy and transparent. There is a portable record player on the bedside table, the lid of the red leatherette box propped open and the cream plastic arm crooked around the silvered rod in the center of the turntable. *Machine Head. Thick as a Brick. Ziggy Stardust.*

You have to promise.

I promise.

Because this is serious.

I said.

Sean tugs at the pine handle of the wardrobe and the flimsy door comes free of the magnetic catch. On tiptoe Sean takes down a powder-blue shoebox from the top shelf and lays it on the khaki blanket before easing off the lid. The gun lies in the white tissue paper that must have come with the shoes. Sean lifts it easily from its rustling nest and Daniel can see how light it is. Scuffed pigeon-gray metal. The words REMINGTON RAND stamped into the flank. Two cambered grips are screwed to either side of the handle, chocolate brown and cross-cut like snakeskin for a better grip.

Sean raises the gun at the end of his straightened arm and rotates slowly so that the barrel is pointing directly into Daniel's face. *Bang*, he says, softly. *Bang.*

Daniel's father works at the local pool, sometimes as a lifeguard, more often on reception. Daniel used to be proud of the fact that everyone knew who his father was, but he is now embarrassed by his visibility. His mother works part-time as a secretary for the county council. His father reads crime novels. His mother does jigsaws which are stored between two sheets of plywood when the dining table is needed. Later in life when he is describing his parents to friends and acquaintances he will never find quite the right word. They aspired always to be average, to be unremarkable, to avoid making too much noise or taking up too much space. They disliked arguments and had little interest in the wider world. And if he is bored in their company during his regular visits he will never use the word *boring* because he is genuinely envious of their ability to take real joy in small things, and hugely grateful that they are not demonstrating any of the high-maintenance eccentricities of many of his friends' retired and aging parents.

They walk across the living room and Sean turns the key before shunting the big glass door to one side. They step into heat and traffic noise. There is a faint brown smog, as if the sky needs cleaning. Daniel can feel sweat running down the small of his back.

Sean fixes the pistol on a Volvo traveling in one direction then follows an Alfa Romeo going the other way. *We could kill someone and they'd never find out who did it.* Daniel explains that the police would use the hole in the windscreen and the hole in the driver's body to work out exactly where the shot came from. *Elementary, my dear Watson,* says Sean. *Let's go to the woods.*

Is the gun loaded?

'Course it's loaded, says Sean.

The woods rise up on the other side of the ring road, a swathe of no-man's-land between town and country. People park their cars at the picnic area by Pennington on the far side of the hill and walk their dogs among the oak and ash and rowan, but the roar of the dual carriageway and the syringes and the crushed lager cans dissuade most of them from coming down its northern flank.

They wait on the grass verge, the warm shock waves of passing lorries thumping them and sucking at their clothes. *Go,* shouts Sean, and they sprint to the central reservation, vaulting the scratchy S-shaped barrier, pausing on the ribbon of balding grass then running across the second carriageway to the gritty lay-by with its moraine of shattered furniture and black rubbish bags ripped open by rats and foxes. All that bacteria cooking slowly. An upturned pram. They unhook the clanky gate where the rutted track begins. Sean has the gun in a yellow Gola bag thrown over his shoulder.

They pass the scrapyard with its corrugated-iron castellations. They pass the Roberts' house. A horsebox with a flat tire, a floodlight roped to a telegraph pole. Robert Hales and Robert Hales and Robert Hales, grandfather, father and son, all bearing the same name and all living under the same roof. The youngest Robert Hales is two years above them at school. He has a biscuity unwashed smell and bones that look slightly too big for his skin. He used to come in with small animals in a cake tin, stag beetle, mouse, grass snake, but Donnie Farr grabbed the last of these and used it to chase other children round the playground before whipping its head against one of the goalposts. Robert pushed Donnie to the ground, took hold of the fingers of his left hand and bent them backward until two of them snapped.

The curtains in the Roberts' house are closed, however, and there is no red van parked outside. They walk on toward the corner where the path narrows and turns into the trees. Slabs of dusty sunlight are neatly stacked between the branches. If it weren't for the smell of exhaust fumes you could imagine that the roar of traffic was a great cataract pouring into a ravine to your left.

They find a clearing that contains the last few broken branches of a den they built earlier in the summer where they drank Tizer and smoked four menthol cigarettes which Sean had stolen from his mother's handbag. *Let's do it here.* Sean finds a log to use as a shooting gallery and sends Daniel off in search of targets. He climbs the boundary fence and searches among the hawthorn bushes which line the hard shoulder, coming back with two empty beer bottles, a battered plastic oilcan and a muddy teddy bear with both arms missing. He feels exhausted by the heat. He imagines standing on the lawn at home, squeezing the end of the hose with his thumb and making rainbows in the cold falling water. He arranges the objects at regular intervals along the log. He thinks about the child who once owned the teddy bear and regrets having picked it up but doesn't say anything.

Sean raises the gun and moves his feet apart to brace himself. A deep cathedral quiet. The traffic stops. He can hear the shuttle of his own blood. He is not aware of the shot itself. The loose rattle of scattering birds. He sees Sean being thrown backward, as if a big animal has charged and struck him in the center of his chest mid-leap. The bear, the oilcan and the bottles are still standing. *Oh my God.* Sean gets to his feet. *Oh my God.* He begins dancing. He has clearly never done anything this exciting in his life. *Oh my God.*

A military plane banks overhead. Daniel is both disappointed and relieved that he is not offered the second shot. Sean breathes deeply and theatrically. He braces himself again, wipes the sweat from his forehead with the arm of his T-shirt and raises the gun. The noise is breathtakingly loud. It seems obvious to Daniel that many, many people will have heard it.

What are you doing? It is the youngest Robert Hales.

They jump, both of them, but Sean recovers his composure quickest. *What do you think we're doing?*

You've got a gun. Despite the heat Robert is wearing a battered orange cagoule.

Duh.

Let me have a go.

Yeh, right, says Sean.

I want a go, says Robert. He steps forward. He is taller than Sean by a good six inches.

Just as he did in the bedroom, Sean lifts his arm until the gun is pointing directly at Robert's face. *No way, José.*

Daniel realizes that Sean may kill Robert. He is excited by this possibility. He will be a *witness to a crime.* People will respect him and feel sorry for him.

Robert doesn't move. Five, maybe ten seconds. *The Good, the Bad and the Ugly.* Daniel can't tell if he's terrified or utterly unafraid. Finally Robert says, *I'm going to kill you,* not in the way they say it to one another in the playground, but in the way you say, *I'm going to the shop*. He walks away without looking back. Sean aims at him till he vanishes. The two of them listen to the fading crunch of twigs and dry leaves under his trainers. *Spastic*. Sean lets his arm slump. *Bloody spastic*. He walks up to the teddy bear and places the barrel in the center of its forehead. Daniel thinks how similar they look, the bear and Robert, uninterested, staring straight ahead. But Sean can't be bothered to waste another bullet. *Shit*. Robert's appearance has made the adventure seem mundane. Sean throws the gun into the Gola bag. *Let's go*.

They walk back through the woods, taking the long route that loops up the hill and comes out on the far side of the scrapyard, avoiding the Roberts' house altogether. Gnats and dirty heat. Daniel has dog shit on his left shoe that he has not been able to scrape off completely.

His sister, Helen, was unexpectedly born breech. The cord became trapped while her head was coming out and she was deprived of oxygen. Daniel is not told about this until he is sixteen. He knows only that there is a light in her eyes which stutters briefly sometimes then comes back on. He knows only that she has trouble with numbers, money, telling the time.

She will leave school at sixteen with no qualifications, living at home and working in a furniture warehouse then in a greengrocer's. She will change doctors and get better drugs. Ethosuximide. Valproic acid. The petit mal will stop. She will be easily confused but she will be plump and blonde and pretty and people will like her instinctively. She'll meet Garry at a nightclub. Overweight, thirty-five, detached house, running a taxi firm, a big man in a small world. They will marry and it will take Daniel a long time to realize that this is a happy ending.

The noise, when it comes, is nothing more than a brief hiss followed by a clatter of foliage. Crossbow? Catapult? Then a second shot. It is the oddest thing, but Daniel will swear that he saw it before he heard it, before Sean felt it even. A pink stripe appears on the skin just above Sean's elbow. He yelps and lifts his arm. *Bastard.*

They squat on the path, hearts hammering. Sean twists his arm to inspect the damage. There is no bleeding, just a red weal, as if he has leaned against the rim of a hot pan. Robert must be somewhere further down the hill. The hole in the windscreen, the hole in the driver's body. But Daniel can see nothing without lifting his head above the undergrowth. They should run away as fast as they can so that Robert is forced to aim at a moving target between the trees, but Sean is taking the gun out of the bag. *I'm going to get him.*

Don't be stupid.

And what's your brilliant idea?

Another hiss, another clatter. They duck simultaneously. For a couple of seconds Sean looks frightened. Then he doesn't. *This way.* He starts to commando-crawl through a gap in the black-berries.

Daniel follows him only because he doesn't want to be alone. Sean holds the gun in his hand as he crawls. Daniel thinks how easy it would be for him to pull the trigger accidentally. They drag themselves between the gnarly bramble trunks. Cracked seed cases, dry leaves and curls of broken bark. Born and bred in a briar patch. He tries to pretend that they are in a film but can't do it. They are moving in the wrong direction, away from the scrapyard. And this is Robert's back garden.

They find themselves under a low dome of branches just big enough for them to lie stretched out, a place where an animal might sleep, perhaps. Improbably, they hear the sound of an ice cream van, far off. No fourth shot.

What do we do now?

We wait, says Sean.

What for?

Till it's dark.

Daniel looks at his watch. At six his mother will call Sean's flat, at seven she will ring the police. He rolls onto his back and narrows his eyelids so that the light falling from the canopy becomes a shimmer of overlapping circles in white and yellow and lime green. The smell of dog shit comes and goes. Is this a safe place or a trap? He imagines Robert looking down at the two of them lying there under the brambles. Fish in a barrel. That weird keening noise Donnie made when his fingers snapped.

After twenty minutes the tension begins to ease. Perhaps this was what Robert intended after all, to scare them then go home and sit in front of the TV laughing. Forty minutes. Daniel hasn't drunk anything since breakfast. He has a headache and he can feel little gluey lumps around the edge of his dry lips. They decide to run for it. They are now certain that Robert is no longer waiting for them but the running will increase the excitement of their escape and recapture a little of their lost dignity.

And this is when they hear the footsteps. A crackle. Then silence. Then another crackle. Someone is moving gingerly through the undergrowth nearby, trying not to be heard. Each heartbeat seems to tighten a screw at the base of Daniel's skull. Sean picks up the gun and rolls onto his stomach, elbows braced in the dirt. Crackle. Daniel pictures Robert as a native hunter. Arrow in the notch, two fingers curled around the taut bowstring. The steps move to the right. Either he doesn't know where they are or he is circling them, choosing his direction of approach. *Come on,* says Sean to himself, turning slowly so that the gun points constantly toward the direction of the noise. *Come on.*

Daniel wants it to happen quickly. He doesn't know how much longer he can bear this before jumping up and shouting, *Here I am!* like Paul used to do during games of hide-and-seek. Then everything goes quiet. No steps. No crackle. Midges scribble the air. The soft roar of the cataract. Sean looks genuinely frightened now.

A stick snaps behind them and they twist onto their backs just as the silhouette springs up and shuts out the dazzle of the sun. Sean fires and the gun is so close to Daniel's head that he will hear nothing for the next few minutes, just a fizz, like rain on pylon wires.

He sees straightaway that it is not Robert. Then he sees nothing because he is kicked hard in the stomach and the pain consumes him. When he uncurls and opens his eyes he finds himself looking into a face. It is not a human face. It is the face of a roe deer and it is shockingly big. He tries to back away but the brambles imprison him. The deer is running on its side, wheezing and struggling in vain to get to its feet. A smell like the camel house at the zoo. Wet black eyes, the jaws working and working, the stiff little tongue poking in and out. Breath gargles through a patch of bloody fur on its neck. It scrabbles and kicks. He can't bear to look but can't make himself turn away. The expression on its face. It looks like someone turned into a deer in a fairy tale. Crying out for help and unable to form the words.

It's weakening visibly, something dragging it down into the cold black water that lies just under the surface of everything. That desperate hunger for more time, more light. Whenever Daniel hears the phrase *fighting for your life* this is the picture that will come back to him.

Sean hoists his leg over its body and sits on its chest. He presses the end of the barrel to the side of its head and fires, *bang . . . bang . . . bang . . . bang . . .* each shot sending the deer's body into a brief spasm. The gun is empty. A few seconds of stillness then a final spasm. It stops moving. *Oh yes,* says Sean, letting out a long sigh, *Oh yes,* as if he has been dreaming about this moment for a long time.

Fingers of gluey blood start to crawl out from under the head. Daniel wants to cry but something inside him is blocked or broken.

Sean says, *We have to get it back.*

Back where?

To the flat.

Why?

To cook it.

Daniel has no idea what to say. A part of him still thinks of the deer as human. A part of him thinks that, in some inexplicable way, it is Robert transformed. Already a fly is investigating one of the deer's eyes.

Sean stands up and stamps the brambles aside, snapping their stems with the heel of his trainers so they don't spring back. *We can skin it.*

He tells Daniel to return to the lay-by to fetch the pram they saw beside the rubbish bags. Daniel goes because he needs to get away from Sean and the deer. He walks past the scrapyard. He wants to bump into Robert, hoping that he will be dragged back into the previous adventure, but the curtains are still closed and the house is silent. He removes the loop of green twine and opens the clangy gate. There is a brown Mercedes in the lay-by. The driver watches him from the other side of the windscreen but Daniel cannot make out the man's face. He turns the pram over. It is an old-fashioned cartoon pram with a concertina hood and leaf-spring suspension. The rusty handle is bent, the navy uphol-stery is torn and two of the wheels are tireless. He drags it back through the gate, closing it behind him.

It's a trick of the light, of course. Time is nothing but forks and fractures. You step off the curb a moment later. You light a ciga-rette for the woman in the red dress. You turn over the exam paper and see all the questions you've revised, or none of them. Every moment a bullet dodged, every moment an opportunity missed. A firestorm of ghost lives speeding away into the dark.

Perhaps the difference is this, that he will notice, that he will see things in this way when others don't, that he will remember an August afternoon when he was ten years old and feel the ver-tigo you feel walking away unharmed from a car crash. Or not quite unharmed, for he will come to realize that a part of himself now exists in a parallel universe to which he has no access.

When they lift the deer onto the pram it farts and shits itself. It doesn't smell like the camel house this time. Daniel is certain that it would be easier to drag the body but says nothing, and only when the track flattens out by the scrapyard and they are finally free of the roots and the sun-hardened ruts does the pram finally begin to roll a little.

The man is sitting against the bonnet of his Mercedes, as if he has arranged himself a better view for the second act. He has shoulder-length black hair, a cheap blue suit and a heavy gold bracelet. Sean shuts the gate and reattaches the loop of green twine. The man lights a cigarette. *Lads.* It's all he says. The smallest of nods. No smile, no wave. He will recur in Daniel's dreams for years, sitting at the edge of whatever else is going on. Cigarette, gold bracelet. *Lads.*

They stand at the side of the carriageway. Hot dust, hot metal. Daniel sees drivers glance at them, glance away then glance back again. *Three, two, one.* The pram is less stable at speed and less inclined to travel in a straight line and they reach the central reservation accompanied by a whoosh of air brakes and the angry honk of a lorry that comes perilously close to hitting them in the fast lane.

Clumsily, they heave the deer and the pram over the barrier. This takes a good deal of time and the strip of yellow grass is not wide. *Police,* says Sean, and Daniel turns in time to see the orange stripe of a white Rover slide past, lights and siren coming on as it goes up the hill. It will turn at the roundabout and come down the other carriageway. They have a minute at most.

Now, yells Sean. And the relief Daniel feels when they bump over the curb of the service road and heave the pram up the bank through the line of stunted trees into the little park makes him laugh out loud. *The warrens,* says Sean, panting, and they keep their momentum up past a gaggle of rubbernecking children on the climbing frame and into the little network of walled paths round the back of the estate. They stop by the peeling red lock-ups and wait. No siren. No squeal of tires. Daniel's head pulses. He needs to lie down in the dark.

They push the pram across the parched quadrangle to Orchard Tower. An elderly lady watches them, transfixed. Polyester floral dress and varicose veins. Sean gives her a jokey salute. *Mrs. Daley.*

The double doors are easy but it takes some juggling to get the pram and the deer into the lift and they leave a lick of blood across the mirror that covers one of the side walls. Sean puts his finger into it and writes the word MURDER in capital letters on the glass at head height. The chime goes, the lift bumps to a halt and the doors open.

Later when he tells the story to people they won't understand. Why didn't he run away? His friend had a loaded gun. He will be repeatedly amazed at how poorly everyone remembers their childhoods, how they project their adult selves back into those bleached-out photographs, those sandals, those tiny chairs. As if choosing, as if deciding, as if saying no were skills like tying your shoelaces or riding a bike. Things happened to you. If you were lucky, you got an education and weren't abused by the man who ran the five-a-side. If you were very lucky you finally ended up in a place where you could say, *I'm going to study accountancy . . . I'd like to live in the countryside . . . I want to spend the rest of my life with you.*

It happens fast. The door opens before Sean can put his key into the lock. Dylan stands in dirty blue dungarees, phone pressed to one ear. He says, calmly, *Cancel that, Mike. I'll talk to you later,* and puts the phone down. He grabs a fistful of Sean's hair and swings him into the hallway so that he skids along the lino and knocks over the little phone table. He puts his foot on Sean's chest and yanks at the bag, ripping it open and breaking the strap. He takes out the gun, checks the chamber, shunts it back into place with the heel of his hand and tosses it through the open door of his room onto his bed. Sean sits up and tries to back away but Dylan grabs the collar of his T-shirt and hoists him up so that he is pressed against the wall. Daniel doesn't move, hoping that if he remains absolutely still he will remain invisible. Dylan punches Sean in the face then lets him drop to the floor. Sean rolls over and curls up and begins to weep. Daniel can see a bloody tooth by the skirting board. Dylan turns and walks toward the front door. He runs his hand slowly across the deer's flank five or six times, long, gentle strokes as if the animal is a sick child. *Bring it in.*

He wheels the pram across the living room and out onto the balcony. Dylan gives Daniel a set of keys and sends him downstairs to fetch two sheets from the back of his van. Daniel feels proud that he has been trusted to do this. He carries the sheets with their paint spatters and crackly lumps of dried plaster back upstairs. Dylan folds them and spreads them out on the concrete floor and lays the deer in the center. He takes a Stanley knife from his pocket, flips the animal onto its back and scores a deep cut from its neck to its groin. Gristle rips under the blade. He makes a second cut at ninety degrees, a crucifix across the chest, then yanks hard at one of the corners so that the furred skin rips back a little. It looks like a wet doormat. Daniel is surprised by the lack of blood. Under the skin is a marbled membrane to which it is attached by a thick white pith. Dylan uses the knife to score the pith, pulling and scoring and pulling and scoring so that the skin comes gradually away.

Sean steps onto the balcony pressing a bloody tea towel to the side of his face. Daniel cannot read his expression. Turning, Daniel sees the radio mast and the sandy slab of the car plant. A hawk hangs over the woods. His headache is coming back, or perhaps he has simply begun to notice it again. He wanders inside and makes his way to the kitchen. There is an upturned pint mug on the drying rack. He fills it with cold water from the tap and drinks it without taking the glass from his lips.

He hears the front door open and close and Mrs. Cobb shouting, *What the bloody hell is going on?*

He goes into the living room and sits on the brown leather sofa and listens to the slippery click of the carriage clock on the mantelpiece, waiting for the pain to recede. There are framed school photographs of Sean and Dylan. There is a wall plate from Cornwall, a lighthouse wearing a bow tie of yellow light, three gulls, each made with a single black tick. The faintest smell of dog shit from the sole of his shoe. Sean walks down the corridor carrying a full bucket, the toilet flushes and he comes back the other way with the bucket empty.

He dozes. Twenty minutes, maybe half an hour. The sound of a saw brings him round. It takes a while to remember where he is, but his headache has gone. So strange to wake and find the day going on in your absence. He walks out onto the balcony. Dylan is cutting the deer up. The legs have been sawn off and halved, hoofs in one pile, thighs in another. Carl from next door has come round and is leaning against the balcony rail smoking a cigarette. *I'll have a word at the chippy. They've got a chest freezer out the back.* Sean is no longer holding the tea towel against his face. His left eye is half closed by the swelling and his upper lip is torn.

Get rid of that, will you? Dylan points to a yellow plastic bathtub. Lungs, intestines, glossy bulbs of purple Daniel can't identify.

He and Sean each take a handle. As they are leaving Dylan holds up the severed head and says to Carl, *What do you reckon? Over the fireplace?* But it's the bathtub that unsettles Daniel. The way it jiggles and slops with the movement of the lift. MURDER in capital letters. The inside of a human being would look like this.

He says, *How are you?*

Sean says, *Fine.*

Neither of them means it. Some kind of connection has been broken, but it feels good, it feels like an adult way of being with another person.

They put the bathtub down and lift the lid of one of the big metal bins. Flies bubble out. That wretched leathery stink. They hoist the tub to chest height. Two teenage girls walk past. *Holy shit.* A little countdown and they heave the bathtub onto the rim. The contents slither out and hit the bottom with a slapping boom.

Upstairs, the oven is on and Mrs. Cobb has put a bloody haunch onto a baking tray. Carl is helping her peel potatoes with another cigarette in the corner of his mouth. Dylan drinks from a can of Guinness. *Come here.* Sean walks over and Dylan puts an arm around him. *If you ever do anything like that again I'll fucking kill you. Understand?* Even Daniel can hear that he is really saying, *I love you.* Dylan gives Sean the half-finished can of Guinness and opens another one for himself.

Your mum rang, says Mrs. Cobb. *Wondering where you were.*

Right. He doesn't move.

Because it has nothing to do with the gun, does it. The gun is one of those dark stars that bend light. This is the moment. If he asks to stay then everything will be different. But he says nothing. Mrs. Cobb says, *Go on. Hop to it, or your mum will worry,* and however many times he turns her words over in his mind he will never be able to work out whether she was being kind to his mother or cruel to him. He doesn't say good-bye. He doesn't want to risk hearing the lack of interest in their voices. He walks out of the front door, closes it quietly behind him and goes down via the stairs so that he doesn't have to see the blood.

Forty years later he goes to his mother's funeral. Afterward, not wanting to seem callous by heading off to a hotel, he sleeps in his old bedroom. It makes him profoundly uncomfortable, and when his father says that he wants things back to normal as soon as possible, he takes the hint with considerable relief and leaves his father to the comfort of his routine, the morning walk, the *Daily Mail*, pork chops on Wednesdays.

There are roadworks on the way out of town and by chance he finds himself diverted along the stretch of ring road between the flats and the woods. It all comes back so vividly that he nearly brakes for the two boys running across the carriageway pushing the pram. He slows and pulls into the lay-by, grit crunching under the tires. He gets out of the car and stands in that same thumping draft that comes off the lorries. Freakishly the gate is still held shut by a loop of green twine. It scares him a little. He steps through and shuts it behind him.

The scrapyard is still there, as is the Roberts' house. The curtains are closed. He wonders if they have been closed all these years, Robert Hales and Robert Hales and Robert Hales, the same person, growing old and dying and being reborn in the stink and the half-light.

That cathedral silence before the first shot. Slabs of dusty sunlight.

He stoops and picks up a jagged lump of broken tarmac. He imagines throwing it through the front window, the glass crazing and falling. The loose rattle of scattering birds. Light flooding in.

A stick cracks directly behind him. He doesn't turn. It's the deer. He knows it's the deer, come again.

He can't resist. He turns slowly and finds himself looking at an old man wearing Robert's face. His father? Maybe Robert himself. What year is it?

The man says, *Who are you?* and for three or four seconds Daniel has absolutely no idea.

Stephen Dixon

Talk

H E HASN'T TALKED TO anyone today. I haven't talked to anyone today. It's not that I haven't wanted to. It's not that he hasn't wanted to talk to someone, but he just never had the chance to. He only realized he hasn't talked to anyone today when he sat down on the bench he's sitting on now. In front of the church across the street from his house. I like to sit on it after a long or not-so-long walk around my neighborhood. I usually take the same route. Almost always end up on the same bench. One of the benches in front of the entrance to the church. It's now 6:45. Closer to 6:47. I haven't talked to anyone today since I woke up more than twelve hours ago, rested in bed awhile, exercised in bed awhile, mostly his legs, and then got out of bed and washed up and so on. Did lots of things. Brushed my teeth, brushed my hair, dressed, took my pill, let the cat out, let the cat in, gave the cat food, changed its water, let the cat out again, made myself breakfast, ate, got the newspaper from outside before I made myself breakfast and ate, same things almost every morning soon after waking up, same breakfast, coffee and hot cereal and toast, maybe blueberry jam and butter on the toast every third or fourth day instead of butter and orange marmalade, same newspaper, different news but some of it the same, same cat, same water bowl for the cat, same kibble in a different bowl for the cat, same plate for the cat's wet food and same wet food till the cat finishes the can in about three days. Then I shaved, did some exercises with two ten-pound barbells, one for each hand, curls, he thinks they're called—the exercises—and so on. No one phoned. The classical music radio station was on when I shaved and exercised and after he was done exercising he turned the radio off. Then he sat at his work table in his bedroom. I could use one of the other two bedrooms in the house to work in or the study his wife used to work in, but I prefer this room, the master bedroom they used to call it to distinguish it from the other bedrooms, the room that was once their bedroom but is now only his since his wife died. She didn't die in that room. She died in one of the other bedrooms. He had a hospital bed set up for her in that room more than a year before she died and she died in that bed. She was unconscious for twelve days in that bed before she died. Do I really want to go into all this again? Just finish it. She was lying on her back in a coma for twelve days in the hospital bed. Or just unconscious for he doesn't know how many days and then in a coma, when she opened her eyes, or her eyes opened on their own, and her head turned to where he was sitting on the right side of the bed and she died. He closed her eyes with his hand. Her eyes struggled to stay open and then, after he closed them a second and third time, they stayed permanently closed. The day after she died I had the hospital bed removed. He bought a new bed for that room a week or two later so his older daughter could sleep in that room again when she visited him. But I was thinking before about my not talking to anyone today. No opportunity to, as I said. He could have made the opportunity to, I suppose, but he didn't. I didn't go out of my way to talk to anyone today, he's saying. He likes these kinds of conversations to happen naturally. He'll be in the local food market, for instance—not to bump into people he knows from around the neighborhood or initiate small talk with employees behind the food or checkout counter with shoppers he doesn't know—but to buy things, mostly food for himself and his cat—and he'll bump into someone he knows. Hi, hello, how are you? and so on. Maybe with someone whose hand he shakes, back or shoulder he pats, cheek, if it's a woman, he kisses. Someone who most of the time stops his or her shopping to talk to me, and whom I like to talk to too. Am I being clear? He thinks so. Anyway: that didn't happen today. It's happened plenty of times in the almost twenty years he's lived in the house and been going to that market. But I didn't go to that market today. No market, and he rarely sees anyone he knows at any other market. He did, after writing in his bedroom for about three hours, go to the Y to work out. I often see someone I know from the Y in the fitness room, or whatever that room with all the resistance machines, he thinks they are, is called. Fitness center. Fitness center. And sometimes he sees two or three people there he only knows from the Y and has a brief conversation with them or just says "Hi" or "Hello" or "How you doing?" to. And he has, in the local market a few times—the one he almost always goes to because it's so close and the prices aren't that much higher than the big chains and they get you out fast because they have lots of working checkout counters for a store its size and just about all the checkout clerks know him—bumped into people he knows only from the Y and chatted with them. Though for the most part these chats are shorter than the ones he might have with the same people in the Y, and one or the other of them will usually say something like "Funny to see you here after seeing you so many times in the Y" or "I almost didn't recognize you out of your gym clothes." As for the weight room in the Y, which is right next to the fitness center, he has fewer conversations there than he does with people in the fitness center, since there are much fewer people working out in it. They also seem more serious and involved in their workouts. But he's still had a few conversations there when both he and the other person working out took a minute-or-so break from the weights and were close enough to talk to each other. Like a few days ago. "I always see you with a book. What are you reading now?" this person asked him, or said something like it: a man; very few women work out in the weight room. Someone he'd seen several times before in both rooms but never spoke with or even said hi to but might have smiled or nodded at. He held up the book so the man could see the cover. "*Gilgamesh?*" the man mispronouncing it the same way he once did till his wife corrected him. "Never heard of it. From the cover, it looks like it could be a fantasy or horror novel." "In a way it sort of is," I said. "But it's a new or relatively new translation of an epic poem, maybe the oldest literary work, or the oldest one found so far. With a long introduction as interesting as the work itself, and with great notes." "What's it about?" He gave a brief synopsis of it, based on the introduction, since he was only a third of the way into the poem. And then—"This might give you a laugh"—why he bought it. "The oldest work—a classic—and the only one in my family never to have read it? My older daughter, who graduated college eight years ago, read it when she was nine or ten and took a special humanities course in grade school. And I was in the bookshop last week, the Ivy on Falls Road, looking for something to read. I always have to have something to read—at home; if I take a walk and think I'll stop to sit and rest. Even here between sets on the sit-down resistance machines for a minute or the stationary bike if it doesn't have on its TV screen something especially good on the movie channel—and I saw it. In the store, this book, and remembered I'd never read it but for many years wanted to. But I've told you more than you probably wanted to hear, and you want to get back to your weights." "No," the man said, "it's interesting. *Gilgamesh.* I'll remember," and we both resumed our workouts. That's how the conversation went, sort of. I know I went on too long. He often does most days because he gets to talk so little. But today there wasn't anyone he knew at the Y to say even a word to, which was unusual. Most times, after he slides his key through the bar-code recorder, or whatever that piece of plastic on his key ring is called, and his name and photo appear on the monitor and an automated voice says "Access granted," someone behind the front desk there will look at the monitor and say "Have a good workout, Mr. Seidel," and he'll say "Thank you." But the one person behind the desk—usually there are two people there—was folding clean towels for members with the more expensive plan and more elaborate locker rooms, and didn't look up. He went into his locker room. Sometimes there's someone there I know from the Y and we'll talk a little. But the room was empty when I first got there and then after my workout. Sometimes, though this doesn't happen much, he might talk with someone in the shower room after his workout, but the one guy showering there today was someone he knows doesn't want to talk. I've seen him in the locker room and shower and at the front desk checking in dozens of times. Never downstairs in the fitness center or weight room. He seems to only come to the Y to swim. And I never saw him communicate with anyone. I don't even think the people at the front desk say "Have a good day" to him, or if they do, he doesn't answer them. First thing the guy does when he gets to the locker room is put his athletic bag on a bench and go around the room closing every locker that might be even just slightly open and make sure every bench is aligned with the banks of lockers. Then he'll walk around the room again and pick up any trash he sees on the floor—tiny pieces of paper, thread, part of a broken shoelace, for instance—and drop it into a trash can there. Then he'll undress and get into his swimsuit and lock his locker and go to the pool with his towel and in his shower slippers. I said hello to him a few times, but gave up. He looked right past me as if I hadn't said anything or he hadn't heard. Today I avoided looking his way once I saw who it was. I feel he doesn't want to be looked at either. I could have gone to the small food shop at the Y and ordered a sandwich to go—chicken or tuna fish salad on rye toast with tomato and lettuce and once each a powerhouse and grilled chicken sandwich, which weren't good—and while it was being made by an employee in back, exchanged a few words with the shop's owner about a number of things. The owner just takes the orders and rings them up and serves the food if anyone's sitting at one of the two tables there, which I've never done. The owner likes to talk. A few days ago it was strawberries. He said he grows them in his garden and they're very small this year, he doesn't understand it. I told him my younger daughter put in a number of strawberry plants two years ago, I got nothing but a few tiny ones last year, but this year they're all over the place and big, "What can I say?" And he once told me, when I asked, how to get the shells off hard-boiled eggs without taking any of the white of the egg with it. "Boil them for thirty to forty minutes. Infallible, and perfect for deviled eggs." But he didn't want to order any kind of sandwich today. He still has in the refrigerator, and it's probably still good but a little soggy, half the chicken salad wrap he got from him yesterday. What were some of the other opportunities to talk today? And by talking, I mean to someone, a human being, not the cat. He talks a lot to his cat. Actually, it's his younger daughter's, but she lives in an apartment in Brooklyn, the cat likes to run around outside, so he's taking care of it for the time being. "Hey, little guy, want something to eat?" Talk like that. "Want to go outside, Rufus?" "Go on, go on," when he's half in and half out the door. "I don't want to catch your tail, and you can come back whenever you want." "It's getting dark, Rufus. Want to come inside?" "Come inside, Rufus. Don't make me have to chase you." "You here to help me with the weeding?" Because sometimes when I'm weed-ing outside, he'll lie down on his stomach beside me and pull a weed out of the ground with his teeth and play with it or try to pull one out of my hand that I just got out of the ground. Also, sometimes when I talk to him it seems he talks back to me with a couple of meows. And when he's at the front door and I let him in, he always meows in a sound he uses no other time as he scoots in or walks past me, as if saying thanks to me for opening the door. He never meows, though, when I open the door to let him out. When he wants to go out he'll stand silently facing the door or stand up on his back paws and scratch the door with his front ones till I let him out. If I don't want him out, he'll walk quietly away from the door after about two minutes. But no other opportunities to talk to someone today? Can't think of any. Usually, during his late-afternoon walks, he'll see at least one person walking his dog and he'll say more than "Hi" or "Good evening" to him. He'll ask the breed of the dog, for instance, and if he asked it the last time but forgot it, he'll say "I forgot what you told me your dog's breed is" or "your dogs' breed is," since several people in the neighborhood have two dogs of the same breed, and one couple has three, and walk them together. I've also asked this person or couple what the dog was originally bred for. Not that I'm really interested, but it gives me a chance, if it was a day I hadn't talked much, to talk more. "Hunting foxes?" "Herding sheep?" "Going after moles or other burrowing animals like that in holes?" He once joked, and regretted it right after, for the guy didn't seem to find it funny, "Catching Frisbees?" But in his walk today he saw no one he's talked to or just said hello to before. Saw no one, period. Oh, people in cars, and a jogger, but she came up behind him without his hearing her and was past him before he could even wave. Maybe when he gets home he'll call his daughters and, if they're in, speak to them. Although it doesn't have to be in their homes. With their cell phones, they could be anywhere: walking on the street; having a drink in a bar. He speaks to them almost every night around seven. Seems to be a good time for them. They're done with work for the day, haven't started dinner. They call him or he calls them. But that's the kind of day it's been. Where he hasn't as yet said a word to anyone. Not one, and it makes me feel kind of strange or odd. It's true. It does. Both of those. But enough of that. Maybe, really, it's better not to dwell on it. If his wife were alive and still relatively healthy, or just not as sick as she was the last three years of her life, he would have spoken to her before he left the house. That would have been nice. "I'm going out for a walk," he would have said; "like to join me?" If she didn't or couldn't because she was still working in her study or something else, then when he got back she might say, as she did a lot, "See anything interesting?" or "Meet anyone on your walk?" Or just "Did you have a good walk?" Or he might volunteer: "I had a good walk. Farther than I usually go. Saw some beautiful and unusual flowers. Our neighbors, especially the church, really take care of their properties. But for the first time in a long time I didn't see anyone else outside except a fleet-footed jogger, who ran past me before I could even say hi to her. And of course people in the occasional passing car, but they don't count." Or if she was too weak to walk and didn't want to be pushed around the neighborhood in her wheelchair—"People stare; I don't like it"—he'd say "All right, then, if I take a brief walk by myself? And I will make it quick. I won't stop to talk to anyone." "Why should I mind?" she said a number of times. "Get out. You need a break. And talk all you want." "So you'll be okay here alone?" and she always said "I told you. I'll be just fine." But he shouldn't think of himself as odd or strange just because he hasn't talked with anyone today. I'm not odd. He's not strange. Thirteen hours? That's not so long. Listen, this is where life has led me, to this point; something. He can't quite put it in words now. But he's trying to say what? What am I trying to say? That it's not his fault he hasn't spoken to anyone today? No, that's not what I wanted to say. Forget it. I think if I had someone to speak to other than myself today, I'd be able to say what I want to say understandably. Coherently. Clearly. Some way. But again: enough. He opens *Gilgamesh* and turns to the page the book-mark's on. I resume reading what I stopped reading when I was on the exercise bike at the Y. Is that the best way to put it? What if it isn't? What's important is that I know what I mean. Or another way could be "He resumes reading at the place he left off when he was on the exercise bike at the Y." Any real difference? Some. Second's better. I'm reading when someone says my name. He looks up. It's my neighbor from up the hill from my house. Karen.

"I didn't want to startle you," she says, "so I called out to you as softly as I could. You seemed so absorbed in your book. Am I disturbing you?"

"Not at all."

"Nice place to read, I'd say. Quiet. Surrounded by all these lovely flowers the church has planted. Best time of day too."

"Yeah, it's a great place. I come here almost every day around this time after a long walk. And I'm thinking, I don't know if I should admit this, and it's kind of laughable, but you're the first person I've spoken to all day."

"Oh, that's so sad," she says. "You know what? Why don't you come by our house tomorrow for a drink? Jim and I have been meaning to have you over for I don't know how long. We've talked about it several times, but as you can see, we're great procrastinators."

"I don't know. Maybe another time. I've become such a hermit, which I know isn't good, although it helps my work, but—"

"Nonsense. Tomorrow. Say around six? Bring your cat. I'm only kidding. What's her name?"

"His. Rufus."

"Rufus. I see him running all around. Once up a tree. He never seems to just walk. And hiding in bushes. But it'll be wonderful talking to you over an extended period of time instead of only these quick chats or when I run into you at the market. By the way, what's that you're reading?"

"*Gilgamesh.*"

"Oh, I remember it from college. You'll have to tell us tomorrow why you're reading it. I mean, what made you, I'm sure, take it up again. Tomorrow then? Sixish?"

"Yes. Thanks."

She smiles and goes. He reopens the book. What page was I on again? He thinks. Eighty-four, I think. He turns to it. I'm right. So, today won't be a day where I can say I didn't talk to a single person, and tomorrow won't be one either. Well, it wouldn't have turned out that way today anyway. He probably would have reached one of his daughters on the phone later. Maybe both.

Tessa Hadley
Valentine

M ADELEINE AND I ARE waiting at the bus stop at the bottom of Beech Grove in our school uniforms: green print dresses, short white socks and sandals, blazers. In the summer, we are allowed to leave off our hated green felt hats. It's June, and summer is thick everywhere, a sleepy, viscous, sensuous emanation; hot blasts of air, opaque with pollen from the overblown suburban gardens, are ripe with smells from bins and dog mess. We are mad with summer, chafing and irritable with sex. We are fifteen, studying for our O levels; we have breasts (small in my case, luscious in Madeleine's) and pubic hair and periods. A breeze, stirring the dust in the gutter, tickles up around our thighs, floats our dresses—we can hardly bear it.

Our talk is rococo with insincerity, drawling, lascivious. Everything seems to have an obscene double meaning, even though it's only quarter past eight in the morning and, behind us in our homes, our mothers are still clearing the breakfast tables, scraping soggy Rice Krispies and burned toast crusts into the bin, wiping the plastic tablecloths. My mother is bending over my little brother, Philip, in his high chair, playing pat-a-cake to trick him into letting her wipe his face and hands, making his mouth spill open with delighted laughter. She lifts up his shirt and kisses his belly; I might be jealous, if I had time to crane that way, back toward home and the cramped circle of old loves. But my attention is all thrusting forward, onward, out of there. I've burned my boats, I can't go back—or, rather, I do go back, dutifully, every evening after school, and do my homework at the same table in the same stale olive-green dining room, and still get the best marks in the class for everything, nearly everything. But it's provisional, while I wait for my real life to begin. I feel like an overgrown giant in that house, bumping up against the ceiling like Alice in Wonderland after she's found the cake labeled "Eat Me": head swollen with knowledge and imagination, body swollen with sensation and longing.

Madeleine is my next-door neighbor and best friend. She and I have never even kissed boys: we have no actual sexual experience except a few things we've done with each other, experimentally, and out of desperation. (Not shamefaced afterward—flaunting and wicked; it is the 1970s, after all. But it's boys we want.) At an all-girls school, we don't get many chances to meet boys, although there are usually some on the bus, on their way to the Grammar School. This is part of our excitement, at quarter past eight. There are certain boys we are expecting to see, and we may even pluck up the crazy courage to speak to them, a word or two; any exchange will be dissected afterward in an analysis more nuanced and determined than any we ever give to poems in English lessons. ("What do you think he really meant when he said that his friend said yesterday that you weren't bad?")

Anything could happen on the bus in the next half hour, even something with the power to obliterate and reduce to dust the double math, Scripture, double Latin, and (worst) PE that lie in wait at the end of the journey—a doom of tedium, infinitely long. And, after PE, the nasty underground shower room with its concentrated citrus-rot stink of female sweat, its fleshly angsts, its tin-pot team spirit, the gloom of girls passed over, the PE teachers ogling, the trodden soaking towels.

Something *has* to happen.
Into our heat that morning comes Valentine.

He walked down to join us at the bus stop. We'd never seen him before: into the suburban torpor his footsteps broke like a signal for adventure on a jaunty trumpet. I loved his swaggering walk immediately, without reserve. His eagerly amused glances around him—drinking everything in, shaking the long hair back from his face—were like a symbol for morning itself. (His energy was no doubt partly a result of the Do-Dos—caffeine pills—he'd have swallowed in the bathroom as soon as his mother got him out of bed. Soon we were all taking them.) A Grammar School blazer, hooked by its loop around one nicotine-stained finger, was slung over his shoulder; his cigarette was cocked up cheekily between lips curved as improbably, generously wide as a faun's. The pointed chin was like a faun's, too, and the flaunting Cara vaggio cheekbones, pushing up the thick flesh under his eyes, making them slanted and mischievous. He was tall, but not too tall. His school trousers slid down his impossibly narrow waist and hips; he tucked his shirt half in, with a careless hand. The school tie that others wore resentfully as a strangled knot became under his touch somehow cravat-like, flowing. The top two buttons of his shirt were undone. He was sixteen.

He grinned at Madeleine and me.

At me first, then at Madeleine—although Madeleine was willowy and languorous, with long curls and a kitten face, pink cheeks. I was too small, too plump and shapeless, and my eyes, I knew, were blackly expressive pits in a too-white face. Madeleine, trying kindly to advise me on my sex appeal, had said that I might be "too intense"—but I didn't know how to disguise my intensity. Valentine stopped and offered us his cigarette, me first. It was not an ordinary cigarette. (We went to school stoned for the first time, but not the last.)

"Hello, girls," he said, beaming. "Does this bus go into town? Do you catch it every day? That's good. I like the look of you."

We met each other's eyes and giggled, and asked him what he liked about us. Thinking about it, surveying us up and down, he said we looked skeptical.

What did he mean, skeptical?

Thank God we weren't wearing our hats.

I longed for the bus not to come. Proximity to his body—a glimpse, via his half-tucked shirt, of a hollowed, golden, masculine stomach, its line of dark hairs draining down from the belly button—licked at me like a flame as we waited. His family, he explained, had just moved to one of the posher streets behind Beech Grove. When the bus did come, he sat on the backseat and took Beckett out of his rucksack: *Endgame.* The very title, even the look of the title—its stark, indiscreet white capitals on a jazzy orange cover—was a door swinging suddenly open into a new world. I'd never heard of Beckett; I think I was plowing through *The Forsyte Saga* then. None of the other boys on the bus read books. Val smiled at us encouragingly, extravagantly, over the top of his.

"He was gorgeous. I liked him," Madeleine conceded as we trudged in a tide of other green-gowned inmates up the purgatorial hill from the bus stop to where school loomed, the old house frowning like a prison in the sunlight. "But I couldn't actually fancy him, could you? There was something weird."

I was disappointed in her; I was already wondering if I'd find Beckett in the local library. (The librarian, warmly supportive of my forays into Edwardian belles lettres, would startle and flinch at my betrayal.) Madeleine didn't insist on her doubt—she never insisted—and I closed the door on that early intimation of danger. I wanted Val because he was different—as I was different. What I'd felt at my first sight of him that summer morning was more than ordinary love: something like recognition. When I read later in Plato about whole souls divided at birth into two halves, which move around in the world ever afterward mourning each other and longing for their lost completeness, I thought I was reading about myself and Valentine.

And it was the same for Val; I do believe that it was. He recognized me, too.

"What a scarecrow," my stepfather, Gerry, said, after Val came to my house for the first time. "I can't believe the Grammar School lets him get away with that hair."

"He looks like a girl," my mother said. "I'm not that keen, Stella."

Following up the stairs behind Val, I had been faint from the movement of his slim haunches in his tight white jeans. How could she think that he looked like a girl? Yet all we did in my bedroom was cozy up knee to knee, cross-legged on the bed, to talk. We swapped our childhood stories. He was born in Malaya; he'd had an ayah.

"What was your family doing in Malaya?"

"You don't want to know."

"I want to know everything."

"My father worked for the government; he was an awful tax expert. Now that he's retired, he's just awful and old. What does yours do?"

"Gerry's not my real dad. My real dad's dead."

Mum brought in a pile of ironed clothes to put away in my chest of drawers. Then she called up to ask if we wanted coffee. Philip came knocking at the door, asking us to play with him. Afterward, Mum spoke to me awkwardly, about self-respect. The familiar solidity of the house and its furniture melted away around Val; after he'd left, I couldn't believe I really lived there. I couldn't hold my two worlds in the same focus. I wanted Val to be brilliant for my parents, and he wouldn't, or couldn't. He never made any concessions to them. If they asked him questions, he sometimes didn't even seem to hear them; his eyes were blank. It was as if he simply paused the flow of his life, in the presence of anyone unsympathetic.

Yet among our friends he was magnetic, commanding, funny. He was a clever mimic. We started getting together at Madeleine's in the evenings—a gang of six or seven of us from the streets round about. Madeleine's father was often away; her mother, Pam, was bored and liked flirting with teenagers. She brought homemade brownies and cheese straws and jugs of weak sangria to Madeleine's room, and we cadged her cigarettes. Madeleine fancied a boy who played the guitar and wrote his own songs; we tried to talk a shy blond girl out of her faith. Madeleine bought a red bulb to put in one of the lamps; we draped the others with colored scarves. When Gerry was sent over to fetch me home, he never stepped across the low fence between our front gardens but went punctiliously via both front paths and gates. He said that if Pam wanted teenagers carrying on under her own roof it was her business.

"What's this?" he joked, when I brought Beckett back from the library.

"He's a play writer. Haven't you heard of him?"

"Playwright." (Gerry did crosswords—he had a good vocabulary.) "Aren't they all waiting for some chap who never turns up?"

Gerry had been so keen for me to go to the High School, yet he was hostile to the power my education brought me. He thought I was putting on airs—and I expect I was. I was probably pretty insufferable, with my quotations from Shakespeare and Gerard Manley Hopkins, my good French accent. (I corrected his: "*Ça ne fait rien,*" not "*San fairy ann.*") He could still usually trip me up, though, in geography or history—my sense of how things fit together was treacherously vague. Gerry knew an awful lot; he was always reading. He subscribed to a long series of magazines about the Second World War, which he kept in plastic folders on a shelf. Already, invidiously, however, I had an inkling that the books he read were somehow not the real books.

He was amused and patient, correcting my mistakes. He did it to my mother, too: as long as he had the upper hand, he was kind. If I had given in gracefully to that shape of relations between us—his lecturing me and my submitting to it—we might have been able to live happily together. My mother didn't care about his corrections; she just laughed at him. ("Oh, for goodness' sake, Gerry—as if it mattered!") But I couldn't give in. I wanted everything I learned to be an opening into the unknown, whereas Gerry's knowledge added up to a closed circle, bringing him safely back to where he began, confirming him.

I took Beckett up to my room.

It wasn't the kind of writing I was used to. I'd taught myself to stir in response to the captured textures of passing moments—the subtle essence of unspoken exchange, the sensation of air against the skin. Now I learned to read Beckett (and then, under Val's influence, Ginsberg, Burroughs, Ferlinghetti) like a convert embracing revolutionary discipline, cutting all links with my bourgeois-realist past.

"Is he your boyfriend, then?" Madeleine wanted clarification.

I was disdainful. "We don't care about those kinds of labels."

"But is he?"

"What does it look like?"

Val and I were inseparable. We saw each other almost every day—not only on the bus going to school and coming back but in the evenings, as often as my parents allowed me to go out or said he could come round. They claimed they were worried about my schoolwork, but I didn't believe them. I saw my mother recoil from what she dreaded—the dirty flare of sex and exposure; my making a fool of myself. (They were so innocent, I don't think they guessed about the drugs until much later.) Sometimes I went out even when they'd forbidden me to, and then there was trouble. When I got home, Gerry took me into the lounge for one of his lectures, screwing up his forehead, leaning toward me, pretending to dole out impartial justice. From my dizzy vantage point (high as a kite), I believed I could see right through him to his vindictiveness, his desire to shoot me down when I was flying. "They hate me," I said to Val. "Under his pretense of being concerned for my future, he really hates me. And she doesn't care." "Don't mind them," Val said, his eyes smiling. He blew out smoke. He was serene, bare feet tucked up on his knees in lotus position. "They're just frightened. They're sweet, really, your parents."

We were talking in his bedroom: a drafty attic where his books and clothes lay around in chaos on a Turkish carpet gray with cigarette ash, so unlike my little pink cell. Val's attitude toward his own parents was coolly disengaged. I was afraid of them—I tried to avoid meeting them on my passages through the rambling house (built when Stoke Bishop was still the countryside). They were both tall and big-boned. His father was stooped, with brown-blotched skin, long earlobes, and thinning white hair. His mother had a ruined face and huge, watery eyes; she wore pearls and Chinese jade earrings at the dining table in the evenings. (Unlike us, Val's family actually ate in their dining room.) They were polite with me, and their conversation was as dully transactional as any in my house, yet in their clipped, swallowed voices they seemed to talk in code above my head.

They never came up to his attic room. Sometimes his mother shouted up the stairs, if a meal was ready or Val was wanted on the telephone. We were private up there. I loved the evening shadows in the complex angles of the sloping ceiling. In summer, the heat under the roof was dense; in winter, we cuddled up for warmth under the blankets on his bed. Our bodies fit perfectly together—my knees pressed into the backs of his, my breath in the nape of his neck, his fingers knotted into mine against his chest; we lay talking, or listening to the Velvet Underground, Janis Joplin, Dylan. The shape of the long, empty room seemed the shape of our shared imagination, spacious and open. I couldn't believe the long strides he made in his mind, all by himself. Sometimes, depending on what pills he'd taken, he would talk and talk without stopping. "How do you know that I really exist, outside you?" he asked me urgently. "I might be a figment of your imagination."

Our heads were side by side then on his pillow. How lucky I was to lie like that, so intimate with his lovely looks that I couldn't see them whole: teasing green eyes, down on his upper lip, curving high hollows in his cheeks. I longed for him to begin kissing me, as he sometimes did, but I had learned that I must not try to initiate this—he didn't like being hurried into it. "I just know!" I insisted, stroking his face as if the feeling in my fingers were proof. "And I'm not a figment of yours, either. I'm really here, I promise."

"I believe in you. I'm not so sure about me. You're solid. You're fierce."

I wasn't as solid as I had been. Since meeting Val, I'd stopped bothering to eat. I couldn't bear my mother's gluey gravy any longer; I drank black (instant) coffee and gave up sugar. The weight had flown off me. Although I was small and Val was taller, we came to look like a matching pair: skinny and striking. By this time, we were on the fringes of a set who gathered at weekends in a sleazy bar behind a cinema in town. Val had a good instinct for the people worth getting to know: a man with freckled hands and a mane of red hair who sold him speed and other things; a clever art student, half Greek, who played in a band (they sounded like art-punk before punk had really happened). These men were older and more powerful, and a lot of people were eager to be their friends, but Val was able to impress them with his quick wit and cultural know-how.

I knew it mattered to Val that I look right. I wore his shirts and his sleeveless vests and his Indian silk scarves, over the tight jeans that he helped me buy. I put kohl around my eyes, and so did he sometimes. We both dyed our hair the same dark licorice color. (My mother was aghast, another scene—"Whatever are they going to say at school?") I paraded up and down the attic in different outfits for his approval, getting the effect just right, and yet when we went out we looked as if we didn't care what anyone thought. Val's idea of me was that I was single-minded, fiery, uncomplicated, without middle-class falsity. ("But aren't I middle-class?" I asked, surprised.) And I performed as his idea, became something like it.

We made plans to live abroad together—in Paris or New York. He'd been to both these places; I hadn't been anywhere except Torquay and Salcombe. He talked about how we'd earn money and rent an apartment, and I believed that he really could make these things happen. There was a rare blend in him of earnestness and recklessness. And he seemed to know instinctively what to read, where to go, what music to listen to. He was easily bored, and indifferent to anything he didn't like. Psychological novels were dreary, he said. The Beatles were consumer culture. I didn't talk to him about the old-fashioned books I'd loved before I met him.

"In New York, I'll work as a waitress," I said. "And you can write."

"Sometimes I think I could do something with my life," he said. "But then, in the middle of the night, something awful happens."

"What kind of awful?"

"I feel as if I'd already done it, this important thing—writing a book, or whatever it is. I feel as if it were a mountain to climb, and I'd toiled up the mountain and achieved the thing and I'm coming down the other side and it's behind me, and it's nothing. It doesn't alter anything in this world by one feather's weight. And then when I wake up I panic that, because I've already dreamed the end of the work, I'll never be able to begin."

But, more often, Val's mood was buoyant and exhilarated— he was impatient to get started. Everyone assumed he would take the Oxbridge entrance exam, go to university. For the moment, he went along with the idea. "My English teacher at school," he said, "he's invested a lot of hopes in me. He's giving me special tuition. I don't know how to tell him I'm leaving, not yet. Soon I will."

"Wherever you go," I said, "I'll follow you."

We ran into him once—the English teacher, Mr. Harper. Val and I were arm in arm, walking down Park Street on a Saturday in the crowds of people milling about and looking in the shops—jeans boutiques, bookshops, places selling Indian and Chinese knick-knacks and silver jewelry. A stubby middle-aged man was staring in a shop window; he veered away from it as we passed, almost walking right into us and then recognizing Val, putting on a show of surprise that seemed contrived, as if he'd actually seen us coming from miles off and prepared for this scene. I thought at the time that he was socially inept because he was such an intellectual. I knew that Val respected him, and that it was he who'd put Val onto Pound and Beckett and Burroughs. But I could see that Val wished we hadn't met him—he seemed shocked by this collision of the worlds of school and home.

"Hello, Valentine," Mr. Harper said. He was staring leeringly at me. "What a good way to spend your Saturdays. Aren't you supposed to be revising?"

"We're on our way to the reference library," Val said sulkily, blushing.

"Oh—then I mustn't get in the way of virtue! God forbid. But I will see you Tuesday, after school?"

"Is it Tuesday?" Val was vague. "I'm not sure."

"You must come on Tuesday. We're broaching the divine Marianne."

I was disappointed. Val had talked about Fred Harper (the boys doing the Oxbridge entrance called him Fred) as if he were a portal to higher things, yet here he was chaffing and prodding about work like any other teacher. Also, he was rumpled and pear-shaped, with pleading eyes, and a bald patch in his hair, which was dark and soft like cat fur. He had a drawling posh voice. I knew that there was a Mrs. Harper and also children; and that Mrs. Harper got bored if her husband and Val talked for hours about poetry. Sometimes she went to bed, leaving them to it.

"Who's the divine Marianne?" I said jealously when we'd walked on.

Valentine shrugged, irritated. "A poet in the A-level anthology."

Mum and Gerry were afraid I was bringing a contamination into their house. When I bought junk-shop dresses, Mum made me hang them outside in case of fleas. Val found an old homburg and wore it pulled down over his eyes.

"What does he think he looks like?" Gerry said.

"What's the matter with that boy?" Mum asked. "What's he hiding from?"

He stood in our neat kitchen with its blue Formica surfaces, as improbable—in his collarless shirt, waistcoat, and broken canvas shoes, with a scrap of vermillion scarf at his neck—as an exotic bird blown off course. Even in those days, when he was fresh and boyish, the drugs left some kind of mark on him—not damage, exactly, more like a patina that darkened his skin to old gold, refining its texture so that minute wrinkles appeared at the corners of his lids when he frowned. His eyes were veiled and smoky. He smelled, if you got up close: an intricate musk, salty, faintly fishy, sun-warmed even in winter—delicious to me.

"Hello? Anybody home behind that hair?" my mother said.

Val looked at me quickly, blissfully. Later, he would imitate her for our friends. While he was with me, everything was funny. Without him, I was exposed, on a lonely pinnacle—afraid of tumbling. They were still strong, my parents. I couldn't, wouldn't yield to their judgment of what I loved, but it weighed on me nonetheless, as monumental as a stone. If I tried to carelessly condescend to them, they found me out. I was clever, I was still doing well at school, but Gerry was clever, too.

"What's so wrong with Communism?" I'd lightly say, trying to be amused at their naive politics. I really was amused—I knew about so much beyond their blinkered perspective. I'd read poets and visionaries and *The Communist Manifesto*. "Doesn't it seem fairer that everyone should start out equally, owning a share of the means of production?"

"It's a nice idea, Stella," Gerry said. "Unfortunately, it doesn't work out in practice. People in those countries wouldn't thank you for your high ideals; they'd rather be able to buy decent food in the shops. The trouble is, a command economy just isn't efficient. Breaks down because of human nature in the end. Every man naturally wants to do better than his neighbor."

Because he knew those words—"command economy"—and I didn't, how could I answer him? His knowledge was flawed, but substantial—an impregnable fortress. My attacks on it—so effective when we were apart, and Gerry dwindled in my imagination to a comic miniature—faltered in his actual presence, so that I battered at the fortress with weak fists. Even in the seventies, the old order hadn't changed much. Young people wore their hair long and had afghan coats and went to music festivals—some young people did those things. But at the top, bearing down on everyone, there were still those ranks of somber-suited men (and the occasional woman): politicians, professors, policemen—inflexible, imperturbable in their confidence about what was to be taken seriously and what was not. You could jeer at them, but their influence was a fog you breathed every day, coiling into your home through their voices on radio and television and in newspapers. Gerry said that Africans suffering in a famine should know better than to have so many children, or that feminists did women no favors when they went around like tramps, or that there was no point in giving to charities because it was well-known that they spent all the money on themselves.

As for my mother, cleverness could never beat her. In my mind, I was convinced that her life—housework and child care—was limited and conventional. But, in my body, I was susceptible to her impatient brisk delivery, her capable hands fixing and straightening—sometimes straightening me, brusquely, even when I had half grown away from her: a collar crooked or a smudge on my cheek, which she scrubbed at with spit on her handkerchief. She was in her late thirties then, and no doubt she was very attractive, though I couldn't see it—compact good figure, thick hair in a short bouffant cut, definite features like strokes of charcoal in a drawing. Probably she was sexy, too. In her withholding and dismissing manner, she seemed to communicate that women knew the prosaic and gritty and fundamental truth that underlay all the noise of men's talk and opinion. Something I ought to know, too, or would come to know sooner or later. I wanted to resist knowing it with all my force.

The summer I got my O-level results (all A's, apart from a C in physics), my uncle Ray got me a job at the chocolate factory where he worked. I wept to Val about how the women there hated me and gave me the worst tasks (I had to take the molds off the hot puddings—at the end of the first day my fingers were blistered), because I was only a student worker and because I took a book to read during my breaks. I wanted him to tell me to give it up, but he didn't. I think that he actually liked the romance of my working there—it was not "middle-class." He said he loved my Bristol accent. Really? Did I have one? I didn't think so; my mother had always strictly policed the way I spoke at home ("'I wasn't doing anything,' Stella, not 'I weren't doing nothing'"). Apparently, however, I said *reely* for *really*, and *strawl* for *stroll.* "Your mother has an accent, too," he said. "Broader than yours. Can't you hear it? But I prefer it to the way my parents speak."

Valentine and I were bored one night with the flirting in Madeleine's bedroom. He rolled a joint—quickly, with the fingers of one hand, as only he could—and we went outside to smoke. The moon, watery white, sailed in and out behind dark rags of cloud blown by the wind; we lay spread-eagled on our backs on Pam's lawn. Only our fingertips were touching—through them we communicated electrically, wordlessly, as if we were emptying ourselves into each other. As the dope went to my head, I thought I felt the movement of the world turning.

Then I was sure that someone was spying on us from our garden next door. Madeleine's garden was perfunctory, compared with ours: there was a patio swing with chintz cushions, and a birdbath on the scrappy lawn, a few plants in the flower beds. Ours was densely secretive behind fences top-heavy with clematis and rose and honeysuckle; it had a trellised arbor and young fruit trees and a rockery, which Gerry had built to make a feature of the old tree stumps left behind by the developers. I despised his prideful ownership, the ceaseless rounds of pruning and spraying and deadheading. And it occurred to me now that he might be hidden in there. He did walk out into the garden in the dark sometimes—"to cool off," he said. If he was there, he'd be skewered with irritation, snooping involuntarily.

Val began to stroke my hand, rubbing his thumb around my palm, then pushing it between my fingers, one by one, over and over, until I was sick with love for him. But I knew better than to make any move toward him—he didn't like me all over him. There was a rustling from among the shrubs next door, and a head like a pale moon-blob rose above the top of the clematis mound.

"My stepfather thinks that I should get a job in a bank, when I leave school," I said aloud to Val.

Surprised, Valentine turned his head toward me. "Do you want a job in a bank?"

"Of course not. I'd rather kill myself. But he thinks it would be good for me, and provide for my future."

"He's a cunt," Valentine said. "What does he know about your future?"

"I know, he's a cunt."

The blob spoke. "Stella, come inside. You'll catch your death. That grass is damp."

Gerry's voice in the night was sepulchral, ridiculous, tight with disapproval. Only when I heard it was I aware of myself sprawled so provocatively on my back, with my legs spread wide apart, my arms flung open. Let him look, I thought. I didn't move. I pretended I didn't see him.

"Did you hear something?" I said to Val, squeezing his hand in mine.

We were going to laugh—I knew we were.

"Come inside, Stella, now, at once," Gerry said—but keeping his voice low, as if he didn't want my mother to know what he had to witness. "I'm telling you. Get up!"

Pointedly, he didn't address Valentine, ignoring his existence.

"I think I heard something," Valentine said. "Or was it cats?"

Leisurely, Val sat up, crouching over the cold end of the joint, his hand held up to shield it from the wind and his hair falling forward, hiding his face. Then came the scratch and flare of the heavy, shapely silver lighter that had been his mother's until she gave up smoking. Fire bloomed momentarily in Valentine's cave; I saw him aflame—devilish, roseate. I scrambled to my feet. I really was stoned. The garden swung in looping arcs around me. "Oh," I cried, exulting in it. "Oh . . . Oh!"

We were laughing now. Under my soles, the world rocked, and steadied itself, and rocked again.

"What's the matter with you?" Gerry hissed. He must have been standing on something—a rock? a box?—on the other side of the fence, because it was too high ordinarily to see over; his two fists, hanging on, were smaller moon-blobs against the night. "Are you drunk?"

(My parents still hadn't understood what we were smoking.)

"You'd better come back the front way. Come round by the front door."

"Back the front way, Stella?" Valentine imitated softly, looking at me, not at Gerry. "Front the back way? Which way d'you like?"

I had always had a gift of seeing myself as my stepfather saw me—only in this vision I used to be a small and thwarted thing, blocking him. Now, in the moonlight, I was transfigured: arms outstretched, veering like a yacht tacking, I was crossing the garden, flitting ahead of the wind, like a moth, weightless.

Valentine and I looked so consummately right as a couple: stylish, easily intimate, his arm dropped casually across my shoulder, our clasped hands swinging together. We looked sexy. I knew that because I saw it in others' faces. But the truth was, we didn't have sex. In all the time we'd spent lying on his bed (or, occasionally, on mine), we hadn't done an awful lot for Mum and Gerry to disapprove of.

We did work ourselves up; there was some touching and fumbling. I touched him, mostly; if he touched me he turned it into a joke, put on a funny voice as if my breasts were little animals squeaking and crawling around on my chest. Kissing, he pecked dry kisses all over my face with a satirical, popping noise, smiling at me all the time with his eyes open. Then sometimes, if his mother banged the gong for supper, or the phone rang and she called upstairs to say that Val was wanted, he grabbed my hand with sudden aggression, pushed it down inside his jeans, and used it to rub himself fiercely and greedily for a moment, before he flung himself off the bed and ran to the phone, zipping up as he went, cursing, pushing his erection away inside. I wasn't disgusted—actually, I'd say I was more fascinated—by my transgression into that crowded heat inside his stretched underpants, his smell on my fingers afterward. But also I was confused: if that was desire, it was unmistakably urgent.

So what was the matter?

Who wants to remember the awful details of teenage sex, teenage idiocy?

I loved him because he was my other half, my twin, inaccessible to me.

One evening I was supposed to babysit while Mum and Gerry went out to a Masonic Ladies' Night. I liked my baby brother very much: Philip was an enthusiast, always entertaining us with

jokes and little performances, looking quickly from face to face
for approval; he sat on his hands to keep them from waving about
and swung his legs under his chair until it rocked. When Mum
came downstairs, perfumed and startling in a silver Lurex bodice
and a stiff white skirt, he and I were laughing at *Dad's Army* on
the telly. She stood clipping on her earrings by feel, giving us her
instructions. The whole process of her transformation, she managed to convey, was just another duty to discharge.

"Stella, I don't want anyone coming round."

"Madeleine said she might."

"I don't want Valentine hanging around Philip if I'm not here."

I wasn't even expecting Val: he was at one of his sessions with
Fred Harper. But out of nowhere—everything had been all right,
the previous moment—I was dazzled by my rage. "What's the
matter with you?" I shouted. "Why have you got such a nasty
mind?"

I knew in that moment that she regretted what she'd said, but
only because she'd miscalculated and hadn't meant to start an
argument. She was afraid it would make them late; she glanced at
the wristwatch on a silver bracelet that had been Gerry's wedding
present to her. "Who you choose as your friends is your own business, Stella," she said stiffly. "But I'm not obliged to have them in
my house."

"Your house? Why d'you always call it your house? Don't I live
here or something?"

My stepfather hurried downstairs in his socks, doing up his
cuff links. He'd heard raised voices. I loathed him for the doggy
eagerness with which he came sniffing out our fight.

"What's going on, Edna?"

He irritated my mother, too. "For goodness' sake, get your
shoes on, Gerry. We're late already."

"I won't let her get away with talking to you like that."

"I'll talk to her how I like," I said. "She's my mother."

Philip went off into a corner, dancing on tiptoe with his

head down, shadowboxing, landing tremendous punches on the air: this was what he did when we quarreled, trying to make us laugh. *Dad's Army* wound up; the ordinary evening melted around us; then they were too late for their dinner dance, their treat spoiled. Mostly, I shouted and they pretended to stay calm. Soon I couldn't remember how it had all started: I felt myself washed out farther and farther from the safe place we usually cohabited. I couldn't believe how small and far away they seemed. It was suddenly easy to say everything. "You think you're so sensible and fair," I protested to Gerry. "But, really, I know you just want to destroy me."

"Don't be ridiculous," he said.

"Oh, Stella. D'you have to make such a performance out of everything?"

Gerry said that I wasn't a very easy girl to like, that I was arrogant and selfish. He crossed the room to close a window, because he didn't want the neighbors to hear us. At some point, Philip went quietly upstairs. I said that I would die if my life turned out to be as boring and narrow as theirs.

"Just you wait," my mother warned. "Boring or not, you'll have to get on with it like everybody else."

Gerry called my friends dropouts and deadbeats, a waste of space.

"That's what we think you are," I said. "We think you're dead."

"I'd watch out for Valentine if I were you," my mother said. "You might be barking up the wrong tree."

Gerry did lose his temper eventually.

"Get out, Stella, if you can't respect this house. Just get out."

Mum remonstrated with him, halfheartedly.

"Don't worry," I said. "I'm going. I wouldn't stay in this house if you begged me."

They didn't beg me. I let myself out the front door, into the street.

Freezing without my coat, and weeping, I went to Val's. His mother let me in and I waited for him in his attic, getting under the blankets to keep warm. When he came home from Fred Harper's, I heard her expostulating downstairs, saying that I couldn't stay, she wouldn't put up with it. So she didn't like me, either. And I heard Val's voice raised, too, yelling awful things. ("You silly bitch. Don't touch me!") An infectious rage was flashing around between us all that night, like electricity.

"I can't go back," I said, when he erupted into the room.

And he understood that it was true. Anyway, he'd had a row, too—with Fred Harper. He was leaving school. We'd both leave school. We'd leave home, too. This, I felt, was the beginning of my real life, of everything I had been waiting for. My real life, in my imagination afterward, always had that attic shape, high and empty and airy, cigarette smoke drifting in the light from a forty-watt bulb. Val said he knew someone who had a flat where we could stay. Tomorrow he'd sort it out. For tonight, I could stay here. He didn't care what his mother thought.

"Poor little Stella," he said. "Poor little you. I'm so sorry."

He was stroking my arms and nuzzling between my shoulder blades, trying to warm me up where I was rigid with cold. And there you are: that night he made love to me, properly—or more or less properly. Anyway, we managed penetration. And we did it another time, too, in the early morning a few days later, in a zipped-up sleeping bag in the front room of a fantastically disgusting ground-floor flat belonging to Ian, the freckled red-haired man who sold Valentine his drugs. We lay in the dawn light, crushed together on our narrow divan in the blessed peace of the aftermath, Val's head on my breast: proudly, I felt the trickling on my thighs. I suppose we must have heard the milkman's float passing—or perhaps by that time we had dozed off.

Then someone threw a full milk bottle through the closed window. I didn't understand at first what had happened: it was just an explosion in the room, appalling and incomprehensible, the crashing glass as loud as a bomb, milk splashed violently everywhere. (It seems unlikely that the drug dealer had a daily delivery—the bottle must have been picked up from someone else's doorstep.)

"What the fuck?" Val struggled up out of the sleeping bag, naked.

Ian came running in, pulling jeans on. "What the fuck?"

He cut his feet on the glass.

I saw in Val's face that he knew what the explosion was, and who.

Some other girl, I thought. Some old love. Someone he loves, or who loves him and is desperate for him the way I am.

But of course it wasn't any girl. It was his English teacher.

I thought—when the whole truth came out, when at last I'd understood about the sex, and Ian was so fucked off with Val about the window and was looking for him everywhere, and Val got some money from his older sister and went to the States, and it was all such a collapse of my hopes—I thought I could still go back, defeated, to my old life. Back home and back to school, and pick up where I'd left off, and be a clever girl again, and get to university. Even if I could never ever again, in my whole life, be happy.

But I wasn't that clever, was I?

Had I forgotten everything they'd taught us at school? That you only had to do it once, just once, to get into trouble. We had even done it twice.

Olivia Clare

Pétur

ASH FELL FROM THE wind. She began to take long walks. Before breakfast, after lunch, she walked the weed-pocked path to the lake. White ash turned the lake's surface to desert and the tops of *fjall*s invisible.

By the third morning, ash from Eyjafjallajökull coated the porch, the porch rail, the seats of the porch chairs, and the rented station wagon. The *hrossagaukur* had disappeared, and the cabin's weathervane creak had stopped. Laura told Adam, again, she was going out. He was her son. She tied a gauze scarf around her nose and mouth.

"I look like a robber," she said.

"No one will see you."

He opened the door for her into the otherworldly weather. She was garish in the ash in her flannel green coat. At the cabin window, he watched her diminish, and like a little boric flame a quarter mile out, her back rose on the path, then shrank and went out.

This dale in Iceland had a permanent population of eighty-six. They had seen almost no one . . . once or twice, until nine or ten at night, they'd heard shouting children. Icebabies, Laura called them. You can't ever see them, of course. They're made only of sound.

Adam was a data systems analyst. He was thirty-six. He lived in a one-bedroom apartment in Palo Alto, where Laura was, in a house she'd once shared with Adam's father on the other side of town. Iceland for two weeks had been her idea for her birthday. She'd just turned sixty-one, and she'd told Adam she didn't believe it, and he shouldn't, either. She'd said, You look in the mirror and acknowledge you're as old as you like. She felt nineteen, mostly. She looked fifty.

She returned from her walk late enough that Adam had made soup. The cabin had five rooms, floors of dull old wood, a kitchen and dining area adjoining the living room. There was a woodstove, a coffee table with a fan of women's fashion magazines, an expensive guitar on its stand, a box of black rocks and cockles from the lake and elsewhere, a striped sofa, a cushion ripped, all owned by the family they rented from.

"On the news they're saying don't go out at all," he said.

"But no one's said anything like that to me." She untied her scarf.

Bits of ash stuck to the silvering blond roots of her hair. She was tall, too slim. She wore blue jeans and tall boots.

"On TV, Mother." He put a roll and a bowl in front of her, soup with halibut and celery from the store in town.

"Well, people are out there," she said. "I talked to some people."

"Who's out there? Rangers?"

"I think it's coming down most at the lake," she said. "Right now it's like the moon. It's not dangerous on the moon." She put her scarf on the small dining room table. "Come with me, come to the lake. There isn't much ash."

"It's unhealthy."

She picked up a chunk of fish in her spoon. "What does *antimatter* mean?"

"What?"

"What's antimatter?"

"Antimatter?" Adam wiped his mouth with his napkin. He

liked when she asked questions he could answer. "Sure, it's like a mirror image, a negative image of matter, like matter's twin. And there are antiprotons. Antielectrons—"

"What happened to all the fish?" she said.

"In the lake? All dead, from the ash."

"I don't think they feel anything."

She walked in, waking Adam from a nap in a chair beside the fire in the woodstove. It had been two days. Her scarf was tangled around her neck. Her green coat off, a rip in her shirt at the elbow. She held her arm to her chest: a bright red cut like a seam showed through the rip. She went into the bathroom with a sleepwalker's involuntary smile and an alien tannic scent, maybe wine.

"You're going to laugh," she shouted, "when I tell you what happened."

"Let me help you," he said, getting up from the chair.

"It's fine," she said. "Sit down. It doesn't hurt."

Maybe she'd stolen a neighbor's skiff, as she'd done the week before, the day they'd argued because he'd looked out the window and said a *fjall* was beautiful. She'd told him not to call things that, told him that one word, *beautiful,* a word his father had used constantly, was limiting. She had learned the landscape, the words *rill, caldera,* and the names of wildflower species. Nights after her afternoon walks, she'd sit with a field guide. I have a birdheart, she'd say, your mother, the bird. Precise knowledge of a *fjall*'s origins, or of the call each bird made, was the closest she felt she had, she said, to wisdom, because *land,* because details, were important. They were solid and finite and felt infinite.

"Let me help you," Adam said again. "Please."

She came back into the room. "I was climbing up that boulder on the shore. I had my camera with me and a bird swooped near my head, and I just tumbled off. Your mother. On the ground."

"No more walks."

"I wasn't going to," she said.

"It's like with those eggs. You forget what you're doing."

"That nest's still in my room at home," she said. "It's one of the few objects I like to own."

She looked at him, expecting a response. She tired him. What did she want? He knew how she thought of him, his "normalcy." She said what she thought, and there was both innocence and maturity in that. When she was eleven, she'd told him, she had watched her brother die from a rare leukemia. She'd spent the rest of her life trying to strike lightning back.

"Don't worry," she said. "The eggs are alive."

"I believe you," he said.

Laura had raised him on her "wisdom and whims"—she'd taken him to museums and operas, he'd had a violin and no television, she'd taught him the names of native ferns and trees around their house. Sometimes she'd invented names. On Adam's first day of high school, she'd taken his face in her hand and told him school was for wolves and sheep, that wolves and sheep ought to be separate, and that she wanted him to be a wolf. She was a wolf. His father was a sheep.

He'd attended college on the East Coast, joined a fraternity, been an average student. He visited her that first Christmas, then stopped. When they talked on the phone, she told him he'd become something else, someone she didn't understand.

Ten years ago, after he graduated, Laura called him: they'd found a small tumor in her neck. He flew to Palo Alto to live with her awhile, to help her. She'd told him it wasn't necessary. She recovered fully, incredibly, and he'd obtained a small apartment and a job there, told himself he'd been planning to live in California anyway and that it was the "right thing to do." Now he saw her every Sunday dinner, some weeks more frequently to help around the house, though she claimed she didn't need him.

He aged uneventfully, a little sadly. Gained a little weight, lost a little hair. He was often ill with some nonthreatening flu or infection; he had problems with his joints. He saw several doctors and specialists. Sometimes he had a girlfriend, and there was a coworker he slept with occasionally.

But Laura—she'd become younger, uncommonly healthy. Woke earlier, stayed up later, ate what she wanted, always hungry. It was as if she were subtracting years. Some days she told him her ecstatic dreams, which never contained people. They both forgot these dreams immediately.

After dinner she stood on the sofa and took down the three framed watercolors on the living room walls.

"Be careful," he said.

"It's just that they're a bit disgusting. Kitsch." She balanced on the back of the sofa, her feet clinging to the edge. She'd painted her toenails pink the night before. "I should have done this a while ago."

"They're not ours."

"I refuse to stare at it anymore. It's unhealthy." She jumped off the sofa without trouble and stacked the watercolors in a corner and looked around the room for anything else that offended her. She took the fashion magazines from the coffee table and put them in a drawer.

"I think I'll go for a walk," she said.

"Please don't."

"Please don't tell me don't."

"Mother. Don't go outside."

"You love scolding me. You think you get something from it. Like your father."

"All right," he said. "Then I'll come with you."

They walked to the lake with scarves tied around their faces—he'd insisted, though the ash had stopped falling. This time of year, the sun did not fully set until ten o'clock at night. The other cabins, spaced around the dale, were out of focus in the northern pre-twilight. Another constellation of cabins, mirroring their own, across the lake. A giant *fjall* above them.

She'd been asking to come to Iceland for years, ever since she'd met an Icelandic man, divorced and in his fifties. A year after she'd recovered from her illness, she had started seeing him, and then had stopped abruptly. But she still needed to visit the place that felt like both "the end of this world and the beginning of another," the man had told her, "a second life." Adam wouldn't let her go by herself. What a good son you are, they'd said to him at work. Your mother's very lucky. He'd felt he had no choice.

He was quiet while they walked, he knew that was important to her, but he wanted to say something about the red blinking light across the lake—the ranger's station—and the sound of the skiffs knocking against one another, tied on the shore. He felt old and practical. He felt he wasn't there.

"God," he said finally.

"What?"

"Everything. The news last night. We're trapped. A volcano erupted, we're trapped."

"We have a car," she said.

"It needs gas. It's a hundred dollars here for a tank, you know. A hundred twenty-five."

"I see."

She didn't. The trip had cost them thousands. She owned her house in California outright, had a small pension from Adam's father, and Adam helped her take care of the rest. She knew nothing of money; she'd forget to pay bills. She'd bought a car she couldn't afford. Here, of course, but even in California, she acted as though currency were foreign to her. At restaurants, she treated money like it was only paper, holding it by the corners. She left waiters incredible tips.

"We're not trapped," she said.

"We are. That's the perfect word for what we are."

"Think of this as something else, meaningful. Maybe this is a land of ash now. This is some kind of other place. Ashland."

She was asking him to concede, to play her game, as she'd

asked him to imagine things when he was a child. He wouldn't anymore, he said nothing, and she looked at him with disappointment, as if he'd played the wrong notes on the piano. But in fact he'd played nothing. For years, he'd only sat silently on the bench in front of the keys.

They'd come to the lake, a layer of ash on the surface, gray-white. Torn bits of paper. She took off one of her shoes and put a toe in the shallow water. Specks of ash stuck to her pink toenails. She let her whole foot sink in.

"Isn't it too cold?" he said.

"We're not trapped," she said.

"We're in a volcano. We're trapped. It's remarkable."

"It isn't remarkable. Nothing is merely remarkable. You think something can be one word," she said, taking off her other shoe and standing with both feet in the lake. "You can enjoy yourself. Not think the way you do. You're not always just who you think you are."

She spoke softly, as if to herself. Her inflections were neutral, anonymous, any evidence of her Midwestern origins gone. She had sung with a band in the seventies in Ohio, she habitually told him. Music producers had been interested, but her own mother had been jealous of any success, of any attention she'd received.

"Look, I'm tired," he said.

"Everyone I know is always tired. Why?"

"I'm sorry."

She looked at him—a stranger's doubt and maternal empathy—and he wanted to ask her either to hug him, as sentimental as it was, or to leave him alone. An act of kindness, or nothing at all. She was incapable.

"Your father said it that way. You never heard him say it."

"We should walk back now," he said.

Adam drove in the morning to the base of the dale with his laptop, on his thighs, bumping against the steering wheel. The wagon's tires crushed sprigs of lupine powdered with days-old ash. Parked across from the ranger station, he leeched the station's Internet and e-mailed clients. He was scheduled to return to Palo Alto in two days, but he knew they couldn't leave by then. The road to Reykjavík was closed indefinitely.

He had been gone a half hour and had driven halfway back, when, rounding a switchback, he saw Laura two hundred feet below, a little green jacket in high boots. She used a bowed branch as a walking stick. She carried a backpack he'd never seen before.

He parked the car on the side of the gravel road, tied his scarf around his face, and followed her down the path to the lake, through the tangle of bushes. She hadn't seen him, he was sure of it, but she walked as if pursued.

At the lake he hid behind a boulder. She crouched amid drifts of ash on the black rock shore. Hands quick as a sharp's dealing cards, she seemed to sort rocks into stacks—minutes of this— then scooped a stack into her backpack and kicked the second into the lake. She was talking to herself—he'd caught her doing this before, at the house, washing her hands at the sink, gesturing to herself with the water running, talking and singing to no one, sometimes without words, cooing. She worried him . . . sometimes he thought she was too forgetful and scattered, too unpredictable or immature, or that she might be approaching a very mild, early form of senility. He worried he couldn't help her.

She left the lake. He followed her down another path, overgrown with wildflowers and weeds. She was walking up a stairway to a cabin. Weather-battered, smaller than theirs, with blue shutters. No antenna on the roof, no car in the gravel driveway lined with walls of bushes. She knocked once, then opened the door herself, leaving stick and backpack on the porch.

Adam was heating soup when she returned, holding her scarf. She had the same preoccupied, sleepwalker's smirk, her blue jeans stained black at the cuffs.

"What happened?" he said.

"I looked for fish, for anything living. There weren't any eggs out there, either."

She'd been gone a few hours since he'd seen her enter the other cabin. Her backpack was gone. She put her scarf on the table and warmed her hands in the steam from his teacup. Sometimes she'd sit still so long she'd turn, not "to stone," as she knew she'd scold him for thinking, but to what? An inanimate vacancy, with eyes, wide-set as an elf owl's, that could blink her alive.

"You were at the lake?"

"I can't see to its bottom. Looking at the lake for so long makes me never want to look at land."

"Where's your backpack?"

She scraped her chair on the floor and stood very quickly. "I'll be back in a minute."

She went to her bedroom. He almost followed her; he went to the bathroom. Her cosmetics, her face powder, her tiny bronze cylinders of perfume, were on the glass countertop. A canister of rouge had spilled. He collected it in a mound and then released the mound into the sink. Ten years ago, when she'd been ill, he'd had to help her to the bathroom. She'd put both arms around his neck while they walked. There is no gulf between humans as wide as between the ill and the well. When she was finished, she'd call for him to help her to the bed. She'd told him she'd been trying to discover something unearthly, being nearer death. She couldn't find it. She'd told him he could have her pearls, her dog. Everything. How remarkable, impossible, that she was completely well now and did not need him.

The light was off in her bedroom, but before he reached the doorway he heard her talking to herself, so softly he couldn't understand it. It seemed as if she was trying to calm herself. He could smell her, the lotion she used on her face: lavender, clean. She sat on the bed, still as a sphinx.

"Mother?"

"Is there soup left?" she said, when she saw him. She looked startled. "For tomorrow's lunch?"

"What were you doing?" he said. He switched on a lamp in the room. He moved to touch her, and her shoulder tensed. He moved away.

"What?" she said.

"I saw you," he said. "In that house. You told me you'd stop going outside."

"I don't think I said that." Lying meant nothing to her.

"I saw you go in that cabin."

"Pétur lives there, by himself. I met him one time, walking."

"But you agreed with me," he said. "It isn't healthy."

He wanted her to say she agreed, to apologize. He could feel himself start to try to take her by the hand.

"Pétur has," she said, "has turned into a friend, I think."

She looked past him, toward the door. She was done talking. He saw in her face she intended to dismiss him. With her, you could risk nothing. She forgave nothing, not the slightest imposition upon the complex world she believed in. She saw that he was simple, he thought, a teenager or a very old man. It scared him to watch her that way. Scared him more to watch her watch him that way.

Adam slept the kind of skeletal, half-sleeping wakefulness that allowed him the belief he was asleep. A car door somewhere in the dale closed, and he looked at the digital clock, then turned on the TV. All European flights were stranded for a week, and cots and cotless irate passengers crowded Heathrow terminals. Eyjafjallajökull had erupted a second time, ash had descended on London and Scotland, and there was concern about Katla, another volcano, in Vík í Mýrdal—"Could you turn it off?" Laura called from her room.

She left before he rose. The tattoo of her boots on the wood floor. He made sure she had gone before he got out of bed and made coffee and built a fire in the woodstove.

He came into a sheer fog at the end of the path. It was very early. There were no lights on in the cabins, most of them probably empty.

He came to the lake, now dusted with faint patches of ash. He hadn't been able to convince himself not to follow her. He stopped at a boulder too tall to sit on and tightened the scarf around his face. The lake was the color of weathered nickel. Small rocks like globules of oil littered a shallow bed at the shore. The water, hitting the edge of the boulder he leaned on, sprayed up in a tiny spire. Across the lake, the other cabins were dark, too. A waterfall, tiny from where he stood, forked a few feet from the top of the *fjall.*

He walked the same path he'd seen her walk the day before. Bugs nagged his arms. He passed abandoned cabins; others had tiny yards with patio furniture. In one yard was a plastic yellow toy car with ash on its roof.

He came to the bottom of the steps he'd seen her climb. "Pétur's" steps. Trees obscured the house. From the bottom of the stairs, Adam could see only the housetop, the woodstove chimney.

There was a table on the porch. A small gas grill. He stepped over an open garbage bag spilled on its side. He decided, without really considering, to crouch below a corner of the screened window and to look in with one eye.

Adam could see his mother at the other end of the house. She was alone, putting pots on the stove, lips in motion. The cabin was one room, much smaller than theirs, with hardly any furniture. A table with chairs, a bed, an armchair in the corner, no refrigerator, dark rhombuses on the wall where frames had been. He could hear her now, talking quickly. He studied the interior, the corners. She was alone.

On the floor were her flannel green coat and the backpack he'd seen the other day. Rocks she'd collected from the shore were stacked in a pyramid and placed as a centerpiece on the table. Cans on the counter, open cans he recognized from their house, cans he'd bought himself at a nearby town's store. She was talking, and he made out not the words, but the tone, the cooing inflection.

She became very quiet. He watched from the window. She brought a bowl of dim liquid to the table and ate, closing her eyes. He watched this a long time. She put her bowl and spoon in the sink. Then she pulled her dress over her head. She had on a pale slip. She took off her rings.

If Adam's life was "ordinary," an average of a series of predictable events, maybe that was why, for him, there was no Pétur. On the bed, she climbed on top of nothing, of no one himself, and moved her hips forward and back.

David Bradley

You Remember the Pin Mill

YOU ARE DRIVING WEST across the state, at the insistence of the commonwealth's Department of Corrections, when you remember the pin mill.

Just a shape when you first saw it, through the windshield of the Goddamn Rambler: a vague but jagged blackness looming in the gray ahead. You turned to warn your mother, but in the predawn light you glimpsed the contours of her face and turned back, only then you saw Whatever It Was rising up and clawing with skeletal appendages at the pearlescent sky.

But then you realized: Whatever It Was wasn't rising; the Goddamn Rambler was coming down a long, steep hill. So maybe Whatever It Was was sleeping and nothing would happen if you went by quietly. Only the Goddamn Rambler would not go quietly. The Goddamn Rambler coughed and sputtered, though you whispered, *Shh, shh, shh.* Then the Goddamn Rambler backfired, and you saw Whatever It Was turn.

But then you realized: *it* wasn't turning; the road was, curving away. Maybe far enough away that Whatever It Was couldn't hurt her, even if it did awake.

. . .

You remember when you learned its name: after a cough-and-sputter climb and a big door opening wide; after an old man with glinting glasses and a gray mustache, in bare feet and a bathrobe, helped her up a flight of winding, waxed wood stairs; after he came back down in blue suit pants and shiny slippers and said he was pleased to meet you and you didn't need to call him sir, plain Grandpa would do fine; after he led you to a kitchen with two stoves in it and sat you down in what he said had been your Grandmother Godrester's favorite chair, and put on a bib apron with magenta flowers on it and said he was going to fix you a real country breakfast.

Then he was doing something in the black stove with MAJES-TIC in silver letters on the door, and you were rocking, back and forth, back and forth, until you smelled smoke and heard a scream and leaped up and shouted, "Who's that? Who's that?" But he said, "Rest easy. Pay no mind. That's just the whistle at the pin mill," and his voice was calm and patient, so you tried, only you still heard it in your head and the chair went back-forth, back-forth.

Then he took you by the hand and pulled you out the kitchen door, across a swath of dew-damp grass, onto a broad, black rock, and you saw the empty air beyond and wondered if he'd throw you over for not resting easy. But he knelt, groaning, beside you, wrapped his arm around you, pointed over the edge, and said, "Look."

And you looked over treetops and steeples and saw the rooftops of a miniature town, like at Wanamaker's at Christmas, with gray paint streets, an Erector Set bridge over a blue paint river, and train tracks on the other side, only instead of Lionelville Station, there was a dark shape wreathed in smoke. "That's the pin mill," he said, and you realized: it all looked small only because you were high above.

He told you a mill was a factory, and pins were wooden screws that held insulators onto telephone poles, and insulators held the wires but were made lots of places; this was the only mill in the whole nation that made pins. And he said, "Some call this the hind end of the earth, but all the telephones, clean to the Pacific, depend on pins made in Raystown."

Then he pointed to freight cars on a siding, and told you how logs came in on bulkhead flats and pins were trucked out in semis, and traced what he called the access road to where it connected with what he called root two twenty, and pointed to a tractor-trailer, bound for the 'Pike, he said, turning onto it and starting up a long, steep hill. But suddenly somehow you were coming down in the Goddamn Rambler, and you realized: the pin mill was what you'd seen maybe sleeping in the night. Only now it was awake.

Then treetops, steeples, rooftops vanished; the pin mill was all that you could see. You felt yourself lean toward it, felt yourself take a step. But then you felt your Grandpa's arm, holding you and turning you, and then magenta flowers were all that you could see.

Now you remember *ring-ring-ring, ring-ring-ring,* and waking in a room a-clutter with dolls and teddy bears, thinking it was night until through a pink-curtained window you saw a porch awash with sunlight and your mother perched sideways on the rail.

Her head was lowered, chin-to-chest, so her hair hid her face, and her blouse was long sleeved, high collared, white—her neck looked like a swan's—and her left arm hung languidly, a cigarette dangling from her fingers.

The *ring-ring-ring*ing stopped. You heard your Grandpa say, "Hello? . . . Yes, Hal, she's here," and she raised the cigarette to her lips and winced, but the tip glowed bright. Then he said, in the calm, patient voice, "No, Hal; she does not wish to speak with you."

Then he said, "No, Hal, I don't intend to interfere between a man and his wife—" and then was quiet, listening, and she lowered the cigarette and you saw the filter, red, as if from lipstick, but no smoke.

Then he said, "Excuse me, Hal, but your wife is also my daughter. She is always welcome in my house, for as long she wishes." Then you heard a *ting* and saw smoke plume silver and her lifting her chin, but her hair swung back and her cheek was like a plum about to burst and you had to close your eyes.

And you remember, when it was really night, hearing your Grandpa upstairs, telling her he didn't know how that darned junker ever made the grade, and suddenly somehow you were in the Goddamn Rambler, with the blazing and bellowing coming from behind, and huge tires howling alongside, and then wind slapping right-left-right-left-right, and her wailing wordlessly. And she said, "It almost didn't, Daddy. Daddy, I almost didn't make it home."

You remember *eeoheeohchkchkchk*, warm air wafting through the window, Raggedy Ann and Aunt Jemima, and a humpback trunk treasured with camphored quilts and a box of eight Crayolas, peeled and sharpened like she'd done with your box of sixty-four.

You remember the black telephone in the alcove in the hall, with no dial and no dial tone but ladies on it talking.

You remember the claw-footed, scaly-legged table in the dining room, and the straight-legged one in the kitchen with your Grandpa behind it, glasses on his forehead, fists crushing a thin newspaper, muttering about whipping horses and dogs, until he saw you and said to pay him no mind, he was just an old bear growling like he still had teeth.

You remember the sounds from the upstairs hall—click of lock, creak of hinge, footfalls, slow and heavy, rush of water in the pipes, footfalls going back, dull thud of closing door.

You remember the cold milk your Grandpa poured from a green glass jar—sweet milk, he called it—and the ham he had to simmer to get the salt out, he said, and the eggs he cracked one-handed, and the onions he sliced underwater so he wouldn't cry, and that though the ham was salty anyway, the milk was sweet as sugar if you warmed it in your mouth.

You remember the porch—the veranda, he called it—that went all around the house, and the chair on chains he called a swing, though it wouldn't go fast or high, and the tree, a-teem with birds, that towered at the forest's edge. He said its name was Quercus Rubra and you, not thinking, said, "Trees don't have names . . . ," and stopped. But he just laughed and said this one did, and in the fall the birds, except the crows of course, held a convention there to decide where to spend the winter, and you could poll the factions because each kind of bird had a different song. And you said, Like *Peter and the Wolf*? but he said, No, these were real country birds; they didn't sing opera.

You remember the doors that slid into the walls, the green glow of bankers' lamps, the big battered desk he said was older than he was, the dictionary—the Lexicon, he called it—so heavy it had its own desk—a lectern, he called it—and the shelves that bowed with books. You asked if you could read them, certain he'd say no, but he said to take a crack at anything you could reach.

You remember him at the black stove—the Majestic, he called it—stirring something steaming in a white-and-blue speckled pot. Broth, he said; good for what ailed you, and he lifted you to see the chicken rolling in the roiling water, and let you add peppercorns, parsley, and thyme.

You remember his calm, patient voice lulling you to sleep with the tale of Indian Eve, who was kidnapped by the Mohawks, indentured by the British, but crossed four hundred miles of wilderness on foot to bring her son home safe to Raystown.

Now you remember the Patrician, your Grandpa's Prussian-blue Packard sedan, with the chrome grille and headlight mounts like his mustache and glasses, and an arch-necked bird on the hood, dropping like a roller coaster past big houses of gray stone;

and him, in the whole suit and a white shirt and blue tie and black shoes with pinholes in the toes, with one foot on the brake because, he said, it was a 15 percent grade.

And he said this was Juliana Street, and you were in Juliana Heights, and you asked was it named for your mother? and he said he'd told her so when she was your age, but in fact it was for William Penn's daughter-in-law, did you know who Penn was? and you did, and that *sylvania* meant woods, and he said you were a smart fella, and the street at the bottom of the grade was Richard, for one of Penn's sons, and lots of Raystown's streets were named for Penns, because the Old Settlers thought sycophancy would forestall a whiskey tax, and you said you knew what whiskey was, but he didn't call you a smart fella again; he just coughed.

Richard Street was like a highway, with a double yellow line and lots of cars and trucks, and a semi made a machine-gun sound when your Grandpa pulled out in front of it, but he said pay it no mind, he had the right-of-way. Then the line disappeared and Richard Street was like a tunnel, roofed by leaves, sided by thick-trunked trees, and behind them were sidewalks and houses of red-orange brick, and in front of one you saw a statue of a monkey in white pants, a red jacket, and a red cap, holding a lantern, only then you realized: it wasn't a monkey—just a man with a brown face. Then you saw another statue: a man with a gray face in a long gray coat, holding a rifle, but he was on a pillar in the middle of the street.

And he said that was the Monument, and now you were in the Public Squares, where respectable lawyers had offices—him too, until he got elected and had chambers in the Courthouse, which was over there, but now he only had the study because he'd retired from everything except the Board of the First National and the Generally Board. And you saw boys running on broad, grassy lawns and climbing on two big black cannons—and then a building white as chalk, with tall columns and wide steps, and a blue-and-orange Rexall and a red-and-gold G. C. Murphy, and then the Patrician stopped and you looked through the windshield and saw a red light and beyond it the Erector Set bridge.

And he was saying how if you went left you'd be on Forbes Road, which, past the Fairgrounds, turned into Route 30, which was how he went to Pittsburgh, but if you went right you'd be on River Road, which went out the East End and through the Narrows, then ran along the Raystown Branch for fifteen miles to Juniata Crossing before it turned into Route 30, and how River Road had been a famous scenic route before the Doggone Democrats built the 'Pike, and even nowadays some folks got off at the Raystown Interchange to drive—and you said, "It's straight ahead."

And he said, "Why, yes, Richard turns into Route 220 and goes straight up to the 'Pike. You *are* a smart fella," only that wasn't what you meant but when the light turned green he stuck his arm straight out the window and went left.

You remember the red-striped pole; the scents of cloves, bay rum, and talc; the trout and whitetail leaping on dog-eared magazines; the slap-swish of razor on strop; the chair like the La-Z-Boy, only it was your Grandpa in it, and his face creamed with lather, and wishing you had whiskers too.

You remember the restaurant wrapped in tinfoil and shaped like a coffeepot, and the men on stools along the counter, and the lady with orange hair behind it who poured coffee into a mug with HIZZONER on it when your Grandpa walked in. He told them you were his grandboy and a real smart fella, and asked the lady to make you a black cow, and she brought you a glass of root beer with vanilla ice cream in it and a thin, long-handled metal spoon, and you ate while the men growled about horsewhipping the Doggone Democrats.

You remember Cohen's Emporium, where a clerk in a black skullcap piled up underwear, socks, shirts in pastel colors with alligators on the pocket, and pants—trousers, your Grandpa called them—of khaki and gabardine, and blue jeans, which he called dungarees, and a blue sweatshirt with NITTANY LIONS in white letters on the chest, and a heavy purple-and-gray plaid jacket he called a mackinaw.

Then the clerk said to put your feet in a machine and, right through your sneakers, you could see your toes in green, but the clerk said you shouldn't be wearing Red Ball Jets because your arch was weak; you needed P. F. Flyers with the Magic Wedge. Your Grandpa said you'd need brogans too, for when you went exploring in the woods, and you liked the high-topped leather shoes with thongs instead of laces but felt sorry for your old sneakers and hoped he wouldn't make you go.

Then the clerk brought out gray fuzzy shoes with no laces he called Hush Puppies and said were the Latest Thing for the Young Man, but your Grandpa called them loafers so you asked for shoes like his, but the clerk said he only carried wingtips for mature gentlemen, and your Grandpa said, "You mean old geezers, don't you?" and the clerk said he only meant . . . and stopped. But your Grandpa just laughed and said send the bill.

And you remember how, when you thanked him for the presents, he said, Oh these were just a few things you'd need since you'd be staying in Raystown, and you realized: you hadn't thought of staying anywhere except away.

You remember swinging back and forth through the hot bright days, listening to birds flittering and tittering in Quercus Rubra, reading books from lower shelves, learning to pay no mind at noon and quitting time.

You remember bedtime tales: of Alliquippa, queen of the Seneca, who sent her braves to save George Washington from the French; of James Smith and his Brave Fellows, who dressed up like Indians and ran the Redcoats out of Raystown while those Sons of Liberty in Boston were still drinking tea; of Jacob Dibert, who found the Lost Children of the Alleghenies; of Davy Lewis, who stole gold from gunrunners, gave it to poor widows to pay taxes, then stole it from the tax collector, and who stopped to visit his mother, though the sheriff was in hot pursuit, and, with just his horse for company, hid out in these very woods in a cave that nobody'd ever found.

You remember the *ring, ring, ring*ing, the *chuff, chuff, chuff*ing of his slippers on the stairs, his voice saying, "Yes, Hal . . . Who else, this time of night? . . . Hal, this is a party line so don't say anything you don't want half the town to hear and the rest to know about by noon."

You remember waking to a stench of vinegar, ammonia, and stale tobacco smoke and seeing your mother in a nightgown, moving gingerly around the room. She clutched her right arm to her side, like she was holding something in, but reached out with her left hand to caress each doll and teddy bear. Watching with half-closed eyes, you envied them her touch, but when she turned her face toward you, you closed them all the way.

You remember the path, warded by briar and thorn, that led from Quercus Rubra into the darkling forest.

You remember the broad, black rock your Grandpa said was part of the Appalachian Bedrock and called the Lookout because Queen Alliquippa's braves kept watch from there, and seeing him, at sunset, keeping watch there too.

You remember the Majestic and the tools he used to tend it: spring-handled lid-lifter, wiry scraper, poker hooked and pointed like a halberd. He showed you how to rouse the fire—to shake the ashes from the embers, set the draft and damper, add a little kindling, and wait patiently for flame—and you shouldn't try it yet, but one day you'd need to know.

You remember the wood in a hodgepodge pile outside the kitchen door—bark-scabbed slabs, skewed oblongs, out-of-kilter cones with broken screw threads at the ends. Chunks of pin-mill scrap, your Grandpa said, cut to stove length so nothing went to waste, and he showed you how to carry them: elbows at right angles and tight to your sides, palms up, fingers crooked. Then he said, "Let's load you up," and began laying chunks across your arms. He said, Say When, but you didn't know what Say When meant, and when he stopped loading you up the weight seemed more than you could bear. But he said, Take it step-by-step, and went beside you, steadying, and then ahead to do the opening and closing, and then he took the weight from you, chunk by chunk by chunk.

You remember going up the winding, waxed wood stairs, balancing a bowl of steaming broth on a silver tray, setting it gently on the table outside her bedroom door, knocking softly, only once, and going down again.

And you remember following him, at sunset, onto the Lookout, feeling it was wrong to let him keep watch alone. Only then you realized: maybe he wasn't, because you saw his lips moving, like he was talking to someone, though he wasn't making any sound. He laid his hand lightly on your head but didn't look at you until the lowering sun touched the mountains to the west. Then he coughed and said, "See the river?"

And you looked and saw a stream of gold flowing through the town and disappearing into the mountain to the east. And he said, "Rivers are lazy. Even famous rivers—the Euphrates, the Nile, the Congo, of course, but even the Mississippi; they all take the easy way. But not the Raystown Branch."

Then he told you how, a billion years ago, Africa encroached on North America and though the Appalachian Bedrock was the hardest rock on earth, it was forced to fold up into ranges of mountains, with ridges running north and south and sheer slopes facing east.

"Geologists call it the Allegheny Front," he said. "Two hundred miles long, two thousand feet high. When the first Europeans crossed the Susquehanna they saw it and called it the Great Wall and said there was no sense in going further. But some heard a Voice calling from beyond and looked for a way through.

"The river'd made it for them. Instead of flowing north or south between the ranges, the Raystown Branch cut what geologists call water gaps, right through solid rock. It took a hundred million years, but the river got through.

"Some Europeans came west through those gaps; a hundred miles against strong current. The gaps were there, but every passage was perilous, all boulders and whitewater, and somebody was always saying there was no sense in going further. But some still listened to the Voice and went on, and gradually they stopped being Europeans and became Americans, and eventually they reached the final gap.

"That's it, where the river disappears. They called it the Narrows because the banks were sheer and close. Some died trying to make that passage. Most didn't even try. But a few got through.

"And they found a beloved country, rich with game and fish and timber, and coal and hematite, and springs of healing water. So they cleared land and sowed crops, and built a town and a fort, and fought off the Indians and the French and the British, and put a scare into the Federals too.

"Those were the Old Settlers. My ancestors, and your Grandmother's, and your mother's . . . and yours. They took their spirit from that river that went the hard way for a hundred million years. We take ours from them. And we'll, by God, get through."

Now you remember your mother coming barefoot down the stairs, in her nightgown, hair a-tangle, shouting it should be her taking you, and stumbling, and your Grandpa catching her and saying, in his calm voice, Rest easy, he guessed he still had pull enough to get a boy into fifth grade, she should stay in until she was feeling better. Then she said, "You mean looking, don't you?" and pushed him away and knelt to tuck your alligator shirt into your khakis, and told you to be brave but all you looked at were black wingtips, gray Hush Puppies, and her pale pink toes.

You remember your Grandpa parking the Patrician beneath a *flap, flap, flap*ping flag, and telling you your ancestors were Old Settlers so you belonged in Raystown and didn't have to give account to anybody. "It's nothing you need be ashamed of," he said, "but folks here love to mind other folks' business, especially People Like Us." Then suddenly somehow you were in the Goddamn Rambler, waking to a toll booth's glare, hearing a man say, "Two dollars," and your mother saying she didn't have any money, but she'd see he got it later. And he said, "Who do you think you are?" and she said, Please, and a man's name, and he said her name, like a question, and she said, Yes, but turned her head when he leaned down to look, and he wouldn't raise the gate until she let him see her face.

You remember the peppermint-breathed principal who kept calling your Grandpa Your Honor, and the white-capped nurse who poked your hair with a toothpick because she said there was no telling where you'd been, and waiting beside Smokey Bear, who said ONLY YOU CAN PREVENT FOREST FIRES, until a teacher with hair like Brillo took you to her classroom, asking questions as you went, and the boys who laughed at your Hush Puppies and the girls who giggled, at what, you never knew, and hot dogs dipped in ketchup for lunch, which they called dinner, and getting picked last at recess, and being called a liar when you said you'd seen the ocean, and the teacher telling you not to brag, even if it was true, and pretending not to know answers already, and the beep they called a bell, and your Grandpa in the Patrician, parked beneath the flapping flag.

You remember him waiting every day, glasses propped up on his forehead and a book in hand, or head drooping, but not sleeping, just resting his eyes, he said. Some days he'd say he needed you to help him run errands, and you'd walk together past the house where George Washington had slept and the church that was where the jail Davy Lewis escaped from twice used to be, to the Post Office, where you'd look at WANTED posters while he got mail from the box, and to the First National, where he'd sign papers while a lady who looked old but wasn't would ply you with horehound slugs and questions until you'd get mad and go make the revolving door go *whupwhupwhup*, and to the grave-yard where the Old Settlers were buried, and your Grandmother too, God rest her.

Other days he'd drive south on Richard, past Juliana and the Inn at Anderson's Springs to where it turned into Route 220, and tell you how, way back when, he'd had a Buick roadster—canary yellow, black rag top, rumble seat, ninety horses—that went like a bat out of . . . a cave, and when he was courting your Grand-mother he'd drive her out this way because the road ran straight and near-level all the way to Mason & Dixon's Line so he could open 'er up, and she loved the speed, even though she wouldn't learn to drive, but she'd pretend she didn't like the top down because the wind blew her hair all wild, but eventually she'd throw her head back and close her eyes and let the wind have its way. Then he'd say, "Let's see what she'll do," and the white line would blur solid, and the Patrician would come up from behind semis and whip around so fast you'd barely hear the bellowing.

Other days he'd go left on Forbes Road and when it turned into Route 30, he'd tell you how Forbes didn't have a thing to do with it, George Washington either, it was the Old Settlers who transformed an old Indian trail into a road for caissons and Conestogas so Colonel Armstrong could run the French out of Pittsburgh and pioneers could reach Ohio, and Republicans who named it the Lincoln Highway and paved it so it could carry Tin Lizzies across the Plains and the Rockies and clean to the Pacific, only then the Doggone Democrats gave the highways numbers, and the people too.

Then you'd feel the land rise beneath you, and the arch-necked bird would fly, and you'd see the hotel shaped like a ship on the mountain's brow. He'd give you nickels for the telescope so you could get the lay of the land and SEE 3 STATES AND 7 COUN-

TIES and the ridges like ocean waves, their hues modulating in the distance—green, green-blue, cadet blue—and blending into periwinkle sky.

Other days he'd drive on rough, recondite roads—Pinchots, he called them—that snaked through gloomed forests before bursting into sunlit coves. Sometimes he'd stop at farms cacophonous with bark and squawk to haggle with white-capped women for scrapple, head cheese, and liver pudding, or at stores sided with rusty signs—HIRES, NEHI, UPPER 10—in slumberous five-house towns, to growl about the Doggone Democrats with gaunt, knob-knuckled men. But generally on those days he just drove, past cattle-clotted pastures, close-filed fields, red tractors, black barns billboarded blue-white-yellow CHEW MAIL POUCH, white churches flanked by gray gravestones. And he taught you the names of every kind of kine and swine and crop, and told you who owned what and always voted how, but said since you weren't running for anything yet, you didn't need to know where the bodies were buried.

And some days he'd go right at the light and out the East End, past the trailer park, the junkyard, the blue-and-white Scenicruisers parked aslant beside the Greyhound Post House, the green combines ranked before the John Deere dealership, and then you'd see the river on your left, frothed by rocky confrontations before disappearing into the mountain ahead.

Then it would seem the mountain parted and on either side you'd see sinusoid stripes—brown, tan, purple, pink, the insides of the earth. Then the road would swing out into the empty air, but you'd hear his voice telling you how engineers, smart fellas out in Pittsburgh, invented a new kind of bridge to get a highway through the Narrows, and rest easy.

After that the road descended to the river's bank, and through a green gauze of weeping willows you'd see the river again, tranquil now, its surface only occasionally V'd by hidden obstructions, and he'd drive slow and talk about how your Grandmother,

God rest her, loved River Road, and how he should have brought her here more often, and how he hoped that when you got to be a man you wouldn't always be rushing no place good for no good reason, and then wouldn't say another word all the way to Juniata Crossing. And you'd long to tell him, in that silence, how you'd failed your mother, but you knew he'd tell you it was nothing you need be ashamed of. Only it was.

But you remember the day you came through the kitchen door and saw her at the white electric range, stirring something steaming in the white-and-blue speckled pot. You saw her face, lumpish, yellow-green, but made your eyes stay open, and when she smiled at you with her mangled mouth you made your mouth smile back. Then your Grandpa came in behind you and she said supper would be *boeuf sans bourguignon* and he said pork made better stew and the range ran up his light bill and she said, "Quit growling, you old bear," and he just laughed.

You remember your mother stowing dolls and teddy bears in the humpbacked trunk and saying she'd make you new curtains; this was your room now.

You remember *cheer-upcheer-a-leecheer-ee-o* and a robin redbreast hopping on the lawn.

You remember asking could you walk to school like the other boys and your Grandpa saying he didn't see why not, it was all downhill, mostly.

You remember doing homework at the kitchen table, and her checking your grammar and spelling and him your arithmetic.

You remember her reading to you like she did when you were little—tales of ladies and their knights, in French, with consecutive interpretation.

You remember boys with a football in the Public Squares, and your Grandpa telling you, Go play, he didn't need help running errands every day, and you said, "You'll still need help some days, won't you?" and he ruffled your hair and gave you fifty cents walking-around money.

You remember the rules of what they called Rough Touch: two hands below the shoulders, no tackling, but shoving was okay. Some boys said you shoved too hard, but when they chose up for another game you got picked third.

You remember your mother saying you had to learn to use the Lexicon because words were both tools and weapons and the difference between the right one and the almost-right one was like lightning and a lightning bug, and when you said the lectern was higher than you could reach she showed you the step stool hidden underneath.

You remember tying up your brogans, braving briar and thorn and entering the forest, going step-by-step along the path until it forked. Then you turned back because by then you knew the Lost Children got found dead.

And you remember birds flocking by hundreds in Quercus Rubra's limbs, chattering sunrise to sunset, sometimes after dark. Stump speeches and midnight caucuses, your Grandpa said; the prothonotary warblers advocating Costa Rica, the robins lobbying for Lauderdale, the orioles proposing Mexico. Your mother said one day you'd look and they'd be gone, and it would mean the end of summer and that always made her sad, but you kept watch and saw it when they rose and flew away together, and it didn't seem sad at all.

Now you remember the dump truck. Just a sound when you first heard it, like the Goddamn Rambler's cough and sputter, only in a lower register. You were at the woodpile, loading yourself up, and looked and saw it as it inched over the crest: white grille pitted with raw sienna rust, pewter air horn tarnished brown, red cab splotched with gray, steel dump bed battered, spattered, corroded to huelessness.

It shuddered, screeched to a stop, sat wheezing awhile, then clanked, coughed, and backed its corrugated hind end wearily into the driveway, stopping only feet from you. Then the cab door opened and a man jumped down.

He wore a kind of uniform—cap, shirt, trousers of forest green—brogans of Indian red, gray gloves that flared at the wrist. His face was brown and rough, like a walnut. His jaw bulged as he chewed—on what, you dared not wonder. He unchained the tailgate, pulled down a blue handle, then said, without looking at you, "You wanta move from there."

You moved; meanwhile he worked a thin red lever, the dump bed rose in fits and starts, and then the tailgate lifted, and chunks came tumbling out. In a minute it was over; he got back into the cab, the truck eased forward, and the tailgate swung-and-banged, swung-and-banged. Then he got out again and worked the red lever and the dump bed stuttered down.

He pushed up the blue handle, rechained the tailgate, then strode past you to the kitchen door, smelling of sweat and Juicy Fruit. He knocked twice, and still without looking at you said, "You live here now?" and you said, "This is my Grandpa's house," and he said, "That, I know."

Then your Grandpa was in the doorway saying, "Thanks, Joe. Same price?" and the man said, "For now, Judge, but it's gonna go up soon. You want another load beforehand? I pick up Saturdays, forenoon," and your Grandpa said, "Well, I don't . . . ," and then your mother came slipping past him with a dip of shoulder and twirl of hip.

Her steps were like a dancer's, swift and light, and she wore makeup that almost hid the bruises, and her voice was like a singer's when she said, "Hello, Joe. Whadaya know?" Then she held out her hand. And he said, "Jewels," and pulled off his glove and took her hand in his, but they didn't shake, they just smiled until your Grandpa stepped between them with money in his hand.

You remember asking, over supper, who that man was, and your Grandpa saying he was just a colored fella who hauled sand, gravel, chunks, and manure, most likely, in a thirdhand piece of truck, and your mother putting her fork down and saying his *name* was Joe Wisdom, and they'd been friends in high school.

And you asked, "Was he your boyfriend?" and your Grandpa choked on his Salisbury steak.

But later, when he came to check your long division, he said he'd meant no disrespect to Joe Wisdom, who worked hard and stayed sober and came from respectable folk. Then he told you how, way back when, colored people came over from Africa to be free, but below Mason & Dixon's Line white men made them slaves, only one white man, named Wisdom, went camping and caught Methodism and wanted to let his colored people go for fear of boils and blains, but other white men wouldn't let him unless he sent them back to Africa. Then Wisdom came to take the waters at Anderson's Springs and found out about Raystown, and bought twelve hundred acres eight miles west and sent his colored people there, and they all took his last name, and called it Wisdom's Notch. Then other colored people started running away from slavery and coming north across the Line, and folks in Raystown would send them to Wisdom's Notch, where they could hide and be safe until Abe Lincoln freed them.

You liked that story so you asked if one day he'd drive to Wisdom's Notch, and he said, "We'll see," and you heard your mother cough, and later, when you were in bed, say, "Daddy, if you're going to tell him stories, tell him the whole story," and he said, "Are you sure you want him hearing the whole story?" and you knew he did leave things out sometimes, so when she came to tuck you in you asked what the whole story was.

She said you shouldn't eavesdrop, and the whole story was that she and Joe took French together in high school, but only for half a year; then she went away to boarding school and hadn't seen him again, or even thought of him, until today. Then you asked why your Grandpa didn't like him, and she said, "Sweetie, try to understand. In Raystown, different kinds of people are supposed to be happy with different things—" and you said, "Colored people?" and she said, "Other kinds of people too. They're all supposed to want what they're supposed to have, and settle for it.

Only, Joe wouldn't settle. He didn't care how hard he had to work for what he wanted, but if anybody told him he shouldn't want it in the first place, he'd make a fuss. Your Grandpa hates fuss."

You asked, Did he want money? and she said, "Joe never cared about money. Joe wanted . . . things to be different. Joe wanted the County Library to have books by colored writers, and gave the librarian a list. Joe wanted the School Board to hire a colored teacher, and gave them a list of colored colleges where they could find one. Joe wanted to take French instead of Industrial Arts. The principal said no, Joe would take shop like he was told to, because no . . . body from Wisdom's Notch was going to Paris. Joe sent a letter to the newspaper that quoted the principal word for word, with copies to the governor and the NAACP. The paper wouldn't print it, but the School Board said Joe could take French.

"Joe made people nervous, wanting things he wasn't supposed to, even some people in Wisdom's Notch. Finally he wanted one thing too much. Some men were going to teach him a lesson, but the sheriff arrested him first, and your Grandpa was the judge and sent Joe to the army instead of jail. It was wartime, but colored men weren't supposed to fight; the army taught Joe to drive trucks.

"Only Joe wanted to fight. So he made a fuss, and eventually the army taught him to drive tanks and sent him to Europe, and he fought for General Patton and won a medal and was wounded at the Battle of the Bulge. After the war he stayed in France. He'd send letters to the principal postmarked Paris—long letters, all in French." She gave a little laugh. "I guess I was as bad as that principal; Joe and I had talked about Paris, and I expected I'd see it someday, but I never thought Joe . . . Only there he was, living on the Left Bank. He could have stayed; a lot of colored soldiers did. But Joe wanted to live in Wisdom's Notch. And he was a hero, so eventually your Grandpa had to let him come back."

You asked, So he'd settled? but she said Joe would never settle, but loved Wisdom's Notch more than . . . anything. So you asked, What was the one thing too much? and she said, "Oh, sweetie, that's ancient history," but you wondered if it was, and if one of the other kinds of people was People Like Us.

You remember cool air billowing blue curtains, but being warm beneath a quilt your Grandmother, God rest her, made.

You remember your mother holding the round box with the white man in the black hat on it, in one hand, and the square box with the colored man in the white hat on it, in the other, asking, Oatmeal or cream of wheat?

You remember *ring, ring, ring*ing, and hearing not his voice but hers saying, "Hello, Hal . . . ," and holding your breath until she said, "I still don't. But it's time I told you myself."

You remember the teacher with the gray crew cut saying he'd heard you liked to mix it up, you should come out for Pop Warner. Your mother said football was too rough but your Grandpa told her he'd buy you one of those newfangled plastic helmets with the bar to protect your nose, and he did, and a jock strap with a cup and clacking shoulder pads.

You remember trading belly punches to see who was in shape, and doing push-ups, sit-ups, leg-ups, wind sprints, and after, going to the fountain at the Rexall, where a skinny teen with pimples would add cherry syrup to your nickel Coke, no extra charge, and give boys who didn't have a nickel plain soda water, free.

But now you remember coming out of the Rexall, jibing and shoulder-jabbing, and seeing the dump truck parked in the alley and Joe Wisdom at the top of the First National's steps, and hearing the door *whupwhupwhupwhupp*ing behind him.

He had on his brogans and green trousers, but his shirt was white, and he wore a lemon-yellow tie with a turquoise-and-cranberry parrot on it. You called out to him, singsong, like your mother had: "Hello, Joe. Whadaya . . . ," and stopped, because his face looked like a picture on a WANTED poster.

And he said, "What did you say?" and the other boys stopped

laughing. Then he said, "What did you call me?" and the other boys ran away. Then he came down the steps and said, "Get your hind end in the truck."

You remember cowering in the corner of the cab, watching his fist jam the gearshift left and right, hearing the engine cough-sputter-roar, the brakes screech, the air horn blare. Then you felt his fingers digging into your biceps as he carried you at arm's length across the lawn, shouting, "Somebody come get this boy." Then he deposited you on the veranda and you heard your Grandpa's calm voice say, "Now, Joe, what's he done?" and he shouted, "He called me by my Christian name, right on the street," and your Grandpa said, "Well, I don't find that sufficient cause to scare the piss out of him."

Then your mother was hugging you, wet pants and all, saying, "Joe, he's sorry, he doesn't understand—" and he said, "Then explain it to him, Jewels." Then your Grandpa said, "Joe, tell you what. Why don't you haul us up another load of chunks come Saturday, whatever your price is now."

You felt your mother hug you tighter, and looked and saw Joe Wisdom staring at your Grandpa and your Grandpa staring back. Finally Joe Wisdom said, "Sorry, Your Honor, but I'm afraid my thirdhand, insufficient-collateral truck would bust a gasket tryin' to make that grade again." Then he yanked off his necktie.

You remember wailing to your mother, as she helped you clean up, that you *weren't* sorry because you did *not* call him a name, but she said, "Sweetie, you called him by his first name; he felt you weren't showing respect," and your Grandpa growled, "Your friend Joe wants too doggone much respect, if you ask me," and she said, "He's proud of his ancestors, like others I could name," and your Grandpa went into his study and pulled the doors out of the walls.

Then she said, "Sweetie, you have to understand. In Raystown, if you live like people think you should—if you work hard, pay your debts, don't talk about your troubles, don't take charity, things like that—people say you're respectable. No matter what kind of people you are, you can be respectable, and other people are supposed to show you respect. That means . . . all kinds of things. They'll bill you later. They'll take your word. They'll call you Mr. or Mrs. if they see you on the street. But if you're not respectable, people say you're trash. Then it's cash before carry, nobody will believe a word you say, and you're lucky if they speak to you at all.

"Only it's not just about you. People might not even know you. But they know your people, going back however many generations. In Raystown, your people stand for you. If your people are trash, you're trash until you prove otherwise—that can take years. If your people are respectable, you're respectable. But you still have to live like people think you should, because what you do reflects on your people. They stand for you, but you stand for them too, and even the most respectable people are just a scandal or two away from trash. In Raystown, you never stand for just you.

"Joe's proud—too proud, some say. But he's not proud of himself, he's proud of Wisdom's Notch; of people who have been respectable for seven generations. Only Joe—Mr. Wisdom— thinks they've never gotten the respect they're due. And if he thinks he's been denied respect he gets angry not just for himself, but on behalf of all seven generations.

"Sweetie, I can call him Joe because we've known each other a long time and he knows I respect him. Your Grandpa can call him Joe because . . . well, because he can. But Joe doesn't know you. He can't know what you think. All he knows is, he's a man and you're just a boy, and you called him by his first name, like you would another boy. So he heard you saying, underneath, that you didn't respect him, or Wisdom's Notch. And it wasn't only you he heard, because in Raystown, you don't just stand for you. Do you see?"

You said you did, but didn't . . . until sunset. Then you saw your Grandpa on the Lookout and thought about him standing like a statue on the veranda and Joe Wisdom standing like a statue on the lawn, and you knew what you'd have to do.

You remember waiting after practice, at the traffic light, hoping he'd pass by and maybe have to stop. But he didn't the first day, nor the next day, nor the next, and that was Friday and you knew where you'd have to go.

You remember winding the alarm clock but not sleeping anyway, and listening to *poor, poorwill,* and *whowhowho* until you couldn't wait anymore, and dressing by touch and climbing out the window and going tiptoe onto the lawn. You felt lost in darkness; you saw no lights, no moon, no stars. But then you felt the lay of the land and let gravity guide you down the grade.

You remember walking through the silent town, where fog haloed streetlights, shrouded statues, and transformed the traffic light into a pulsing ruby wrapped in cotton.

You remember waiting on the bridge, the river sluicing sibilantly below, you trying out words—short ones, long ones—wondering which would be only almost-right. Then the fog was sheered to airy thinness by a sudden breeze, and light lanced through the Narrows, raying the sky crimson, vermillion, rose, and you knew why your Grandpa called it the crack of dawn.

You remember going step-by-step along the access road, eyes on your P. F. Flyers, expecting the whistle yet flinching when it sounded. Then you looked and saw the pin mill, and realized: it was cloaked not with smoke, but dust, and wasn't black, or even dark, but an almost gay patchwork of orange, green, and blue, though every patch was streaked with rust the color of dried blood.

You remember crouching beneath a bulkhead flat, watching huge hooks descend and grapple logs and hoist them dangerously aloft, listening to conveyors clank, cables twang, saws whine and ching, wondering if the white shirt meant he didn't pick up on Saturday anymore. But then you saw the dump truck trundling along the access road and pulling up beside the pin mill, beneath a metal chute, and Joe Wisdom leaning out of the cab and pumping his fist in the direction of a window in the mill. Then you heard a rumble that swelled into a roar, and chunks came cascading down, making the truck rock side to side, then settle on its springs.

You walked toward it, watching chunks coming down into the dump bed and a few bouncing back out onto the ground. Then a lot started bouncing out and Joe Wisdom drew his hand like a knife across his throat and the chunks stopped coming, and you realized: he was loaded up, and you began to run. But then he jumped down from the cab, pulling on his gloves, and bent and started picking up fallen chunks and tossing them back into the bed.

He didn't look up, so you thought he didn't see you, but when you got close he yelled, "What do you want?" and you thought he was angry but then you realized: he had to yell on account of the pin mill's din, and that the long words wouldn't work, so you just yelled back, "I'm sorry, Mr. Wisdom. I meant no disrespect."

He tossed another chunk and yelled, "She tell you to say that?" and you yelled, "No, sir. My Grandpa either," and he yelled, "That, I believe," and tossed another chunk. Then he straightened up, looked around, and yelled, "How'd you get here?" and you yelled, "I walked." And he yelled, "That's two miles," and you yelled, "It's all downhill, mostly." He gave you a cockeyed look, then yelled, "You wait till I'm loaded up 'cause it's all uphill from here." Then he bent and started tossing chunks again.

But it felt wrong to wait while he worked alone, so you picked up a fallen chunk and tried to throw it into the bed. Only you didn't get it high enough and it banged off the side, and you heard him shout a bad word. But you tried again, this time doing it as he had—bending low, swinging your arm back before the throw, following through after—and the chunk went up and over. That felt right, so you tossed another, and another. Then you heard him yell again, calling you by name.

And you looked and saw him holding out another pair of

gloves. You took them, pulled them on, and realized: they weren't that much too big. You nodded. He nodded. Then you worked together until the ground was clear.

You remember riding high beside him in the cab, over the river and through the town, wishing, hoping he'd just drive, maybe all the way to Wisdom's Notch. But he braked approaching Juliana, so you thanked him and told him you'd walk up so he wouldn't bust a gasket, and he gave you that cockeyed look again, but pulled over. Then you said, "Mr. Wisdom? Are you still my mother's friend?"

And you thought you'd done something wrong because instead of answering, he shifted to neutral, set the brake, and said, "What did she tell you?" And you said, "The whole story. She said it was ancient history but I think she needs friends now." And he said, "She don't need me; she's got you."

Then it all came up, like vomit: how you'd found hiding places big enough for you, but not her too; how when you realized it only happened to her, even if it was you who did whatever made him mad, part of you was glad; how you'd made believe it was TV, or people in the street, and in the morning got yourself dressed and off to school, never knocking on her door to see was she okay; how in daydreams you lifted her, up, up, and away, but in nightmares you dropped her and flew on alone; how when she lifted you and carried you away, you couldn't keep watch and fell asleep and let her face the blazing and bellowing alone; how you'd closed your eyes because you didn't want to see.

He let you say it—all of it. Then he was quiet awhile. Then he cleared his throat and said, "Maybe you did more than you know. She always talked about the son she hoped she'd have one day and how he'd grow up to be a different kind of man. You didn't want to see, but maybe she didn't want you to have to see. Maybe she left because she didn't want you to grow up thinking that's how things ought to be. Maybe she wanted to save you enough to save herself. But you've got to save her now.

"Raystown's short on sympathy. They say, 'You made your

bed, lie in it.' Especially if the sheets are silk." He was staring through the windshield, as if at something distant, and his voice too seemed far away. "A High Church wedding. Reception at the Inn. Caterer from Philadelphia. Champagne, caviar, hors d'oeuvres—food folks here couldn't even pronounce. So now they'll say they're sorry to hear, but they'll be glad to listen, and whisper about richer or poorer and better or worse, and pray for her so they can gossip with God."

Then he looked at you again. "They'll hurt her," he said. "They always could. But they could never make her change her mind. What could is if she thought Raystown was hurting you.

"Whenever we'd talk about coming home I'd say Raystown was too crooked. But she'd say, 'Raystown's straight, it's just not true.' Straight, to her, meant following rules. True meant doing what's right. True was what she cared about, so that's what you've gotta be. But you've gotta be straight too, so those party-line biddies won't have dirt to throw in her face. Be straight for them, true for her; maybe then she'll stay here where she's safe, and what you coulda done but didn't will be ancient history."

Then he looked through the windshield again and said, in that far-off voice, "She was right. Raystown *is* straight. Trouble is, it leans. Nobody notices because we all lean the same way. If you're born here, you grow up at an angle. If you leave, you can look back and see it's out-of-kilter, but if you wanta come back, you've gotta learn to lean again. But comes a time you've gotta square up." He looked at you again, and, for the first time, smiled. "Leaning's a man's problem," he said. "You just worry about straight and true."

And you remember what he said before you left the truck: "I'll always be your mother's friend. If she needs help, pick up the phone and tell the operator, eight-three-nine-R-four. If I don't answer, somebody will; that whole line is Wisdom's Notch."

You remember quitting the comfort of the quilt and going tiptoe sockfoot to rouse the fire so the kitchen would be warm when she came down.

You remember the County Library, where you'd check out *Real Books About* so you could explain things to her—Indians, helicopters, birds, the sea—while she washed and you dried.

You remember *ring, ring, ring*ing and hearing her say, "Never, when you're like this," and, "Hal, don't lie. I can practically smell it through the phone."

You remember the forking of the path. One way, rocky and indefinite, went switchback uphill; the other, worn to smooth certainty, ran straight and almost level. You set your brogans on the upward way, thinking of the Old Settlers, but step-by-step that path grew fainter and finally disappeared. You stopped, thinking of the Lost Children, but then you looked and saw a mark emblazoned on an oak, higher than you could reach, and then another further on, and you followed the blazes on up to the ridge.

You remember hearing your Grandpa tell her, her friend Joe was making a fuss and was going to be persona non grata, and looking it up in the Lexicon and wondering if your Grandpa still had pull enough to send Joe Wisdom back to France.

You remember learning to assume the three-point stance— head up, tail down, weight balanced on staggered feet and the knuckles of one hand—ready to fire out low and hard when you heard the snap count.

You remember offering to buy Cokes for boys who didn't have walking-around money, and they said it was white of you but wouldn't take charity.

You remember hearing your Grandpa tell her, her friend Joe had hired a Semite shyster from Pittsburgh, and her saying, Wasn't that what judges wanted people to do, hire lawyers instead of taking matters into their own hands?

You remember learning to not jump offsides, to clutch your jersey with your fists so you wouldn't hold, to hit your man in the numbers so you wouldn't clip, to get your shoulder into him and always keep your legs driving, to focus all your feelings—hate, rage, shame, fear, frustration, pain, even love—into five seconds of furious contact.

You remember hearing her say, "Hal, it's two a.m., he's ten years old. Where do you think he is? . . . You demand to speak to your son? Call before closing time."

You remember the bruises on your shoulders, chest, and arms, and the awed looks in the locker room, and your Grandpa's smile when you said they didn't hurt, and how he took you to the Rexall and bought you Absorbine Jr. and to the Coffee Pot and told the men you were one tough customer, and asking him for long-sleeved shirts so she wouldn't have to see.

You remember hearing him tell her, her friend Joe needed reminding he was colored, and her saying, "What does that mean, exactly?" and him saying, "It means his children won't be white, no matter who their mother is."

You remember hearing his voice shout your name when you ran onto the field, and it didn't matter that she was sorry, sweetie, she just couldn't face Raystown yet, because you were standing for her.

And you remember realizing: what you craved was not the contact, but the instant before; when, balanced in your three-point stance, you knew exactly what to do: drive and keep on driving, until the whistle blew.

Now you remember how the forest flared and the mountains looked like quilts, and the town grew fat with tourists come for the Foliage Festival, and the Public Squares were chockablock with booths selling cob corn brushed with butter, fried dough dusted with sugar, funnel cakes, pickled eggs, friendship bread, blood sausages, slabs of shoofly pie.

You remember the Patrician descending from the Heights, your mother at the wheel, smelling of Jergens and White Rain. And her mouth was straight and her cheek was smooth and her hair was pinned up high, and she looked as lovely as the lady on the soap she used.

You remember her holding your hand tight as you pulled her toward the crowd, and squeezing tighter when some ladies saw her and whispered to each other. But then an old man spoke her name and she spoke his, and an old lady patted her arm and said it was good to see her home, and she didn't squeeze so tight.

Then you walked together, hand in hand, and she spoke to people, and some spoke back but some didn't and she said they must be hard of seeing, and she bought you a mug of hot spiced cider and, because she said you had to take sour with sweet, some pickled watermelon rind. A group of men was making music on a violin, banjo, bass, and sideways guitar, going fast and taking turns with the melody, and she let go of your hand to clap her hands in time. Some people were grumbling that it wasn't real country, but she said, Pay them no mind, it was bluegrass and they'd like it once they got used to it. Then you saw Joe Wisdom.

He had three girls with him, one holding each hand, one riding on his shoulders, and a tall woman with high caramel cheeks and long black braids. You said, "Hello, Mr. Wisdom," and your mother stopped clapping and took your hand again and said, "Hello, Joe," but there was no music in it.

He said, "Jewels. You remember Margo," and the woman said, "Juliana," and your mother said, "Why, yes. Margo, from Home Ec. What sweet little girls!" Then she pulled you in front of her and said, "This is my *son*."

The woman gave Joe Wisdom a cockeyed look, then knelt and looked you in the eye, and hers were deep and black, but soft. And she said, "I hear you're a man who's not afraid to get his hands dirty," and you said, "Yes, ma'am, I mean, no, ma'am, I mean, I'm just a boy," and your face got hot and she smiled but didn't laugh, and you realized: she was as lovely as your mother.

But now you remember your mother on the veranda, bundled in your Grandpa's overcoat, arms crossed across her chest like she was holding something in. Silver plumed before her face and you thought she was smoking again, but then you realized: she was breathing hard. And you wanted to tell her to pay no mind, that you'd been straight and true, but then the *ring, ring, ring*ing started, and she left the veranda, and you heard her say, "Yes, Hal, I suppose it is time we talked."

Now you remember *caw, caw, caw,* and cold air slashing between sash and sill, and dead leaves raked into crackling piles, and gray smoke defiling the air, and her saying, over supper, your father had a new job, a better job, and your Grandpa asking, Better than the ones he'd got fired from or the ones he couldn't get?

You remember guns booming in the forest and your Grandpa saying not to go exploring, it was hunting season, but going anyway, forsaking paths and trail marks because nobody'd ever found it, only you had to because if there was room for Davy and his horse there'd be room for both of you.

You remember him telling her, her friend Joe had settled out of court.

You remember her asking, as she tucked you in, Didn't you miss your room, your bunk bed? and wondering if she'd forgotten scooping you out of it, whispering, *Shh shh, shh,* going tiptoe barefoot past the La-Z-Boy, the shivaree of snore and static, the stink of whiskey and cigarettes. Then you realized: she didn't want to see.

And you remember the Patrician parked beneath the flag and your Grandpa waiting, but not reading or resting his eyes or saying anything.

Now you remember the Thunderbird—blank-faced, boxy, Doeskin Beige over Colonial White, the bird flattened on the hood—and your father's big-voiced brags of Cruise-O-Matic, Master Guide, dual headlights, dual horns, dual everything, and his demonstrations of the push-in cigarette lighter on the central console, and the lever that made the electric turn signals go *tock-tick, tock-tick, tock-tick*—no more horse-and-buggy, hand-out-the-window jazz, he said. And he said they called it the Car Everyone Would Love to Own, and when your Grandpa said he'd liked the roadster better, he said, "Well, Dad, as usual, you're a few model-years behind."

You remember your Grandmother's handmade tablecloth above and dragon legs below, and your mother asking was there too much lemon in the aspic, was the roast too done, did he want more of this or that, and jumping up to get it before he could say yes or no, and how when he said, "Julie, sit down and shut up," your Grandpa left the table, but part of you was glad.

You remember your Grandpa on the Lookout, staring across the valley to the mountain opposite, where head- and taillights on the Turnpike moved swiftly east and west. And he said, "This is Appalachian Bedrock. It's been here a billion years. It'll always be here, any time you need it," and you knew what he meant. But you heard him saying, underneath, that he didn't intend to interfere, and you despised him for it.

And you remember waiting there, in your mackinaw and brogans, looking over treetops, steeples, rooftops, and smelling tobacco smoke and hearing your father say, "Well, don't you look like Dan'l Boone. Kilt you a b'ar yet?" And you, not thinking, said, "That's Davy Crockett . . . ," and stopped.

He stepped out onto the rock beside you, took a drag on his cigarette. Then he said, "You're confused. Your mother brought you here, and you've had her all to yourself. Your Grandfather buys you anything you want; you're the son he couldn't have. Now you don't want to leave.

"Well, let me unconfuse you. It doesn't matter what you want. What matters is, I'm your father, and I demand respect. You will go where I say, when I say. You will look at me when I speak to you, and say *sir* when you speak to me. And don't you dare ever correct me again. Do you understand?" And you said, "Yes, sir."

Then he stepped closer to the edge, looked down and said, "Man, this truly is the ass end of the earth." And then he flicked his cigarette butt into the empty air.

You watched it trace a glowing arc toward the bare treetops

and thought, *Only you can prevent,* and dropped into your three-point stance, knowing but not caring that you'd go over too. You waited for him to turn, not to follow any rule, but so he'd see it coming when you fired out low and hard, and you felt it inside you: the blazing and the bellowing.

Only then you realized: the bellowing was outside too. And you looked and saw a dump truck appear at the crest: cab and bed of forest green, bumper and grille of polished steel, twin air horns chromed and radiant, silver bulldog statant on the hood.

It paused beside the Thunderbird, snorted once and hissed. Then it backed, grumbling, into the driveway, stopping at the woodpile, and magically the bed rose up on a thick, oily piston, and the tailgate lifted, and chunks came avalanching down, filling the air with dust and thunder.

You straightened and went toward it, seeing your Grandpa, then your mother, coming out the kitchen door, and still the chunks came roaring down, covering the old wood with new, piling higher than you could reach. Then they stopped. The bed subsided. Joe Wisdom climbed down from the cab.

Your Grandpa said, "Well, Joe, that Mack does haul quite a payload. I expect the price is double." But Joe Wisdom said, "No charge, Judge. This boy earned one last load for you." And he looked at you and said, "God keep you, son." Then he looked at your mother and said, *"Au revoir,* Jewels. *Un baiser de benediction."*

But then you realized: you'd failed her again, because your father stepped from behind you and said, "Who the *hell* do you think you are, speaking to my wife like that? And he's not your son, he's mine."

Only, you realized: you still had a chance. Because if you said what you wanted, what you wished, that would make it happen, and not to her—to you. And maybe if she saw she'd stop making believe, and maybe if he saw, your Grandpa would interfere.

But then you realized: you couldn't. Because Joe Wisdom would surely interfere, but what might most matter, afterward, was that he wasn't People Like Us, and you couldn't trust your Grandpa to be true instead of straight, and maybe not your mother either. And then you realized: you couldn't let them stand for you.

So you stepped in front of your father. You held out your hand. And you said, "Thank you, Mr. Wisdom, sir. Thank you for the wood."

They're gone now. First your mother, of manner and cause detailed in the trial transcript; then your Grandpa, of grief, some said, and, you'd hoped, guilt, but probably just too many real country breakfasts; now your father, the twenty having turned out to be longer than the life.

That should have ended it. But the Department of Corrections, while willing to cremate, insisted you come in person to perform the rites you requested. So you set out at the crack of dawn for the Western Penitentiary to receive the ashes, dump them in a toilet, urinate, and flush.

With three hundred horses under the Firebird's hood, you figured to get from the Delaware to the Ohio and back by supper, but after you crossed the Susquehanna you saw the Allegheny Front and could almost hear your Grandpa cribbing Kipling, and between Blue Mountain and Kittatinny you remembered the pin mill. Now you see the sign for Juniata Crossing, and without thinking, downshift, slip between jake-braking semis, take the off-ramp, pay the toll.

Juniata Crossing is not as you remember: two off-brand gas stations, one greasy spoon, one ten-cabin motor lodge. Now it's a junction of the Turnpike with a north-south interstate, and Route 30 is a four-lane lined with outlets of every oil company, fast-food franchise, and cheap motel chain known to man.

But a mile west two-lane asphalt reappears, ascending sharply then descending in switchbacks through a green profusion of pine, oak, and sugar maple, to where River Road still runs along the north bank of the Raystown Branch, brown and swollen from recent rains. The valley spreads in herded pastures and husbanded fields, and you can almost hear your Grandpa naming the strains: Yorkshire, Berkshire, Poland China; Guernsey, Jersey, Holstein, Black Angus; timothy, alfalfa, black medick, white Dutch, yellow dent, Tuscarora white. The Firebird grumbles in third gear, but you feel yourself resting easy, recalling how, here, forward, backward, left, and right mean less than up and down. Too soon you see the fresh green of weeping willows, the mountain rearing ahead.

But instead of swinging into empty air to bridge the Narrows, the road suddenly ascends through a raw cut blasted through the mountain, then widens into an expressway on a high embankment. The river and the town must be below and to your left, but all you can see are treetops and no sign for an exit.

You shift the Firebird into top gear, thinking it's better this way; you don't really want to see what's faded out, fallen in, been modernized to charmlessness or tarted up for tourists. Still, you find yourself looking up, hoping to glimpse the houses on the Heights. But suddenly somehow you are in the Thunderbird, looking through the rear window at your Grandpa on the veranda, then through the windshield at the statues, brown and gray, the bank, drugstore, and five-and-dime, the traffic light turning red. You see your father's hand pushing in the lighter and picking up his Camels from the center console. You see his lips sucking a cigarette out of the pack. You hear *tock-tick, tock-tick*, and your mother saying, "No, go straight . . . ," and stopping.

You remember part of you was glad. Because it was going to happen sooner or later, so let it happen here, where half the town would see and the rest would hear by noon, where you could tell the operator eight-three-nine-R-four.

But it didn't happen then or there. Instead, you heard him telling her things were going to be different, that they'd start by taking that scenic route the old man was always going on about. Then you heard the lighter *twang* and smelled tobacco burning.

Only now you remember something more: him holding out

the cigarette and her accepting it, inhaling deeply and exhaling, then leaning, stretching, twisting, contorting her whole body across the console to place the cigarette precisely between his lips. And you realize: there was nothing you could have done to save her.

And now you see it, through the windshield: spanning frame sagging, guy wires snapped, gantries fallen, catwalks dangling like broken arms. Now you're past it and see a sign warning of the expressway's end, then another, offering a connector to the 'Pike. You double-clutch downshift, flick the lever, hear *tock-tick, tock-tick, tock-tick.*

But suddenly somehow you realize: you're rushing no place good for no good reason, when the road you're on will get you where you need to go. And before that it will lift you to a summit from where the land looks like the sea, and after, it could take you anywhere—the Plains, the Rockies, clean to the Pacific.

Kirstin Valdez Quade

Nemecia

THERE IS A PICTURE of me standing with my cousin Nemecia in the bean field. On the back is penciled in my mother's hand, Nemecia and Maria, Tajique, 1929. Nemecia is thirteen; I am six. She is wearing a rayon dress that falls to her knees, glass beads, and real silk stockings, gifts from her mother in California. She wears a close-fitting hat, like a helmet, and her smiling lips are pursed. She holds tight to my hand. Even in my white dress I look like a boy; my hair, which I have cut myself, is short and jagged. Nemecia's head is tilted; she looks out from under her eyelashes at the camera. My expression is sullen, guilty. I don't remember the occasion for the photograph, or why we were dressed up in the middle of the dusty field. All I remember of the day is that Nemecia's shoes had heels, and she had to walk tipped forward on her toes to prevent them from sinking into the dirt.

Nemecia was the daughter of my mother's sister. She came to live with my parents before I was born because my aunt Benigna couldn't care for her. Later, when Aunt Benigna recovered and moved to Los Angeles, Nemecia had already lived with us for so long that she stayed. This was not unusual in our New Mexico town in those years between the wars; if someone died, or came upon hard times, or simply had too many children, there were always aunts or sisters or grandmothers with room for an extra child.

The day after I was born my great-aunt Paulita led Nemecia into my mother's bedroom to meet me. Nemecia was carrying the porcelain baby doll that had once belonged to Aunt Benigna. When they moved the blanket from my face so that she could see me, she smashed her doll against the plank floor. The pieces were all found; my father glued them together, wiping the surface with his handkerchief to remove what oozed between the cracks. The glue dried brown, or maybe it dried white and only turned brown with age. The doll sat on the bureau in our bedroom, its face round and placidly smiling behind its net of brown cracks, hands folded primly across white lace, a strange and terrifying mix of young and old.

Nemecia had an air of tragedy about her, which she cultivated. She blackened her eyes with a kohl pencil. She spent her allowance on magazines and pinned the photographs of actors from silent films around the mirror on our dresser. I don't think she ever saw a film—not, at least, until after she left us, since the nearest theater was all the way in Albuquerque, and my parents would not in any case have thought movies suitable for a young girl. Still, Nemecia modeled the upward glances and pouts of Mary Pickford and Greta Garbo in our small bedroom mirror.

When I think of Nemecia as she was then, I think of her eating. My cousin was ravenous. She needed things, and she needed food. She took small bites, swallowed everything as neatly as a cat. She was never full and the food never showed on her figure.

She told jokes as she served herself helping after helping, so that we were distracted and did not notice how many tortillas or how many bowls of green-chili stew she had eaten. If my father or little brothers teased her at the table for her appetite, she burned red. My mother would shush my father and say she was a growing girl.

At night she stole food from the pantry, handfuls of prunes, beef jerky, pieces of ham. Her stealth was unnecessary; my mother would gladly have fed her until she was full. Still, in the mornings everything was in its place, the waxed paper folded neatly around the cheese, the lids tight on the jars. She was adept at slicing and spooning, so her thefts weren't noticeable. I would wake to her kneeling on my bed, a tortilla spread with honey against my lips. "Here," she'd whisper, and even if I was still full from dinner and not awake, I would take a bite, because she needed me to participate in her crime.

Watching her eat made me hate food. The quick efficient bites, the movement of her jaw, the way the food slid down her throat—it made me sick to think of her body permitting such quantities. Her exquisite manners and the ladylike dip of her head as she accepted each mouthful somehow made it worse. But if I was a small eater, if I resented my dependence on food, it didn't matter, because Nemecia would eat my portion, and nothing was ever wasted.

I was afraid of Nemecia because I knew her greatest secret: when she was five, she put her mother in a coma and killed our grandfather.

I knew this because she told me late one Sunday as we lay awake in our beds. The whole family had eaten together at our house, as we did every week, and I could hear the adults in the front room, still talking.

"I killed them," Nemecia said into the darkness. She spoke as if reciting, and I didn't at first know if she was talking to me. "My mother was dead. Almost a month she was dead, killed by me. Then she came back, like Christ, except it was a bigger miracle because she was dead longer, not just three days." Her voice was matter-of-fact.

"Why did you kill our grandpa?" I whispered.

"I don't remember," she said. "I must have been angry."

I stared hard at the darkness, then blinked. Eyes open or shut, the darkness was the same. Unsettling. I couldn't hear Nemecia breathe, just the distant voices of the adults. I had the feeling I was alone in the room.

Then Nemecia spoke. "I can't remember how I did it, though."

"Did you kill your father too?" I asked. For the first time I became aware of a mantle of safety around me that I'd never noticed before, and it was dissolving.

"Oh, no," Nemecia told me. Her voice was decided again. "I didn't need to, because he ran away on his own."

Her only mistake, she said, was that she didn't kill the miracle child. The miracle child was her brother, my cousin Patrick, three years older than me. He was a miracle because even as my aunt Benigna slept, dead to the world for those weeks, his cells multiplied and his features emerged. I thought of him growing strong on sugar water and my aunt's wasting body, his soul glowing steadily inside her. I thought of him turning flips in the liquid quiet.

"I was so close," Nemecia said, almost wistfully.

A photograph of Patrick as a toddler stood in a frame on the piano. He was seated between my aunt Benigna, whom I had never met, and her new husband, all of them living in California. The Patrick in the photograph was fat cheeked and unsmiling. He seemed content there, between a mother and a father. He did not seem aware of the sister who lived with us in another house nine hundred miles away. Certainly he didn't miss her.

"You better not tell anyone," my cousin said.

"I won't," I said, fear and loyalty swelling in me. I reached my hand into the dark space between our beds.

The next day, the world looked different; every adult I encountered was diminished now, made frail by Nemecia's secret.

That afternoon I went to the store and stood quietly at my mother's side as she worked at the messy rolltop desk behind the counter. She was balancing the accounts, tapping her lower lip with the end of her pencil.

My heart pounded and my throat was tight. "What happened to Aunt Benigna? What happened to your dad?"

My mother turned to look at me. She put down the pencil, was still for a moment, and then shook her head and made a gesture like she was pushing it all away from her.

"The important thing is we got our miracle. Miracles. Benigna lived, and that baby lived." Her voice was hard. "God at least granted us that. I'll always thank him for that." She didn't look thankful.

"But what happened?" My question was less forceful now.

My mother shook her head again. "It's best forgotten, hijita. I don't want to think about it."

I believed that what Nemecia told me was true. What confused me was that no one ever treated Nemecia like a murderer. If anything, they were especially nice to her. I wondered if they knew what she'd done. I wondered if they were afraid of what she might do to them. Perhaps the whole town was terrified of my cousin, watching her, and I watched Nemecia too as she talked with the teacher on the school steps, as she helped my mother before dinner. But she never slipped, and though sometimes I thought I caught glimmers of caution in the faces of the adults, I couldn't be sure.

The whole town seemed to have agreed to keep me in the dark, but I thought if anyone would be vocal about her disapproval—and surely she disapproved of murder—it would be my great-aunt Paulita. I asked her about it one afternoon at her house as we made tortillas, careful not to betray Nemecia's secret. "What happened to my grandfather?" I pinched off a ball of dough and handed it to her.

"It was beyond imagining," Paulita said. She rolled the dough in fierce, sharp thrusts. I thought she'd go on, but she only said again, "Beyond imagining."

Except that I could imagine Nemecia killing someone. Hell, demons, flames—these were the horrors that I couldn't picture. Nemecia's fury, though—that was completely plausible.

"But what happened?"

Paulita flipped the disk of dough, rolled it again, slapped it on the hot iron top of the stove, where it blistered. She pointed at me with the rolling pin. "You're lucky, Maria, to have been born after that day. You're untouched. The rest of us will never forget it, but you, mi hijita, and the twins, are untouched." She opened the front door of her stove with an iron hook and worried the fire inside.

No one would talk about what had happened when Nemecia was five. And soon I stopped asking. Before bed I would wait for Nemecia to say something more about her crime, but she never mentioned it again.

At night I stayed awake as long as I could, waiting for Nemecia to come after me in the dark.

Any new thing I got, Nemecia ruined, not enough that it was unusable, or even very noticeable, but just a little: a scrape with her fingernail in the wood of a pencil, a tear on the inside hem of a dress, a crease in the page of a book. I complained once, when Nemecia knocked my new windup jumping frog against the stone step. I thrust the frog at my mother, demanding she look at the scratch in the tin. My mother folded the toy back into my palm and shook her head, disappointed. "Think of other children," she said. She meant children I knew, children from Tajique. "So many children don't have such beautiful new things."

I was often put in my cousin's care. My mother was glad of Nemecia's help; she was busy with the store and with my three-year-old brothers. I don't think she ever imagined that my cousin wished me harm. My mother was hawkish about her children's safety—later, when I was fifteen, she refused to serve a neighbor's aging farmhand in the store for a year because he whistled at me—but she trusted Nemecia. Nemecia was my mother's niece, almost an orphan, my mother's first child.

My cousin was fierce with her love and with her hate, and sometimes I couldn't tell the difference. I seemed to provoke her anger without meaning to. At her angriest, she would lash out with slaps and pinches that turned my skin red and blue. Her anger would sometimes last weeks, aggression that would fade into long silences. I knew I was forgiven when she would begin to tell me stories, ghost stories about La Llorona, who haunted arroyos and wailed like the wind at approaching death, stories about bandits and the terrible things they would do to young girls, and, worse, stories about our family. Then she would hold and kiss me and tell me that though it was all true, every word, and though I was bad and didn't deserve it, she loved me still.

Not all her stories scared me. Some were wonderful—elaborate sagas that unfurled over weeks, adventures of girls like us who ran away. And all her stories belonged to us alone. She braided my hair at night, snapped back if a boy teased me, showed me how to walk so that I looked taller. "I'm here to take care of you," she told me. "That's why I'm here."

After her fourteenth birthday, Nemecia's skin turned red and oily and swollen with pustules. It looked tender. She began to laugh at me for my thick eyebrows and crooked teeth, things I hadn't noticed about myself until then.

One night she came into our bedroom and looked at herself in the mirror for a long time. When she moved away, she crossed to where I sat on the bed and dug her nail into my right cheek. I yelped, jerked my head. "Shh," she said kindly. With one hand she smoothed my hair, and I felt myself soften under her hands as she worked her nail through my skin. It hurt only a little bit, and what did I, at seven years old, care about beauty? As I sat snug between Nemecia's knees, my face in her hands, her attention swept over me the way I imagined a wave would, warm and slow and salty.

Night after night I sat between her knees while she opened and reopened the wound. One day she'd make a game of it, tell me that I looked like a pirate; another day she'd say it was her duty to mark me because I had sinned. Daily she and my mother worked against each other, my mother spreading salve on the scab each morning, Nemecia easing it open each night with her nails. "Why don't you heal, hijita?" my mother wondered as she fed me cloves of raw garlic. Why didn't I tell her? I don't know exactly, but I suppose I needed to be drawn into Nemecia's story.

By the time Nemecia finally lost interest and let my cheek heal, the scar reached from the side of my nose to my lip. It made me look dissatisfied, and it turned purple in the winter.

When Nemecia turned sixteen, she left me alone. It was normal, my mother said, for her to spend more time by herself or with older girls. At dinner my cousin was still funny with my parents, chatty with the aunts and uncles. But those strange secret fits of rage and adoration—all the attention she'd once focused on me—ended completely. She had turned away from me, but instead of relief I felt emptiness.

I tried to force Nemecia back into our old closeness. I bought her caramels, nudged her in church as though we shared some secret joke. Once at school I ran up to where she stood with some older girls. "Nemecia!" I exclaimed, as though I'd been looking everywhere for her, and grabbed her hand. She didn't push me away or snap at me, just smiled distantly and turned back to her friends.

We still shared our room, but she went to bed late. She no longer told stories, no longer brushed my hair, no longer walked with me to school. Nemecia stopped seeing me, and, without her gaze, I became indistinct to myself. I'd lie in bed waiting for her, holding myself still until I could no longer feel the sheets on my skin, until I was bodiless in the dark. Eventually, Nemecia would come in, and when she did, I would be unable to speak.

My skin lost its color, my body its mass, until one morning in May when, as I gazed out the classroom window, I saw old Mrs. Romero walking down the street, her shawl billowing around her like wings. My teacher called my name sharply, and I was surprised to find myself in my body, sitting solid at my desk. Suddenly I decided: I would lead the Corpus Christi procession. I would wear the wings and everyone would look at me.

Corpus Christi had been my mother's favorite feast day since she was a child, when each summer she walked with the other girls through the dirt streets, flinging rose petals. Every year my mother made Nemecia and me new white dresses and wound our braids with ribbons in coronets around our heads. I'd always loved the ceremony: the solemnity of the procession, the blessed sacrament in its gold box held high by the priest under the gold-tasseled canopy, the prayers at the altars along the way. Now I could think only of leading that procession.

My mother's altar was her pride. Each year she set up the card table on the street in front of the house. The Sacred Heart stood in the center of the crocheted lace cloth, flanked by candles and flowers in mason jars.

Everyone took part in the procession, and the girls of the town led it all with baskets of petals to cast before the Body of Christ. On that day we were transformed from dusty, scraggle-haired children into angels. But it was the girl at the head of the procession who really was an angel, because she wore the wings that were stored between sheets of tissue paper in a box on top of my mother's wardrobe. Those wings were beautiful, gauze and wire, and tied with white ribbon on the upper arms.

A girl had to have been confirmed to lead the procession, and was chosen based on her recitation of a psalm. I was ten now, and this was the first year I qualified. In the days leading up to the recitation I surveyed the competition. Most of the girls were from ranches outside town. Even if they did have a sister or parent who could read well enough to help them with their memorization, I knew they wouldn't pronounce the words right. Only my cousin Antonia was a real threat; she had led the procession the year before, and was always beautifully behaved, but she would recite an easy psalm. Nemecia was too old and had never shown interest anyway.

I settled on Psalm 38, which I chose from my mother's cardboard-covered *Manna* for its impressive length and difficult words.

I practiced fervently, in the bathtub, walking to school, in bed at night. The way I imagined it, I would give my recitation in front of the entire town. Father Garcia would hold up his hand at the end of Mass, before people could shift and cough and gather their hats, and he would say, "Wait. There is one thing more you need to hear." One or two girls would go before me, stumble through their psalms (short ones, unremarkable ones). Then I would stand, walk with grace to the front of the church, and there, before the altar, I'd speak with eloquence that people afterward would describe as unearthly. I'd offer my psalm as a gift to my mother. I'd watch her watch me from the pew, her eyes full of tears and pride.

Instead, our recitations took place in Sunday school before Mass. One by one we stood before our classmates as our teacher, Mrs. Reyes, followed our words from her Bible. Antonia recited the same psalm she had recited the year before. When it was my turn, I stumbled over the phrase "For my iniquities are gone over my head: and as a heavy burden are become heavy upon me." When I sat down with the other children, tears gathered behind my eyes and I told myself that none of it mattered.

A week before the procession, my mother met me outside school. During the day she rarely left the store or my little brothers, so I knew it was important.

"Mrs. Reyes came by the store today, Maria," my mother said. I could not tell from her face if the news had been good or bad, or about me at all. She put her hand on my shoulder and led me home.

I walked stiffly under her hand, waiting, eyes on the dusty toes of my shoes.

Finally my mother turned to me and hugged me. "You did it, Maria."

That night we celebrated. My mother brought bottles of ginger ale from the store, and we shared them, passing them around the table. My father raised his and drank to me. Nemecia grabbed my hand and squeezed it.

Before we had finished dinner, my mother stood and beckoned me to follow her down the hall. In her bedroom she took down the box from her wardrobe and lifted out the wings. "Here," she said, "let's try them on." She tied the ribbons around my arms over my checked dress, and led me back to where my family sat waiting.

The wings were light, and they scraped against the doorway. They moved ever so slightly as I walked, the way I imagined real angel wings might.

"Turn around," my father said. My brothers slid off their chairs and came at me. My mother caught them by the arms. "Don't go get your greasy hands on those wings." I twirled and spun for my family, and my brothers clapped. Nemecia smiled and served herself seconds.

That night Nemecia went up to bed when I did. As we pulled on our nightgowns, she said, "They had to pick you, you know."

I turned to her, surprised. "That's not true," I said.

"It is," she said simply. "Think about it. Antonia was last year, Christina Garcia the year before. It's always the daughters of the Altar Society."

It hadn't occurred to me before, but of course she was right. I would have liked to argue, but instead I began to cry. I hated myself for crying in front of her, and I hated Nemecia. I got into bed, turned away, and fell asleep.

Sometime later I woke up to darkness. Nemecia was beside

me in bed, her breath hot on my face. She patted my head and whispered, "I'm sorry, I'm sorry, I'm sorry." Her strokes became harder. Her breath was hot and hissing. "I am the miracle child. They never knew. I am the miracle because I lived."

I lay still. Her arms were tight around my head, my face pressed against her hard sternum. I couldn't hear some of the things she said to me, and the air I breathed tasted like Nemecia. It was only from the shudders that passed through her thin chest into my skull that I finally realized she was crying. After a while she released me and set me back on my pillow like a doll. "There now," she said, and arranged my arms over the covers. "Go to sleep." I shut my eyes and tried to obey.

I spent the afternoon before Corpus Christi watching my brothers play in the garden while my mother worked on her altar. They were digging a hole. Any other time I would have helped them, but tomorrow was Corpus Christi. It was hot and windy and my eyes were dry. I hoped the wind would settle overnight. I didn't want dust on my wings.

I saw Nemecia step out onto the porch. She shaded her eyes and stood still for a moment. When she caught sight of us crouched in the corner of the garden she came over, her strides long and adult. "Maria. I'm going to walk with you tomorrow in the procession. I'm going to help you."

"I don't need any help," I said.

Nemecia smiled as though it was out of her hands. "Well." She shrugged.

"But I'm leading it," I said. "Mrs. Reyes chose me."

"Your mother told me I had to help you, and that *maybe* I would get to wear the wings."

I stood. Even standing, I came only to her shoulder. I heard the screen door slam, and my mother was on the porch. She came over to us, steps quick, face worried.

"Mama, I don't need help. Tell her Mrs. Reyes chose me."

"I only thought that there will be other years for you." My

mother's tone was imploring. "Nemecia will be too old next year."

"But I may never memorize anything so well ever!" My voice rose. "This may be my only chance."

My mother's face brightened. "Maria, of course you'll memorize something. It's only a year. You'll get picked again, I promise."

I couldn't say anything. I saw what had happened: Nemecia had decided she would wear the wings, and my mother had decided to let her. Nemecia would lead the town, tall in her white dress, the wings framing her. And following would be me, small and angry and ugly. I wouldn't want it next year, after Nemecia. I wouldn't want it ever again.

Nemecia put her hand on my shoulder. "It's about the blessed sacrament, Maria. It's not about you." She spoke gently. "Besides, you'll still be leading it. I'll just be there with you. To help."

"Hijita, listen—"

"I don't want your help," I said. I was as dark and savage as an animal.

"Maria—"

Nemecia shook her head and smiled sadly. "That's why I am here," she said. "I lived so I could help you." Her face was calm, and a kind of holiness settled into it.

Hate flooded me. "I wish you hadn't," I said. "I wish you hadn't lived. This isn't your home. You're a killer." I turned to my mother. I was crying hard now, my words choked and furious. "She's trying to kill us all. Don't you know? Everyone around her ends up dead. Why don't you ever punish her?"

My mother's face turned gray, and suddenly I was afraid. Nemecia was still for a moment, and then her face clenched and she ran into the house.

After that, everything happened very quickly. My mother didn't shout, didn't say a word. She came into my room carrying the carpetbag she used when she had to stay at the home of a sick relative. I made my face more sullen than I felt. Her silence was frightening. She opened my bureau drawer and began to pack things into the bag, three dresses, all my drawers and undershirts. She put my Sunday shoes in too, my hairbrush, the book that lay beside my bed, enough things for a very long absence.

My father came in and sat beside me on the bed. He was in his work clothes, pants dusty from the field.

"You're just going to stay with Paulita for a while," he said.

I knew what I'd said was terrible, but I never guessed that they would get rid of me. I didn't cry, though, not even when my mother folded up the small quilt that had been mine since I was born and set it into the top of the carpetbag. She buckled it all shut.

My mother's head was bent over the bag, and for a moment I thought I'd made her cry, but when I ventured to look at her face, I couldn't tell.

"It won't be long," my father said. "It's just to Paulita's. So close it's almost the same house." He examined his hands for a long time, and I too looked at the crescents of soil under his nails. "Your cousin has had a hard life," he said finally. "You have to understand."

"Come on, Maria," my mother said gently.

Nemecia was sitting in the parlor, her hands folded and still on her lap. I wished she would stick out her tongue or glare, but she only watched me pass. My mother held open the door and then closed it behind us. She took my hand, and we walked together down the street to Paulita's house with its garden of dusty hollyhocks.

My mother knocked on the door, and then went in, telling me to run along to the kitchen. I heard her whispering. Paulita came in for a moment to pour me milk and set out some cookies for me, and then she left again.

I didn't eat. I tried to listen, but couldn't make out any words. I heard Paulita click her tongue, the way she clicked it when someone had behaved shamefully, like when it was discovered that Charlie Padilla had been stealing from his grandmother.

My mother came into the kitchen. She patted my wrist. "It's not for long, Maria." She kissed the top of my head.

I heard Paulita's front door shut, heard her slow steps come toward the kitchen. She sat opposite me and took a cookie.

"It's good you came for a visit. I never see enough of you."

The next day I didn't go to Mass. I said I was sick, and Paulita touched my forehead but didn't contradict me. I stayed in bed, my eyes closed and dry. I could hear the bells and the intonations as the town passed outside the house. Antonia led the procession, and Nemecia walked with the adults; I know this because I asked Paulita days later. I wondered if Nemecia had chosen not to lead or if she had not been allowed, but I couldn't bring myself to ask.

I stayed with Paulita for three months. She spoiled me, fed me sweets, kept me up late with her. Each night she put her feet on the arm of the couch to stop the swelling, balanced her jigger of whiskey on her stomach, and stroked the stiff gray hair on her chin while she told stories: about Tajique when she was a girl, about the time she snuck out to the fiestas after she was supposed to be asleep. I loved Paulita and enjoyed her attention, but my anger at my parents simmered, even when I was laughing.

My mother stopped by, tried to talk to me, but in her presence the easy atmosphere of Paulita's house became stale. Over and over she urged me to visit her in the store, and I did once, but I was silent, wanting so much to be drawn out, disdaining her attempts.

"Hijita," she said, and pushed candy at me across the counter.

I stood stiff in her embrace and left the candy. My mother had sent me away, and my father had done nothing to stop her. They'd picked Nemecia, picked Nemecia over their real daughter.

Nemecia and I saw each other at school, but we didn't speak. Our teachers seemed aware of the changes in our household and kept us apart. People were kind to me during this time, a strange, pitying kindness. I thought they knew how angry I was, knew there was no hope left for me. I too would be kind, I thought, if I met myself on the road.

The family gathered on Sundays, as always, at my mother's house for dinner. That was how I had begun to think of it during those months: my mother's house. My mother hugged me, and my father kissed me, and I sat in my old place, but at the end of dinner, I always left with Paulita. Nemecia seemed more at home than ever. She laughed and told stories, and swallowed bite after neat bite. She seemed to have grown older, more graceful. She neither spoke to nor looked at me. Everyone talked and laughed, and it seemed only I remembered that we were eating with a murderer.

"Nemecia looks well," Paulita said one night as we walked home.

I didn't answer, and she didn't speak again until she had shut the door behind us.

"One day you'll be friends again, Maria. You two are sisters." Her hand trembled as she lit the lamp.

I couldn't stand it anymore. "No," I said. "We won't. We'll never be friends. We *aren't* sisters. She's the killer, and *I'm* the one who was sent away. Do you even *know* who killed your brother?" I demanded. "Nemecia. And she tried to kill her own mother too. Why doesn't anyone *know* this?"

"Sit down," Paulita said to me sternly. She'd never spoken to me in this tone. "First of all, you were not sent away. You could shout to your mother from this house. And, my God, Nemecia is not a killer. I don't know where you picked up such lies."

Paulita lowered herself into a chair. When she spoke again, her voice was even, her old eyes pale brown and watery. "Your grandfather decided he would give your mother and Benigna each fifty acres of land." Paulita put her hand to her forehead and exhaled slowly. "My God, this was so long ago. So your grandfather stopped by one morning to see Benigna about the deed. He was still on the road, he hadn't even made it to the door, when he heard the shouting. Benigna's cries were that loud. Her husband was beating her." Paulita paused. She pressed the pads of her fingers against the table.

I thought of the sound of fist on flesh. I could almost hear it. The flame of the lamp wavered and the light wobbled along the scrubbed, wide planks of Paulita's kitchen floor.

"This wasn't the first time it had happened, just the first time your grandfather walked in on it. So he pushed open the door, angry, ready to kill Benigna's husband. There must have been a fight, but Benigna's husband was drunk and your grandfather wasn't young anymore. Benigna's husband must have been closer to the stove and to the iron poker. When they were discovered—" Paulita's voice remained flat. "When they were discovered, your grandfather was already dead. Benigna was unconscious on the floor. And they found Nemecia behind the woodbox. She'd seen the whole thing. She was five."

I wondered who had walked in first on that brutality. Surely someone I knew, someone I passed at church or outside the post office. Maybe someone in my family. Maybe Paulita. "What about Nemecia's father?"

"He was there on his knees, crying over Benigna. 'I love you, I love you, I love you,' he kept saying."

How had it never occurred to me that, at five years old, Nemecia would have been too small to attack a grown man and woman all at once? How could I have been so stupid?

At school I watched for signs of what Paulita had told me, but Nemecia was the same: graceful, laughing, distant. I felt humiliated for believing her, and I resented the demands she made on my sympathy. Pity and hatred and guilt nearly choked me. If anything, I hated my cousin more, she who had once been a terrified child, she who could call that tragedy her own. Nemecia would always have the best of everything.

Nemecia left for California three months after Corpus Christi. In Los Angeles, my aunt Benigna bought secondhand furniture and turned the small sewing room into a bedroom. She introduced Nemecia to her husband and to the miracle child. There was a palm tree in the front yard and a pink-painted gravel walkway. I know this from a letter my cousin sent my mother, signed with a flourish, *Norma*.

I moved back to my mother's house and to the room that was all mine. My mother stood in the middle of the floor as I unpacked my things into the now-empty bureau. She looked lost.

"We missed you," she said, looking out the window. And then, "It's not right for a child to be away from her parents. It's not right that you left us."

I wanted to tell her that *I* had not left, that I had been *left*, led away and dropped at Paulita's door.

"Listen." Then she stopped and shook her head. "Ah, well," she said, with an intake of breath.

I placed my camisoles in the drawer, one on top of the other. I didn't look at my mother. The reconciliation, the tears and embraces that I'd dreamt about, didn't come, and so I hardened myself against her.

Our family quickly grew over the space Nemecia left, so quickly that I often wondered if she'd meant anything to us at all.

Nemecia's life became glamorous in my mind—beautiful, tragic, the story of an orphan. I imagined that I could take that life, have it for myself. Night after night I told myself the story: a prettier me, swept away to California, and the boy who would find me and save me from my unhappiness. The town slept among the vast, whispering grasses, coyotes called in the distance, and Nemecia's story set my body alight.

We attended Nemecia's wedding, my family and I. We took the long trip across New Mexico and Arizona to Los Angeles, me in the backseat between my brothers. For years I'd pictured Nemecia living a magazine shoot, running on the beach, stretched on a chaise longue beside a flat, blue pool, and it was a fantasy that had sustained me. As we crossed the Mojave Desert, though, I began to get nervous—that I wouldn't recognize her, that she'd have forgotten me. I found myself hoping that her life wasn't as beautiful as I'd imagined it, that she'd finally been punished.

When we drove up to the little house, Nemecia ran outside in bare feet and hugged each of us as we unfolded ourselves from the car.

"Maria!" she cried, smiling, and kissed both my cheeks, and I fell into a shyness I couldn't shake all that week.

"Nemecia, hijita," my mother said. She stepped back and looked at my cousin happily.

"Norma," my cousin said. "My name is Norma."

It was remarkable how completely she'd changed. Her hair was blond now, her skin tanned dark and even.

My mother nodded slowly and repeated, "Norma."

The wedding was the most beautiful thing I'd ever seen, and I was wrung with jealousy. I must have understood then that I wouldn't have a wedding of my own. Like everything else in Los Angeles, the church was large and modern. The pews were pale and sleek, and the empty crucifix shone. Nemecia confessed to me that she didn't know the priest here, that she rarely even went to church anymore. In a few years, I too would stop going to church, but it shocked me then to hear my cousin say it.

They didn't speak Spanish in my aunt's house. When my mother or father said something in Spanish, my aunt or cousins answered resolutely in English. I was embarrassed by my parents that week, the way their awkward English made them seem confused and childish.

The day before the wedding, Nemecia invited me to the beach with her girlfriend. I said I couldn't go—I was fifteen, younger than they were, and I didn't have a swimming suit.

"Of course you'll come. You're my little sister." Nemecia opened a messy drawer and tossed me a tangled blue suit. I remember I changed in her bedroom, turned in the full-length mirror, stretched across her pink satin bed, and posed like a pinup. I felt older, sensual. There, in Nemecia's bedroom, I liked the image of myself in that swimming suit, but on the beach my courage left me. Someone took our picture, standing with a tanned, smiling man. I still have the picture. Nemecia and her friend look easy in their suits, arms draped around the man's neck. The man—who is he? How did he come to be in the photograph?—has his arm around Nemecia's small waist. I am beside her, my hand on her shoulder, but standing as though I'm afraid to touch her. She leans into the man and away from me, her smile broad and white. My scar shows as a gray smear on my cheek. I smile with my lips closed, and my other arm is folded in front of my chest.

Until she died, my mother kept Nemecia's wedding portrait beside her bed: Nemecia and her husband in front of a photographer's arboreal backdrop with their hands clasped, smiling into each other's faces. The photograph my cousin gave me has the same airless studio quality but is of Nemecia alone, standing on some steps, her train arranged around her. She is half-turned, unsmiling, wearing an expression I can't interpret. Neither thoughtful nor stony nor proud. Her expression isn't unhappy, just almost, but not quite, vacant.

When she left for Los Angeles, Nemecia didn't take the doll that sat on the bureau. The doll came with us when we moved to Albuquerque; we saved it, I suppose, for Nemecia's children, though we never said so out loud. Later, after my mother died in 1981, I brought it from her house, where for years my mother had kept it on her bureau. For five days it lay on the table in my apartment before I called Nemecia and asked if she wanted it back.

"I don't know what you're talking about," she said. "I never had a doll."

"The cracked one, remember?" My voice went high with disbelief. It seemed impossible that she could have forgotten. It had sat in our room for years, facing us in our beds each night as we fell asleep. A flare of anger ignited—she was lying, she had to be lying—then died.

I touched the yellowed hem of the doll's dress, while Nemecia told me about the cruise she and her husband were taking through the Panama Canal. "Ten days," she said, "and then we're going to stay for three days in Puerto Rico. It's a new boat, with casinos and pools and ballrooms. I hear they treat you royally." While she talked, I ran my finger along the ridges of the cracks in the doll's head. From the sound of her voice, I could almost imagine she'd never aged, and it seemed to me I'd spent my whole life listening to Nemecia's stories.

"So what about the doll?" I asked when it was almost time to hang up. "Do you want me to send it?"

"I can't even picture it," she said, and laughed. "Do whatever you want. I don't need old things lying around the house."

I was tempted to take offense, to think it was me she was rejecting, our whole shared past in Tajique. I was tempted to slip back into that same old envy, for how easily Nemecia had let those years drop away from her, leaving me to remember her stories. But by then I was old enough to know that she wasn't thinking about me at all.

Nemecia spent the rest of her life in Los Angeles. I visited her once when I had some vacation time saved, in the low house surrounded by bougainvillea. She collected Dolls of the World and Waterford crystal, which she displayed in glass cases. She sat me at the dining room table and took the dolls out one by one. "Holland," she said, and set it before me. "Italy. Greece." I tried to see some evidence in her face of what she had witnessed as a child, but there was nothing.

Nemecia held a wineglass up to the window and turned it. "See how clear?" Shards of light moved across her face.

Dylan Landis

Trust

"WE'RE JUST PRACTICING," SAYS Tina.

"We're just playing," says Rainey.

"We're just taking a walk."

"Yeah, but we're walking behind them," says Rainey. She and Tina have turned right about twenty feet behind a couple who lean into each other, slowly strolling, and here is something Rainey has noticed: couples don't attend to their surroundings the way solo walkers do. She wonders if the gun in her purse has a magnetic pull, if it wants to be near people.

"We're losing them," says Tina.

They're playing robber girls. Before they took the gun out for a walk, she and Tina were up in Rainey's room wrapping tie-dyed scarves around their heads to disguise their hair. They put on cheap lime green earrings from Fourteenth Street to take attention off their features, and T-shirts from Gordy's room to hide their own tops.

Gordy Vine lives in the West Tenth Street town house too, in the room next door to Rainey's. He is Rainey's father's best friend and a horn player, and he is as pale as the moon. His eyes are blue, but his hair is the color of milk. Gordy says shit like You don't need to understand jazz. You are jazz.

The earrings and T-shirts will go in the trash right afterward, that's the idea.

Would go. They're just playing.

The man and the woman amble on through the purpling evening, walking single file past the trees that encroach on the sidewalk.

"Gordy didn't mind you going through his stuff, huh?" Tina's T-shirt says LARRY CORYELL on the front and THE ELEVENTH HOUSE on the back. Rainey's says CHICK COREA. Hers is signed.

Rainey regards Tina as they walk. She wonders if the question is loaded. Tina is the only person on earth whom Rainey has told about Gordy's night visits. But they are best friends. Tina must not mean anything. Plus, Rainey doesn't want to be what her father calls those eggshell people.

She says, guardedly, "If he figures it out, he'll be pissed. But he might not. I'm never in his room."

Ahead of them, the couple slows to look up at the window of a town house, and Rainey stalls by bending over to retie her sneaker lace.

Tina makes a little smirk-sound in her nose. "Yeah, why would you be," she says. "He gets into your room every night." Her face darkens. Her hand fastens to her mouth. "Oh, no," she says through her fingers. "I fucked up. It just came out. I'm sorry, Rain."

Inside Rainey's purse, the gun beats like a heart. Its workings are a mystery. She and Tina were afraid to check if it had bullets because of the little lever that looks like another trigger. Rainey thinks the round part might be called a chamber, which sounds romantic.

"It's okay," says Rainey, not breathing. What else is it her father says? Fuck 'em if they can't take a joke.

Through the darkness that drapes them all, she studies the

woman who walks ahead of them. She's tucked her sleek hair into her collar, implying some magnificent length—Like mine, thinks Rainey—and she wears Frye boots, which make a lovely, horsey click on the sidewalk. It's not enough for this chick to hold the man's hand; she has to nestle both of their hands into the pocket of his leather jacket, a gesture that irritates Rainey and makes her think, bizarrely, of the airlessness of that pocket, of lying under her quilt at night, waiting to see if her door will open, and faking sleep.

How do you say no to an innocent back rub? She has asked Tina that. "Do you want to say no?" Tina asked back, and Rainey wanted to sock her.

"It's not okay," says Tina. "I can read you. It was a shitty joke, Rain. It just came out. I don't know why."

As they walk on, Rainey can see what the man and woman stopped to admire: a red room hung floor to ceiling with paintings. "Really," says Rainey. "It's okay." She smiles sweetly at Tina. It isn't clear who's being punished by the sweetness.

What kills her is the woman's extraordinary cape. It flaps serenely around her calves like a manta ray.

"Swear it's okay," says Tina.

"I swear." She is still smiling and it is like smiling at Tina from across a long bridge. Rainey ought to get over it—seriously, fuck her if she can't take a joke.

Tina exhales. "Okay." They both watch the couple for a moment. Then Tina says, "It's not like I need the money."

Rainey opens her mouth and closes it. She's tempted to make a crack but she holds it in. Tina goes on about her grandmother a lot—how she gets paid to live with her. How she can't bring anyone home because the grandmother doesn't like strangers. How the grandmother is blind. Best friends for five years and Tina has never invited Rainey home, so Rainey's not buying. She's never probed, though. Tina might detonate, or cry.

They've sped up, and now Rainey slows, partly so their footsteps won't be heard, but partly because she is pissed off and wants to consider the ramifications—that she is one of those eggshell people and fuck her because she cannot take this particular joke, and she suddenly has had it with the twenty-dollars-a-week grandmother story, because Tina has never had a twenty in her pocket once. A perverse urge to find the fuse in Tina rises up in her. And it would be so easy. Tina is like one of those sea corals they saw in a bio class movie that plant themselves any damn where they please, but close up tight as a fist when brushed by something they mistrust. In fact the only thing they do trust is this one fish called a clown fish. Rainey isn't anyone's goddamn clown fish.

She says, "I know, Tina. You get twenty dollars a week to live with your grandmother."

Tina looks at her slantwise and reaches deep into the bag on Rainey's shoulder—for the gun, Rainey thinks crazily, but it is only for the pack of Marlboros.

"Check out that cape," says Rainey. "That's mine."

"What's that supposed to mean, about my grandmother?" Tina lights a cigarette and drops the pack back in the bag.

Rainey wonders if she should be reeling Tina in right now, since they are playing robber girls. Besides, the grandmother is sacred territory. Rainey knows that without being told. Tina is tougher than Rainey but she is also easier to hurt. She knows that without being told. Rainey listens to the slow, steady hoofbeat of the Frye boots, satisfying as a pulse. Can you rob someone of her boots and cape? It's okay to think these things, because they are just playing. They will veer off any minute. The woman looks back, appraises them with a glance, and dismisses them.

"I asked you what it means about my grandmother," says Tina.

"It means your cup runneth over." Rainey uses her musical voice. "If you're getting twenty dollars a week."

"I don't have a cup." Tina's voice is low. "I have a savings account. I'm not supposed to touch it."

"You must be rolling."

Now Rainey too reaches for the cigarettes, which they jointly own, and lets her knuckles bump the gun. "What bank?" She's ultracasual. The gun is cold and bumpy and could shoot off her foot, but the weight of it feels good. Already she knows she will stash it at the bottom of her school backpack, with her picture of Saint Catherine of Bologna, patroness of artists.

"What bank? What is this, a fucking quiz? You don't believe me," says Tina. Reflexively, she passes over her cigarette so Rainey can light hers.

"I want that cape, Teen."

The couple turns left on Greenwich, walks a block, and crosses Barrow. Then they turn right on Morton. Rainey and Tina pick up their pace and fall back again, spooling out distance like kite string. It's perfect; they're all headed closer to the Hudson, where only true Villagers live and tourists rarely stray. Even from a half block back Rainey knows the man is handsome, his hair dark and thick, the shape of his head suggesting broad cheekbones that ride high. Rainey wants this man to desire her even as he looks at the gun and fears her. If she can make him desire her, she'll erase the feeling of Gordy's fingers where they don't belong, where he can still call it a back rub when he makes his night visits. Right now the feeling is like a dent at the edge of her left breast. It's a pressure along her neck where he starts stroking her long hair. She wants the cape, and she wants some other things that the man and the woman have. The money doesn't interest her.

"I have over a thousand dollars in Marine Midland Bank," says Tina.

"I'm going to take her cape," Rainey says. "You can have all their bread."

"If you don't believe me," says Tina, "I'm not taking another step."

"Oh?" says Rainey in the dangerously charming voice she saves for the final minutes with a victim in the girls' room. "Do you really live with your grandmother? Or do you just not want me to meet your family?"

Tina stops. Let her, thinks Rainey, she won't stop long. She keeps walking. By the time she makes half of Morton Street by herself she is trying not to trudge; she is missing Tina acutely, missing the way she bumps into her sometimes, the slight brushing of her jacket sleeve. Tina doesn't go in for hugging but she finds other ways to make contact, the affectionate shove, the French braiding of each other's hair, touching the hand that holds the match—anything that can't be called lezzy, which suits Rainey fine. At school there are teachers who insist they sit on opposite sides of the classroom, who make them play on separate teams: Rainey Royal and Tina Dial. When Rainey finally hears Tina approaching at a scuffing trot, she stops and waits, happy and faintly ashamed.

Tina says, "Gimme the goddamn bag, Rain."

Rainey passes it over. She waits to see if Tina is going to detonate and what that will look like. She waits to see if Tina can take a joke.

"I'm sorry, Teen."

Tina looks into the bag as she cradles it in front of her, and Rainey knows she is looking at the darkly radiant gun, a gun Rainey stole from her father's filing cabinet days earlier after one of his obnoxious sex talks. She's spent a lot of secret time in Howard Royal's room. She's excavated the postcards her mother sends from the ashram. She's stolen family photos from Howard's albums, one at a time. She's found boxes of Ramses and a pair of leopard-print underwear for men and the dispensers of birth-control pills from which Howard administers one pill every morning. I know what girls your age are doing. She hates those talks, Howard loosely strung across a brocade parlor chair while she's curled into her carapace to hide her breasts.

"I believe you," says Rainey. "I do."

In addition to the gun, Rainey stole her birth certificate from a file marked "Legal." Rainey Ann Royal. Who the fuck picked Ann, anyway? A girl named Ann would dance badly and her hip-huggers wouldn't hug. If anyone kissed her, she'd wonder where the noses go. In dodgeball, if you were feeling mean, Ann would be the girl whose anxious face you'd aim for.

Maybe Ann is the reason her mother left.

No one knows Rainey's middle name, not even Tina, and she knows every single other thing about Rainey. Tina knows it is a lie when Rainey says she plays jazz flute. She knows it is true that Rainey technically may have lost it to her father's best friend. She knows it is a lie that Rainey will move to the ashram when she is sixteen. She knows all this, and she doesn't judge.

Ahead, near the corner of Washington, the couple sits on a town house stoop. They kiss and lean into each other.

"She's blind," says Tina. It takes Rainey a second to realize they are still talking about the grandmother. "I told you." They are standing less than half a block from the couple, watching obliquely. The man lights two cigarettes and passes one to the woman. Maybe they are just playing too, playing at being robbed, Rainey thinks. The man glances up the sidewalk and watches Rainey and Tina, still in conference.

"I get it," says Rainey. "I believe you. I get it, Teen."

They resume a slow walk toward the town house stoop. Rainey could swear she hears Tina thinking hard in her direction. She could swear she hears something like I'm lying, she's not blind. The twenty dollars, that's bullshit too, and Rainey thinks back, It's okay, Teen, I love you anyway, and we're going to just walk by these people, right? and she hears Tina think, Of course we are, we're just playing, when Tina drops her hand into the bag and says, "You don't get anything."

They are about a quarter block away. Less.

Alarmed, Rainey looks straight at the beautiful leonine man. "Don't do it," she says in a low voice. And then, because she knows it is too late, because it is not in her control and because she wants to do it too, she whispers, "Don't hurt anyone."

Now the woman looks up. In about fifteen steps, if they keep walking, Rainey and Tina will reach the man and the woman on the town house stoop.

They keep walking, slowly.

Tina whispers, "There's a safety, right? That's what it's for, right?" Her elbow is cocked, it's obvious she's about to draw something out of the bag, and now they are right there, steps from the man and the woman sitting and smoking on the town house stoop, and Rainey has no idea if there's a safety or what a gun was doing in Howard's filing cabinet. She wants the man to look at her and lose all awareness of everything that is not Rainey, and he is, now, looking at her, but with the wrong expression. Quizzical. He looks quizzical, and the woman is checking his face to see what's changed. Tina stops. Rainey stops behind her. She has no idea what will happen if Tina steps any closer and the man twists her wrist so that the gun falls to the sidewalk and explodes, shooting someone in the ankle. She does want that softly gliding cape, which she will wear to school, inciting fabulous waves of jealousy.

She could go somewhere around the treetops and look down from there. It's a gift she has, one she likes to think her mother left her. The moment hurtles toward them. She has to decide fast. Tina faces the woman as if she were going to ask her directions. Her two hands shake around the gun, which is abruptly half out of the bag.

"This is a stickup," she says, trembling, her voice hoarse, and Rainey is far from the treetops, she is right there, feeling the concrete through her shoes.

The woman claps a hand over her mouth, stopping a laugh. "Central casting," she whispers from under her hand.

"The gun's real," says the man. "Shut up, Estelle." Rainey has no idea what wuthering means, but she thinks he must have that kind of face: brooding and gorgeous, from some dreamy old novel.

"Yeah, shut up, Estelle." Tina sounds like she does in the girls' room but with an undertow of fear. "You guys live here or what?" Rainey feels the approaching moment thundering right up to her. She feels like someone who can take any kind of joke, now. She can't wait to find out what her job will be.

The man and the woman say no and yes at the exact same moment. "Take our wallets," says the man. "You don't have to hurt anyone."

"Be nice," says Tina. "Invite us up."

"If you're going to do anything do it here," says the man. Estelle's hand remains plastered to her mouth, but her eyes are rounded.

Rainey feels ravenous for what is about to happen. The sidewalk is pushing through her shoes now. "I'm feeling kind of antsy down here," she says in a voice that sounds like smoke and jazz. She has it down. "Take us upstairs, baby," she tells the man.

Tina walks up to the stoop and jabs the gun against Estelle's knee. Saint Tina of the Girls' Room—are they really in the same place, doing the same thing? Is it possible that Tina feels purification as she does this bad act? Rainey's father's words unspool from her body as if she is expelling a magician's silk scarf: They talk about this at school, don't they? How girls your age are approaching the height of their sexual powers? She feels the nape of her neck sealing itself against Gordy's hand, and she looks at Estelle's neck with rising irritation.

"Okay okay okay okay okay," says Estelle, and gets up fast from the stoop.

"Hey, listen," says Rainey, batting Tina on the arm. She almost says her name but catches herself. "I totally believe you. I do. I had one crazy moment of doubt but it's over. I'm sorry." She watches as Tina closely scans her face as if she's not sure she's seen it before.

"You still think I'm bullshitting," says Tina, locking her gaze back onto the boyfriend and Estelle. "And you're still mad from what I said about Gordy."

Rainey is not afraid of Tina. She might be afraid of hurting Tina, though.

"I believe you to death," says Rainey. "And it's okay about Gordy. Come on. I'll prove it. Let's do something crazy."

"Oh my God," says Estelle. "Oh God oh God oh God."

The brick building's entry hall is lit with bare bulbs and its stairs are thickly carpeted. Glossy black doors, greenish walls—Rainey feels like she is at the bottom of a fish tank. "Go," says Tina harshly, and the man looks at her jamming her purse, with the gun half in it, into Estelle's back. "Don't touch her," he says, and immediately starts up the stairs. Rainey listens for sounds from other tenants and hears none. "I'm aiming right at Estelle's spine," says Tina, and while it seems to Rainey that the man could lunge back down the stairs at them, it also seems that the word *spine* sounds menacingly like bone porcelain, and she is not afraid.

They climb, first him, then Estelle and Tina in a kind of lock-step, then Rainey, the shag carpeting hushing their progress, till the man stops at a door on the third floor and Estelle sags against it. She says, "You don't have to come in. You could just turn around. We'll give you everything."

Tina holds the gun close to her own side, aimed at Estelle. "Oh, we can't wait to see your apartment," she says in a pretend-guest voice.

Rainey holds her hand out for both sets of keys; she senses Estelle and the boyfriend trying not to touch her palm. It makes her powers grow, holding their keys and key chains: such intimate objects. She opens the shiny black door, feels for a switch, and turns on the light.

"You're not kidding we want to see it," she says.

The apartment, a large studio with two tall windows, is painted a deep violet, as if an intense twilight has settled. In contrast, the trim and furnishings—a bureau, a table with chairs, and a curvaceous bed frame—are painted bridal white. Rainey can't believe it. She walks down a violet hall into which a Pullman kitchen is notched, flicking on lights as she goes. At the end, she opens the door to a violet bath. She wants to steal all the walls.

Behind her, she hears Tina telling the boyfriend and Estelle to sit on the bed, and how far apart.

"What color is this?" she calls from the bathroom, where the white shower curtain manages to look like a wedding gown against the violet walls.

"I mixed it." Estelle is breathing hard. "I'm a set designer."

Rainey walks back down the hall into the main room and props herself against a white dining chair. Tina moves cautiously around the room, always watching Estelle and the boyfriend, lifting small objects off the mantel and nightstands and amassing a little pile of goods on the hearth. Rolls of coins. Earrings. The gun never wavers. Rainey asks Estelle, "Yeah, but what do you call it, this color?"

"Amethyst," says Estelle. "It's a glaze."

"It's incredible," says Rainey. "It's the most beautiful color I've ever seen."

Estelle hugs herself and shivers. "Please point that somewhere else," she asks Tina. "I swear I won't do anything."

"God, I love this place," says Rainey. "Would you light me a cigarette? And may I have your cape, please?"

Rainey watches Tina collect sixty-three dollars from the two wallets tossed on the table and a fistful of earrings from a bureau drawer. It takes Tina only a minute. The gun never wavers and she never stops watching Estelle and the boyfriend. She jams her prizes in the pocket of the boyfriend's leather jacket, which she is now wearing. Then she positions herself by the white marble hearth. Estelle and the boyfriend are not playing at being robbed. They sit on the edge of the bed about as far apart as they can while still holding hands—the holding hands was Tina's concession.

Glancing at Tina, Rainey catches sight of herself in the mirror over the hearth, luxuriant hair spilling out the back of the tie-dyed scarf. "Look at us," she says, giving Tina a light nudge. "Even with all this shit on, we're still cute. We should take a Polaroid. You got a Polaroid, Estelle?"

Tina keeps the gun aimed straight at Estelle as she turns quickly to look at herself in the mirror, then at Rainey. Her shoulders slump a little. She looks back at Estelle but says, "How can you tell it's still us?"

Rainey laughs. "You're tripping, right?" Tina shrugs. They both know she hasn't tried acid yet. "'Cause it looks like us," says Rainey. "Right?"

"I'm not sure," says Tina.

"You're on blotter," says Rainey, and waits for her to stop being spooky. Rainey once licked blotter off Gordy's palm and spent hours watching the walls quilt themselves exquisitely, kaleidoscopically.

"Who else would I think you are?" Rainey says. "Jimi Hendrix?"

"I know what Jimi Hendrix looks like. Don't move," she snaps at the boyfriend, who is edging closer to Estelle. "I am tripping," she says. "I don't recognize myself."

Rainey isn't sure she recognizes this Tina either, the one who sees a stranger in her own face. "Ever?"

"That would be retarded. I mean, with the scarf on."

It's Rainey's turn to nosey around, as her father would say. She takes her time. Tina's weirding her out. The nightstand alarm clock says they've been there only four minutes. Surely they can stay another four. She could swear that in the silence she can hear the clock whirr. The cape hangs heavy from her shoulders; it is too hot for the apartment but the weight feels terrific.

On a closet shelf she finds a stack of typed and handwritten letters rubber-banded in red. She takes it down and sets it aside on the bureau. "You don't want that," says Estelle, half rising. "It's old, it's just junk—"

"I don't always recognize people on TV, either," says Tina. "Or at school. You think there's something wrong with me?"

"Yes." Rainey goes back to the hallway Pullman kitchen for a pair of shears.

"Well, then fuck you," calls Tina.

"But there's plenty of shit wrong with me too," says Rainey, walking back in with the scissors.

Rainey snips buttons from Estelle's blouses, lace and ribbons from her nightgowns. She puts those on the bureau with the letters. "In winter?" says Tina. "When you put a hat on? I'm not a hundred percent sure it's you till you say something." She takes a deep breath and locks it up somewhere for a while. "At least I always know my grandmother." She smiles; it's a private, knowing smile. Rainey could almost swear there's pride in it.

She bites her lip. She prowls the room more aggressively. She finds two photo albums at the foot of the hearth and begins robbing them of photographs. "Not my father," says Estelle, and starts to cry. "Not my grandfather."

"Who is this?" Rainey holds up a square color photo of a woman pretending to vamp in a one-piece bathing suit. Her smile is playful, as if she is somebody's mother who would never really, actually vamp. Mothers interest Rainey: their presence, their absence, the way they react to the heat waves her body gives off in the proximity of their husbands and sons.

"No one," says Estelle.

Rainey adds it to the stack. Estelle makes a high-pitched sound in her throat. Rainey, moving on, seizes two black journals from a nightstand drawer.

"Oh my God, no," says Estelle, but then she looks at Tina and the gun and closes her eyes.

Rainey turns abruptly to face Tina. "Look," she says, "if you ever don't know who someone is, just ask me, okay?"

"Do you think I'm crazy?"

"Just ask me."

"Are we okay?"

Rainey sighs like of course they're okay, but she still hears it. He gets into your room every night.

"Do you think I have schizophrenia?"

"Just ask me," Rainey says.

She goes down the hall again, cape flapping behind her; she salvages a grocery bag from under the sink, unclips the receiver from the hallway wall phone and drops that in first. Then she drops in the letters, the cuttings, the photos, and the journals that she has piled on the bureau. The door lock, miraculously, requires a key on each side. She and Tina can actually lock these people in.

"Who's the woman in the photo?" demands Rainey.

Estelle, crying, just shakes her head.

"Take my watch," the boyfriend tells Tina. "Leave her papers and take my watch. You'll get fifty dollars for it, I swear."

"Thanks," says Tina, as if startled by his generosity. She makes him give it to Estelle, who holds it out, shrinking from the gun.

"The papers?" he says. But Tina's admiring the watch in quick glances, and Rainey's lost in a vision. She sees a tapestry made from scraps of handwriting and snippets of photos, tiny telegrams from the heart: patches of letters, strips of confessions, grainy faces of people who have, in one way or another, perhaps like her mother, split. She'll sew buttons at the intersections, layer in some lace. In Rainey's hands, such things will reassemble themselves into patterns as complex as snowflakes. She will start the tapestry tonight, in her pink room. What would Estelle do with this ephemera anyway, besides keep it closeted away?

"You have Paul's watch," whispers Estelle. "Can I have my papers?"

"Oh, it's Paul?" Rainey looks at the boyfriend. "I don't have Paul's watch." She swirls the cape and turns theatrically to Tina, who appears delicate in the leather jacket. "You have the watch, right?" Rainey sighs dramatically and runs her hands down the curves of her body, staring at Paul, who looks back at her with the directness of someone who respects the gun too much to move but is not exactly afraid. This intrigues Rainey tremendously.

"I thought Paul would like me better, but she got the watch, so apparently not." She's just playing, but it seems to her that Tina looks at her sharply. "Listen," she says to Tina, "let's go. I'm great. I have every single thing I need."

She is surprised to see hurt flash across Tina's eyes.

"You're great?" says Tina. "Why are you great? What've you got that you need?"

Paul sits forward with interest.

"Shut up," says Tina, though he hasn't said anything.

"Don't," says Rainey. She is holding her grocery bag with one arm and has her left hand on the doorknob. "I said I believe you. Let's go." But Tina remains plastered to the hearth.

"What've you got that you need?" says Tina. When Rainey doesn't answer, she says, "What? You've got an albino freak who—" She stops, possibly because Rainey is staring her down, possibly out of restraint.

"An albino freak who what?" says Paul.

Rainey looks at Tina, flaming against the amethyst walls, radiant in her distress. She feels the gaze of Paul upon her, and she flushes. "I have everything I need from this apartment," she says, as if talking to someone from a distant land.

"Oh." Tina visibly relaxes, as if warm water were being poured through her. "I don't." She turns a slow, thoughtful quarter circle, looking around the room.

"Oh no," says Estelle. "Please go. Please please please go."

"Get those scissors, would you?" says Tina, taking a few steps toward Estelle.

Rainey picks them up off the nightstand, where she set them down after taking souvenir snippets from Estelle's clothes, and swings them from one finger. "What are you going to do, cut her hair?"

Tina smiles. "No, you are."

"Really? Seriously"—again she almost says Tina's name—"what are you planning to do with her hair?"

"Same thing I was going to do without it," says Tina.

Estelle lets go of Paul's hand and clamps both her hands around her hair. "For Christ's sake," says Paul.

Rainey wonders if the gun belongs to Tina now. Estelle's hair belongs to Estelle, that much is true. "No," she says. "This is between me and you."

"You said everything was okay," Tina says. "You said you believed me. You said, 'I'll prove it.' "

"I think she's proven quite a bit," says Paul.

"Whose boyfriend are you? Be quiet," says Tina.

Rainey sets the grocery bag on the floor and puts her face in the bowl of her hands, scissors still dangling, so she can think. Tina is telling the truth now. It's Rainey who's lying: she does not believe a word about the grandmother, and things are not okay. She looks through her fingers from Estelle, who has wrapped her long hair protectively around her fist, to Tina, who waits to see if trust can be restored.

She almost asks again about the woman in the picture. It's the right moment: she holds the scissors and Tina holds the gun. Instead she takes a deep breath of amethyst air. "Forgive me," she says, and for a moment, while neither Tina nor Estelle knows whose forgiveness she requires, she feels nearly free.

"Here," she says. She bends over quickly, so the tie-dyed scarf falls forward and the violet room swings back, grabs a thick sheaf of her own long, dark hair, and cuts.

Allison Alsup

Old Houses

As they gather for the spring block party on the Peabodys' extra lot, the residents of Hillcrest Way think how lucky they are to live in old houses and among the kind of people who understand old houses and their architecture—Tudor, Colonial, Spanish Mediterranean. Every house on the street is different but in keeping with the neighborhood, scaled and proportioned. *Houses that know who they are,* Dennis Petersen calls them in an effort to distinguish them from the ones down the hill. The homes on the roads below are smaller, built on stingier lots and, in some cases, built too late to have the kind of distinct identity that old houses do. His own house is Norman, the first on the block, and built over a century ago.

The latecomers make their way down the sidewalks toward the Peabodys' lot, the women holding cheese trays and pasta salads, the men bottles of wine. They are all grateful to Richard and Katherine for having purchased the lot and for having saved it from the builders. They have seen what developers can do. When fire swept through the hills across town, the builders razed everything and erected rows of white boxes with no room for gardens or yards for children to play in. So after they place their offerings on the folding-table buffet on the Peabodys' lawn, they all compliment Katherine on her growing collection of irises. They note, as always, with genuine delight, how the lot opens the view in just the right spot: a slice of steel-blue bay and beyond, the studded grid of downtown San Francisco. The view is better, they note, from this side.

They are fond of the phrase *original to the house.* Moldings and inlaid oak floors original to the house. Built-in cabinets, box beams, coved ceilings and stained glass original to the house. Bannisters, mullions, muntins, French doors, glass knobs, telephone niches, carved mantels, fireplace grates, chandeliers, porthole windows and *working* shutters, all original to the house. The little bedroom on the ground floor, original to the house. All the old houses on Hillcrest have one—just a few steps from the kitchen and the back stairs. They don't call it a maid's room, except in private. Of course, no one has a maid anymore, only a woman who cleans and a gardener who comes once a week to mow and round up the leaves. Live-ins are for those in the hills above, people who can't be bothered to walk their own dogs.

In some of their houses, the little room has been converted into an office, sometimes into a discreet spot for the television. Five years ago, the Welshes lined the back wall with double-glazed windows and made a music studio where he could play the violin and she the French horn. The children played too, before they went to college and moved away. Since their remodel, Judith Goldman times her evening walks to coincide with the Welshes' practice hour; sometimes Suzanne Collier joins her and they share news of their daughters who attend neighboring colleges in Massachusetts. Sometimes, however, Judith prefers to walk alone. The faint sound of the Russian composers and the sight of the cool evening fog weaving through the tall pines make her think of summers spent as a girl in upstate New York. She had her own little room remade into a library complete with a gas fireplace and matching high-back chairs. When she closes the door, her husband knows not to bother her.

They stand clustered about the grass, sampling salads and refilling wineglasses. They like to think about all that their houses have witnessed. They all know the story of the Petersens' house— built for a bachelor sea captain at the turn of the last century. Of course, there had been sea captains then. They all agree that with his thick sweaters and ruddy face, Dennis Petersen does indeed resemble a sea captain.

You never own an old house, they agree, you just safeguard it for the next generation.

By this, they mean their children, the eldest of whom have scattered. And really, given the way prices and taxes have risen, inheriting a house on Hillcrest is the next generation's only hope for an old house in a good neighborhood. Of course, they themselves will never leave. They'll have to be carried out feetfirst, they say, though they are careful to speak softly so that the old doctor won't hear. His house, just across the street from the Peabodys' lawn, rises above the thick clump of Katherine's yellow irises. He is very old now and must decline the invitations to the block party. He sends his wishes from behind the closed curtains of his white stucco Spanish Mediterranean. They do not say so, but the other residents of Hillcrest are relieved. They have never understood why he chose to stay after what happened. They wouldn't have been able to.

Occasionally, an article appears in the paper, marking the tenth, twentieth, now thirtieth anniversary of the killings—the doctor's first wife and older daughter, home from college for a visit between semesters. The case remains unsolved; the articles end with the usual plea for information. They have written to the paper and asked that the name Hillcrest be withheld from the article; it gives the wrong impression of the neighborhood. But of course, the paper still prints the street name and inevitably one of their kids learns of the crimes and they're forced to tell the version they've agreed upon. They assure their children all this happened long before they moved in, another era really. They're more careful now. It's why Madeleine Welsh was right to phone the police about the stranger looking over the Colliers' garden gate. Below them is a different city, where hooded youths with guns roam the flat streets. There isn't a wall between them and the rest of the world. They must all watch out for one another. It's why the block parties are so important. Still, what's past is past.

They omit certain details. They don't tell the children the way the killer bound the two women with their own stockings or what he did to the girl. They don't mention that it was the younger daughter, the one still in high school, who walked home from class to find her mother and sister on the living room floor just a few feet from the piano. Nor do they say that the front door had not been forced open or that the prime suspect lived just two doors down, in what is now the Dillingers' house: a shaggy-haired, hollow-eyed teenage boy whose second-story window faced the doctor's house. They do not admit what they have all imagined from the black-and-white photo of the victims reprinted in the paper each year: the scrubbed coed opening the door, her pressed miniskirt, her straight smile and full brunette hair. *Please, come in.* They especially do not like to think about that. As parents, they have aimed to instill good manners in their own children. The police investigated, but couldn't make a case against the boy. That hasn't changed, the adults agree. Even with all the technology now, they have no faith in the cops. Instead, they tell their children, That was a long time ago. They've learned to be more careful now. They watch out for one another.

Everyone claps encouragement as James and Madeleine Welsh arrive carrying their instruments in black armored cases. Each year they learn a new piece just for the party. James has never told his wife this, but he believes their music placates ghosts. Nor has Suzanne Collier ever revealed that years ago, after she saw the girl's picture in the paper, she began to hear odd noises. She said nothing of it, even to Anne Dillinger, who had confided that she once hired a woman to burn sage in every room of their house. Judith Goldman keeps most thoughts to herself. Sometimes when she closes the door to her small library, she sits in her high-back chair and thinks about when the house was new. She imagines the young girls who once slept in her little room. She pictures their raw fingers and plain faces, the way they rose from narrow beds early in the morning to pin back mop-straight hair and light the fireplace. She imagines the routine of their days, cooking and cleaning for a family not their own, and how the girls must have longed for the few dark hours to themselves in this tiny room. She thinks of her own daughter, now three thousand miles away in a little dorm room. When Judith calls, her daughter does not seem relieved to hear from her or interested in news from the neighborhood. Judith doesn't understand it, but she detects accusation, even disdain, in her daughter's voice.

Wineglasses are refilled, then everyone quiets as James and Madeleine settle their music stand on the grass. Anne Dillinger gently guides her husband away from the spinach dip. The first tendrils of the evening fog have crept in and some of the women slip on jackets they have knowingly brought. There is a general murmur about *San Francisco summers*. And there's a breeze; the sheet music ripples. Dennis Petersen steps forward and, with thick, pink fingers, steadies the sheets. His tall frame looms to the side of the metal stand and they all smile, certain that in a past life, he held the pitted wood of a ship's wheel with the same measured calm.

Keeping their backs to the doctor's house, they tell themselves that any place as old as Hillcrest has stories. All old houses do. It's part of their character. The older neighbors stand smiling as the younger parents gather their children, pull them close and whisper, *Listen.* Then Madeleine's lips nestle into the brass mouthpiece of her horn, and James lowers his bow to the strings.

Halina Duraj
Fatherland

MY MOTHER'S PARENTS KEPT four cows. Each had a heavy chain around its neck. When my mother got home from school at two, she brought the ends of the chains together in one thick strand, looped them around her arm, and led the cows to pasture. She held on to the chains until dinnertime. She couldn't let go, not even for a second, because the cows might wander off into the rows of cabbage. To pass the time, she made up poems. She was so good at Polish that the boys in the row behind her called her Pani Poetka—Little Miss Poet. So good her teacher told her she could be a teacher if she went to high school.

But to go to high school she would need a new pair of shoes. Her mother would not buy them. Instead, her mother sent her to be a nanny for a rich couple in a nearby town. You don't need new shoes to run after children, her mother said. But of course she did not only run after children. She cooked, she cleaned, she helped them with their lessons, repaired their clothes—all in tattered, too-tight boots. By the time she saved enough money for a new pair, she was too old for high school. She became a seamstress instead, in a factory that made heavy black overcoats for the Communists in China.

After ten years of sewing coats, she wrote to the beekeeping nuns of Szczecin. She'd bought their honey at a market once; it was sweeter than the honey she remembered from home. She thought she'd be an excellent nun, even if she were afraid of bees, except for the fact that she wanted children. She was thirty, old for getting married. She was getting ready to accept that children weren't meant for her, even though it twisted her to think she'd never know the peculiar sensation of life inside. The nuns told her to wait until spring, when the snow would melt and the trains would be safer for journeying through the mountain passes.

On the cool April day she planned to give notice at the factory, she stepped off a curb on her way to work and got hit by a speeding bakery truck.

So much depends on a new pair of shoes, my mother liked to say.

When my father was two years old, his father drove his horse and cart home from a New Year's Eve *sylvestra* at a neighboring farm. Drunk, my grandfather passed out behind the reins and slipped sideways into the snow. The horses went on without him, pulling the empty cart all the way home to my grandmother's barnyard. They stamped their hooves lightly and snorted steam until my grandmother came out to milk the cows in the morning. She saw the horses and sent my uncles down the road to find their father. It was not the first time.

Only this time the New Year brought an unexpected snowfall, and in the hours between my grandfather's fall and my grandmother noticing the horses, two inches of snow fell steadily and softly onto the road and my drunk grandfather, who froze solid and died.

When my father was sixteen, SS men drove up to his farm in southern Poland, outside a tiny town named Golonog, and tore the brothers out of their beds. It was four in the morning. They demanded employment papers. Only my father did not have them; his job had been to help his widowed mother on the farm. The SS men loaded him onto the transport. The dog barked in the barnyard, so the SS men shot it dead. The dog's name was Kukusz.

The SS took my father to four labor camps, the last and worst of which was Auschwitz. Night after night, for company or just for us kids, he reenacted the story in the middle of our kitchen: In a twilight march back to camp after a day of digging ditches, my father breaks from the line and bolts into the forest. He is twenty, but in our kitchen, in the forest, he is sixteen, frozen in time at the age he was torn from bed. He throws himself on the forest floor, on the yellow linoleum. He rolls under the branches of a fir tree, under the legs of the table. Soldiers shout, guns fire; my father trembles. Flashlights glance off boughs. In our kitchen, he leaps to his feet. He shouts in German, stomps—SS boots crunch pine needles. He is hunter and hunted, all at once.

The SS men search awhile, then give up. What is one Pole? Not worth a cold night. Not worth a bullet. They will tell the commandant that they shot him and left him for dead. The Pole would die out here anyway, in the forest, in the cold.

By morning light, my father creeps from beneath the branches of the tree. He crawls to the edge of the forest. He skulks toward a farmhouse. He steals a bike and rides three days to his mother's farm. In the barnyard, a new dog barks and strains at the end of its chain. My grandmother carries milk pails out of the house. She doesn't recognize him. Then she does. She drops the pails and splashes through milk to hold him tight, her boy, her baby, her youngest.

My father must keep moving; he must leave Poland. He clings to the underbelly of a train and rides it into the American Zone—a day's journey. When he emerges from beneath the train, he can't straighten his arms, can't unclench his fists.

He lives under an alias in West Germany for eleven years,

scraping together a living, sometimes as a lookout for back-alley con artists, sometimes as a machinist—a trade he learned in one of the camps.

In Munich he goes hooliganing. He works odd jobs and makes enough to buy a radio, his only possession. It plays such beautiful music that some mornings he doesn't want to get out of bed for work. The radio is made of highly polished wood with golden swirls in the grain. It has a gold brocade face and yellowed plastic keys like a piano. If you press a key it makes the little gold ticker jump from city name to city name: Berlin, Dresden, Frankfurt, Warsaw, Paris, London, Rome, Moscow, Budapest, Amsterdam.

In the house I grew up in, the radio sat on top of my father's dresser. As a child, I pressed the keys and listened for sounds from another continent, but the radio no longer worked. One day my mother discovered a family of mice living inside it. They had chewed through the pressed-board backing and made a nest for themselves among the wires. My mother carried the radio into the backyard and let the mice scamper across the lawn. The cat looked up, blinked, and went back to sleep.

Eventually, my father boards a ship that stops in Copenhagen. He buys a small blue-and-white plate with a farm scene. It will hang above our kitchen sink, beneath the exposed wires of a torn-out light fixture. My mother would like a little light by which to wash the dishes, but my father never repairs it. During my father's last days in the hospital, my brother extracted the wires and installed a new light. Ceramic, with little painted flowers. Then he repainted the walls and hung valances above the curtains. The Danish plate remains.

My mother's accident left a scar on her head—a wild zigzag above her left temple. When I was little I assumed that a scar like a lightning bolt could mean only one thing: my mother had been struck by lightning.

She recovered in a sanatorium called Kudowa-Zdroj in south-western Poland, where people stroll down a boulevard flanked by elms and take the waters in mineral baths of different temperatures, some so hot that steam curls from them all year long. These sanatoria held dances, and my father, between jobs back in America, devoted six months of his life to scouting those dances for a wife.

My father admires my mother across the room. Here is a woman hit by a truck—a truck!—and look at her dancing, laughing, holding a porcelain cup with her littlest finger extended. A real lady, but peasant stock. Look at those hips, begging to bear children. No stranger to farm work either, he can tell. He'll call her boss at the factory in a couple of days: a good worker, her boss says. Good at taking orders, never lazy, almost never sick. At worst a little nearsighted—she should have seen that truck.

My mother is stunning and demure in black gabardine and pearls, low black heels. She has wide cheekbones and a kind, steady gaze. Her hair is piled high in a stiff bouffant, carefully arranged over her brow to conceal the scar. She sits at the edge of the checkered stone dance floor. My father extends his hand. She likes his suit: good quality, American-made. He wears a striped silk cravat, has a closed-lipped smile, a large nose, sharp eyes, a slick black widow's peak. When he speaks, his new gold tooth winks in the light.

They dance. But he jerks her around the dance floor to some other music—some rhythm in his head that beats faster and sharper than the music played onstage. He will ask why the lady is trying to lead—it's his job to lead—and my mother will blush, lower her gaze, apologize. She will say she didn't mean to lead. She will try harder to surrender to his rhythm—no rhythm at all.

The next day they meet for a walk, but my father won't enter the lobby of her dormitory, where other people wait. She doesn't know, of course, that he can't abide a crowd, can't abide people. She doesn't know about the camps, won't know until much later.

At dinner, he raises his hand and snaps his fingers to get the waiter's attention. Boy, he calls. Over here. My mother's temple begins to throb. She lifts her fingertips to the scar and rubs, but she ignores the signs. He's a rich American citizen who owns a house in California. There may be other reasons: physical attraction, some sense of destiny. Love at first sight, even. In French—*coup de foudre*.

I began reading my older sister's Harlequin romances in the sixth grade, when I no longer shared a room with my parents. I read them in bed late at night by flashlight, so my father would not see the overhead light glowing through the drapes on the glass-paned double doors separating his room, the dining room, from my room, the den. Every night I read until I heard my father's mattress springs and then his heavy footfall on the kitchen floor. I plunged my book and flashlight under the covers and pretended to sleep, while my father came to check that my windows were locked.

One night I was too slow to get the book under the covers in time. The book lay facedown inches from my hand. When my father passed the foot of my bed, he paused. The pages rustled as he examined the book in the light through the door. He snorted, then shut the door. He took the book with him.

The next evening, he called me over to his chair at the kitchen table and patted the seat beside him. "Sit down," he said. "I have something to tell you."

He told me never to marry for love. He told me to marry a hard worker, a good provider, someone like him. He told me how he'd decided on my mother. He brought his brother to the train station and told my mother to walk a few paces ahead of them. "Because," he said, "you wouldn't buy a horse without checking its legs first."

While my mother was in labor with my brother, my father planted a redwood sapling at the edge of the yard, so it would grow up alongside my brother. The next year he planted one for my sister, then one for my other sister, then one for me. But after I was born, he did not stop. He lined the perimeter of the yard in redwood saplings. Most of them he dug out of other people's gardens at night. Sometimes he took all of us on long drives north to the redwoods, shovels in the bed of the truck, wet cloths in a bucket for wrapping the roots. Everyone dug.

The day my brother came home from the hospital, my father put on his Sunday suit and fedora and carried him up and down the block, ringing doorbells. My son, he said, with a fat cigar in his mouth. When my brother began learning to walk, the bare wood floors bruised his knees, so my father went to the flea market in Sebastopol and bought Oriental carpets.

But also, imagine this: An eleven-year-old boy wants to buy his father a birthday present. His mother gives him a little of her secret money. He rides his bike to the drugstore and walks to the back, jingling his one dime and his mother's coins in his pocket. He runs one grubby finger along the edge of a dusty metal shelf. It holds the cheap little paperback joke books. One of these books might be perfect for his father, who does not smile often, who is, in fact, angry rather often. Maybe the father needs to hear more jokes.

He sees that the books are organized by country: *The Little Book of Irish Jokes, The Little Book of Italian Jokes, The Little Book of Polish Jokes.* Of course! Here is something that will make his father laugh and thank the boy and love him. His father will be proud of how smart and clever he is. The boy bends his head to count the coins in his palm. His father cuts his hair every month in the kitchen; he gives him a tidy little buzz cut with a cowlick in front.

The boy has enough to buy the book. He rides home and wraps the book in Sunday comics and gives it to his father. His father looks at it and puts it down on the table. He gets up and takes his belt from the peg inside the basement door and takes the boy into the garage and locks the door from the inside. The mother rattles the knob and yells that the boy is only eleven, he doesn't understand, he doesn't know any better. But she can't save him.

Nor can she save him a year later, when the father takes the boy to Poland, to see the place in which he worked, the place where work would set you free. He stands at the gates, beneath the iron sign, and with a pointed finger directs the boy's gaze. *Arbeit macht frei,* the father says. Repeat after me. *Arbeit macht frei.* The boy squints up into his father's face, which partially blocks the bright summer sun. The boy puts his hand to his forehead to shield his eyes, as if he were saluting.

Arbeit macht frei, the boy repeats.

The father strikes the side of the boy's head so hard he tumbles onto his knees in the dirt. A passing tourist gasps. *Czego tak ostro,* she says. Why so harsh?

In America, the boy begins sleeping in his yellow dirt-bike helmet, because you never knew when. Or why.

When we were children, my mother occasionally caught my father lost in thought at the kitchen table, extending his hand palm-down at the side of his chair, as if imagining the height of a child changing over the years. But he didn't have to imagine our heights. Beside the swinging door of the dining room, which was actually my parents' bedroom and mine until I was in the sixth grade, my father periodically marked our height in ballpoint pen. We stood as motionless as possible while he drew an unsteady line above our heads and noted the date beside it.

My father blamed his stunted height on being the runt of twins and malnourishment in the camps. Nightly he lined us up at the kitchen table and poured milk from the carton. We all drank out of the same glass, to save dishwater. The line started with the eldest, my brother, then my two sisters, and finally me.

My brother left for college when I was ten, and after my sisters left, my father told me to get the milk and pour a glass myself. I would spend those last six years at home alone with my parents, sleeping in the room next door to theirs, separated by French doors covered on both sides with wine-red drapes. It was a substantial improvement over sleeping in the trundle drawer between my parents' twin beds in the dining room. We had all always slept downstairs, so the upstairs rooms could be rented out to "young professional men," as our ad in the paper said.

In the room my sisters had vacated—formerly a den—my bed was actually a bed, not a drawer. It was pushed up against the French doors, and my father's bed was pushed up against the other side. Several of the panes of glass were broken; my father inserted a large sheet of cardboard behind the drapes so that I would not throw my hand up against the glass in my sleep and break a pane or cut myself. The cardboard did nothing to prevent the travel of sound. I could hear everything—my father calling my mother a cripple, my mother's alarm clock beeping at six every morning, my father snoring through the night and rattling the glass panes with his nightmare screams. Every sound was as loud as if we were sleeping in the same bed.

At work, my father made parts for machines that made missiles. When he miscalculated a setting on his lathe—even a sixteenth of an inch—the part could not be used. The faintest mis-shaving of metal destroyed the utility of the piece. My father brought those ruined parts home, and laid them beside his plate on the kitchen table.

When my mother saw my father's truck pull into the driveway, she ladled his soup into one bowl, sloshed it into a second bowl, and then sloshed it back into the first bowl, to help it cool.

While he ate, I removed his shoes and socks as he'd taught me. I carefully peeled the edge of each sock from his calves and rolled them down his leg to the heel. Then I hung the socks over the edge of the sink for my mother to wash after dinner.

My mother carried his loaded plate from stove to table, while my father ranted about the German who stood at the lathe next to his. I never learned the man's name; my father called him only *Niemiec,* "the German." The German tended to speak just as my father began shaping a hunk of metal. How are your kids? May I borrow your level? My father's ruined parts were always the German's fault.

Sometimes, when the soup was still too hot, my father swept the bowl off the table so that it shattered around my mother's feet. Sometimes he didn't. Sometimes he yelled: *Ty kaleka, ty krowo, ty bydlo.* Always my mother went from being a cripple to being a cow to being cattle. When she became a cow, I wondered, was she still crippled, or suddenly intact? And how could she be both cow and cattle, singular and plural?

When the bowls shattered on the floor, my mother would not let me pick up the shards. I might cut myself.

My mother taught me how to sew buttons onto shirts. She taught me how to change a pillowcase and to cut strawberries with a plastic knife so they wouldn't taste of metal. She taught me how to make glue by mixing flour and water. She tried to teach me how to knit. She taught me to put a burned finger to my earlobe instead of running cold water over it; earlobes don't have many nerves, she said. They'll absorb the pain.

I tried to stop my father's words at my ears but they would not stick. I knew they weren't meant for me, but I was half my mother, my father had said so himself. Like any good soldier, my father shot bullets through the air toward a target, but did not understand collateral damage.

I asked my mother why my father was the way he was. I wanted him to be an alcoholic, but he rarely drank. A little wine with holiday dinners, a Coors Light heated in a saucepan with a little sugar on a Saturday afternoon. My mother said he didn't have a father, so he didn't know how to be one. Also it could have been the camps. Or the electroshock therapy after the war. Or maybe he was born this way—something in his wiring, she said. But probably it was the camps.

And how to deal with him?

A little philosophy, my mother said.

While I was growing up, my mother read Rousseau's *Confessions*, Bertrand Russell, Thomas Merton. As a single woman in Poland, she'd loved reading adventure, mystery, romance. She read translations of *The Count of Monte Cristo, Dr. Zhivago, A Tale of Two Cities.*

My father read two newspapers a day but when he saw my mother sitting with a book, he walked around the house and looked for cobwebs clinging to corners of the ceiling. He pointed them out to her. She stood up and went for a rag to wrap around the broom, but under her breath, she said, "I hope a goose kicks you."

My father loved American folk songs. Every night before I went to bed, he said, "Good night, Kathleen," and I said, "No, Dad, it's 'Good night, *Irene.*'" Sometimes he asked me to get out my violin and play "This land is your land, this land is my land." He loved Woody Guthrie. He loved Lawrence Welk. He loved Charlie Chaplin. He loved the movie *How Green Was My Valley.*

He loved Joseph Conrad, Marie Curie, Copernicus. He loved Einstein, Goethe, Marlene Dietrich. He visited Schiller's birthplace. A civilized German, he said. Not like the rest of them.

When my father napped, my brother lifted his huge bunch of keys (sixty-four—we counted once) off the kitchen counter. The keys hardly clinked. He tiptoed past my father sleeping in the dining room–bedroom and unlocked the top drawer of my father's desk, where we all knew my father kept stacks of twenties. My brother put a finger to his lips when he saw me watching. I nodded.

Some nights my brother stole one of my father's old Buicks to drive to Jack in the Box and buy cheeseburgers for my sisters and me. He put the car in neutral; my sisters pushed it down the driveway and into the street. My brother cranked the steering wheel and coasted to the stop sign. There he turned the key in the ignition. My job was to stand at the kitchen sink and run the tap to cover the sound of the engine rumbling to life at the corner.

"Who's wasting water?" my father yelled from his bed.

Imagine: The family drives the young man to college. His dormitory is at the edge of town and campus, near the bovine research facility. Fields stretch west to a line of low coastal hills. It is late September, hot. The air smells of hay and manure.

The young man smiles and waves as the truck drives out of the parking lot. With his other hand, he wipes his eyes.

He walks the campus until dawn that first night. He breathes deeply; even the manure smells sweet.

Back home the father wanders up the stairs to the young man's abandoned room. It is empty except for furniture—a bed, a desk, a dresser. He opens the door to the closet. Inside: a stack of high school yearbooks and a yellow dirt-bike helmet. The father tries it on. It's tight, but it fits. From then on, he wears it while driving. Even in a dual-cab, dual-rear-wheel Chevy Silverado, you are not safe. Who knows when? Who knows why?

In his retirement, my father devoted entire days to concocting health potions. A favorite: skunk cabbage, garlic, lemon, and honey in giant sun tea jars. He drank a gobletful every morning. He told me, again and again, how I needed to do the same. How after the camps, in the American Zone, when he was sick for years, he'd cut himself shaving and the blood beaded on his chin or cheek so slowly—thick and dark, like jam, he said. But within months of eating a clove of garlic a day, his blood ran thin and red and fast, the way blood should run.

He feared men with guns, yet after Auschwitz, the only real danger lurked in his blood, with its propensity to clot. His own cells conspired against him, though if you asked them they'd say they were doing only what they were designed to do—to clump, to gather, find safety in numbers at the first sign of breach. But the problem was, there was no breach, no outlet from which the blood might spill. The cells had simply aggregated, and traveled through his arteries. And decided to settle in the brain, depriving it of oxygen, and that was why my father collapsed, why he devolved, step-by-step, in crossing the kitchen one morning in his thermal undershirt tucked into his Fruit of the Looms. His knuckles nearly brushed the linoleum, my mother noticed, when he stumbled at her feet.

After the brain surgery, my father remained in a coma for weeks. When he woke up, he could make sounds but not language. At first, we tried to make meaning of the guttural noises from deep in his throat. We lined up by his hospital bed. We bent our ears to his cracked lips and listened as if he were an oracle. All we heard were echoes of ourselves. My brother heard, "Do what you have to do." My mother heard, "You never learned a thing in your life." I listened hard, too, but nothing made sense to me.

On the night before my father's stroke, my mother dreams that two large black cows stand in their bedroom, grazing the carpet. She is a little girl again, in Zarebki, and it is her job to take the cows out to pasture and bring them home. If she loses one, she'll be beaten, of course, but it is so boring out there in the fields, always too hot, or too cold, and her shoes are full of holes. She wakes from the dream, looks at the center of the room—nothing. Then she gets up, takes a little tincture of valerian to calm her nerves, and goes back to bed. Her husband sleeps, but she won't, not with that kind of snoring.

My mother always slept lightly, because of her nerves. She used to wake in the middle of the night just from the sudden light cast by the refrigerator door opening in the kitchen, adjacent to their dining room–bedroom. She turned quietly and saw my father silhouetted by the fridge light, head tipped back and milk carton tipped high.

Then she knew why there was never enough milk for all the children at the end of the week. It was he who drank in the middle of the night and yelled at her on the night before shopping day if only a few drops fell in the youngest child's cup. She didn't know how to ration the milk, she must drink it all herself, that was why she was such a fat cow.

My mother still has not fallen back to sleep when my father gets up at six to go to the bathroom. She puts the kettle on the stove, and when he collapses at her feet, she is too afraid to call an ambulance—if he has to pay for it, he'll probably kill her. Instead, she calls one of her daughters, who calls an ambulance.

In fifteen minutes, two large men in black pants and black jackets hunch over my father. They shift him onto the stretcher, raise its collapsible legs, and wheel it out of the kitchen.

"Come with us, please," one of the paramedics says, and my mother thinks that she can't possibly go with them. Her shoes are full of holes. But when she looks down, she's wearing her new white Reeboks. She's not sure how they got on her feet. She takes her purse and follows the cows out to pasture.

Chanelle Benz

West of the Known

M Y BROTHER WAS THE first man to come for me. The first
man I saw in the raw, profuse with liquor, outside a brothel
in New Mexico Territory. He was the first I know to make a
promise then follow on through. There is nothing to forgive. For
in the high violence of joy, is there not often a desire to swear
devotion? But what then? When is it ever brung off to the letter?
When they come for our blood, we will not end, but go on in an
unworldly fever.

I come here to collect, my brother said from the porch. If there
was more I did not hear it for Uncle Bill and Aunt Josie stepped
out and closed the door. I was in the kitchen canning tomatoes,
standing over a row of mason jars, hands dripping a wat'ry red
when in stepped a man inside a long buckskin coat.

I'm your brother, Jackson, the man smiled, holding out his
hand. I did not know him. And he did not in particular look like
me. I'm Lavenia, I said, frantic to find an apron to wipe upon.

I know who you are, he said. I put my hands up.

Dudn't matter, he said, and the red water dripped down his
wrist, We're kin.

With the sun behind him, he stood in shadow. Like the white

rider of the Four Horsemen come to conquest, and I woulda cut my heart out for him then.

Jackson walked to the stove and handed me down an apron from a hook, saying, I reckon we got the same eye color. But your shape's your ma's.

I couldn't not go. Uncle Bill and Aunt Josie saw me fed but were never cherishing. I did not dread them as I did their son, Cy.

What comes in the dark?

Stars.

Cooler air.

Dogs' bark.

Cy.

Always I heard his step before the door and I knew when it was not the walking-by kind. I would not move from the moment my cousin came in, till the moment he went out, from when he took down my nightdress, till I returned to myself to find how poorly the cream bow at my neck had been tied. In the morning, when Cy was about to ride into town and I was feeding the chickens, we might joke and talk, or try. I had known Cy all my remembered life. We had that tapestry of family to draw upon.

That night Jackson came for me, I heard Cy's step. My carpet-bag, which I had yet to fill, fell from my hands. Hush said the air, like a hand in the dark comin for your mouth. Cy came in and went to my bedroom window, fists in his pockets, watching the ox in the field knock about with its bell. Drunk. Not certain how, since no one at dinner had any spirits but Jackson, who'd brought his own bottle and tucked in like it was his last meal.

You gonna go with him, huhn? Cy spoke through his teeth, a miner having once broken his jaw.

He is my brother, I said.

Half brother, Cy said, turning toward me.

He's older'n me so I guess I best listen, I said, suddenly dreadfully frightened that somehow they would not let me leave.

Jackson an me're the same age. Both born in 'fifty. You remember when he lived here? It was you and Jackson and your ma.

I don't remember Ma and I don't remember Jackson, I said.

It were a real to-do: your Pa joining up to be a Reb, leaving us his kids and squaw. She was a fine specimen tho. A swacking Indian gal. They lost you know. . . . Cy sat me down on the bed by my wrist. . . . The Rebs. His hands pinching the tops of my arms, he laid me back. You know what kind of man he is? I heard Cy ask. He was a damned horse thief. Old John Cochran only let your brother off the hook cause of my pa.

You done? Jackson leaned in the doorway, whittling a stick into a stake.

I jumped up. I'm sorry I'm just gittin started, I said, kneeling to pick up the carpetbag.

Get a wiggle on, girl, Jackson said, coming in.

Cy walked out, knocking Jackson's shoulder as he passed.

Jackson smiled, saying, His existence bothers me. Hey now, I don't wanna put a spoke in your wheel, but how in hell you think you are gonna load all that on one horse?

I'm sorry. Is it too much? I whispered and stopped.

Why are you whispering? he asked.

I don't want them to think we're in here doing sumthin bad, I said and lifted open the trunk at the bottom of my bed.

Look here, Jackson said, You're gonna come live with me and my best pal, Colt Wallace, in New Mexico Territory. And Sal Adams, if we can locate the bastard, so pack only your plunder.

Jackson made like he was gonna sit on the bed, but instead picked my bustle up off the quilt. I got no notion how you women wear these things, he said.

I don't need to bring it, I said.

You know, Lavenia, you weren't afraid of nothing. When I was here you was a game little kid. He spun the bustle up and caught it.

I disremember, I said.

He looked at me, the tip of his knife on his bottom lip, then went back to picking. When I'm with you, I won't let no one hurt you. You know that? he called back as he walked toward the kitchen.

. . . .

Jackson threw me up on the horse, saying, Stay here till I come back. An don't get down for nuthin. Promise me.

Yessir. I promise, I said, shooing a mosquito from my neck, I swear on my mother's grave.

Don't do that, he said.

Why? I asked.

Cause she weren't a Christian.

Wait.

What?

Nuthin.

The dark of the Texas plain was a solid thing, surrounding, collecting on my face like blue dust. The plain and I waited in the stretched still till we heard the first gunshot, yes, then a lopsided shouting fell out the back of the house. The chickens disbanded. A general caterwauling collapsed into one dragged weeping that leaked off into the dogs the stars and the cool.

The horse shifted under me. Please, I asked, What did you do?

Jackson tossed the bloody stake into the scrub and holstered his pistol. I killed that white-livered son of a bitch, he said, jerking my horse alongside his.

And the others? I asked.

You know they knew, don't ya? Aunt Josie and Uncle Bill. He let go and pulled up ahead, They knew about Cy. Now you know sumthin, too, he said.

Through the dark I followed him.

A few mornings after, we rode into a town consisting of a general store, two saloons, and a livery. We harnessed the horses round the back of one of the saloons. Jackson dug a key out from under a barrel and we took the side door. He went behind the empty bar and set down two scratched glasses.

You used to be more chipper, he said, Don't be sore. An eye for an eye is in the Bible.

There's a lot of things in the Bible. Thou shalt not kill, for one, I said, sitting up on a stool.

Waal, the Bible is a complicated creature, he said, smiling, You and I're living in Old Testament times. He poured me a double rye. I can't warn a trespasser not to rustle my sheep with no sugar tongue. I have to make it so he don't come back and you don't go bout that cordially, mindin your manners. I have to avenge harm done pon me. Yes, ma'am, what you witnessed t'other day was a vendetta cause I can tell you that I don't kill wantonly.

And I don't drink liquor, I said, pushing the glass back across the wood still wet from the night.

Truth is, he clinked my glass, I shouldn't have left you. When I run away I mean. It's jest bein you was a girl, and so little, a baby almost, I figured Bill an Josie'd take to you like you was their own, especially after your ma and our pa went and died. But those folks didn't do right. They didn't do right at all. We can agree on that much, can't we?

I don't know, I guess we can, I said and a rat run under my feet.

Those folks, they weren't expecting me to come back. Naw. But no one's gonna hurt you when I'm around—that there is a promise.

I picked up my glass. We'd run out of food on the trail the morning before and as we broke camp, Jackson'd made me a cigarette for breakfast.

But I didn't know what you were fixing to do, I said, runnin my tongue over the taste of ash in my mouth.

You didn't? Let me look about me for that Bible cause I'd like to see you swear on that.

Can you even read?

Enough. Cain't spell tho. He refilled my glass, Look, it ain't your fault this world is no place for women.

But us women are in it, I said.

Have another, he said. Don't dwell.

A bare-armed woman appeared in a ribboned shift, breasts henned up; she went into Jackson and said Spanish things. He smiled, givin her a squeeze, Go on then, he said to me, Go with Rosa, she'll take care a you. Imma go get a shave and a haircut. Should I get my mustache waxed and curled like an Italian?

I laughed despite myself. The whore held out her hand, Come with me, Labinya.

Upstairs, she poured water in a washstand. Some slipped over the side and spilled onto the floor; she smiled then helped me take off my clothes heavy with stain. Her nose had been broken and she was missing two top teeth on either side. I stood there while the whore washed me like a baby. I wondered if this was somethin she did to men, lingering on their leafless parts for money.

On the bed, divested, I could not care what next would befall me. There was no sheet only a blanket; I covered my head with the itch of it and cried. I cried cause as sure as hell was hot I was glad Cy was gone, cause I could not understand why when first Jackson took my hand I had known he was not good but bad, I knew that right then I was good but would be bad in the days to come, which were forever early and there as soon as you closed your eyes.

The whore was still in the room. But when I grew quiet, the door shut, and I could not hear her step, for the whore was not wearing shoes.

Since I was between hay and grass, my brother dressed me as a boy. It only needed a bandanna. I's tall for my age and all long lines so it was my lack of Adam's apple he had to hide if I was gonna work with him and not for the cathouse, since my face was comely enough tho never pleased him, it looking too much like my mother's (he said and I do not know).

In the back of the saloon, the bandanna Jackson was tying bit the hair at the nape of my neck. Lord, I think you grew an inch these last few months, Jackson said then turned my chin to him. Why're you making that face?

Cause it pulls, I said, playing with my scabbard. Jackson had gotten me a whole outfit: a six-shooter, belt and cartridges.

Waal, why didn't you say so? Needs to be shorter, he whipped the bandanna off, Hey Rosa, gimme them scissors again. Gal, what d'ya mean no no por favor? She said you got pretty hair, Lav. Rosa, why don't you make yourself useful and get us some coffee from the hotel—Arbuckle if they got it—and have that barkeep pour me another whiskey on your way out. Lavenia, I am gonna cut it all off if that is all right with you.

I shrugged as Colt Wallace of the white-blond hair who could speak Dutch and play the fiddle came into the saloon with Sal Adams who always wore a big black hat and had told me when he taught me three-card monte that his father in New York City had but half a stomach and lived on raw onions and sugar.

Hey boys, you feeling ready for a hog-killing time tomorrow? Sit down here, honey. See Rosa, Lavenia don't mind! Jackson shouted to the whore who was going out into the night and across the street in her tinsel and paint.

Jackson, said Colt, dragging a chair to our table away from the games of chance. What are you doing to the fair Lavenia Bell?

Keeping her from launching into a life of shame, an helping her into one of profit, Jackson said, and my black hair fell down around me. Sal, gimme her hat. Lavenia, stand up. Go on. There. She looks more like a boy now, don't she?

Sal smiled and said, Tomorrow Lavenia will be a woman of masculine will.

Colt gave an old-fashioned Comanche yell, then laughed, Sure cause she's flat as an ironin—

Jackson had both hands round Colt's throat. The table tipped and Sal stepped in the middle of them, steadying it. Fall back, Jackson, Sal said, Colt misspoke. Didn't you? You understand, Colt, how such words might offend?

Choking, Colt tried to nod.

Please don't, Jackson! I ain't hurt none by it. Truly, I said. Listen, I don't even want tits.

Why not? Jackson turned to look at me.

I don't know—guess they'd get in the way of shootin?

Jackson laughed and let him loose.

Sure Sal, coughed Colt. I mean, yessir, I—I didn't mean nothing by it, Jackie. I meant to say yeah they'll think Lav's a boy long as they don't look her too long in the eyes.

What the hell you mean by that now? Jackson asked, rounding on Colt again.

He means she's got long eyelashes, Sal said, taking our drinks from one of the whores.

Shucks Jackie, ain't we friends? Here, Colt toasted, To good whiskey and bad women!

It was a day's ride. Sal stayed to guard the town square and watch for any vigilant citizens with guns, while Colt and I went with Jackson into the bank, the heft of worry in my bowels. There was only one customer inside, a round man in spectacles, who Colt thrust into and said, Hands up, with his loud flush of a laugh, as Jackson and I slid over the counter, six-shooters out, shouting for the two bank tellers to get down on their knees.

Open up that vault, said Jackson.

We can't do that, sir, the older teller said. Only the bank manager has the key. And he's not here today.

Get the goddamn money. Damn, this whole town knows you got a key.

Sir, I would if I could but—

You think I got time for this? Jackson hammered the older teller in the face with his pistol, and the man thrashed over, cupping his nose. He straddled him as he lay on the ground, saying, Now you open that vault right quick.

The older teller blinked up at him through bloody hands, I won't do that for ya. . . . I refuse to be . . .

Jackson thumped the older teller's head with the butt of his right pistol and that older teller began to leak brain. There was a sting in my nose as I watched him drip into the carpet. Until then, I had no notion that blood was child-book red. Jackson turned to the younger teller, who looked frantic at me.

Son, you wanna live? Jackson asked.

I willed him to nod.

Gesturing to me, Jackson said, Give this boy here all the bonds, paper currency and coin in these bags.

Hurry it up back there! hollered Colt, forcing the customer to his knees and peeking out the front door, Sumthin's up! Sal's bringin the horses!

Me and the younger teller, Jackson's pistol cocked on him, stuffed the burlap sacks as Jackson climbed backward through the bank window. That's enough. Now get on your knees, he said.

As I tossed Jackson the first sack, the young teller rose up and grabbed me from behind, snatching my gun, waving it at us, shouting, You yellow-bellied bushwhackers, attacking an unarmed man! You a whore herder—this girl is a girl!

Jackson shot the young teller in the chest, dove through the window and got back my gun. He slapped it into my stomach, Shoot him, he said.

Who? No, I pushed the gun away.

Hey! Colt shouted, What in hell is going on? They're gonna have heard them shots!

I looked to the young teller rearing in his blood. Please Jackson, don't make me do that, I said.

Put him out of his misery, honey. He's gonna die either way.

I raised the gun then just as quick lowered it. I cain't, I said.

You're with us, ain't ya? Jackson was standing behind me, the warm of his hand went on the meat of my back, After all Lavenia, you just done told that boy my name.

Colt's gun sounded twice from the front.

And so I shot the young teller dead through the eye and out of that bank we rode into the bright forever.

Alone, jest us two, in what I had by then guessed was her actual room, tho it had none of the marks of the individual, the whore put the whiskey between my fingers.

Èl no debería haber hecho esto, she said, locking the door and loosening my bandanna.

Leave it, I stared in her mirror. Make me drunk, I said. I want the bitter of that oh-be-joyful.

Drink. She put the glass to my lips, then took it back and topped it off, asking, How old you?

Fifteen. Sixteen in June, I said. The whiskey tore a line down my stomach to let the hot in. Wait. If you can speak English, then why don't you?

She shrugged, handing me back a full glass, Is more easy for men to think the other.

And I ain't a man, I said.

She nodded. Why you brother dress you like one?

So when we ride no man messes with me and I don't mess with my bustle. Is it hard bein a—a soiled dove? I drank, It's awful hard on one bein a gunslinger.

She smiled with her missing teeth, took off my coat and shirt then sat down inside the bell of her ruffled skirt, My husband die when I you age. I make good money this place.

Money . . . I repeated, and took the whiskey off her bureau where it sat next to a jeweled dagger and a small bottle of Best Turkey Laudanum. I got money now I guess, I said and laid a few dollars down, If you don't mind, I said and droppered laudanum into my whiskey, I hope this will stupefy me. I drank it and flopped back on the bed.

Where you mama?

Died. When I was three. My pa's sister raised me. Aunt Josie. You papa?

I shook my head, Dead from the war.

Solo Jackson, she said.

Hey Rosa, what if somethin bad happened that I did?

The door handle turned, then came a knocking and my brother: Hey Rosa, lemme in there. I gotta see her. Lavenia?

I scrambled up.

Rosa put her finger to her lips, Lavenia no here.

She's gotta be—hey, Lavenia, Lavenia! C'mon now. Come out and jest let me talk to ya for a minute, honey.

I swallowed more whiskey'd laudanum. Hey Rosa, I whispered, holding out my free hand.

No now, Jackie, Rosa said, taking it.

If you did a bad thing but you didn't mean to? Cause he was gonna die anyways either way. I pulled till her head went under my chin. But he was alive and then he wasn't and I did that, I said, I did.

Jackson no good.

No, no good, I said.

You have money? You take and go away. Far.

But I'm no good, I said.

Open this damn door! Jackson pounded, Listen gal, your pussy ain't worth so much to me that I won't beat your face off.

Hush up! I shouted, Shut your mouth! The shaking door stilled. I don't want you, I said.

Lavenia, I heard him slide down the door, Hey gal, don't be like this.

I leaned my forearm and head onto the wood. Why? I asked.

Baby girl, he said, don't be sore. Not at me. I cain't.

Why did you make me? I asked.

Darlin, those men done seen our faces. What we did we had to do in order to save our own skins. That there was self-defense. Necessity, sure, it's a hard lesson, I ain't gonna falsify that to you.

But I'm wicked now, I said, feelin a wave of warm roll me over. I slid.

Hey, I heard him get to his feet, Hey you lemme in there.

Rosa put her hand over mine where it rested on the lock. The augury of her eyes was not lost on me. As soon as I opened the door, Jackson fell through, then tore after her.

Jackson don't, I yanked him by the elbow as he took her by the neck. You—she didn't do nothing but what I told her to!

He shook me off but let her go. Go on, get out, he slammed the door and galloped me onto the bed, tackling me from behind and squeezing until I tear'd. I did not drift up and away but instead stayed there in what felt to be the only room for miles and miles around. He spoke into my hair, saying, We're in this together.

Jackson, I sniffed and kicked his shin with the back of my heel, Too tight.

He exhaled and went loose, The fellas are missing you down there.

No, they ain't.

They're sayin they cain't celebrate without the belle of the Bells.

I rolled to face him, pushing the stubble of his chin into my forehead, Why do you want to make me you?

Would you rather be a daughter of sin?

I *am* a daughter of sin.

You know what I mean. A—a . . . Jackson searched his mind, A frail sister.

I could not help but laugh. He whooped, ducking my punches till he wrestled me off the bed and I got a bloody nose. You hurt? he asked, leaning over the edge.

Lord, I don't know, I shrugged in a heap on the floor, sweet asleep but awake. I cain't feel a thing. Like it's afternoon in me, I said.

Jackson glanced over at the laudanum bottle and backhanded me sharp and distant, Don't you ever do such a thing again, you hear?

My nose trickled doubly but I said, It doesn't hurt. I tried to peel Jackson's hands off his face, Hey it truly truly doesn't!

I laughed and he laughed and we went down to the saloon drinking spirits till we vomited our bellies and heads empty.

The next night two deputies walked into the saloon and shot out the lights. In the exchange of dark and flash, a set of hands yanked me down. I'd been drinking while Jackson was with Rosa upstairs. I got out my six-shooter but did not know how to pick a shadow. A man hissed near my head and I crawled with him to the side door.

Out of the fog of the saloon, Colt stood, catching his breath, saying, There ain't nothing we can do for Jackson and Sal. If they take them to the hoosegow, we'll break them out. C'mon.

I cain't, I said, getting up.

A couple bystanders that had been gawking in the saloon were now looking to us.

Lavenia, Colt took me tight by the shoulder, and swayed us like two drunkards into the opposite direction. In the candlelight of passing houses, Colt's hand, cut by glass, bled down my arm.

At the end of the alley, Colt turned us to where three horses were on a hitch-rack. We crouched, untying the reins, and tho my horse gave a snort, it did not object to the thievery, but we were not able to ride out of town unmolested. There, our ingenuity had been anticipated and the sheriff and his deputy threw us lead. Buckshot found my shoulder, and found Colt too, who slid like spit down his horse and fell onto his back, dead.

Hey there Deputy, said Jackson through the bars, How much for a clean sheet of paper and that pen?

The men outside the jail began shouting louder. The silver-haired sheriff sat at his desk, writing up a report, ignoring us all.

This un? the deputy stopped his pacing.

I'll give you twenty whole dollars, Jackson said, I'll be real surprised if I make it to trial, so least you could do is honor my last request.

There were a few scattered thumps on the door. Won't we make it to trial? I asked.

Well darlin, there's a mob out there that's real loco'd about me shooting that bank teller and that marshal and that faro dealer and that one fella—what was he? A professor of the occult sciences! Yes that's sure what he looked like to me!

I laughed. The men kicked at the door. The sheriff checked his Winchester.

Jackson chuckled, I'm writin against the clock. The windows smashed as if by a flock of birds. Jackson didn't look up from writing.

Now sheriff, you won't let them hurt my baby girl will ya? You gotta preach to them like you was at the gospel mill before Judgment Day. Gotta tell them that this young girl here was jest following me, was under a powerful family sway. Here, Deputy, would you kindly give this to her.

The deputy took the letter.

The sheriff said, Son, there are about forty men out there with the name of your gang boiling in their blood. By law the two of us must protect you and that child. I jest hope we don't die in the attempt.

Mi DReaM-

> *dremP'T i, wAS, with YoU, Lav,*
> *Near Your BrEATh, so DEar:*
> *id, neVEr, saw, none, so BeAuTiFull,*
> *And I, wisht You Were NEar:*
> *No Angel, on eaRrTH, or, HeAven,*
> *CoUlD rivall Your HeaRT,*
> *no DeaTH, or distancE, can uS PArt*
> *if, Any, should TelL You,*
> *They Love You eTerNAly,*
> *There, Is, no onE, You tell Em,*
> *Who Loves You like Me*

Fare! Well! My Dear SisTer..anD FrIEnd
Al.So. My Belle oF The Bells

> *Yours Hopefully*
> *Jackson Bell*

The forty exited the street and entered our cells.

They dragged Jackson and I into the dogs the stars the cool and the night. Their hands in what hair I had; my hands underbrush-burned and bound together in baling wire.

In an abandoned stable somewheres behind the jail, they made Jackson stand on a crate and put the noose hanging from the rafters round his neck. They were holding down the deputy and the sheriff, who looked eyeless cause of the blood, having been beaten over the head.

I was brought to Jackson and saw the rope round his neck weren't even clean.

Hey gal, my brother said, Guess what? This is my final request. Now honey, what do you think? *Don't* you think I kept my promise? You'll be all right. If you cain't find Sal, Rosa will take care a you.

I nodded and the men pulled me back.

Hey you ain't cryin, are ya? Jackson called out, swallowing against the rope, C'mon, quick—you got any last little thing to say to me?

The men brought me to a crate and tied a noose around my neck. What the hell's goin on? Jackson asked.

You all cannot murder a woman without a fair trial, the sheriff started up.

No now fellas, it ain't s'posed to go like this. Listen to the sheriff here—Jackson said and the men walloped him in the belly.

Lavenia Bell, the men asked, crowding me, What is your final request?

Sometimes I wish I were just a regular girl, not a whore or an outlaw or playactin at man. I had a father for two years and a mother for four, but I cannot remember what that was like, if they care for you better or hurt you less or if they keep you no matter what it costs them.

The girl first, the men said.

I am not afraid. You kept your promise good. Thank you for you, I said.

Have you no wives, no sisters or daughters? shouted the sheriff.

I felt the thick of hands on my waist.

Wait! Don't y'all see? She woulda never done nothin without me not without me—

The noose tightened.

The sheriff was struggling to get to his feet, hollering. Boys this will weigh heavy on your souls!

Hey I'm begging you to listen, boys—look, it weren't her that killed them tellers it was me—only me!

Up on the crate, it was that hour before sun, when there was no indication of how close I was to a new morning. I waited for the waiting to break, for the dark of the plain in my face to bring me to dust.

William Trevor

The Women

GROWING UP IN THE listless 1980s, Cecilia Normanton knew her father well, her mother not at all. Mr. Normanton was handsome and tall, with steely gray hair brushed carefully every day so that it was as he wished it to be. His shirts and suits gave the impression of being part of him, as his house on Buckingham Street did, and the family business that bore his name. Only Mr. Normanton's profound melancholy was entirely his own. It was said by people who knew him well that melancholy had not always been his governing possession, that once upon a time he had been carefree and a little wild, that the loss of his wife—not to the cruelty of an early death but to her preference for another man—had left him wounded in a way that was irreparable.

Remembered by those who had known it, the marriage was said to have echoed with laughter, there'd been parties and the pleasure of spending money, the Normantons had appeared to delight in one another. Yet less than two years after the marriage began it was over; and in the Buckingham Street house Cecilia heard nothing that was different. "Your mother wasn't here any-more," her father said, and Cecilia didn't know if this was his way of telling her that her mother had died and she didn't feel she could ask. She lived with the uncertainty, but increasingly believed there had been a death from which her father had never recovered and which he could not speak of. In a pocket-sized yellow folder at the back of a drawer there were photographs of a smiling girl, petite and beautiful, on a seashore and in a garden, and waving from a train. Cecilia's father, smiling, too, was sometimes there, and Cecilia imagined their happiness, their escapades, their pleasure in being together. She pitied her father as he was now, his memories darkened by his loss.

Dark-haired and tall for her age, her slim legs elegant in schoolgirl black, Cecilia was taken to be older than she was. Eighteen or nineteen was the guess of the youths and men who could not resist a second glance at her prettiness on the street: she was fourteen. She didn't know why she was looked at on the street, for an awareness of being pretty was not yet part of her. It wasn't something that was mentioned by her father or by Mr. Grace, the retired schoolmaster whom her father had engaged as her tutor in preference to sending her to one of the nearby schools. It wasn't mentioned by the Maltraverses, who daily came to the house also, to cook and clean.

Among these adult people Cecilia was lonely, and friendless, too, on Buckingham Street. At weekends her father did his best, making an effort to be interesting on their strolls about the deserted City streets—the Strand and Ludgate Hill, Cheapside and Poultry, Threadneedle, Cornhill. He pointed out the Bank of England, the Stock Exchange; he said that London's City was a village in its way. Sometimes, as a change, he booked two rooms at a small hotel in Suffolk, usually at Hintlesham or Orford.

Cecilia enjoyed these weekend excursions, but the weekdays continued to pass slowly, for Mr. Grace came only in the mornings and the Maltraverses were not given to conversation. In the afternoons, when she had completed the work she'd been set, she had the spacious rooms of the house to herself and poked about in drawers, watched television, or opened the yellow folder to look again at the photographs of her mother. When she had money she went out to buy licorice allsorts or Kit Kat.

She was fortunate, she knew. No one was unkind to her, no one was angry. She imagined nothing would change, that Mr. Grace would always come, the Maltraverses would always be too busy for conversation, that always there'd be the silent afternoon house, the drawers, and being alone. But her father, sensitive to the pressure of duty where his child was concerned, did not demur when he was advised that the time had come to send her away to boarding school, to be a girl among other girls.

"You shall have a flower bed," Miss Watson said.

Smart as a mannequin, she was delicately attractive in different ways. Her voice was, her slimness, the gentleness in her eyes. A softly woven scarf—a galaxy of reds and rust against the gray of her dress—was loosely draped and almost reached the ground.

"We are happy people here," she assured Cecilia. "You shall be, too."

Amhurst the school was called, and Miss Watson, who was its headmistress, explained how the name had come about, told how the school had been the seat of a landed family, how outbuildings had been transformed into music rooms and laboratories, art rooms and the weaving room, only the classroom blocks being a new addition. She took Cecilia to a small brick-walled garden, which was, and always had been, the headmistress's. She opened an ornamental iron gate in an archway, then latched it again as if shutting away everything of the school itself. She pointed at a flower bed with nothing growing in it and said it would be Cecilia's own, where she could cultivate the flowers she liked best. Old Trigol was the school gardener, she said, a dear person when you got to know him.

Cecilia disliked the place intensely, felt lonelier and more on her own than she ever had on Buckingham Street. She wrote to her father, begging him to come and take her away. She was the only new girl that term, and no one bothered with her except a senior girl whom Miss Watson had ordered to. "You pray?" this older girl asked her, and suggested that they might pray together. "Every meal's inedible," Mr. Normanton read. "A girl was sick after pilchards."

But as time went on Cecilia's letters became less wretched. She discovered Mozart, Le Douanier Rousseau, and—recommended by the religious girl—St. Teresa of Lisieux. She found *The Moon and Sixpence* and *The Constant Nymph* among the well-used books in the school library. Two girls, Daisy and Amanda, became her friends. The religious girl reported to Miss Watson that settling in had begun.

Mr. Normanton came often during that first term. He took Cecilia out on weekend jaunts—lunch at the Castletower Hotel, tea in the tearooms on the river. He met Daisy and Amanda, and before the term ended took them out, too. He was glad he had listened to the advice he'd been given, had realized what he hadn't on his own: that his child would benefit and be happy as a girl among other girls.

Cecilia grew lilies of the valley in her flower bed, having decided it was her favorite flower. She picked the first bunch on her fifteenth birthday and offered it to Miss Watson.

"You are a person we take pride in, Cecilia," Miss Watson said.

The two women who were watching the hockey were on the other touchline, directly opposite where Cecilia, with Daisy and Amanda, was watching it, too, since attendance at home matches was compulsory. Cecilia remembered the women being on the touchline before, because when the hockey ended they'd passed close to where she and Daisy and Amanda were looking for Amanda's watch, which had slipped from her wrist without her noticing. "Someone'll stand on it!" Amanda was wailing, and the two women had hesitated as if about to look for the watch, too. Daisy found it, undamaged, on the grass, and the women went on. But when they hesitated they'd stared at Cecilia in a way that was quite disconcerting.

There was sudden cheering and clapping: Amhurst had scored. St. Hilda's—in their unbecoming brown jerseys a glum contrast to Amhurst's jolly red-and-blue—looked defeated already and probably would be, for Amhurst never lost. It would have been Elizabeth Statham who'd scored, Cecilia imagined, and hoped it wasn't or it would mean a lot of showing off later on. But Amanda said it was. "Bloody Statham," Daisy muttered.

They wanted St. Hilda's to win. Favoring the other side eased their indignation at having to stand in the cold for an hour and a half on a winter afternoon. They hated watching hockey almost more than anything.

"I tried to read 'Virginibus Puerisque,'" Amanda said. "Ghastly."

Daisy agreed, and recommended *Why Didn't They Ask Evans?*

Cecilia wondered who the women were who'd come back again only a few weeks after she'd seen them before. They wouldn't be Old Girls because Old Girls always hung around Miss Watson or Miss Smith and they weren't doing that. They wouldn't be supporters of St. Hilda's because the visiting team hadn't been St. Hilda's the other time. She wondered if for some reason they enjoyed watching hockey matches, the way Colonel Forbes enjoyed watching cricket on Saturday after Saturday, in the summer term. Or like Trigol, who was allowed to take the afternoon off from the garden for Sports Day because he'd once been a high-jump champion, which wasn't easy to imagine, Trigol being in his seventies now.

When the two women stared at Cecilia the smaller one had smiled. Cecilia had smiled back, since it would have been rude not to, but Daisy and Amanda hadn't seen that any more than they'd seen the staring, and afterward Cecilia hadn't said anything because it was embarrassing, and silly to go on about.

Miss Chalmers blew the final whistle and there were three

cheers for St. Hilda's and then for Amhurst, followed by clapping when the two teams walked off the pitch. The people who'd been watching followed, groups breaking up and new ones forming as they made their way back to the school buildings. The two women became lost in the crowd and Cecilia was aware of feeling relieved. But they were there again, by the cattle grid, where cars were parked on match days. The St. Hilda's bus was there, too, the driver folding away the newspaper he'd been reading. The two women didn't get into a car and drive off, as Cecilia thought they would. They stood about as if they had a reason to, and Cecilia avoided looking in their direction.

They had taken the path through the trees and, emerging from what had become a small wood, they marveled at the open land, as that morning they had marveled at sunshine in February, misty though it was. Nothing as tiresome as rain had spoiled their walk from the railway station or their returning to it now.

"I would have traveled a million miles for this afternoon," Miss Keble summed up their outing as they approached the first of the bungalows on the town's outskirts.

Miss Cotell—less given to exaggeration than her friend—said nothing, but in her reticence there was no denial that the afternoon had been a pleasure. How could it not have been, she thought, their presence for the second time unquestioned, and the feeling as well that they had been right to return? How could all that not have been a treat?

Miss Keble, sensing these thoughts, kept the subject going, marveling that so little achieved should seem so much a triumph, yet understanding that it should be. She would not easily forget the faces of the girls, their voices, too, and how politely they stood back, respecting strangers. All of it was impossible to forget.

Miss Cotell again was silent but still no less impressed and then, quite suddenly, affected in a different way, an urge to weep restrained. On the homeward train her tears, permitted now, were not of sorrowing or distress but came because her friend understood so much so well, because agreement between them, never faltering, had been today more than it had ever been before.

Guessing all this, Miss Keble watched Miss Cotell recovering her composure. For some minutes they both gazed out at the landscape and the image of a prehistoric animal cut into the limestone of a distant hill.

"I'm sorry," Miss Cotell apologized. "Stupid."

"Of course it wasn't."

Miss Keble went in search of tea, but there wasn't any to be found. Miss Cotell fell asleep.

The two—of an age, at fifty-five—had retired early from a government department. They had met there thirty-odd years ago, and their friendship had flourished on the mores of office life ever since, Miss Keble remaining in Benefits (Family), Miss Cotell making a brief foray into Pensions and then returning to Benefits. They had been together since, as close in retirement as they were before it.

The landscape Miss Cotell was unaware of, while she dreamed instantly forgotten dreams, faded into winter dusk. Miss Keble failed to interest herself in a newspaper someone had left behind and instead thought about the house they were returning to, and the rooms in which their two lives had become entangled over the years, for which furniture, piece by piece, had been chosen together, where childhood memories had been exchanged. Miss Keble, as she sometimes did when she was away from the house for longer than usual, saw as if in a vision the reminders it held of foreign places where there'd been holidays: the Costa del Sol; the beach at Rimini; Vernon, where they'd stayed when they visited Monet's garden; and the unidentified setting where an obliging stranger had operated Miss Cotell's Kodak, allowing them to pose together. The house, the rooms, these images of themselves in places visited meant everything to Miss Keble, as equally they did to Miss Cotell.

The house, in a terrace, was small, without a garden. At the back, the feature of a concrete yard was a row of potted plants arranged against a cream-distempered wall. Curtains of fine net protected the two downstairs front windows from the glances of passing pedestrians; at night, flowery chintz was drawn across; upstairs there were blinds. Everything—and in the yard, too— had been made as Miss Cotell and Miss Keble wanted it, an understanding that became another element in their relationship. Nothing had been undertaken, no changes made, without agreement.

This house, in darkness, became theirs again when the train journey ended. It was cold and they switched on electric fires. They discussed what food should be cooked, or not cooked, if tonight they should open a tin of salmon or manage on sandwiches and tea. Both settled for a poached egg on toast.

"It was good of you, Keble," Miss Cotell said when, snug in their heated kitchen, they sat down to eat. "I have to thank you."

Their calling one another by surname only was a habit left behind by office life, for although they did not regret their early retirement office life clung on. They had wondered about other clerkly work, but it wasn't easy—and was in the end impossible—to find anything suitable, especially since they stipulated that they should not be separated.

"Both times I wanted to come with you," Miss Keble said. "And I will again."

Tidily, Miss Cotell drew her knife and fork together on her empty plate. "I wonder, though," she said, "if I have the heart for going there again."

"Oh, what a thing, Cotell! Of course you have!"

"What more can come of it?" And whispering as if she spoke privately, although there was no privacy between them, Miss Cotell softly repeated, "What more?"

Miss Keble knew and did not say. Warm and pleasant, the euphoria brought about by the day still possessed her. She wished

Miss Cotell no ill will, wished her all the peace in the world, but still could not help welcoming in a way that was natural to her the exhilaration she experienced. She did not press or urge: they were neither of them like that. Resisting the flicker of satisfaction that threatened to disturb her features, she gathered up the cups and saucers.

Miss Cotell folded the tablecloth and put away the salt and pepper. "How difficult," she murmured, "to know what's right."

"Of course," Miss Keble said.

It wasn't until the following term that Cecilia again saw the two women. Summer had come, the long, light evenings, the smell of grass just cut, the flower beds of Miss Watson's brick-walled garden bright with *Crocosmia* and sweet pea, with echium and *Geranium sanguineum*. When she was younger, Cecilia had preferred the coziness of winter, but no longer did. She loved the sunshine and its warmth, her too-pale skin lightly browned, freckles on her arms.

She saw the women when she was returning from taking the afternoon letters to the postbox, a fourth-form duty that routinely came once a fortnight. She had called into Ridley's when the letters were posted—honeycomb chocolate for Daisy, Mademoiselle's bonbons. The women were on the path through the trees, coming toward her.

They must live nearby, Cecilia thought. Probably they went for walks and had found their way to the hockey pitch. But hockey was over now until September.

Sunlight came through the trees in shafts, new beech leaves making dappled shadows on the women's clothes. How drab those clothes were! Cecilia thought. How ugly the taller woman's features were, the hollow cheeks, her crooked teeth, one with a corner gone. Her friend was dumpy.

They had stopped, and Cecilia felt she should also, although she didn't want to.

"What weather at last!" the dumpy woman said.

They asked her her name and said that was a lovely name when she told them. Violets were held out to her to smell. They said where they'd picked them. A dell they called the place, near the fingerpost. They could have picked an armful.

"We hoped we'd see you," the taller woman said. "For you, my dear."

Again the violets were held out, this time for Cecilia to take.

"We're not meant to pick the flowers."

Both smiled at once. "You didn't pick them, you might explain. A gift."

"Look this way, Cecilia," the dumpy woman begged.

She had a camera, but the distant chiming of the afternoon roll-call bell had already begun and Cecilia said she had to go.

"Just quickly, dear." They both spoke at once, saying they mustn't keep her, and when she hurried away Cecilia heard the voices continuing, a monotone kept low, hardly changing from one voice to the other. She could tell she was being watched, that the women were standing there instead of going on.

"Who are they?" Elizabeth Statham was in her games clothes, returning from the run she went on every afternoon. "Friends of yours?" she asked.

"I don't know them at all."

"Funny, they'd take a photograph."

Cecilia didn't attempt to reply. Frightened of Elizabeth Statham, she was at her worst with her, never knowing what to say.

"Funny, they'd want to give you flowers."

Cecilia tried to shrug, but her effort felt clumsy, and Elizabeth Statham sniggered.

"Poor relations, are they?"

"I don't know them."

She couldn't hear the women anymore and imagined they must have gone. She didn't look back. Elizabeth Statham would go on about it because she had a way of doing that, sitting on your bed after lights-out, pretending to be nice.

"Funny, they'd know your name," she said now, before she continued on her run.

"Come now," Miss Keble said that same evening, when they were home again and it was late.

Miss Cotell, not at first responding, said when the pause had become drawn out, "A dullness settles on me when I try to think. 'I'll think it through,' I tell myself, and then I can't. That dullness comes, as if I've summoned it."

"It's called being in two minds," Miss Keble said.

"I feel I have no mind at all."

"Oh, now!" Miss Keble smiled and firmly shook her head.

"How good you are to me, Keble." Miss Cotell thanked her before she went upstairs.

Miss Keble did not deny it.

Miss Cotell undressed and for a moment before she reached for her nightdress stood still, her nakedness reflected in a looking glass. How old she seemed, the flesh of her neck all loops and furrows, her arms gone scrawny! The hair that Broughton had called her crowning glory was grayer and thinner than it should be. She blamed herself, but blaming didn't help. "How could I!" she had protested, laughing almost, when Broughton had asked if she would show herself to him. "Please," he begged. "Oh, please." He wouldn't now. He'd held her to him, the buttons of his jacket cold. Shy as a bird she'd heard him called, but oh, he wasn't. With her he could not be, he'd said.

Slowly Miss Cotell drew on her nightdress, then felt the sheets, the pillow, cold. He'd warmed her, and tonight she had known he would again. The caressing of his murmur did, and his touch was more than she could bear, his hands so soft, as if all his life he had done no physical work. The blue of his eyes was a paler blue than she'd ever seen in eyes before, his hair like down, wheat-colored, lovely. He whispered now as he had then and she did, too, in the dark, since always they wanted that. She dried his tears of shame.

She loved his body's warmth. He'd chosen her. She'd wanted no one else.

Miss Keble, who had not experienced this aspect of life, was aware without resentment that she lived at second hand. Her friend had done things: their reminiscences, so often exchanged, allowed no doubt about that. Yet Miss Cotell, while seeming to lead the way, did not. Miss Keble, through listening and knowing what should be done, had years ago taken charge. "How little I would be, alone!" Miss Cotell had a way of saying, and Miss Keble loved to hear it. Accepting her lesser role, she knew that it was she, in the end, who ordered their lives and wielded power.

She turned the pages of an old book she had never thrown away and knew almost by heart, *Dr. Bradley Remembers*. But her thoughts did not connect with the people it again presented to her. What innocence there was in the girl's eyes! She closed her own and saw the unspoiled features still a child's, the dark, dark hair, the blue-and-red blazer, the pleated gray skirt. Vividly, recollection refreshed for Miss Keble all that the day had offered, and the joy that should have been her friend's became her own.

Miss Cotell dreamed. When she answered the doorbell Father Humphrey was standing there, his back to her at first. "All done," he said, his voice stern, his handshake firm. "Thank you," he said, not opening the envelope she gave him.

Because Cecilia was to be Thisbe, Mr. Normanton was given a seat in the front row. His daughter's ambition, he knew, was one day to be an actress, a secret shared only with him. There had been such intimacies since Cecilia had gone away to Amhurst, as if each separation and each pleasurable reunion had influenced a closeness that had not been evident or felt before. He understood Cecilia's reluctance to reveal to her friends the presumption of a talent, to keep from them her English teacher's prediction that she would in time play Ophelia, and one day Lady Macbeth. It delighted Mr. Normanton that all this had come about, that his solitary child had been drawn out in ways he had not been able to find himself, that in spite of his awkwardness as a father she had turned to him with her confidences.

Miss Watson took her place beside him, whispering something he couldn't hear. The house lights dimmed, all chatter ceased.

Afterward, Miss Cotell and Miss Keble talked about the evening, tickets for which Miss Keble had discovered could be purchased by the public when the requirements of friends and parents had been satisfied. They'd been at the back and more than a little cramped but hadn't minded. They had noticed the honoring of Mr. Normanton, placed next to the headmistress, and when someone asked Miss Keble who he was she was able to say he was the father of the girl who had been enthusiastically applauded as Thisbe.

It was almost midnight now, and in their bed-and-breakfast lodgings their beds were close enough to allow conversation that would not disturb if their voices were kept low. Tonight had felt like the height of what they could hope for, Miss Cotell reflected, the end at last of what had been a beginning, when, alone, she had visited what Father Humphrey called the priest house on a cold April afternoon a long time ago. "He'll come to you when he's ready," a slatternly woman with a bucket and mop curtly informed her, and didn't answer when Miss Cotell remarked on the weather. "Well, now?" Father Humphrey greeted her, when he came, a big, tall man who asked her how she had heard of him, and she explained that another girl in Pensions had mentioned him.

Awake, Miss Keble also was drawn back to the memory of that afternoon, to the slovenly woman, to the priests who'd passed silently through the room where Miss Cotell waited. Both had thought it likely that tonight they would talk again about that time, but found they didn't. A lorry clattered by on the street outside, somewhere a dog ceased to bark.

Miss Cotell and Miss Keble slept then. Period costumes colored their unconscious, and the rhythms of period music were faintly there again; and Mr. Normanton's dark-blue suit was, his polka-dotted tie, the hat he carried with his coat.

"I cannot leave," Miss Cotell confessed at breakfast. "I cannot without saying how all of it was wonderful. I cannot, Keble."

They bought two gifts, Miss Cotell's brooch a circle of colored stones set in silvered plate, Miss Keble's a selection of chocolates she was assured were special. They had become familiar with the bells of the school, the one that ended classes, the lunchtime summons, the roll-call bell at half past four, the hurry-up one five minutes later. They knew a clearing in the woods and brought the sandwiches they'd made there. They could see the path, but no one appeared on it all day.

It had to be said, Miss Keble, impatient, told herself while they waited. It had to be, and Cotell was not the one to say it, for it was not her way. Cotell did not ever press herself, never had, never would. Too easily she went timid. But even so, and more than ever, Miss Keble could see in her friend's eyes the longing that had so often been there since they'd first begun to come here. She could sense it today, in gestures and intimations, in tears blinked back.

At twenty past four they walked to the school.

Cecilia caught a single glimpse of the two women and looked away and didn't look again. Whoever was on afternoon duty would surely ask them what they wanted, why they were here in Founder's Quad, where visitors never were without a reason. She heard a prefect asking who they were, and someone saying she didn't know. It was a relief at least that Elizabeth Statham was excused this roll call because every afternoon now she had to train for Sports Day.

"We wanted just to say how much we enjoyed last night," the taller of the women said, and the dumpy one added that wild horses wouldn't have stopped them from coming back to say it.

"These are for you," the tall one said.

They held out packages in different-colored wrapping paper, and Cecilia remembered the flowers they'd pressed on her, which she'd had to throw away. It was Miss Smith on duty, but she appeared to be unconcerned by the women's presence, even acknowledging it with a hospitable nod in their direction as if she remembered them from last night. They murmured to one another, their voices low when the roll was called and while Miss Smith read out two brief announcements.

"Cecilia, if you visited us, you would like our house," the dumpy woman said then. "We're not that far away." She said that the packages, which Cecilia had not accepted, were gifts, that the address of their house was included with them, the phone number, too.

No one was near enough to hear, and the curiosity about the two women had dissipated. Already girls were moving away.

"They are for you," the tall woman repeated.

Cecilia took the packages, then changed her mind and put them on a nearby bench. "I don't know you. It's kind of you to give me presents, but I don't know why you want to."

"Cecilia," the dumpy woman said, "you'll have heard of Father Humphrey?"

"I think you're mistaking me for someone else."

The tall woman shook her head. She had looked startled when the name was mentioned, had held a hand out as if protesting that it shouldn't be, anxiety in her eyes.

"Father Humphrey died," she nonetheless went on. "Miss Cotell heard. And when she went back to the priest house she asked me to be with her for support. The same cleaning woman was there and I said that any papers left behind might concern Miss Cotell. The woman had her objections, but she let us peruse the papers for five minutes only and, truth to tell, five minutes were enough. Father Humphrey was a man who wrote everything down."

Cecilia wondered if the women were unbalanced, if they had

found a way of wandering from a home for the deranged. For a moment she felt sorry for them, but then the smaller one began to talk about their house, about a cat called Raggles, and flowers in pots, and after a hesitation the tall one joined in. They didn't sound then as Cecilia imagined the mad would sound, and the moment of pity passed. The cat had strayed into their backyard as a kitten. Their house was called Sans Souci. If she came she could spend a night, they said. They spoke as if they were suggesting she should come often and described the bedroom she would have, which they had wallpapered themselves.

"How much we'd like it if you came!" Through the anxiety that had not gone away, the tall woman smiled as she spoke, her chipped tooth, crooked and discolored, sticking out more than the others.

"My dear, Miss Cotell is your mother," Miss Keble said.

Cecilia went away, leaving the two packages on the bench, but she had gone only a few yards when she heard the women's voices, raised and angry as she never had heard them before. She looked back once and only for a moment.

They were not as she had left them. They confronted one another, trying to keep their voices down but not succeeding. "I gave my sworn word," the woman who had been called her mother was bitterly exclaiming.

The voices clashed in accusation and denial, contempt and scorn; and there was the sobbing then of the woman who felt herself deprived. She had wanted only to be near her child, all she deserved. "No more than that." Cecilia heard the words choked out. "And in your awful jealousy how well you have destroyed the little I might have had."

Cecilia hurried then. "We cannot come back," she heard, but only just. "Not once again. Not ever now."

There was a protest furiously snapped out, and nothing after that was comprehensible. Cecilia kept trying again to think of the women as unbalanced, and then she tried not to think of them at all. Afterward she told no one what had been said, not even Daisy and Amanda, who naturally would have been interested.

That summer Mr. Normanton took his daughter to the Île de Porquerolles. In previous summers he had taken her to Cap Ferrat, to Venice and Bologna, to Switzerland, making time on each journey for a stay in Paris. It was on these excursions that Cecilia first came to know her father better. More of his life was revealed, more of a past that he'd thought would not interest her. His childhood added a dimension to his lonely father's role; his young man's world did, too. Every time Cecilia returned from school to Buckingham Street she was aware that melancholy disturbed him less than it had. On their holidays together it was hardly there at all.

At Porquerolles, while every bay of the island's coast, every creek, every place to swim was visited, Cecilia felt her company relished; and her father's quiet presence was a pleasure, which it had not always been. Silences, a straining after words to keep a conversation going, uncertainty and doubt too often once had become the edgy feeling that nothing was quite right.

It was hot in August, but a breeze made walking comfortable and they walked a lot. They talked a lot, too, Cecilia especially— about her friends at school, the books she had read during the term that had just ended, the subtle bullying of Elizabeth Statham. She hadn't meant to say anything about the women who'd been a nuisance and when something slipped out she regretted it at once.

"They wanted money?" her father asked, stopping for a moment on their walk along the cliffs to look for a way down to the rocky shore below, and going on when there was none.

"No, not at all," Cecilia said. "They were just peculiar women."

"Sometimes people who approach you like that want money."

He was dressed as he never was in London, casually, without

a jacket, in white summer trousers, a colored scarf at his throat which she had given him, his shirt collar open. Cecilia, who particularly noticed clothes, liked all this much better than the formality of his suits. She said so now. The women were not mentioned again.

But that evening when his whiskey had been brought to him on the terrace of the hotel he said, "Tell me more about your women."

Cecilia bit into an olive, cross with herself again. He was curious, and of course bewildered, because she'd left out so much— the women being there at the hockey matches and then appearing on the way through the woods, and how she'd thought they might suffer from a mental affliction. Now she described their clothes and the way they had of speaking at the same time, each often saying something different, how they related in detail the features of their house and spoke of their cat. Her father listened, nodding and smiling occasionally. She didn't tell him everything.

Shreds of the day's warmth were gaudy in the evening sky as the terrace slowly filled and new conversations began. A dog obediently lay down beneath a chair and was no trouble even when the couple with him finished their drinks and went off to the restaurant without him. A Frenchman, relating an experience he had recently had, brought it to an end and was rewarded with quiet laughter. Cecilia, puzzled by *jeu blanc,* overheard several times, missed the point.

"I played a lot of tennis once," her father remarked when they were being led to their table in the restaurant. "I doubt I ever told you that."

"Were you good?"

"No, not at all. But I liked playing tennis. *Jeu blanc*'s a love game."

On their last morning, walking to the harbor, as every day they had during their stay, Cecilia talked about becoming an actress and heard more than she had before about her father's work and his office colleagues, about the house on Buckingham Street when first he knew it, about his being married there. Passing the farm that was the beginning of the village, he said, "The marriage fell to pieces. When we tried to put it together again we couldn't. I let you believe as you did because it was the easier thing and sometimes, even, I pretended to myself that it was true. I was ashamed of being rejected."

Bougainvillea hung over garden walls. Across the street from the crowded fruit stall the café they liked best hadn't come to life yet, their usual table not taken, as often it was. Their coffee was brought before they ordered it.

"I thought that perhaps you guessed," her father said. "About the marriage."

Old men played dominoes in a corner, the waiters stood about. A woman and a child came hurrying in. The girl who worked the coffee machine pointed at a door.

"During all your life as I have known it," Cecilia's father said, "you have made up for what went wrong in mine."

On the quays they watched the slow approach of the ferry. There was a stirring in the crowd waiting to embark, luggage gathered up, haversacks swung into place. A ragged line formed when two ticket collectors arrived. The newcomers who came off the ferry trundled their suitcases to where the gray minibus from the hotel was parked.

"We should call in at the Tourist Information," Cecilia's father said, but when they did they found they didn't have to because the times of the early-morning boats to the mainland—on one of which they hoped to be tomorrow—were listed in the window.

They bought a baguette and thinly sliced ham in the village, and peaches and a newspaper. They had another cup of coffee in the café.

"I'm sorry," her father said. "For hating the truth so much, and for so long."

On the walk back to the hotel Cecilia didn't say what she

might have said, or ask what she might have asked. She didn't want to know.

They rested in the shade, beneath dry dusty trees. People on bicycles cycled by and smiled at them and waved. Faintly in the distance they could hear the rattle of the minibus returning to the harbor.

"Shall we go on?" her father suggested, his hands held out to her.

She drew the curtains in her room, darkening the lit-up brightness of the afternoon. She thought she might weep when she lay down, and spread a towel over her pillow in case she did. Fragments made a whole: the photographs that were lies, the marriage that fell apart. No child was born, they'd hoped one would be. As best they could they had made up for that, but what had been was over. Suitcases instead were in the hall, coats and dresses trailing from hangers piled together. A taxi drove away. He watched it go, alone but for a child who, by chance belonging nowhere, now belonged to him.

Maids came to turn the bed down. Cecilia said to leave it and thanked them for the chocolate they had put out for her on her bedside table. She called out, apologizing when her father knocked softly on the door. She had a headache, she would not come down tonight. He didn't fuss. He never did. His footsteps went away.

The night didn't hurry when it came. She did not want it to. Tomorrow he would finish what he had begun: she had no thoughts except that now. "I have to tell you this as well," gently he would say, and ask to be forgiven when he did. She didn't blame him for what he had withheld. She understood; he had explained. But still he would complete what wasn't yet complete because he felt he should.

They were early at Toulon for their train to Paris and took it in turns to walk about the streets so that their luggage wouldn't be left unattended. Morosely, Cecilia gazed into the shop windows, hardly seeing their contents. Again the women hovered, as in reality they had. Their voices did, their clothes, the clergyman they talked about, their house, their cat. Her father's silence would not hold; he did not want it to. He would tell her on the train.

Or even now, Cecilia thought when they waited together on the platform. In a strange place, among hurrying people, there'd be a moment that seemed right and he would choose his words. He would say again her presence in his house made up for his unhappiness there, and tell her what she had to know.

But when next her father spoke it was to praise the train they were waiting for. "The best trains in the world," he said. "And we can have a croque for lunch."

They had it standing at the counter of the bar and their talk was about the island and how they would always want to return to the little bays, the clear deep water, their daily explorations, the café they had liked. Cecilia's panic receded a little and then a little more; her father's politeness was measured and firm, as if he'd been aware of her brooding and understood it. He drew the conversation out and kept it going. She could read in his face that he had changed his mind.

Afterward, in an almost empty carriage, where their seats faced one another, they were on their own, and quiet. Her father read *Bleak House,* a book he liked to go back to, and she didn't feel neglected by his absorption in it as on other journeys. His occasional smile of pleasure, his delicate fingers turning the pages, his summer clothes uncreased in spite of travel reflected the ease with himself that had been slow in becoming what it was. He had borne his bitterness well. Somewhere, today and every day, the wife he had not ceased to love enjoyed the contentment he had been unable to give her. With cruel fortitude he might have allowed himself to dwell on her life without him, but he preferred an emptiness, and made of it something better than the truth. Cecilia knew it; and emulating his skill in living with distress, abandoned stern reality for what imagination more kindly offered. Might it not be that the women in their lonely lives nurtured a fantasy that dressed things up a bit, befriending girls without a mother in order themselves to be befriended? Had they, together, discovered the excitement of a shadowland and kept it alive in the bluster of daring and pretense?

Shakily challenging the apparent, the almost certain, this flimsy exercise in supposition was tenuous and vague. But Cecilia knew it would not go away and reached out for its whisper of consoling doubt.

Colleen Morrissey

Good Faith

WE CAME ACROSS THEIR broken-down auto while we were on our way from Sikeston, Missouri, to Dexter—a glossy red Stanley Steam with a white cloud streaming from its front. In 1919, I was twenty years old, born just before the century turned, and this June traveling across the Midwest would be the first time I saw a twenty-dollar bill, and the second time I got bit by a rattler.

My sister, Jessica, and I leaned out the window of our family's wagon, trying to see why we had stopped. Papa got down off the front to talk to the two men who were standing by the auto. Their faces were half-hidden by caps, but next to erect, squinting Papa, their bodies seemed loose and relaxed. The one nearest, talking to Papa, was smiling.

"They look rich," Jessica said to me.

I looked over my shoulder, down the line of wagons behind us, and they also had multitudes of heads protruding from them— all except the reptile wagon, which had no windows. I pulled my head back inside and swung open the door.

"Where are you going?" Jessica said, at the same time as Mother, who had been fanning herself in the shadows, lounging deeply on the green love seat. "Rachel!" she said. "Don't be fool-ish. Let Papa take care of this."

I stopped at the threshold, the dusty summer air dry on my face. Daniel, who was sleeping with his head on Mother's lap, moaned at the breeze. "Close it," Mother said. "You're disturbing Daniel."

I closed the door and rejoined Jessica. A few men of the Church were standing around the auto with Papa and Mr. Forrester, the master handler. They were talking to one of the well-dressed men, who gestured and smiled with an easiness that seemed to verge on impertinence. Papa walked past our window without a word, then returned with a tank of water. He hauled it over to the auto, and the other well-dressed man, unsmiling, helped him lift it to the crown of the auto's grille. Papa's legs splayed under the load, and so did the man's. His trousers pressed tightly against his legs. This man would give me my first and only twenty-dollar bill, and his name was Samuel Pattinson, but all I knew of him in that hot afternoon was the cut of his trousers and the square of a wallet in his back pocket. I could not yet see his face.

The smiling, unoccupied man who was not Samuel Pattin-son broke from the Church men and began sauntering down the line of wagons. As he neared, Jessica pulled her head inside and tugged on my elbow, but I stayed where I was, watching him. He purposely scuffed his burnished leather shoes against the dirt as he came, and finally lifted his head so I could see him. His face was pointed and handsome, his hair a deep brown beneath his cap. He gave an openmouthed smile and tugged at the brim of his hat when he saw me.

"Miss," he said. He seemed to be chewing on something, tobacco or gum. I watched his eyes moving over the side of the wagon, reading what was painted there. " 'Free Church of the Savior,' yep, I've heard of you. Who're you free from?" He had a Yankee accent, like everyone in those parts—dry and clipped and nasal. I was brought up in Mississippi, in our own meek, secluded town along the Pearl River, going to the piney church house for school and town gatherings and everything, only leaving to sleep or to go on our summer tours.

"False religion," I replied, "which calls itself Christian." Jessica pinched the skin near my elbow, but I wrenched my arm away from her.

"Who you talking to?" Mother asked from within the wagon.

"You one of the folks that charms snakes?" the man asked.

"I said *who* you talking to?" Mother said, upsetting Daniel as she stood up and charged over to the window. Jessica dodged away as Mother leaned out and saw the well-dressed man. "Who are you?" she asked imperiously.

He touched his cap again. "Christopher Brown, ma'am. Your man up there is helping my friend cool down his engine. My friend Samuel Pattinson." He said his friend's name as if it should mean something to us. He waited for us to react, but when we did not, he said, "I wanted to know if your girl here can charm snakes."

"Many of us, by the grace of the Lord, handle serpents and do not fear the bite," Mother said.

"Yeah," he laughed, "but does she?" He nodded in my direction.

"Our worship is not entertainment, Mr. Brown," Mother said, and I slid back into the shadows of the wagon, knowing already how the conversation would proceed. I went to sit on the love seat, where Daniel was rubbing his eyes and pouting. I let him lay his blond head on my lap, and I watched Mother's dress shimmy with the vehemence of her words as she said out the window, "If you desire the cleansing touch of the Lord, and approach our worship with a pure and contrite heart, then you may see us handle serpents in Dexter, like everybody else." She angrily shut the window.

"Oh, Mother, it's *hot* in here," Jessica complained, but Mother ignored her. She roughly moved Daniel's legs so that she could sit down on the love seat, then put his legs in her lap, stroking them like she would a dog. Soon, we were moving again. The love seat was too low for me to see anything out the window but the sky.

When we arrived in Dexter at five that evening, I found out that Mr. Pattinson and Mr. Brown had followed us. The two of them were talking to some of the Church men again, Mr. Brown smiling away. I got a good look, for the first time, at Mr. Pattinson. He was bigger than Mr. Brown, both in height and weight, with a solid middle that had just a little fat to it, but he looked strong and youthful. Beneath his cap, he had freckles and wiry eyeglasses, which were strange in combination. He could've been a man in his forties or just a big teenager. As I helped Daniel down the back steps of our wagon, Papa came walking up. He didn't look at Mother, but he made a dissatisfied, suspicious noise to her, staring in the direction of the two strangers.

The other handlers were unloading the reptile wagon, bringing out box after box of snakes, their containers decorated with beads and glass and renderings of the Lord Jesus. I knew I should help, but I stayed near our wagon and watched the strangers. Papa said a few words to them, then waited while Mr. Pattinson said something in return. Then Papa pulled his straw hat deeply over his forehead and walked away. Mr. Brown was still smiling. He clapped Mr. Pattinson's back, and I heard him say to the other Church men, "We'll see you all at the show!"

"Our worship is not a show, Mr. Brown," said Mr. Malcolm.

I turned away and went to the reptile wagon. The handlers were carefully moving the boxes to the bed of our black Ford truck, the only auto the Church had in its possession. I could hear the snakes hissing as Mr. Forrester, who was standing in the wagon, gently passed the boxes down into waiting hands. When the wagon was nearly empty, Mr. Forrester passed me a crimson box, one I'd painted myself, carefully covering up the COCA-COLA and then spelling out my favorite passage in black: TO THIS END WAS I BORN, AND FOR THIS CAUSE CAME I

INTO THE WORLD, THAT I SHOULD BEAR WITNESS UNTO THE TRUTH. EVERYONE THAT IS OF THE TRUTH HEARETH MY VOICE. Inside, sliding around, was a six-foot-long diamondback rattler, my rattler.

"They sluggish 'cause they so hot," Mr. Forrester said. "Best set up the tent and get them cool right quick."

There was already a crowd. Our services had become quite popular during our summer travels, and we didn't have to go into the towns and shout out in the squares to attract people—they already knew we were coming. Mother looked more and more heartened at each new crowd, saying things like, "Well, maybe the Lord's voice is still heard after all," but I knew what they really wanted to see. No one had been bitten so far in this tour— none of the faiths of the handlers so far had been anything but exceptional, no one had yet wavered—but I knew the looks in the eyes of all the strangers who watched us twine the snakes around our bodies. They did not come to see our faith. They came to see if tonight would be the night when one of us got bit.

This audience watched us with anticipation, some of the younger children in a tight cluster about ten feet from the truck that held the snakes. Once every few minutes, the bundle nudged a single child toward the truck, but each lost his nerve immediately and pushed back into the group. People were admiring the Stanley Steam, running their hands over the smooth red hood and talking to Mr. Pattinson as if they knew something about cars. Mr. Pattinson and Mr. Brown, meanwhile, leaned against it, their feet up on the running board. Mr. Brown had a cigarette that put firelight on his cheeks, and Mr. Pattinson leaned over so that he could light his own, balanced in his lips, on Mr. Brown's match.

By sundown, we lit the torches and invited everyone inside the big tent. There was a lot of excited talking as they fanned themselves and glanced eagerly around, but that all stopped when Papa mounted the platform. I sat to one side with the other women, listening to Papa, and looked over the crowd. Mr. Pattinson and Mr. Brown were in the front row. Mr. Brown was smiling with insolent constancy, but Mr. Pattinson was listening intently to Papa. His face did not have the rapt, frightened look that most people wore when they heard Papa's truth. Rather, he looked as though he were a foreigner with a broken understanding of our language and customs, and he wanted to have things explained.

When Papa finished, there was applause, thunderous from the other Church members and scattered from the crowd. "Let me tell you now, people," Papa said, "that the great Lord does not leave his would-be servants without assurance, without *great* assurance, without signs." This was the cue for the handler of the night, and tonight·it was me. I stood up and moved to the center of the stage, and Papa moved to the side. Mr. Forrester picked up the crimson box sitting at his feet, the box that the crowd had been eyeing all night, and approached me. "This is my daughter Rachel," Papa said, putting his hand on my shoulder hard and squeezing. "She has put her *faith*"—he drew a breath—"in the Lord. And *because* she has such *rock-hard* faith, she fears *no* evil, *no* pain."

Mr. Forrester lifted the top of the box at its hinge and presented it to me like a piece of jewelry. The crowd leaned forward. Directly in front of me were Mr. Brown and Mr. Pattinson. Mr. Brown had the salivating look I was familiar with, but Mr. Pattinson was watching me with an expression like worry. He leaned forward and half raised his hand as if to stop me. For some reason, his expression and gesture filled me with fear, and I looked away from him and into the box. There was my rattler, coiled, making a bull's-eye pattern in black and white with his diamond-speckled hide. I could not pick up the snake in fear—it showed a lack of faith in the Lord, and lack of faith got you bitten. I heard people creaking in their seats as they waited for me. I prayed hard. *Holy Spirit, Holy Spirit, descend on me.* Finally, I felt the last bit of the strange fear wash away and reached into the box. Ignoring the gasp of the crowd, I lifted my rattler and draped him over my neck, wrapping his tail around my waist. Careful of his head, I wound his front end around my right arm and then held up my hands.

I had been handling snakes for five years, and sometimes it was just an expression of faith where the rattler stayed the rattler and I stayed me, but sometimes the Holy Spirit would come upon me. I never knew when. It would swoop down and take me without warning. That night, as my rattler filled my palm with his snout, his tongue darting between my fingers, I began to smile as I felt the Holy Spirit coming. Some of the handlers would flail and loll, even as their snakes coiled around them, but I didn't like that. I kept completely still as the Holy Spirit settled upon me like snow, filling my eyes with whiteness, making everyone and everything around me disappear, bringing down sweet silence. My snake had become a rope of fire that it didn't hurt me to touch, and then the fire melted into me so that I was empty-handed and unafraid. Then I began to melt away too. The Holy Spirit was blotting me out, taking me in. But then it withdrew, and I began returning to the platform in the tent, piece by piece. I once again felt the weight of my rattler on my shoulders, became aware of his sour smell. I found that I was on my knees in front of the crowd.

"By their fruits ye shall know them!" Papa shouted as the crowd erupted into applause. Mr. Forrester bent over the edge of the stage to give the collection plate to the woman at the end of the first row. My rattler slowly tightened himself around my waist and arm. I got to my feet and looked down at Mr. Pattinson. He was applauding, his colliding hands making his shoulders shake as he frowned.

When the worship was over, after we had taken down the tent and put away the snakes safe and sound in their wagon, I gathered with Mother, Jessica, and Daniel to go to sleep. Our wagon was very small, and Jessica and I shared a bunk built along the top of the wall. Mother unrolled a mat and slept on the floor while Daniel slept on the love seat. We were surprised on this night by

Papa knocking on the door. He usually slept out in the open. It made him feel closer to God. But it soon became clear that he hadn't come to sleep.

"The two strangers, Pattinson and Brown, will follow us when we leave tomorrow." He looked right at Mother, spoke to no one but her, and stayed in the open doorway.

"*Why?*" Mother asked.

"They are curious about our ways. I won't turn away men who want to love the Lord." He turned his head and spat on the ground behind him. "Answer their questions." He looked at Jessica and me. "But guard yourselves against them."

"You think they will be respectful?" Jessica whispered to me once we were in our bunk.

"One might," I murmured back.

They did follow us, from town to town, in that red shellacked car. They ate with us, and they helped us put up the tent and take it down again. If we were near a town, they spent their nights in the local hotel or inn, and if we were on the road, they slept in the Stanley Steam. A few people—like the uppity Mrs. Malcolm— were angry with Papa for a while, complaining about the cost of feeding two full-grown men three times a day, and after a few hours of silence, Papa finally told them that the men were paying for their keep and anybody who questioned his judgment again could just stay at the next town we came to.

I don't know how everyone got over the initial distrust so fast. After a day or two, they all liked Mr. Pattinson, though his excessive questions sometimes annoyed them. They generally disregarded Brown. Right away, I knew that Mr. Brown's sole purpose in coming along was to mock us, and on the second night, I whispered to Jessica in our bunk, "How can Papa let something like money make him keep unbelievers around to make fun of us?" She shushed me and breathed, "Mama's not asleep yet."

I couldn't make up my mind about Mr. Pattinson. Mr. Brown kept smiling, as if he thought it was a grand joke, but Mr. Pattinson was intensely interested in us. I watched him during the first supper he ate. He was seated down the table from me, leaning over a chicken bone, asking Mr. Forrester question after question. I was just waiting for them to lose their interest and head back home, wherever they came from. The days passed by, though, and they stayed.

Out of the forty-some members of the Church, only about ten were between the ages of fifteen and twenty-five. Besides Jessica and me, there were four other girls. Even the sillier ones knew better than to go out of their way to talk to Brown and Pattinson, but they talked about them behind their mothers' backs. The strange men had a multitude of clothes—the girls counted four separate outfits—jackets, waistcoats with watch chains hanging out of the pockets, and these queer short trousers that buttoned below the knee, which they wore with tall, light socks. Once, Mr. Brown, cigarette in hand, came over to us as we were washing clothes in the half-dozen wooden washtubs we carried with us, and he asked us if we had a light. But Mr. Pattinson appeared right quick and took him away by the elbow, asking us to excuse them. The other girls softly exclaimed about his nerve while grinning at each other, but then I said, "Just think of how many poor folks could eat if he sold his suit," and they stopped.

I didn't avoid Mr. Pattinson and Mr. Brown, but I didn't go out of my way to see them, either. After a week, they both knew my name and had spoken to me a few times. Once, as I was alone in the wagon, braiding my hair before breakfast, Mr. Pattinson knocked on the door, looking for Papa.

"My father is hardly ever in here," I told him. I stood in the doorway looking down at him.

"I see," he said. "If you see him, will you tell him I'm looking for him?"

"I will."

He smiled at me. The sunlight hit his eyeglasses, turning the lenses white. His smile created two bowing lines on either cheek, perpendicular to his mouth. "Thank you. Rachel?"

"Yes."

"Thank you, Rachel."

I closed the door.

It was not until we approached the Ozarks that I had an extended conversation with Mr. Pattinson. We had stopped at high noon for dinner, and I was sitting on a fallen tree just out of sight of the road but not out of hearing. My rattler's crimson box was open on my knee, and I was watching him swallow a squirrel.

"Is it almost your turn again?" Mr. Pattinson asked, coming from the direction of the road. "To perform?"

"It's not a performance," I said. "It's worship."

"Ah, that's right. I'm sorry," he said, looking at the box. "Not like any worship I've ever seen. I'm from Chicago, originally, and—"

"Why are you following us, Mr. Pattinson?" I said. "No one's been able to tell me."

"Frankly," he said, his hands in his pockets, "you all fascinate me. I figure I'll leave when all my questions are answered."

"How do you afford it?" I asked. He smiled, and I continued, "It's easier for a camel to pass through the eye of a needle than for a rich man to enter the Kingdom of Heaven."

"What makes you think I'm rich?"

"The way your friend said your name when I first saw him. Are you a man of faith?"

"I'm Catholic," he said.

I shook my head. "Oh, Mr. Pattinson, I am sorry to hear that. I am sorry that you are enslaved to an evil, false prophet. Won't you worship God instead of your pope, Mr. Pattinson?"

He laughed. "Your people are very Protestant, aren't they?"

"We do not align with any of the false religions that call themselves Christianity. They are Pharisees, pretenders."

"You believe only your father's interpretation of the Bible is correct? That the entire rest of the Christian world has it wrong?"

"They do have it wrong," I said.

He looked at me like I was a child caught in a lie, then said, "May I sit next to you?"

"If you're not afraid," I said. He smiled, and I added, "Of the snake."

"He's a diamondback?" Mr. Pattinson sat on the tree at a respectful distance.

"Yes. A six-footer. My father caught him on the day I turned fifteen." I had a fierce pride of my rattler, one of my everlasting failings. "Most handlers only keep their snakes for a season, but I've had mine for five years now. He has a special beauty, a special grace."

Mr. Pattinson cocked his head and peered into the box. "It's not tame by now?"

I drew myself up a little. "They never tame."

"And the reason you can handle him is because of your unwavering faith?"

"Yes."

"Have you *ever* been bitten?"

I laughed at his audacity, wrapped in such an innocent tone, almost like a child's. "I'm not going to talk about that."

"Why?"

"I'm not going to dwell on the past."

"Are you ashamed of having been bitten?"

All at once, I was conscious of the fact that I was alone with Mr. Pattinson, without Mother or Jessica or even the other girls to draw strength from. "We all go through our period of temptation, a period of questioning," I said. "That time for me has come and gone." I raised the sleeve of my dress, exposing my wrist and the two round scars just beneath the back of my hand. Mr. Pattinson leaned over my wrist and lifted it with his own hands, studying it. His fingertips had new calluses on them from the tent ropes.

"When *will* your turn come again to worship?" he asked, dropping my wrist.

"Not for a few weeks now," I said, shutting the lid of the box. "We have many faithful."

"Would Jesus approve of this little twosome?" said Mr. Brown. He had come up silently and was leaning against a tree, smoking. I stood up with my rattler, embarrassed and irritated, and began to walk back toward the wagons.

"Don't be a swine, Chris," said Mr. Pattinson from behind me.

"Pshaw, Sam," Mr. Brown said with a grin.

"I mean it."

"I can see you do," said Mr. Brown. The way he said it made him sound like the devil himself. "Pardon me," he said as I passed.

I stopped and said, "Remove far from me vanity and lies." Mr. Brown spewed smoke out his nostrils and mouth in laughter. I began walking quickly away again, my face tingling.

"You're going to stop that, Chris," I heard Mr. Pattinson say. "These people are sensitive about their women. Their women are sensitive."

My rattler hissed agitatedly at the way I was jostling him, so I slowed down.

The next morning, I was in the wagon, alone again, before breakfast. I was sitting on the love seat, buttoning my shoes. I hadn't yet braided my hair, and it was loose over my back. Someone knocked. I pushed my hair out of my face and opened the door. Mr. Pattinson was looking up at me.

"I told you my father is not often here," I said.

He pushed his cap back, squinting in the light, and said, "Yes, I know. I was coming for you. To apologize for my friend."

I looked out across the road, to where they were putting up the tables. "Why are you friends with him?" I asked.

"We went to college together," he said. I shook my head. "I guess that doesn't mean much to you," he continued.

"I've never been to college," I said.

"We were in the war, too," he said.

"Never been to war either."

He pulled his cap back and forth over his head, as if scratching with it. Then he said, "Is there anyone you're friends with only because they've been through a very important, or a very difficult, experience with you?"

I thought for a moment. We must have made a queer picture, me standing above him with my hands on my hips, the ends of my hair twitching in the wind, and him below, looking up through his eyeglasses.

"I guess the whole Church is like that to me," I said.

He looked as though I'd said words he'd never heard before. "I guess you understand, then."

"I guess I do," I said.

"Have you eaten yet?" he asked.

"No."

He stepped to the side and paused. "Are you coming?"

"I have to braid my hair," I said, bringing up a hand to finger it self-consciously.

"Oh, all right." He nodded at me with a small smile. "Good morning." He went away.

I closed the door and stood for a moment, still fingering my hair. Then I smoothed down my dress, frowning at the small brown burn mark from when I had my back too close to the supper fire one night. I stood near the window as I braided my hair, watching the breakfast preparations, people gathering around the fire and setting out plates. I couldn't see Mr. Pattinson, but Mr. Brown was there, in suspenders and a shirt with no jacket or waistcoat. There was a bump in his breast pocket from his pack of cigarettes. He seemed to be rubbing his face down with water from a cup in his hand. I refocused my eyes so that I didn't see him anymore, but saw my faint reflection—my dishwater hair, my flat moon face and hook nose. There was movement in the window, Mr. Pattinson approaching Mr. Brown and putting a hand on his shoulder. Mr. Brown grinned and lifted his chin up

206 / COLLEEN MORRISSEY

to the sky. I licked my lips, which were dried out with the hot air, and put my hair into its braid.

Everyone had grown accustomed to Mr. Pattinson and Mr. Brown by the time they had been with us for two weeks. When we were near a town, Mr. Brown would sometimes disappear for several hours, but Mr. Pattinson always stayed close. He began talking with my mother about the details of the Church, since Papa was always too occupied with other things to have conversations. She liked him, and began saying to me or to Jessica, after they'd finished talking and parted, "I believe he is truly growing to love the Lord." I felt uneasy whenever she said that.

Daniel became very fond of Mr. Pattinson and took to clumsily explaining Bible passages to him, and Mr. Pattinson played along as if he knew nothing about any of it. Once, when Mother and I returned to the wagon from gathering the dried laundry, Mr. Pattinson and Daniel were sitting on the love seat inside.

"Daniel has made me a list of rules," Mr. Pattinson said.

In his hands Daniel had a torn piece of newspaper he must have picked up somewhere, and over the print he had written with a pencil, "Rules for Mr Patinsin."

"Read them, Daniel," Mother said.

Daniel haltingly began: "'One, be good. Two, do not blaspheme. Three, don't lie. Four, don't be a Catholic. Five, don't be a fornicator.'" As he stumbled over *fornicator,* I felt my face grow warm. Mr. Pattinson looked at Mother with surprise and said, "He's six and he knows *fornicator?*"

"We don't hide the evils of the world from him," Mother said. "He must know them to denounce them."

Mr. Pattinson looked down at Daniel. "Do you know what that word means? *Fornicator?*"

I covered my cheeks with my hands as Daniel said, "It, ah, it means don't, ah, don't do bad things and—and Mr. Brown is a fornicator." Mr. Pattinson leaned back in the love seat and rubbed his face with his hand, but he was smiling. I felt like I would cry.

"Daniel, we'll talk about what it means later, but you did a good job," Mother said. Daniel continued to murmur about sinning, trying to stumble on the right meaning. I went out and walked down to the reptile wagon. I unhitched the back panel and climbed inside. I found my rattler's box near the back, at the bottom of a stack. I sat in the narrow, dim aisle created by the two rows of boxes, at least four high and six deep. I leaned my ear toward one of the air holes to hear my rattler's hissing over the hissing of the other snakes.

A shadow darkened the aisle. Mr. Pattinson was standing outside the wagon. "Did that upset you?" he asked. "Your brother is not incorrect about Mr. Brown. May I come in?"

I rested my forehead against one of the boxes and looked down. I could feel the snake inside the box slide against the other side. "You think it's funny to bring your disgusting friend into our midst," I said. "You think my brother's concern for the state of your soul is funny. Why are you still here, with your false religion and your questions—to mock us?"

"No," he said from across the wagon's floor. "I want to see if you're right." I raised my eyes, and from my odd angle, he was just a black shape in the sunlight. He hoisted himself up into the wagon, and I brought my knees closer to my chest. He raised his arms above the stacks of boxes so that he wouldn't accidentally nudge any of them, and he murmured, "I'm taking my life into my hands." Then he lowered himself to the floor. It was a squeeze for him, and once he was sitting, his wide shoulders blocked out the sun and put me in shadow. He had his legs out in front of him, bent, with his forearms resting on his knees. He was wearing long trousers that day, and the way the legs hiked up when he sat, the tops of his tan socks were exposed, along with their garter strings, and I could see just a little bit of his bare shin and its light-colored hair. It felt obscene, and I looked back at my rattler's box.

"I respect your people, Rachel," Mr. Pattinson said. "I respect your religion. I want to find out what feeds the kind of faith you have."

"The Lord does," I said.

"No, he doesn't," Mr. Pattinson said. "If he did, what worth would it have? You know better than that."

"Why don't you ask my mother about it? She knows better than me."

"I don't think so. I don't think she's thought about it in that way."

"You're right," I said, beginning to trace the painted letters on my rattler's box. "I don't think she's ever doubted. That's why you want to talk to me?" I could hardly make my voice loud enough to be heard. "Because you think I've doubted?"

He didn't say anything for such a long time that I raised my eyes to him again. He'd taken off his cap and was slowly smoothing out his hair, his hand working through it while he looked at me. "No," he said. "Because, for a second, on that first night, you seemed afraid of the snake. That's why."

I looked down and squeezed my wet eyelids shut.

I heard a smile in his voice when he spoke next. "None of the other young ladies will talk to me."

"Well, what do you expect?" I said, rousing myself and swiping the bottoms of my palms across my eyes. "You're an unmarried man, an outsider. And I don't talk to you that much."

"How do they expect to meet young men, then?" Mr. Pattinson said. "There aren't very many at all in the Church. If they want to get married, they'll have to look outside."

"No girl of real faith will marry outside the Church."

"They're going to have to if they want to have a new generation in it," he said. "Do you want to get married?"

I looked at him askance, before I could stop myself.

He smiled. "Not to *me*," he said. "I mean in general. Silly girl," he added quietly, rubbing his knees with his hands.

"I very likely won't get married," I said, looking back at my finger tracing the box's lettering. "Even though our worship seems attractive, we're speaking harsh truths for the world, and those truths do not attract anyone but the righteous, and there aren't many righteous. My sister and I have accepted that."

"Your mother and father got married, though."

"They were lucky."

"Don't you want to have children someday?"

"I will do whatever the Lord wants of me."

"Be fruitful and multiply," he said. "That's what he wants of you."

"Don't make fun of me."

"Then don't reply to me with platitudes, with quotes from your father's sermons," he said.

"The only reason you're allowed to stay with us is because you're paying my father," I said.

He put his cap back on and sighed. "I suppose that's true enough."

I rested my cheek against my knee. "I could never marry a man from outside," I said, "because I have a true and unrelenting faith. So I will not marry."

I felt Mr. Pattinson's shadow stretch over me as he leaned closer. "You're afraid that a man from outside would not accept that part of you," he said.

"It's all of me," I said.

Daniel was sick that night. He woke us up with his retching— he'd vomited all down the side of the love seat, into Mama's hair. She'd scolded him as she used her blanket to wipe it out, but Daniel just vomited again. Finally, she took him outside. We could hear him through the open doorway, out of sight, retching every two minutes or so while Mother murmured angrily.

Jessica and I were lying in our bunk, with me on the inside, my arms pressed up against her back, as always.

"Poor Daniel," Jessica whispered. "It must have been something he ate."

I watched the narrow plane of Jessica's back, her nightdress shifting as she breathed.

"I was thinking about home," I murmured.

"Are you homesick?" she said.

"Yes, I think so," I said. "I was thinking about the way Mother keeps Papa's shaving kit all lined up by the kitchen window, and she won't let anyone move it. And she can do that because it's her house, with her husband. I was thinking about how—there's no place that we can do that."

Jessica was quiet. Then, she whispered, "Do you mean how we're not going to get married?"

I buried my face into the corner created by Jessica's back and the bottom of our bunk. "Yes."

"Do you want to pray?" Jessica said.

I wanted to say no, but I said, "All right," and I gave her my hand.

Over the following days, I was not quite right. I thought it was about to be my delicate time, which is the only thing Mother would ever call it. My senses were acute like they became just before my time—the air was hotter, the sunlight whiter. When we traveled, I stayed inside the wagon with Mother, Jessica, and Daniel for as long as I could before I had to get out. I walked alongside then, staying in the shade. I didn't mind the dust rising up from the wheels, and I let the flies flick against my face without shooing them away. But I checked every morning, and I wasn't bleeding. I wasn't like Jessica, who could mark down the calendar and be prepared—I never knew when it would come. To this day, I never know.

Half a day away from Aurora, our Ford broke down. I was walking beside the wagon when Mr. Malcolm came running past, up to the front, and shouted something to Papa. Papa turned and signaled the rest of the line to stop. As he walked back with Mr. Malcolm, he said to me, "What are you doing outside?" But he did not wait for me to answer.

The Church ladies milled about the road irritably as every single one of the men went down the line to the Ford to help. We could see them all crowded around the car like ants around a dropped watermelon. Two hours passed, and the ladies gave up on the day. "We won't reach Aurora until well past dark, even if we leave right this minute," each said in turn, and they began moving the wagons off to the side of the road, setting up for an early evening. Near sunset, one by one, the men came wandering toward the smell of creamed corn, ambling like milk cows in the heat, chewing tobacco and fanning themselves with their hats, until most of them had come to get their supper. When it was getting dark, Mother sent me to fetch the rest.

Mr. Forrester was sitting in the driver's seat of the Ford, swiping a handkerchief over his face, and Mr. Brown was in the passenger side, rolling a cigarette with concentration in the diminishing light. Papa and Mr. Pattinson were bent under the raised hood. They were both sweating in their shirtsleeves, dirty with engine grime, hatless. Papa grunted something, and Mr. Pattinson said, "Maybe not."

I stayed a little distance away until Papa noticed me. He straightened up and pushed his shoulders back with his hands on his hips, frowning at an ache. "Yes, Rachel?"

"Mother says supper's ready. Do you want it?" I asked. Mr. Pattinson stayed bent over the engine.

"The carburetor's blown," Papa said, tensing his lips so that his clenched teeth showed. I turned around to go back, but Papa said after me, "Some water."

"Yes, Papa."

I brought back two cream tins full of water.

"I'll leave before sunup, take my car into Aurora," Mr. Pattinson said as Papa took one of the tins. "Get back to you before noon with a mechanic, hopefully."

Papa spat on the ground. "Whole day lost. Mechanic will rob us blind." He took a drink.

From inside the car, Mr. Brown said, "Damn!" He was trying

to light the cigarette he'd just rolled. "I need some Luckies. I can't roll these damn things."

Mr. Forrester chuckled and said, "Mind your language," as he took a pinch from his tin of chew.

"We do not speak of damnation idly here, Mr. Brown," Papa said.

I took the second water tin over to Mr. Pattinson, and he thanked me. His sweat made a glossy layer on his face and neck, and his glasses slipped up his nose as he lifted his head to drink. I could see the muscles of his throat move as he took big swallows. He had a coppery, warm smell after all of his work with the engine in the sun. When he lowered his head and handed back the tin, he nodded at me.

"Won't you eat, then?" I said, trying to speak low so Papa wouldn't get angry with me.

"Will you bring me a plate?"

By the time I brought him a bowl of the creamed corn with a piece of corn bread, the only one still there besides Mr. Pattinson was Mr. Brown, lying across the seat of the Ford, his heels resting on the base of the passenger window. Mr. Pattinson was sitting on the running board.

"Chris is taking a little sleep," he said. "Tuckered out from rolling that cigarette, poor darling. Mr. Forrester went to get some supper, and your father went to count how much money he has to pay the mechanic with." I handed him his bowl and his bread and began to go away, but he took hold of my wrist and steered me back. "Wait a minute." He gently pulled until I was sitting beside him on the running board. "Have you eaten?"

"Yes," I said.

He mixed his creamed corn with his spoon, blew on it, and finally took a bite. "It's burnt," he said.

"I know," I said, smiling. "Mrs. Malcolm made it."

"And who made the corn bread?" he asked.

"I did."

He took a bite of the bread and pretended to choke. I buried my face in my upraised knees. "It's delicious," I heard him say.

"You always make fun of me," I said into my knees. "Your mother should have raised you better."

"My mother raised me *Catholic*, remember?" he said.

I straightened myself up. "Are you Irish?"

He raised his eyebrows. "I suppose your people dislike Irish as well as Catholics?"

"Irish *are* Catholics, aren't they?"

He laughed. "I was born in Chicago. Would you like to see a picture?" He put his bowl on the ground and went off with his corn bread toward the Stanley Steam. It was very dark now, and we were sitting on the side of the Ford facing away from the supper fire and the torches. Mr. Brown hadn't made a sound. Mr. Pattinson returned—I heard him before I saw him. He sat down again and put something light and thin into my hands.

"Just a moment," he said, and he struck a match and brought it close, shielding it with a cupped palm. In my hands was a photograph of three people, a man, a woman, and a child, in a cardboard frame.

"Oh, you were photographed!" I said.

"Dozens of times," he said. From the clothes, it looked like it was taken about twenty-five years before. The man had immense whiskers, and the woman was fingering a long white dress. Her other hand was lightly touching the shoulder of the young child, maybe three years old, who was smiling with a wide-open mouth, riding an ornate rocking horse. The child had a light tuft of hair and tiny eyeglasses.

"Even then you had eyeglasses," I said, resting my cheek in my hand.

"Yes. I'm very helpless." The match went out, and he lit another one. "My father," he said, pointing to the whiskered man, "is a newspaperman. He's getting quite old now, and I think soon he'll ask me to take over the paper. So I figured I'd have one last hurrah, drive down to New Orleans, before I have to take up the family mantle. We were on our way down when we came across you."

"Are you going to go to New Orleans once you're—finished with us?"

"I'm not sure," he said. The match went out again, and this time he didn't light another.

"New Orleans is a sinful city," I said.

"Have you ever been there?"

"No."

"Then how do you know?"

"I don't need to taste the ocean to know its water is bad."

He leaned forward, and the air he moved brought with it a milder smell of sweat and engine oil. "Where you come from, your home, is it just—full of good people?"

"Yes," I said.

"Is it just you in your town, just the Church?"

"Just the Church. My father owns *all* the land."

"He owns all the land?"

"Yes. He's landlord to everyone."

"So he's the police, the law and order."

I did not like the way he said it. "Papa upholds *God's* law."

"And no one breaks it. Rachel, what if you married a man who beat you?"

I put my hands over my heart. "What?"

"Would you break your marriage vow to leave him? What if you had children, and he beat them too?"

"I would—pray for God's help."

Mr. Pattinson put his head in his hands and said, "Jesus."

I dropped my hands to my sides, pressing my palms down against the bumps on the running board. "Don't swear," I said.

Mr. Pattinson abruptly raised his head and said, "Let me tell you what you will do if someone hurts you. You will run away from them, no matter who they are." I had never heard him angry before. I got up and went away toward the supper fire, and I looked back only once, but all I could see were Mr. Brown's feet in their burnished leather shoes. Smoke was now sleepily drifting out of the window.

When I woke up in the morning, everyone was waiting for Mr. Pattinson to return from Aurora with the mechanic. At noon, he did return, and all the men clustered around the Ford again. I stayed in the wagon, watching from the window. In an hour, we were moving.

After another week, Mr. Brown lost his smile. He seemed to grow increasingly agitated, and his politeness suffered. The worst was when he swore at Mrs. Malcolm after she stepped on one of his shoes, and Mr. Pattinson had to drag him away by the shirt collar with both hands and have words with him. That is what Jessica told me—I stayed in the wagon most of the week, because it was my delicate time. Sometimes in the morning, I would lie on the green love seat after everyone had gone to breakfast, and I was afraid that Mr. Pattinson would knock. I didn't like anybody to look at me when it was my time, but the thought of him seeing me made my stomach clench.

The night came when we were camped outside Webb City, just shy of Kansas, and it was my turn again to worship. My delicate time was over by then, so I was fit and pure. I got my rattler from the reptile wagon, and I took him someplace quiet so I could look at him for a little while before it was time to begin. He was awake and lively, trying to slide up out of the box. I smelled cigarette smoke, so I closed the lid and looked up at Mr. Brown. He had no hat, and his dark hair was in his eyes. One hand was up by his mouth holding his cigarette, the other hanging limp at his side.

"What's his name?" Mr. Brown gestured to the box with his cigarette.

"He doesn't have a name," I said.

"No *name?*" he almost shouted. I could see then that he was drunk.

"No, Mr. Brown," I said. "No name."

"All of your crazy show, and the snake has no name? Why *not?*"

"Because," I said, standing up, "he is not a pet."

When the worship started, I sat with my hands on my lap, looking only at Papa. He said the old words from Luke, "Behold, I give unto you power to tread on serpents and scorpions, and over all the power of the enemy: and nothing shall by any means hurt you." When it was time, I stood up and went over to Mr. Forrester, and he opened up my rattler's box like a sacred gift, like he'd done every time before. I lifted my rattler, and as I stood with him wrapped around me, his firm, dry body sliding over my skin, I looked into the crowd. Mr. Brown was not there, but Mr. Pattinson was. He was near the back, but I could see him clear as day, and it was the same as the first time. The fear on his face jumped across the people between us like a lightning bolt, and struck me. I froze, praying that God would have mercy, because I was handling this snake without faith.

The rattler's hatchet head was pointed toward my shoulder, and his white mouth nudged me as he lifted himself up toward my face. I turned my head as he came nearer to my neck, but he did not bite me. I took him up in my hands and put him back in his box, like always, like it hadn't mattered.

And as everyone was taking down the tent and the townspeople meandered away into the night, I went to the Stanley Steam, which was off by itself in the darkness at the back of the wagon line. I sat in its backseat, running my palms up and down over the leather. After only a short time, I could hear someone coming, and I knew it was Mr. Pattinson. I did not look up, but I heard and felt him lean against the outside of the car, one hand on the roof and one on the top of the backseat door.

"Chris is angry with me because he wants to stop following you and your people around," he said. "He wants to go home."

"Why doesn't he just go?" I said, still without looking up.

"Well, for one thing, the car is mine. But even if I did drop him off someplace with a train station, he says he won't leave without me."

I didn't say anything. He abruptly rounded the car, opening the other backseat door, and he sat beside me. "I have a daughter," he said, "and I'm not married to her mother." I looked up into his face, which was covered in wide swipes of shadow so that I couldn't properly see it. "I was very young, and I thought I wanted to marry her. She died in childbirth. I wanted—"

I opened the car door and was about to get out when he raised his voice. "Do you think I'm going to hell, Rachel?"

I looked back at him. "Yes."

"You do?"

"Yes, I do."

"You want me to go to hell?"

"It is—a pleasure to think that God rewards the righteous and punishes the wicked."

"You are happy that I'm going to hell?"

"I am happy in all of God's works."

"You're smiling."

I was, involuntarily, without knowing why. "I'm smiling because you're making me uncomfortable."

"I'm sorry. But maybe you're uncomfortable because—"

I laughed, shaking my head. "I don't want to talk about this anymore."

"Why do you laugh? Because you don't actually believe I'm going to hell?"

"I laugh because I know you. You are a blasphemer and a fornicator. You have scoffed at all of us." He leaned toward me. I looked up at the car ceiling. "And I rejoice to think that God will punish you," I said.

"I never scoffed at you," he said softly. We sat for a little while. There was moonlight on the top of his legs and over his stomach. His right shoulder was beside my left, not touching, and his face was bent downward, his eyeglasses shadowing the sharp outline of his nose. All of these things were painful to me. "Rachel," he said at last, "can you look at me, please?" I did, even though it put a stone in my throat. "You're twenty years old," he said. "You can have a say in your own life. I can see the conflict in you."

"There is no conflict," I said.

"I can see it. This—please listen to me, all the way through, because this will sound . . . *intensely* forward to you. I am leaving with Chris tomorrow, driving to Springfield. Once we arrive in Springfield, I will wait there for three days." He dug into his pocket and pulled out a twenty-dollar bill, then put it into my hand. I stared at it. I had never seen one before. "I'll wait in Springfield for three days, at the train station, from six in the morning until midnight. After three days, I'll go on to St. Louis. But before that, I'll wait for you. You know I have money. There will be people to help you. You won't be alone." He put his hands on my shoulders and squared me up so I was completely turned to him. "This comes from a place of good faith, Rachel," he said. "I don't mean anything more by it than I say." I looked at his face, at the thin bags beneath his eyes, magnified by his eyeglasses, and the faint freckles along the bridge of his nose. He let go of my shoulders and got out of the car.

In the morning, I watched out the window of our wagon as Mr. Pattinson and Mr. Brown shook hands with the Church men, then turned the Stanley Steam around and drove away, tossing up dust behind them. I hadn't even let myself think about it. Even when I lay awake in my bunk while Jessica and Mother and Daniel slept quietly, I had not weighed my options. I did not have any. Perhaps for a small moment in the night before he left, I thought about Chicago and New Orleans and having my photograph taken, but if that moment had happened, it was struck down by Daniel sighing in his sleep.

As the Stanley Steam grew obscure in the distance, I leaned

back into the shadows and sat beside Mother on the love seat, putting Daniel's feet in my lap while he laid his head in Mother's.

"Shame," Mother said. "I thought perhaps Mr. Pattinson at least . . ."

I figured the trip to Springfield would take them about a day. I didn't know how fast his car went, but a day was a little less than it would take a fast, light wagon. I kept the twenty-dollar bill inside my shoe, beneath my heel, and I could feel it slide when I walked. It stayed there for two years before I put it in between the pages of my Bible, in the book of Ruth, once I stopped going on the summer tours.

Four days after Mr. Pattinson left us, we were outside Pittsburg, Kansas, and while everyone was setting up the tent, I took my rattler's box out of the reach of the torchlights, and I sat on the ground with it in my lap. I lifted the lid and looked down at him, fearing that he would kill me dead if I so much as put one finger against his diamond-patterned scales. My tears dropping on him made him twitch.

In three weeks, we were in Coldwater, Kansas, and it was my turn again. I did not tell Papa or Mother or Jessica anything about it. My hands were steady as I took up the snake, my rattler, and I put his middle around my neck, but he only wound himself down my arm. I had been so sure that I would never feel the touch of the Holy Spirit again, but the whiteness began to descend, and the silence came down around me, but my rattler didn't turn to fire. As I watched him move lazily, refusing to be truthful and bite me, I was full of fear, and I began to gasp. *Then* he bit me.

He bit me on the forearm, on the soft, hairless underside. The women in the crowd screamed, people crowded the stage, and I fell to the floor, my rattler still wrapped around me. The crowd pushed backward and away, like an undertow. Mr. Forrester's wide brown hands clamped down behind my rattler's head, and I passed out.

Mother told me that Mr. Forrester yanked the rattler off of me, Papa sucked all the venom out—spitting it onto the dirt like it was chewing tobacco—and everyone in the crowd applauded as soon as they'd gotten the bite wrapped up and loaded me into the Ford to take me to the Coldwater hospital. That night they got the largest contribution to the collection plate they'd ever had. I had to stay in the wagon the rest of the summer. Jessica brought me my meals.

I went on the summer tours twice more, but I couldn't handle my rattler anymore. I was afraid of him. Papa was angry with me at first, saying that I must have sinned very gravely, maybe I had shamed myself with one of those faithless men, and I should pray and humble myself before God. He did not ask me to pick up a snake again. After two years, I asked Papa if I could stay behind with the very old people and the mothers with very young babies during the summer, and he did not pause before saying that I could.

He gave my rattler to Daniel when he turned ten. He's never been bit, not even once. Mother died of influenza in 1923, so now I am the first woman in my father's house. I keep Papa's shaving kit lined up along the kitchen windowsill, but nothing in this house is mine. I continue to faithfully worship the God of Abraham, of Isaac, the God of my fathers. I lead a blameless life, far from the sins of adultery and fornication. I have no husband, but I am a mother to my sister and brother.

Samuel Pattinson, what is your daughter's name?

Robert Anthony Siegel

The Right Imaginary Person

WE WERE PART OF a large group of people at a *yakitoriya* in Shinjuku, celebrating somebody or other's birthday, but we'd both gotten stuck at the wrong end of the long table, cut off from the main conversation, which was drunken and flirty.

"I bet everyone tells you how great your Japanese is," she said, lighting a cigarette.

"They do," I acknowledged.

"Then let's talk about something else."

It was 1985, almost the end of summer. Sumiko told me she was nearing the end of a long, boring adolescent period in which she was trying to become the opposite of her mother. She didn't want to become a good cook, or keep the house clean, or be loved by children—or be nice to anyone, for that matter—or cultivate any of the traditional arts expected of a young lady of marriageable age from a good family. "Calligraphy?" she said. "Can you think of anything more boring? And flower arranging? It makes me want to throw up." Instead she drank a sort of white lightning called *shōchū* and smoked Golden Bat cigarettes and wrote science fiction stories in which androids took on unplanned human emotions, slept with each other, had imaginary pregnancies, and gave birth to children that were strings of computer code.

"But what about you?" she asked. "It's not fair if you don't tell me anything."

I looked at her hand, the delicate fingers smudged with ink. There were nights when I rode the Yamanote Line in a circle, jammed against the other passengers, just to feel someone else's pressure on my skin.

But what I told her about was my trip to Shikoku, how I went alone with a backpack over the vacation, taking old buses from village to village, and how in one of those villages a group of kids had formed a circle around me and asked to touch my hair. I had kneeled down on the grass beside the road, closed my eyes, and felt their hands running over my head. Small, gentle hands reading my otherness like braille.

"Was that creepy?" she asked.

"No, it felt deep."

Later, after the party broke up, I walked her to the train station, and in the shadows by the entrance where I was going to ask for her phone number she unexpectedly reached up and brushed my bangs from my face. "It does feel a little different," she said. "Softer than Japanese hair."

We went to her place, a six-mat *tatami* room with a little kitchen she never used and a single window that looked out on the courtyard in back. We stood in the middle of the tiny space and kissed, bodies slowly softening like candles. Her mouth tasted like *shōchū* and smoke. She pulled off her shirt and her breasts were in my palms, the nipples long and thick, the color of chocolate. And then she was melting to the *tatami*, pulling me down on top of her. With each touch of her hand I felt like I was being sewn back together.

Afterward, we bathed in her tub, which was square and deep, the water so hot that her hand on my thigh felt like a bruise. Then we stretched out naked on top of her futon, and I watched the steam rise from her body into the air. She had a mole in the hollow at the base of her neck, a small half-moon scar on her calf, and silver polish on her toes. "Do you ever get homesick?" she asked.

"Never," I said, though of course I did. A part of my mind was stuck roaming the big Victorian my parents had so painstakingly restored and now left only when they had to, for the pharmacy or the liquor store.

"I don't think I could live in a foreign country," said Sumiko. "I get lonely too easily, and then I end up doing things like this."

Resting her head on my chest, she read me a story she'd written about a group of children who live in a colony on another planet and are taken care of by parents who are nothing but computer-generated holograms. The story wasn't science fiction at all, or not what I thought of as science fiction; it felt honest and emotional, full of the yearning to touch and the sadness of not being real. "That's just so beautiful," I said, thinking of the letters I wrote to my parents, packed with fabrications about my life in Tokyo: how I had discovered an ancient scroll with the work of a lost poet; how I had an audience with the emperor and he handed me a silver tray of bonbons with his own hands, scandalizing the officials around us . . . I never actually mailed those letters, just collected them in a box in the closet.

"The secret is to pretend you're someone else," said Sumiko, taking my fingers from her hair and holding them in her hand, kissing them one by one. "You can't be the person who worries what other people think."

"Who's left then?"

"The imaginary person who tells the truth."

The next day, I left the library early, went to the market, and carried the groceries to her place, where I made dinner using the one pan that she owned. While I cooked she read me a story about an alien race that is being destroyed by a plague of dreams so beautiful that the sleeper refuses to wake. The cure for this plague can only be made from the hearts of human children who have never known love, so a scientist is sent to Earth to collect as many sad orphan hearts as she can. Wearing the body of a teenage girl like a space suit, she goes from orphanage to orphanage, killing children and extracting their hearts, even as spring comes to Tokyo, the cherry trees bloom, people get drunk in the park, and the last signal from her planet dies away forever.

Sumiko didn't have a table, so we ate at the lovely Japanese-style desk where she did her writing—sitting side by side and looking out the window at the evening light bluing the courtyard. "Do you ever feel like the alien in your story?" I asked.

"Sometimes," she said.

I thought of the children in Shikoku, how they had touched my hair and run off, leaving me at a bus stop that was nothing but a patch of grass by the roadside. "I never realized Japanese people got lonely in that way."

"You speak the language, but you don't know anything about real Japanese."

"You're a real Japanese, and I know you."

"That's what I like about you, that you need me so badly. You're a being from another planet, and I'm your human guide, like in a sci-fi movie." She rested her hand on my knee, very lightly. "I want to be the only one on Earth who understands you," she said.

"It's not like there's a lot of competition." But I could feel something happening inside me, a slowing down, like when the kids touched my hair.

"And I want *you* to be the only one who understands *me*," she said.

"I would like that."

She gave a little laugh. "No, you wouldn't, not really. If you did, you'd realize this is all just playacting."

"What is?"

"All of this—dinner, my stories, you and me. In less than a year I'll graduate from school and get a job teaching kindergarten in some suburb or other while looking for an eligible man to marry."

"You don't have to do what everyone else is doing."

"Resistance is futile in a country like this, because the thing you reject isn't just out there, it's in here." She tapped her head. "Obedience is encoded in us through two thousand years of inbreeding."

"Are you saying that you are genetically unable to stop yourself from becoming a kindergarten teacher?"

"Can a sunflower refuse to follow the sun? Can a girl refuse to grow breasts?" She got up and placed the notebook with her story back in the bookcase: four shelves of cheap notebooks dating back to grade school, their covers imprinted with red hearts or Hello Kitty cartoons. "You'll never understand," she said, running her finger over the spines. "You don't want to."

Sumiko wasn't completely wrong; deep down I couldn't understand. That made her furious and she broke up with me often, usually late at night, when the trains had stopped running and I had to walk two hours back to my place. I'd call and leave messages, and we'd meet the next day, or the day after that, to argue and then kiss so that we could see how exactly we fit together, her body pressed to mine.

But one night in February I looked up from my book and found her observing me with a hard, clinical expression, as if I were a beetle and she were going to pin me to a board. "I know what the problem is," she said.

"What problem?" I asked.

"You think I'm ugly."

Sumiko looked like she'd come off a scroll from the Heian period, the era of aristocratic women in flowing robes and long hair: a pale round face, full lips, and eyebrows so elegant I would sometimes trace them with my finger. "That's ridiculous," I said.

"I've been teased all my life about my fat face."

I had no idea that her looks weren't the general ideal anymore, that they hadn't been the ideal for about a thousand years. "I think you're beautiful," I told her.

I could see that she knew I meant it, and that she despised me for it. "That's because you're a foreigner and don't really know what Japanese women are supposed to look like."

"So you think you're ugly too?"

"Obviously."

"And what does that make me?" I asked, not sure I had a right to be hurt when the subject was her looks.

"Blind."

The walk home was so cold that it felt like ice crystals were forming inside my heart. I couldn't erase the look of contempt Sumiko had given me. Back in my tiny four-mat room, I lay shivering under the quilts, unable to sleep, and then in the empty space before dawn I began thinking about my sister, Daisy, remembering how I'd stood in our backyard in New Jersey and watched her climb out of her bedroom window onto the roof of the house to scream at her boyfriend. *That's right, you better run,* she yelled down at him as he jogged across the grass toward the gate. *You better fucking run.* She stood at the very edge of the roof, giving him the finger with both hands, and when he was gone she lay down on the black shingles, her arms and legs spread as if claiming space.

"Hey," I yelled up.

"Leave me alone."

She was vice president of the drama club at school, and still bitter about losing the presidency. She wrapped scarves around her neck and played dress-up and made faces in the mirror: her Marilyn Monroe face, her Jean-Paul Belmondo face, with a cigarette drooping from the corner of her mouth. She had a maddening way of narrowing her eyes at me, as if she knew something about adulthood that she wasn't telling. She wrote messages to herself in felt-tip pen on her arms—*Only 10 miles to Broadway, you can walk if you have to.* She was seventeen, and I was fourteen, and we'd just found out that she would need another round of chemo.

I got up and called Sumiko and left a long, rambling message—

left messages every day for a week till she finally picked up the phone. "I'm angry at you because you left," she said to me.

"You told me to leave."

"If you really loved me, you would have found a way to convince me to let you stay."

I was sitting with my legs in my *kotatsu,* a little table with an electric heat lamp on the bottom, surrounded by a quilted skirt to hold in the warmth. A half-finished letter was spread on the Formica tabletop, destined, like all the others, for the pile in the box. I'd taken Sumiko's advice and pretended someone else was writing it, one of my professors, an elderly man with a vague manner and white chalk dust on his baggy suit. *Dear Mr. and Mrs. Nussbaum,* it ran, *I regret to inform you that your son, Benjamin, seems to have fallen ill. He sits in the library with a book in front of him, but he never turns the page . . .*

I'd picked that professor because he always seemed so serene, sipping tea in his little office, which was lined with novels in three languages. But I'd clearly made some kind of mistake. He could tell you the plot of every story by Balzac or Chekhov or Tanizaki, but he couldn't explain why I'd suddenly begun remembering my sister, particularly the last few months of her illness. I'd tried to make him write to my parents about her, about the way she looked sitting in the big armchair in her hospital room, her head tilted to the side, her eyes closed, resting in the sun coming through the window. Her face was all eyes by then. I got up to go for a walk—anything to get out of that room. "Stay," she said, and I sat back down.

I'd wanted the professor to tell my parents all of that, everything, but each time he lifted his pen, the words disappeared.

"Remember what you said to me about an imaginary person writing your stories?" I asked Sumiko.

"Why are you asking me this when we have serious things to discuss about you and me and this relationship?"

"How do you know it's the right imaginary person?"

I heard her light a cigarette, as if considering the question, but what she finally said was, "My parents want to meet you."

She'd told me once that if she ever brought a foreigner home her father would probably force her to leave school and move back to Kamakura. "Do you think meeting them is a good idea?" I asked.

"Don't you think it's time?"

I'd heard her talk to them over the phone at night: conversations about relatives and school and her internship at the kindergarten. I'd stop whatever I was doing and watch her press the receiver to her ear with her shoulder. She'd be in nothing but a towel, shaving her legs or rubbing in moisturizer or brushing her hair as she talked, her face slowly changing back to some earlier version of herself: placid and contented, the face of a girl.

"Your parents aren't going to like me," I said.

"They need to know who *I* like."

We took the train out to Kamakura that Saturday afternoon, carrying overnight bags. I'd cut myself shaving—a long, stinging cut too big for a Band-Aid. It had occurred to me that meeting the parents must mean something more than it did in New Jersey, but I didn't want to think about that. Instead, as the endless suburbs rolled by the window, I practiced with the flash cards I'd made, each one containing a polite phrase I'd found in an old grammar book, the sort of phrase so arcane, so excessively, self-abasingly polite that it was almost never used anymore, even by the most punctilious of native speakers.

"You don't have to worry," said Sumiko. "Just be yourself and everything will be fine." She was dressed in a prim outfit I'd never seen before: wool tights, a gray flannel skirt and cashmere sweater, a string of pearls, a headband. She lit the end of one cigarette with another all the way to Kamakura, and then threw out the remainder of the pack as we pulled into the station. "Just don't say anything about me smoking or drinking or you staying over at my place," she told me.

"I'm not an idiot."

"And don't say anything about my writing, either."

"They don't know about that?"

"Of course not."

Sumiko's parents were bigger, bulkier versions of her, with the same round faces and elegant eyebrows. They ushered us into the family car and took us to an ancient Buddhist monastery, where we walked the grounds, pretending to sightsee, our breath making steam in the air. Gravel paths, delicate wooden temples that seemed to sit weightlessly, like birds ready to take flight: the place was so beautiful that it felt otherworldly, and that aura transferred to Sumiko's parents, who looked as if it all belonged to them, as surely as their camel-hair coats and kid-leather gloves. I walked beside them with a mixture of anxiety and hunger, waiting for a chance to use one of the phrases from my flash cards, waiting for the chance to be loved. Sumiko kept close, pitching in with the small talk, but after a while she drifted off with her mother, the two of them talking together in low, conspiratorial voices. Her father turned to me, smiling. "They've left us alone for a man-to-man talk, haven't they?" His tone was bemused, but I could see that it was put on for my sake, a form of delicacy.

"You are far too kind to an undeserving wretch like myself," I said, finally using one of the flash-card phrases.

"What marvelous Japanese," he said, giving an embarrassed little laugh. "I understand you plan to become a professor?"

"Yes, that's my intention." But as soon as I heard the words out loud I knew that I wouldn't, that I would never be able to follow through. I didn't want to do anything but watch the late movie with Sumiko, and listen to her stories, and run out and buy roast potatoes from the cart pushed by the old man with the plaintive call.

"And will you seek a post here, or in America?"

"Here, definitely."

He fell silent, and I listened to the gravel crunch underfoot as we walked, waiting for him to tell me that I was full of shit and he knew it. But he just kept smiling his troubled smile, and a moment later we had rejoined the women. They were examining a line of stone Buddhas, heartbreakingly beautiful things worn smooth by the years, stippled with yellow lichen. "Lovely, aren't they?" said Sumiko's mother.

"So peaceful," I said, looking at their bald heads and serene baby faces, their eyes closed against the world. They were images of the Buddha called Jizō, guardian of children and travelers. I'd seen smaller versions of them now and then at the side of the road, marking the spot of a traffic fatality, or in temple cemeteries, pinwheels and plastic toys left by their feet as offerings.

"It's getting late," said Sumiko's father, looking at his watch.

"We should probably head home for dinner," said Sumiko's mother, and the four of us started up the path, walking slowly in the falling light. After a little ways, I veered off to examine a stone marker, pretending to read the characters running down the side but really watching the others as they continued on: Sumiko between her mother and father, her father with his hands behind his back, her mother gripping her pocketbook. They had that aura families have, of existing in a self-enclosed world, tucked inside this one but separate. At the big front gate, they turned back to view the grounds, looking as if they'd momentarily forgotten my presence.

Sumiko's parents fussed over me during dinner, her mother picking out the best things and putting them on my plate, her father filling and refilling my glass with beer, both of them asking questions about my family back home. I had no choice but to tell them about my father, the math professor; my mother, the cruciverbalist, meaning a designer of crossword puzzles. But I didn't tell them that my sister had died when I was sixteen, and that the remainder of the Nussbaums had never quite recovered the ability to speak to each other. I didn't mention the antidepressants and the antianxiety meds and the sleeping pills and the time my mother took too many by accident and we had to call an ambulance.

"And do you have any brothers or sisters?" asked Sumiko's father, finally, smiling his patient smile.

"No, I'm an only child."

"It must be hard for your parents, having you so far away," said Sumiko's mother, choosing yet more things for me with the long chopsticks used for serving.

"I write to them all the time."

Her face was like Sumiko's, but with deep creases around the eyes, which were humorous and kind and disappointed all at once. "I don't think we could stand Sumiko being so far. I'd worry too much."

"Even Tokyo's too far," said Sumiko's father, pouring me more beer. "But then a girl's different from a boy."

I glanced over at Sumiko to see how she was taking this. She sat by her mother, a glass of tea cupped in her hands, nothing showing on her face.

I excused myself to go to the bathroom, but really just wandered the house, trying to breathe. Down a long polished hall, I came across Sumiko's old bedroom, a Japanese version of my sister's: anime posters on the walls, shelves with dolls and stuffed animals, a shoe box full of mix tapes.

That night, Sumiko slept in her old bedroom, seemingly a world away. I slept in the guest room, which, like the rest of the house, expensive and elegant, smelled of new *tatami* and varnished wood. But I couldn't really sleep, and I kept imagining that I heard Sumiko's footsteps coming down the hall, forbidden and dangerous. Eventually I got up and went to the window to look at the moon, which was just a cold sliver.

In the last year of her life, my sister and I used to sneak out onto the roof of our house at night to smoke weed. This was in Leonia, New Jersey, right across the George Washington Bridge from Manhattan, in a neighborhood of big oaks and old Victorians restored by a generation in search of cheap real estate—our parents and their friends. Daisy and I made a big show of turning up our noses at their hand-painted Italian kitchen tile, their charcoal water filters and basement radon detectors, their inexpensive but highly drinkable wines—everything they used to convince themselves that they were exempt from the dangers outside. We would climb out the bay window and sit on the rough black shingles, looking up at the spray of stars above our heads, feeling the rush of the river beyond the black silhouettes of the trees, and beyond that the dense presence of the city, where life really happened. We never talked much; we had already picked up the habit of silence. We would pass the joint between us, a little star traveling from her hand to mine and back, and the house would seem to float beneath our weight like a ship on the water, traveling with the current, faster and faster into the darkness.

Back in Tokyo on Sunday, we went straight to Sumiko's apartment and flopped onto her futon, too tired to take off our coats. We hadn't touched all weekend, had hardly spoken, and now we lay inches apart, staring up at the ceiling. "Your parents aren't so bad," I said, unable to lift my head, which was still full of polite Japanese conversation, spinning around and around. I'd played *Go* with her father, had allowed her mother to teach me calligraphy in a studio full of morning light at the back of the house. Before we left for the station, her mother had given me a scroll with an example of her own writing, surprisingly thick and muscular, full of sharp angles and mad splatter. I'd felt like she was declaring something about herself, something that secretly linked us together. "I think they liked me," I said, wanting to believe it, testing the sound of it.

Sumiko turned to look at me. "In Japan, politeness is a wall. The more polite, the higher the wall."

"And how high was their wall?"

"It was electrified, with barbed wire on top."

I thought of Sumiko's mother serving me at dinner before any-one else, thought of Sumiko's father refilling my glass with beer over and over, though etiquette required the reverse, that I pour for him. I had tried once, but he had grabbed the bottle from me. "At least they weren't rude," I said.

"In the kitchen, my mother turned to me and said, 'Don't give me blue-eyed grandchildren.'"

Everything inside me got very quiet; I could feel the blood moving through my heart. "You're not pregnant, are you?"

"Don't be stupid."

"You don't think that they know that we—"

"I don't care what they know, and anyway, they're not idiots."

And then I felt the delayed sting of her mother's comment. "My eyes are brown, not blue," I said, remembering Sumiko's mother handing me the brush, guiding my hand over the paper, showing me how to write the long dripping letters that looked like rain on the window. I had thought she liked me, maybe she even had, but the more important thing was that I had liked her: her gentleness, which was akin to melancholy, her ability to instruct without saying a word. "I don't think anyone in my entire family has blue eyes."

Sumiko sat up. "You don't want to marry me. You would never even consider marrying me."

"What are you talking about?" We had never used the word together, and it seemed startling, naked.

"You won't marry me," she said.

"I would marry you," I said, phrasing it as a hypothetical.

"No, you wouldn't."

So frightened it almost seemed to be happening in a dream, I asked her to marry me. She burst into tears and asked why I hadn't proposed sooner.

"Because I didn't know you'd say yes," I lied.

"I'm not *saying* yes." She put her head down on my lap, hiding her wet face with her hands. "Poor sweet boy, I feel sorry for you."

. . .

Sumiko went to her first job interview dressed in a blue suit and cream blouse and carrying a leather portfolio tucked under her arm, like all the other soon-to-be-graduated job seekers I saw on the subway. Afterward, she came back and lay on the *tatami* with her eyes shut while I kissed her face and neck and shoulders. "Why don't you write something?" I suggested. "Writing always makes you feel better."

"There's no point," she said, her eyes still closed.

"Write something gory, about aliens who hollow people out and lay eggs inside their skulls."

"It would only make me sad."

"I'll do dinner and the dishes, and you can work till we go to bed."

"That me is gone. I have to be the other me now, the one who pretends to like children."

The job interviews became routine. Sumiko would iron the cream-colored blouse and the blue suit, then spend a long time in front of the mirror, painting her face into a heavy mask. Back at home, she would wash it all off and change into jeans and we would go out for ramen, then watch TV till late at night, as if waiting for some undefined miracle to happen, something that would put a stop to graduation forever. Sitting in the blue glow of her little TV, I wanted to close my eyes against the world, like the beautiful statues of Jizō in the monastery, and imagine us back at the beginning, when she had laid her head on my chest, reading me a story.

And then one night, she shook me awake in that dead space before morning, saying that there was something we had to do. I got dressed in the dark, feeling lucid but not really awake, as if I were just a guest inside her dream. She gave me a big black garbage bag to carry, then grabbed a bottle of *shōchū* from the kitchen counter and opened the front door. I followed her out onto the open-air veranda, dragging the bag, which was surprisingly heavy.

The street was motionless, like an artifact contained in a museum case. The only thing alive was the thrumming of the cicadas, a metallic sound like the whirring of an engine deep inside the world. I followed her around back to the courtyard, a square of concrete on which sat a row of garbage cans, frosted by the light of a single streetlamp.

"Dump the stuff in there," she said, pointing to a big metal tub used for burning leaves.

I carried the bag over and undid the twist tie. Inside were her notebooks, their covers decorated with hearts and Hello Kitties. "Hey, wait a second," I said.

"We're celebrating." She reached into the pocket of her sweatpants and pulled out a very official-looking piece of correspondence. "I got a job. I'm now a kindergarten teacher." She opened the bottle of *shōchū*, took a swig, and handed it to me.

"You can't burn your work," I said.

"Kafka did."

"He asked Brod to do it, knowing full well that he wouldn't. And Kafka was dying, not graduating."

She lit a Golden Bat. "You know what, you're not my husband, so you don't tell me what to do."

"You're going to regret this."

"What do you know about me, anyway?"

Maybe she was right. Was this a test? Did she want me to stop her? I watched her use two hands to dump the notebooks into the metal tub, scooping them out of the trash bag in heaps, as if they were fallen leaves. Her cigarette bobbed between her lips as she worked. When she was done, she lifted the bottle of *shōchū* from the ground and took another swallow.

"Writing was just a stupid fantasy, anyway," she said.

"I love your stories."

"But you don't love me."

"I wish you'd stop saying that."

I watched Sumiko pour *shōchū* onto the notebooks in the tub and then use her lighter to set the acceptance letter ablaze. For a second, it was like a little handkerchief of fire between her fingers. She held it aloft as if waving good-bye to someone leaving on an invisible cruise ship, and then dropped it into the tub to light the rest.

There were some loose pages that caught and curled first. The flames burnt green and then orange. I could see Sumiko's handwriting twisting, turning brown. Bits and pieces of paper flew off into the darkness. The cardboard covers burnt, curving like smiles. I passed the bottle back and forth with Sumiko, feeling the heat from the fire on my face and hands.

In that moment, I knew that I would pack in the morning and go back to my place, and that I would quit grad school and get on an airplane and fly back to America. I knew that my parents would meet me at the airport, looking boozy and frail. I knew that I would go with them for the very first time since the funeral to visit my sister's grave in the big cemetery next to the highway, where the headstones were lined up like millions of chessmen. I knew that I would have to do something to start my life.

Till then, I was just watching.

About a year later, living in New York, I got a letter from Sumiko. It was our first communication since I'd left Japan, and my chest tightened as I opened the envelope and saw the handwriting I knew from her notebooks, that swift native speaker's hand that I could never imitate:

Dear Poor Sweet Boy,

> *The cherry blossoms are falling, and for some reason I think of you.*
> *The school where I teach looks exactly like the one I went to as a child: the concrete building, the playground with the metal climbing set and swings. On the first day, I got there very early, and as I walked the empty hall I had the feeling that I had gone back in time to become a kindergartener again—worse, that I had some-*

how fallen asleep in the middle of class and dreamed that I was an adult. Though the dream had seemed to take twenty-two years, it was really only a few minutes long, and in a second I was going to wake up in my little-girl body, and my mother would be waiting outside at the end of the day to take me home. I got so confused that I had to sit in my chair at the front of the empty classroom and put my head between my knees and breathe, wondering when I would wake up and be my real self again in the real world, not the dream world.

But I've grown used to teaching since then, and I find that I now take a great deal of comfort in the daily routine. There is a working agreement here that makes life reassuring: I pretend to be a teacher and the children pretend to be my students. Parents and teachers agree to forget that children are in fact lunatics, and that what we call growing up is just learning to hide it better so nobody will lock us away.

Oh, did I mention that I'm engaged to be married? He works at the same insurance company as my father, which is convenient. The only problem is that he has a good heart, so we have some trouble communicating—just like I had with you. But I'm trying to learn how good people talk, so I can fake it.

I don't miss you at all.

My first thought was to tell her that she should leave her fiancé and come join me in New York. In America we would switch roles: she would be the space alien and I would be the human guide, the one whose job it was to explain the world. But I knew she would never listen to me.

I sat with the letter in my hand, remembering the sound of her voice as she read me a story for the first time. We were naked, her head resting on my chest. The story was about children whose parents are nothing but holograms, beams of light, and the words were so full of sadness that I knew then and there that I could love her if she let me—if I let myself.

The story was long, and it wasn't till I realized that I could hear every word of it that I grabbed a notebook and a pen and began to write. My fingers ached as they chased her voice, the voice that had made me feel free and alive and frightened all at once, whether we were hiding in the shadows outside the train station or soaking in her deep tub, the water so hot I couldn't breathe. I was going to save her story from the fire, save it and send it back to her as a wedding gift, save all the stories in all the notebooks. But when I came to the end, what I had written was about the night my sister and I sat on the roof of my parents' house in Leonia, right before she went into the hospital for the last time: Daisy and me, staring at the stars, those tiny points of light, and feeling as if we were falling upward into the sky.

Louise Erdrich

Nero

H<small>E WAS THE SECOND</small>, or perhaps the third, Nero owned by my grandparents. With a grocery store that included a butcher shop and a slaughterhouse, they could feed as many dogs as they liked. Nero, a mixture of fierce breeds in a line known locally as guard dogs, was valued for his strength, his formidable jaws, and his resonant bark. At night, he was turned loose to guard the cash register in the front of the shop, where he paced the waxed linoleum, a ghostly white. Other unbanked valuables were kept in a safe in my grandfather's bedroom. He slept behind a locked door with my grandmother on one side of him and a loaded gun on the other. This was not a place where a child got up at night to ask for a glass of water.

I was taken to stay with my grandparents because my mother was about to have a baby. The plan was for me to stay there until the baby was established at home—a period of only two or three weeks. While there, I must have lived at a more intense pitch. Or perhaps the novelty of everything that happened caused each day to imprint itself deeply on my mind. I believe I could still draw the stippled print on my grandmother's homemade shifts, or even reproduce the maps of blood that appeared and disappeared on my grandfather's bleached, starched, ankle-length aprons. I was seven years old, wore boy's clothes, and was often mistaken for a boy, a sickly one. "Don't you feed him?" the customers would say, laughing. My grandmother stopped giving me jobs out front. Every day, I climbed the trestle fence to watch Uncle Jurgen, a skinny, awkward figure in steel-toed boots, bring pigs, sheep, even steers and heifers to a stilled submission. My grandfather, a real wrestler, had taken prizes in Germany. But Jurgen had his own ways. He grappled with each animal without exerting, it seemed, much effort. When the animal had tired itself out and stopped kicking, he'd use a razor-sharp knife to cut its throat with a technique so precise that the blood could be collected for black sausage.

Now the scalding tub for pigs is rusted, thistles have grown through the wire chicken cages, and somewhere in the field behind the closed shop the bones of Nero whitely petrify.

"Throw down the guts if he rushes at you," my grandmother said, handing me a bent pie tin heaped with offal. Nobody argued with her, ever. Sometimes Nero buried his dishes in the fenced backyard after emptying them, or, if acutely bored, tossed them high in the air with his great muzzle. He caught these objects and chewed them to lethal shreds of metal, which littered the ground, along with his dung, and had to be picked up by one of the old men who worked odd jobs in exchange for schnapps. As instructed, I threw down the guts and backed away. Nero snapped down his food and stared at me. His eyes were nobly set in his broad brow. I stepped behind the screen door, but Nero held my gaze.

As I looked into his eyes, which were the same brownish gold as mine, I had my first sensation of self-awareness. I realized that my human body, my human life, was arbitrary. I could have been a dog. An exhilarating sadness gripped me, and then I felt the first intimations of sympathy for another form of creation, for Nero, who had to eat guts from an old pie tin. In the kitchen, there was a ceramic cookie jar in the shape of a fat baker. It was always filled with gingersnaps that had gone stale in the shop. The jar was kept on top of the refrigerator, but was easily reached if I stood on the table. I took two cookies to the back door, opened it a crack, and tossed one of them toward Nero. He caught it with a jump. He caught the second one, too. After that, it became my custom to take a few gingersnaps to the door and toss them to Nero, in the spirit of secretly aiding a fellow prisoner. For I had a confused sensation that we were both captive—in different bodies, true, but with only one dark way out.

Every animal had its use. Most, of course, were there to be slaughtered or, in the case of chickens and guinea hens, to lay eggs and then be slaughtered. The smaller dogs were there to keep my grandparents' feet warm and to accompany them on deliveries. They were given a few pats and scratches, but Nero, as a guard dog, wasn't treated with human affection. Therefore he never begged, wagged his tail, smiled with his tongue lolling, or pricked up his ears with excitement at certain words. He knew no human words except the one I taught him: *gingersnap*. The only sign of his understanding was a keener look in his eyes, a stiller stillness, a slight crouch for the midair catch. But it is probably impossible for our two species, interdependent since the dim beginning of our ascendancy on this earth, not to communicate. Staring at each other, we were exchanging some signal. After being fed or catching his daily gingersnaps, Nero trotted away to lie underneath a rogue pine that had grown up close to the door. When his food was digested, he usually returned to his primary daytime task—attempting to break out of the backyard.

It was well known that Nero was not just looking for freedom. He was infatuated with a mean snub-nosed cocker spaniel named Mitts. She lived on the other side of the fairgrounds with Priscilla Gamrod, the shop's bookkeeper. Her father owned a bar and was known to fling men twice his size out the door by their collar and belt. Priscilla was twenty-five, but she still lived with him.

Her mother had died, leaving the two of them bound by a grief that eased with time but was replaced by Mr. Gamrod's jealous dependence. This had got so bad that he insisted on fighting any man who tried to court her. He'd beaten them all, and Priscilla had put up with it because she hadn't found a man she liked yet anyway. She doted on Mitts and took her everywhere, brushed and beribboned. Once a year, she bred Mitts to Lord Keith, a papered stud who lived on a farm near Long Prairie. She sold the purebred pups only to people who met her standards, and cried when the last one left the house. Nobody knew if Mitts preferred Lord Keith to Nero, because she bit every dog and person within her reach. Priscilla, with her bandaged fingers, often had to cope with Nero's longing, but she never called the city dogcatcher.

Every time Nero broke loose, Jurgen built the fence higher. He used a combination of materials—old pickets, long staves, chicken wire, and spare rebar. He had it up to seven feet now, but the haphazard nature of its construction made the outcome almost certain; there were always bits of wood or metal jutting out on which Nero could gain purchase. For a couple of days now, he had been practicing his ascent. Over and over, he rushed at the fence, each time gaining a few inches of height. From one side of the yard to the other, using subtle variations in each approach, Nero strove. He kept at this for an entire afternoon and could be heard before dawn the next day, throwing himself upward.

When I read the words "dogged pursuit" I see the literal efforts of Nero. The grown-ups in the family were used to this and confident in the seven-foot fence, so I was the only one watching when Nero clambered to the rickety top, balanced, and leaped into space. It was early in the morning, and the shop was already busy, so in theory an entire day could elapse before Nero's services were required and his escape was discovered. I filled my pockets with gingersnaps, told my grandmother I was going to play out in the field, and went straight across the sleepy fairgrounds to Priscilla Gamrod's house.

When Priscilla answered the door, Mitts barked viciously and darted for my ankle, but Priscilla elegantly kicked her dog down the hall with the pointed toe of her shoe. Mitts rolled, skidded, and trotted sullenly before us into the kitchen. She slumped in her pillowed corner, glowering as only a cocker spaniel can glower, while Priscilla sat me at the table and warmed some sugared milk with a bit of coffee in a small blue pan. She also made me cinnamon toast. The kitchen table was white enameled steel, painted with swirling green lines. The chairs were of curved aluminum with fat plastic cushions, green, too. The wallpaper was decorated with little black roosters.

When I told Priscilla that Nero had cleared the fence, she said that she had the hose ready and would give him the works. She said this affectionately and even glanced at Mitts with a sort of amused pride, as if her dog's attractions reflected upon her, too, though she needed no help. Priscilla was round-figured, silky-skinned, rosy, with black curls and great dark pixie eyes. The way her lashes curled, reaching nearly up to her curved brows, entranced me. Her eyes were a warm hazel. It was no wonder that her father fought off boy after boy. I said something about this without thinking.

"Oh, you heard about that," she said, smiling. "He'll have a hell of a time fighting off the man I'm seeing now!"

I wanted to ask who this man was, but right then Mitts yapped. Priscilla looked out the window, and, sure enough, there was Nero. He stood gravely in the scraggle of grass and sand pickers that passed for a yard. I stepped out the back door. "Ginger-snap," I said. Nero's ears pricked up. I was elated. He knew me. He snatched cookies from the air while Priscilla made the phone call, then he turned, listened intently, and loped off. A moment later, my uncle pulled up in the shop's meat truck. I stepped into the kitchen and, it so happened, entered at an angle from which I could just see the front door. Priscilla opened it for my uncle, who kissed her with a fast, furtive gesture, locking his hand for a moment in her black curls.

My uncle was tall and spare, handsome only if you liked thin cheeks and big teeth. He had a protruding Adam's apple, bulging temples, big ears. I didn't think he'd be any match for Priscilla's father. I was sure that their love was doomed, and my uncle was likely to be maimed or killed.

"Any coffee left?"

Uncle Jurgen walked into the kitchen, winked at me, then opened the refrigerator, which held half a frosted lemon layer cake. He grinned as Priscilla entered.

"You'll have your cake and eat it, too," she laughed.

As she cut the cake, she said, teasingly, "Happy birthday to us." Jurgen reached down to pick up Mitts, who bit his hand. Instead of withdrawing his hand, my uncle stuck his fingers out and flicked her nose. He reached for her again. She bit him. He flicked her nose. This happened one more time, but the fourth time he reached for Mitts she didn't bite. She allowed him to pick her up and she sat across his thighs as he ate a piece of cake and scratched her long silky ears.

Uncle Jurgen said that he'd have to spend the rest of the afternoon building the fence higher.

"You should make sure you've got your dog back first," Priscilla said.

"Oh, he won't go far. He's too hung up on poor Mitts."

"Poor Mitts?" I said. "She tried to bite off your fingers!"

My uncle laughed and held up his hand. His long, thin fingers were heavily callused.

"Mitts's teeth can't dent this hide," he said. He stroked the dog's throat, scratched her chin, and made soft clicking noises with his tongue. Mitts looked up at him with wet, adoring eyes.

Priscilla took his plate to the sink. While her back was turned, Jurgen nudged me and nodded at the door. I went outside to sit on the back porch. They talked low for a while, laughed, and then Uncle Jurgen called out that I could catch a ride back with him. The warm truck smelled of scorched foam rubber, smoked sausages, and stale cigars. On the way, he told me that he had plans to marry Priscilla Gamrod. He'd asked her and she'd said yes.

"Won't you have to fight her father?" I asked.

Jurgen said he wasn't worried. I was too shy to disagree with an adult out loud, but what muscles my uncle had were thin and ropy. He even had a slight stoop. Mr. Gamrod stood upright as a fireplug, and his muscles were thick and hard.

At my grandparents' house, I helped my uncle carry some odds and ends of wood to the backyard so that he could add another foot or so to Nero's fence. Jurgen stood on top of the stepladder.

"This is as far as I can work without buying an extension ladder," he said. "And I'm saving for a ring."

The fence was now close to eight feet. When Nero finally turned up, hungry for his supper, I was disappointed that he hadn't kept on running, found his way up north, and joined a wolf pack.

A couple of days later, there was an explosion in the bookkeeping office. Not the usual explosion, which was of papers—toppling stacks, tipping files. This explosion involved a lot of shouting and swearing as Mr. Gamrod strode around the counter and into the office, where Priscilla was writing out invoices.

I was helping my grandmother unpack boxes to restock the cleaning-supply section with glossy cardboard cylinders of Comet and bars of Lava soap. Uncle Jurgen and my grandfather were out on a delivery. When the yelling commenced, my grandmother rushed to the office, slippers flapping, and stood for a moment in the doorway with her hands on her hips.

"Psia krew!"

My grandmother was the daughter of a Polish coal miner, and her one curse, rarely uttered, always silenced the Germans.

Mr. Gamrod held out the wedding-announcement page from the local newspaper. My grandmother took it from him and read it.

"You coulda told us," she said to Priscilla, then nodded at Mr. Gamrod. "They coulda told us."

Mr. Gamrod, happy to take on her hurt indignation along with his own fury, nodded soberly.

Suddenly, there were tears in my grandmother's hard eyes. As we all stood immobilized by those tears, we heard Uncle Jurgen and my grandfather drive to the back entrance. The truck's motor quit, and there was a slide of suspense. They entered the house and came down the hall talking casually, but when they saw us they stopped.

My grandmother rammed herself toward Jurgen and pushed the paper into his chest. She continued down the hall without speaking. We heard the door to the sacred bedroom slam, the dead bolt thwock.

"Well, Mr. Announcement Page," Gamrod said to Jurgen, rolling up his sleeves. "When's it going to be?"

"You'll fight me first," my grandfather said. His sleeves were already rolled up and his thick forearms bulged. Everyone knew about his prize wrestling, but also that his heart was weak.

"If Gamrod needs a fight, I'll fight," Jurgen said. He folded his gangly arms, with the cuffs of his blue plaid shirt neatly buttoned. Even I could tell that the statement was made with a certain irony, pointing out the absurdity of Mr. Gamrod's challenge.

"Daddy," Priscilla said. "I could've eloped!" She shook her black curls at her father and cradled Mitts, whose eyes rolled toward Jurgen.

All of a sudden, Nero set up a quavering high howl from the backyard. His howling was a liquid gargle that mesmerized us until my grandmother opened the bedroom door and shouted at me to run out and throw a bucket of water on the damn dog.

I went into the kitchen and took all the gingersnaps out of the jar. Then I stood in the backyard tossing them to Nero. I ate a couple, too. By the time they were gone, the Gamrods had left and my grandparents and my uncle were sitting in the kitchen, drinking beer and eating slices of summer sausage with dill pickles and rye bread. They were discussing the upcoming fight between Jurgen and Mr. Gamrod. It turned out that they'd agreed to host this fight out in the back field, where there was a sandy spot. They'd meet around dusk. The spectators would bring flashlights. Because the fight was on private property, shielded from the road, it probably wouldn't draw the police. Something in the calm and even good-natured way they discussed the upcoming battle, their laughter at how Mr. Gamrod had roared in, should have reassured me.

During my first full year of school, a lyceum show had been held in the school gym. This show, one of many small educational productions that toured our state, had had a powerful impact on me. The subject was dangerous exotic creatures. It was not a slide show or a movie; the performance featured the animals themselves.

The man who ran the show had a confident air and a polished, domelike head. He was probably called Mr. Johnson, like so many men in the Midwest. He wore a gray three-piece suit and had a young Burmese python draped over his shoulders. He seemed to feed on our shocked murmuring as he proudly carried the patterned bronze loop of muscle to an open blue suitcase. He laid the snake inside and lowered the lid. From another case, he removed a large jar with enough white sand in the bottom to bury a tarantula. Sure enough, when he opened the jar and set it down on its side, an enormous brown spider tiptoed out. Miss Sillet, the fourth-grade teacher, fainted in her chair. None of the children noticed. Mr. Johnson had removed a soft plume from his vest.

"A feather is the only thing that should ever be used to coax along a tarantula," Mr. Johnson said. "They do not like to be poked."

As he brushed the tarantula along, encouraging it to climb the leg of his pants, he described how tarantulas use their long fangs to inject paralyzing venom into their prey. He explained how this venom liquefied the insides of insects, rodents, even small birds. The spiders sucked out this inner soup, leaving only the creature's husk. He told us that tarantulas could live to be thirty years old. The spider paused at his belt and then tested the cloth of Mr. Johnson's sleeve. It continued climbing, with only the lightest touches from the feather, until it was poised on Mr. Johnson's shoulder. There were gasps as its eerily jointed legs used the tip of Mr. Johnson's ear to ascend. Once it had reached the top of Mr. Johnson's head, the tarantula braced its awful legs and lowered its abdomen. There it rested. We were riveted. Mr. Johnson told us that the bite of a tarantula is no more dangerous to a human than a bee sting, but we didn't believe him. After a few minutes, he slowly tipped his head, signaling to the tarantula that it was time to make its way back down his body to the jar of sand. But just as the tarantula was testing the cuff of his trouser leg all hell broke loose.

The lid popped up on the blue suitcase. The young snake writhed through the air like living electrical current and connected with Mr. Johnson. The jolt, as it threw its coils around Mr. Johnson's hips, sent the tarantula spinning like a flailing discus. When the spider hit the ground, it rose to show its fangs and danced aggressively to the front of the stage. In the meantime, Mr. Johnson was trying to stave off the snake's crushing hug. All this occurred just as his two assistants, plus the janitor and our gym teacher, Miss Oten, were carrying in what was supposed to be the show's grand finale, the African rock python.

They were bringing it down the aisle in the longest carrying case I'd ever seen. It was specially made of leather, with mesh windows through which the snake's mottled bulk could be glimpsed. The front of the case had been opened so that all the children could behold the spectacular somnolent indifference of the python's face. But we barely noticed it—we were watching Mr. Johnson. His snake had got the wrap on him and was squeezing tighter with every breath. Mr. Johnson had fallen to the stage floor and was kicking the boards resoundingly, with useless desperation, and not even the air to yelp. The tarantula had stopped prancing about on its hind legs and now picked its way down the side of the stage, away from the dangerous vibrations and toward the screaming children. At that point, the four people carrying the long python case dropped it and rushed to the assistance of Mr. Johnson. They vaulted onto the stage and were trying to pry Mr. Johnson free when the python glided into the mob of children.

Most of us were now standing on our chairs. The cheap tin folding chairs were rickety, and children were crashing to the ground right and left. The teachers didn't know what to do. They kept picking children up and shoving them toward the doors. One was using a collapsed chair to stave off the tarantula. The python slid among the chair legs, and, as if in a nightmare, I fell right in front of it. I looked straight into its wise, primordial face. Its tongue flickered, sensing the currents of pandemonium, and then the forked tip touched my cheek. That's all. It did not open its jaws to try to swallow me whole or attempt to squeeze the life out of me first. It moved away. I thought perhaps I would be marked forever with the python's kiss, but there was no sign of it when I looked in the bathroom mirror. In any case, it was the other snake that dominated my thoughts the night that Uncle Jurgen fought Mr. Gamrod.

My grandfather drew a ring in the sand, and directed the men with flashlights to position themselves just outside the wide circle. That afternoon, I had gone out to the field and cleared the area of sand pickers. The spectators were mostly in favor of Mr. Gamrod's showing a certain leniency. There was talk of not being too harsh on the young man, of cutting him up just a bit, of doing only small damage to his face. They were telling Mr. Gamrod to have his fun but not go overboard. Mainly, they were worried that Priscilla would show up.

Mr. Gamrod divested himself of his shirt. He handed it delicately, by the tip of its collar, to his beer supplier and asked the man to hold it carefully so as not to ruin Priscilla's starching. Uncle Jurgen was wearing a T-shirt and a pair of old dungarees. Both men went barefoot and gloveless. I thought Jurgen was keeping his T-shirt on so as not to reveal his skinny physique, but it turned out that he had another reason. Mr. Gamrod wanted Jurgen to cry quit, or signal quit if he couldn't speak. This was supposed to be a fight to submission, although the fact was that it could be stopped at any time by my grandfather. Or if my grandmother were to charge across the field and yell her Polish curse—it would most certainly stop then. So I was allowed to stay. Jurgen had even argued for it. I stood spellbound at my grandfather's hip.

Dukes up, head down, Mr. Gamrod advanced. His face darkened as he searched out an opening for the punch he would use to knock Jurgen out. That was the plan I'd heard from Gamrod myself: "I'll show mercy, all right—one punch should do it." A shudder rose in me at the look of him with his barbell-trained muscles. He was Mad Dog Vachon—a neckless peg of hairy power. But Jurgen was no Vern Gagne—the straight-arrow champion TV wrestler of those days. He edged out with his fists raised, too, but instead of hopping around he studied Mr. Gamrod with an infuriating professorial air that had no place in the sandy ring. Mr. Gamrod hopped closer; punched the air, as if to test it; then slammed forward to connect with his famous left hook. But Jurgen ducked. In fact, he not only ducked but in a bizarre blur folded his gangly body into a ball, rolled behind Mr. Gamrod, and came back up with an air of calm readiness. Mr. Gamrod whirled, his eyes narrowed, and he charged. Again Jurgen slid from his fists—this time to the far side of the ring. *Badapuckpuck!* Someone made chicken noises. A smile creased Mr. Gamrod's face, the flashlights flickered, and I thought my uncle was finished. Mr. Gamrod plunged at Jurgen and managed to grab hold of his T-shirt so that he could punch him. But after a bit of thrashing about, the punches always missing their target, Jurgen was out of the shirt and had neatly wrapped Mr. Gamrod's arms together with it. Gamrod managed to pull away.

It was what happened next that brought the Burmese python to mind. Jurgen moved. But to say that he simply moved doesn't capture it. He moved the way that that snake had flung itself from the unlatched case. He was one long stream of electric, muscular motion that connected beneath Mr. Gamrod's fists. A twist of Jurgen's leg behind Gamrod's solid calf and the two continued onward, borne down into the sand. Mr. Gamrod was a wrestler also, known for his early years as a champion Greco-Roman grappler on the college circuit. So it was no surprise when he flipped Jurgen onto his back and seemed to pin him down, but as this was not a regular wrestling match, with scorekeeping, Jurgen would have to signal for the match to be over.

It was over in the minds of most of the flashlight holders. A few yelled out that Jurgen was beat. But my grandfather reminded everyone of the rules. In the meantime, Jurgen had wrapped his legs around the bulging mound of Mr. Gamrod, hooking his ankles into the small of Gamrod's back. Perhaps Gamrod was feeling claustrophobic. With an enormous groan of effort, he reared back and tried to punch Jurgen in the head, but Jurgen now pressed his legs together even more tightly, pulling Gamrod down again. This time you could see that Gamrod didn't want to be pulled down. His eyes rolled. He struggled the way Mr. Johnson had struggled. Jurgen's legs, arms, and feet were constantly maneuvering Mr. Gamrod, squeezing at him, positioning him. I thought of the many animals that Jurgen had subdued. Every time Mr. Gamrod strained against him, Jurgen used that energy to his own advantage. He was exhausting Gamrod, pacifying Gamrod, letting Gamrod know what the animals eventually knew: Jurgen was inevitable. His arms were clasped, tight as a drowning child's, around Gamrod's neck. Jurgen's eyes were clear, dispassionate. He wasn't breathing hard, though his face was suffused with color. He was simply waiting for Mr. Gamrod's dizziness to turn into amazement and for Mr. Gamrod to beat his arm on the sand when he understood that his amazement could turn into death.

Mr. Gamrod struck his arm on the ground. Jurgen slid out from under him. He stood and helped Priscilla's father to a wobbly crouch. Then Priscilla herself elbowed in through the circle of men and stood there, holding Mitts. She bent over, made sure her father was all right.

"There's a meatball hot dish still warm in the oven, Dad," she said. "I'll be home late. Get some sleep." She took Jurgen's arm, and they walked about fifty paces before confronting Nero.

"Aw, not you," Jurgen said to the dog.

A length of rope dangled from Nero's collar and he didn't growl when Jurgen picked it up.

"It's time to let him loose in the shop anyway," Jurgen said. He walked him into the store, tossed in a couple of dried-up wieners, and locked up. He and Priscilla left me there, too, in my grandparents' house, and walked off to plan their new life.

The next morning, Jurgen stared at the fence for a long time before leaving in the truck. He returned with a roll of wire and the equipment to attach it to the top of the fence. He tinkered around with the spot on the side of the house where the electrical current fed in from the power pole. He was on the ladder all the rest of the morning, carefully threading the wire. He wouldn't let me near. Nero rested in the shadow of the pine tree.

It was noon by the time Jurgen had finished and flipped the breaker. My grandparents closed up the shop for an hour and each had a beer as they watched from the kitchen windows. It took no time at all. Nero launched himself, scrambled up the fence exactly the way he'd puzzled out the day before. When the electrified wire touched him, he yelped like a puppy and fell, twisting. He lay still a moment, then rose and began to walk in wobbly, widening circles, until he reached the other side of the yard. He stood, panting, then suddenly gathered himself and bounded forward. Again Nero made his peculiar way up the fence, only this time when he reached the wire he snatched it between his teeth before he fell.

Nero shorted out the lights in the house and in the display cases, the fridge, the freezers, and everything else that didn't run off the generator. Then he lay on the ground with the dead cord beside him.

My grandparents and uncle ran around madly trying to restore the power. I went to Nero. He was still breathing. I sat down next to him, and for the first time put my hands on him. I stroked his forehead and scratched behind his ears. When at last he could rise, he dragged himself to the corner of the yard and curled up in the rust-colored pine needles, his nose hidden in his tail. I watched over him for the rest of the afternoon. He was beautiful, like a white wolf in the forest.

Mr. Gamrod could not stop talking about his trip to the other world. To Priscilla, to my grandparents, to the patrons of the bar, and to anyone else who would listen, he would describe how in the clutch of Jurgen's limbs he had died and come to life again. He had not walked into the light. He had not seen Jesus. The only way he could explain it was to say that he had been suspended in a timeless present that held the key to . . . something. He'd felt his arm pound the earth just as he was about to grasp the meaning of it. A few days later, he realized he was no longer afraid. After death he would understand the answers to questions that in this life he couldn't even put into words. Aside from this new assurance, Mr. Gamrod didn't seem much changed.

I didn't get to see a change in Nero, either. He was still quietly recovering when I left, sleeping long days in the pine needles. I went home to my new baby brother.

Six months or so passed before we returned for a Christmas visit. It hadn't snowed for weeks, and the ground was covered with what Midwesterners call "snirt." Everything was gray and grainy, like a blurred old movie. Nero no longer lived in the backyard but in a cage constructed out of the chicken run. The wire had been replaced with a thicker grade and it even ran beneath the ground, Jurgen said. The chicken-wire roof, which had once foiled hawks, now kept Nero from jumping out.

It was one thing to walk out the back door into the yard where Nero lived. It was another thing entirely to walk into his cage. He seemed more dangerous now. His coat had yellowed. He didn't recognize me. Didn't come forward for a gingersnap, didn't even notice the cookies I threw onto the trampled shit-strewn dirt. He was obsessed with an old iron cauldron, which he flipped up and down with jerks of his massive head. He wrestled with it. Rolled it, bit at it. He was raw energy with just one focus.

It was early summer the next time we visited. Nero was losing his winter coat, and clumps stuck out in filthy puffs. He was still rolling his cauldron around but now with only stubs of teeth—he'd broken them on the iron. Jurgen no longer took Nero out to guard the shop. He still worked there but was married to Priscilla now, living several blocks away. My grandparents had installed an electrical alarm system.

One day, with no word to anyone, Jurgen went to the chicken run and shot Nero. I saw him hauling the dog to the back field, by his tail, like a scrap of rug. He carried a shovel. I grabbed another. Together we dug deep into the ground. We lowered Nero down as far as our arms could reach, and dropped him into the timeless present.

Rebecca Hirsch Garcia

A Golden Light

AFTER HER FATHER DIED Sadie stopped moving.

It started with her throat. The day her mother called and told her he was dead she opened her mouth to scream or cry or shout or something, and nothing came out. She pushed her throat muscles together and moved her tongue around until she felt ridiculous and then, at last, a bubble of sound slowly pushed its way out of her mouth. It was a tiny, tinny "no" quickly buried underneath the sobs, which flagged in and out from the receiver. She tried again to say something more, but this time she spoke only silence.

Hello? her mother called over the receiver. Sadie, hello?

I will never be able to talk again, Sadie thought mournfully, and she thoughtlessly placed the phone back in its cradle.

But the loss of sound was only the beginning. It was soon followed by a loss of movement. Walking up and down a flight of stairs became an insurmountable effort; soon even walking on the flattest of flat sidewalks seemed an undertaking too painful to bear. She began to feel like she was struggling underwater each time she stood up on her own two feet. By the time of the funeral her hands and feet had become slow and dimwitted, clumsy and uneasy to maneuver.

At the burial Sadie stood in the front row and, as they lowered the casket into the ground, she realized that she could no longer hear the morbid sounds of the coffin scratching along the dirt. She strained her head forward, listening for the sounds of tears and the unwholesome noise of noses being blown, but there was nothing except a strange humming void.

I've misplaced my ears, she thought, and tried to remember if she had put them on that morning or had simply gone out without them.

She looked around for her sister, or her mother or her brother-in-law; instead she caught the wandering eye of a middle-aged woman, some variant of cousin or family friend. She touched Sadie's hand, her eyes watering in a fresh wave of tears. Be strong, she read off the woman's lips. Sadie nodded vaguely and let her hand be clutched, let herself be dragged into the sea of black cloth that wept and reminisced on her shoulder. They all seemed so sad, but Sadie, dazed from the loss of her senses, kept forgetting what they were being sad for.

After the burial, she fell under a wave of exhaustion. She couldn't even make it out of the cemetery to the car; on the way out she simply sat down to rest on a little bench marked VINER and never got up. If it wasn't for her brother-in-law, who noticed her absence in the car and came looking for her, she might have remained there forever, crouched on the bench like a small frightened creature. He found her sitting there, her fingers roaming desperately over her ears, as if to reassure herself she had not lost them. He had known Sadie since she was a little girl and when he saw her sitting there, looking for her lost ears, it was as if they had fallen through time and they were children again. He plucked her up from the bench and carried her to the car, where her mother and sister were waiting. She fell asleep in his arms before he had even finished buckling her seat belt.

The next thing she knew she was back in her parents' house, surrounded by people she did not know who all seemed to know her. Her mother did not know what to do with her, so she was ensconced among the nearly dead, a group of forgotten wheezing elderly people who pinched her cheeks roughly with their papery fingers and patted their leaking eyes with wrinkled handkerchiefs. Sadie could tell from the force of their expirations on her cheeks that they were shouting their words into each other's dim ears. She was grateful that she could no longer hear them and slid her eyes away to avoid reading their lips. And then, as she waited, hearing nothing and feeling nothing except the slow, mournful reverberations of many feet on the living room floor, she felt her limbs petrifying. Her eyelids began falling slowly down, then up, then back down again. Terrified, she somehow managed to excuse herself and stumbled away toward the stairs. She crawled up the steps to the warmth of her old bed, kicking off her shoes and curling, blissful-deep, under the covers. When she woke up it was dark outside and the warm, familiar body of her sister was curled catlike around her.

Get out, she said, or tried to say. She found she could still at least turn over and so she did that and wedged her elbow cruelly into her sister's side, wriggling deeper and deeper until she woke up. What? her sister queried in the raspy voice of the newly awoken, but Sadie was deaf to her pleas.

In a quick minute the last of Sadie's patience was lost, run off perhaps to join all the sounds which she could no longer hear or make. Rallying the last of her strength she planted her feet firmly into her sister's back and pushed her off the bed.

She could feel her sister's tears as she got up off the floor and walked out of the room. She could feel the slam of the door even though she had gone deaf. When her sister had gone and she could not hear even a trace of angry feet stomping down the hallway she began to regret having pushed her out. She felt very small and alone in the dark of her room and for a while there was no difference between her opened eyes and her shut ones. She thought she had gone blind. She wanted to go and hug her sister and beg her forgiveness for her own selfishness and say, I'm sorry I can't cry with you, I'm sorry I can't give you what you need, I love you, but it was already too late for that. She had grown roots, she was immobile, and her vocal cords had died away, so rather than try to uproot herself she fell asleep instead.

When she woke up again her mother was there. It was morning and she was smoking and staring out the window, smoking as if nothing had happened, as if she belonged there in Sadie's room by her window, as if Sadie were a little girl again and her mother had come in to check on her daughter, the most natural thing in the world to check on your daughter, leaving her husband alone in their bedroom to sleep. She tried to think of the last time that they had been together in this room and she fell upon a memory of long ago. When she was little she had lost her sister's hat and her sister had yelled at her and her father was gone, as usual. It had been her mother who had coaxed her into opening the locked door of her room, who had pulled her onto her lap and told her that there was no use crying over spilt milk or lost hats and kissed her until all the tears ran away.

She willed her mother to come to her again as she had come to her before and run her hands through her hair and hold her as she cried. Instead she stood there smoking as if she hadn't realized that Sadie had woken up and that she needed her. She was filled suddenly with an insensible hatred, a pulse of anger which coursed through her body making her flush with fatigue. Get out, she started to say, and fell asleep halfway through saying it.

The psychiatrist that her mother lured up to Sadie's room told her that this was normal. She wore a beautiful plum skirt suit and round-toed brown shoes, the same shoes that Sadie owned, the same shoes she had worn to the funeral and then kicked off her feet on her way to bed. Sadie thought their matching shoes were a sign, from God, the universe, or whoever, and so she stared at the shoes as the psychiatrist told her that there was no normal reaction to grief, which, conversely, meant that any reaction was normal. As she said this, Sadie realized that she could hear again. The suddenness of this abrupt return of sound and sense startled her so that she almost began to laugh. Instead the laugh turned into a yawn that went on for a century in which everything stayed exactly as it was. The psychiatrist blinked and the yawn was broken, the century over in a second. The psychiatrist asked Sadie all sorts of questions which Sadie might have answered had she been able to speak. I need to sleep, Sadie thought as her eyes closed and she drifted off. The psychiatrist seemed to understand.

Sadie's mother and sister and brother-in-law all took turns watching over Sadie. Our Sleeping Beauty, they called her as they watched the slow rise and fall of her sleep breath. They humored her for a few weeks. A sleeping girl, after all, requires nothing but a little food and a little worry, and the worry was a blessing, a reason to look in front of themselves, and not into their own hearts. They prodded her gently into wakefulness and tried to feed her the lightest of foods: juice and Jell-O, dried toast and soups. She nibbled at them in a daze then fell into sleep again and again. They tried to get her to talk or to move or to see, but it seemed she could no longer do any of these things very well at all. They brought in doctors, who sometimes said her soul was sick, or that she was a medical mystery, or that there was nothing wrong with her at all. The latter type of doctor they considered to be a complete quack and they would be sure to always smile and nod, being kinder and gentler than they would have with someone they considered sane. No matter their opinion of Sadie, no one knew how to fix her. Her family began to believe she was broken forever and adjusted themselves accordingly.

And then a strange thing happened. Sadie woke up one evening to find her room lit up in gold. It was the magic hour, the last hour of sunlight in a day, when everything was bathed in golden light and the warmth of the fading sun made the colors of the sky glow ember bright. She wondered suddenly if she had read that in a book or if her father had told her that. And as she thought that word, the word *father*, a golden flicker burst into the golden room and danced across her legs and arms and face before settling gently on the wall beside her bed. She reached out and placed her hand upon the dancing flicker. Papa? she asked.

It was the first word she had spoken in a year.

In the morning she was a little better. She sat up in bed and said please and thank you to her mother's shock and amazement. For a few minutes strung together she had a brief, quotidian conversation about breakfast foods with her sister. But her mind was elsewhere; she could think of nothing but the flicker of light, a beam of brightness in a field of gold.

From then on, every night at the magic hour, the golden flicker danced into Sadie's bedroom. She placed her hands on the light and let it thread through her fingers. She found that the flicker let her fall asleep with her heart at ease and wake up in the morning with the strength to last through the day. She could get up and get dressed and go downstairs and eat breakfast with her mother like a normal person. She could hear and speak and move her limbs, her flesh no longer cold as a statue. She could be good for her mother and strong for her sister, she could count on both hands over and over again the good things that she did every day. Yes, she was good. One morning they ran out of milk at breakfast and she volunteered to go to the corner store and buy more. When the cashier flirted with her she flirted back and gave him the first smile she had been able to give since her mother had called her that long, long time ago. She was happy, in a way.

One night she went to her room at the hour only to find her sister already there. She was sitting there on Sadie's bed with a book in her hands and when she heard her footsteps she looked up at her with a smile that reached out to Sadie's heart. She opened her mouth to speak only to close it again and Sadie wondered wildly if her former disease was catching and her sister had gone suddenly mute as she once had.

The sun was setting and the room had turned a brilliant gold. Look, her sister said suddenly.

It was the magic hour and the flicker danced in a beam of light between them. Sadie's sister reached out her hand and Sadie's light, a glimmer of brilliance in a room of gold, played across her fingers. Suddenly Sadie felt happy; happy that her sister was in her room and that she had seen the light and that Sadie could explain everything to her. She felt sure quite suddenly that her sister would understand, that she was the only one who *could* understand and that even if she hadn't stumbled into her room unexpectedly like this, she would have brought her here eventually in order to show her the flicker. Sadie reached out for her hand and saw suddenly that she wasn't looking at the flicker at all anymore, but out, out through the window. She turned to see what her sister was looking at and saw her little next door neighbor, a child named Tanya, whose room was directly across from her own. She was playing with a little pocket mirror, flicking it lazily back and forth, now catching the light, now letting it go. It flashed across Sadie's face and for a blissful second she was blind.

Do you see that? her sister asked, pointing. Can you see?

Chinelo Okparanta

Fairness

W E GATHER OUTSIDE THE classroom, in the break between
morning and afternoon lectures, all of us girls not blessed
with skin the color of ripe pawpaw. We stand there, on the concrete steps, chewing groundnuts and meat pies, all of us with the
same dark skin, matching, like the uniforms we wear. All of us,
excepting Onyechi of course, because her skin has now turned
color, and we are eager to know how. It is the reason she stands
with us, though she no longer belongs. She is now one of the others, one of the girls with fair skin.

Clara looks at Onyechi, her eyes narrow, a suspicious look.
Boma chuckles in disbelief. She claps her hands, her eyes widen.
She exclaims, "Chi m O! *My God!* How fast the miracle!" Onyechi shakes her head, tells us that it was no miracle at all. It is then
that she tells us of the bleach. Boma chuckles again. I think of
Eno, of returning home and telling her what Onyechi has said.
I listen and nod, trying to catch every bit of the formula. Clara
says, "I don't believe it." Onyechi kisses the palm of her right
hand and raises it high toward the sky, a swear to God, because
she insists that she is not telling a lie. Our skin is the color not of
ripe pawpaw peels, but of its seeds. We are thirsty for fairness. But

even with her swearing, we are unconvinced, a little too disbelieving of what Onyechi has said.

Hours later, I sit on a stool outside, in the backyard of our house. I sit under the mango tree, across from the hibiscus bush. Ekaite is at the far end of the backyard where the clotheslines hang. She collects Papa's shirts from the line, a row of them, which wave in the breeze like misshapen flags. Even in the near darkness, I can see the yellowness of Ekaite's skin. A natural yellow, not like Onyechi's or some of the other girls'. Not like Mama's.

Eno sits with me, and at first we trace the lizards with our eyes. We watch as they race up and down the gate. We watch as they scurry over the gravel, over the patches of grass. When we are tired of watching, we dig the earth deep, seven pairs of holes in the ground, and one large one on each end of the seven pairs. We take turns tossing our pebbles into the holes. We remove the pebbles, also taking turns. We capture more and more of them until one of us wins. The game begins again.

The sounds of car engines mix with the sounds of the crickets. It is late evening, and the sky is gray. Car headlights sneak through the spaces between the metal rods of the gate. The gray becomes a little less gray, a little like day. Still, mosquitoes swirl around, and I slap them, and I slap myself, and Eno stops with the game, unties one of the two wrappers from around her waist, hands it to me.

At the clothesline, Ekaite is slapping too. She is slapping even more than Eno and I. Her skirt only comes down to her knees; she is not wearing a wrapper with which she can cover her legs.

I say, "They bite us all the same."

Eno says, "No, they bite Ekaite more. Even the mosquitoes prefer fair skin." The words come out like a mutter. Her tone is something between anger and dejection. I imagine the flesh of a ripe pawpaw. It is not quite the shade of Ekaite's skin, but it, too, is fair. I throw Eno's wrapper over my legs.

Emmanuel walks by, carrying a bucket. Water trickles down

the side. A chewing stick hangs from the side of his mouth. His lips curve into a crooked smile. He stops by Ekaite, maybe they share a joke, because then comes the cracking of his laughter, and then hers, surging, rising, then tapering into the night sounds, at the very moment when it seems that they might become insufferable. I look at Eno. Eno frowns.

Emmanuel pours the water out of the bucket, at the corner of the compound where the sand dips into the earth like a sewer. The scent of chlorine billows in the air, and I think of Onyechi and her swearing. I exhume the memory of the morning break, toss it about in my mind, like a pebble in the air, as if to get a feel for its texture, its potential, its capacity for success. And then I tell it to Eno.

When the sky grows black, I hand Eno back her wrapper, and we enter the house. We go together to the bathroom. First we pour the bleach into the bucket. Only a quarter of the way full. Then we watch the water bubble out of the faucet. We inhale and exhale deeply, and the sound of our breathing is weirdly louder than the sound of the running water. We caress the buckets with our eyes as if we are caressing our very hearts. The bucket fills. We turn the faucet off and gaze into the tub. We are still gazing when Ekaite calls Eno. Her voice booms down the corridor, and Eno runs off, because she knows well that she should not be in the bathroom with me. Because Eno knows that she must instead use the housegirls' bathroom, outside in the housegirls' quarters in the far corner of the backyard. But mostly, when Ekaite calls, Eno runs off, because dinner will be served in just an hour, and Eno will have to help in the preparation of it.

At the dining table, Papa sits at the head, Mama by his side. The scent of egusi soup enters through the kitchen. Mama picks up her spoon, looks into it, unscrews the tiny canister, still with the spoon in her hand. It is lavender, the canister, and the lipstick in it is a rich color, red like the hibiscus flower; and it rises from the container, slowly, steadily, like a lizard cautiously peeking out of a hole. Overhead the ceiling fan rattles and buzzes. The air conditioner hums, like soft snoring. In the kitchen we hear the clang-clanging of Ekaite's and Eno's food preparation: of the pestle hitting the mortar, yam being pounded for the soup. Off and on, there is the sound of the running faucet. We listen to the clink of silverware on glass. I imagine the plates and utensils being set out on the granite countertop, and then I hear a sound like the shutting of the fridge, that shiny, stainless steel door all the way from America. And I wonder if Ekaite ever takes the time to look at her reflection in the door. And if she does, does she see herself in that superior way in which I imagine all fair people see themselves?

A bowl of velvet tamarinds sits at the center of the table, a glass bowl in the shape of a dissected apple, its short glass stem leading to a small glass leaf. Mama got it on one of her business trips overseas. She returned from that trip with other things too— silk blouses from Macy's, some Chanel, Bebe, Coach, some Nike wear. The evening she returned, she tossed all the items in piles on her side of the bed. She tossed herself contentedly, too, on the bed, on a small area on Papa's side, the only remaining space. She held up some of the overseas items for me to see. One blouse she lifted up closer to me, held it to my chest. It was the yellow of a ripe pineapple. "Will lighten you up," she said. She tossed it to me. I didn't reach for it in time. It dropped to the floor.

The first magazine arrived two weeks later, *Cosmopolitan*, pale faces and pink lips decorating the cover, women with hair the color of fresh corn. Perfect arches above their eyes. Next was *Glamour*, then *Elle*. And every evening following that, Mama would sit on the parlor sofa for hours, flipping through the pages of the magazines, her eyes moving rapidly over and over the same pages, as if she were studying hard for the JAMB, as if there were some fashion equivalent to those university exams.

I stare at the dissected apple, at the velvet tamarinds in it. I imagine picking one of the tamarinds up, a small one, something smaller than those old kobo coins, smaller than the tiniest one of them. Ekaite shuffles into the dining room, Eno close behind. They find themselves some space between me and the empty chair next to me. Ekaite sets the first tray down, three bowls of pounded yam.

She lifts the first bowl out of the tray. She sets it on the place mat in front of Mama. Mama smiles at her, thanks her. Then, "Osiso, osiso," Mama says. "*Quick, quick,* bring the soup!" Ekaite hurries back to where Eno is standing, takes out a bowl of soup from Eno's tray, sets it in front of Mama. Mama says, "Good girl. Very good girl." The skin around Mama's eyes wrinkles from her deepening smile. Ekaite nods and does not smile back. Eno, by my side, is more than unsmiling, and I can hardly blame her. But then I remember the bucket in the bathroom, and I feel hope billowing in me. Hope rising: the promise of relief.

It is Eno who serves Papa and me our food. She puts our dishes of pounded yam and soup on our place mats, still unsmiling. Papa thanks her, but it is a thank-you that lacks all the fawning that Mama's for Ekaite had. He thanks her in his quiet, aloof way, as if his mind is in his office, or somewhere far from home.

Mama waves Eno away. I watch her hand waving, the gold rings on her fingers, the bracelet that dangles from her wrist. I take in the yellowness of her hand. I think of the bucket in the bathroom, and I feel that hope again in me.

"Uzoamaka," Mama says, when Eno and Ekaite have disappeared into the kitchen. "You are looking very tattered today."

Papa squints at her. I don't respond.

"It's no way to present yourself at the dinner table," she says. The words tumble out of her mouth, one connected to the other, and I imagine rolls of her pounded yam all lined up on her plate, no space between them. Like her words, I think, that American way, one word tumbling into the next with no space between.

Papa looks at me for a moment, taking me in as if for the first time in a long time. "How was school today?" he asks.

"Fine," I say.

Mama says, "A good week so far. A good month even. Imagine, an entire month and no strike! Surprising, with the way those lecturers are always on strike."

"No, no strike so far," I say.

"In any case," Mama says. "Not to worry." She pauses. "Arrangements are already being made."

Papa shakes his head slightly, barely perceptibly, but we both see, Mama and I.

"She needs a good education," Mama says to him, as if to counter the shaking of his head. She turns to me. "You need a good education," she says. It is not a new idea, this one of a good education, but she has that serious look on her face, as if she is weighing it with that thoughtfulness that accompanies new ideas. "That is what America will give you," she says. "A solid education. And no strikes. Imagine, with a degree from America, you can land a job with a big company here, or maybe even remain in America. Land of opportunities." She smiles at me. Her smile is wide.

Papa stuffs a roll of soup-covered pounded yam into his mouth. He keeps his eyes on me. Mama turns back to her food. She rolls her pounded yam, dips it into the bowl of soup, swallows. For a while, no one speaks.

"In the meantime, you can't walk around looking tattered the way you do, shirt untucked, hair unbrushed. As for your face, you'd do well to dab some powder on. It will help brighten you up."

Papa clears his throat. Mama turns to look at him. His eyes narrow at her. She starts to speak, but her words trail into a murmur and then into nothing at all.

There is another silence. This time it is Mama who clears her throat. Then she turns to me. She says, "Even Ekaite presents herself better than you do. The bottom line is that you could learn a little something from her. Housegirl or not."

I roll my eyes and feel the heat rising in my cheeks.

"Very well-mannered, that one. Takes care of herself. Beautiful all around." It is not the first time she is saying this.

I roll my eyes like I always do. "Eno is pretty too," I counter. It is the first time that I am countering Mama on Ekaite. I only intend to mutter it, but it comes out louder than a mutter. I look up to find Mama glaring at me. I catch Papa's eyes on me, a little sharper than before.

"Eno is pretty too," Mama repeats, singsongy, mockingly. "Foolish Eno. Dummy Eno." She has to say "dummy" twice, because the first time it comes out too Nigerian, with the accent on the last syllable instead of on the first. She tells me that Eno is no comparison to Ekaite. Not just where beauty is concerned. What a good housegirl Ekaite is, she says. She adds, an unnecessary reminder, that when Ekaite was around Eno's age, which is to say fourteen, the same age as me, Ekaite already knew how to make egusi and okra soup. And what tasty soups Ekaite made as early as fourteen! Even Ekaite's beans and yams, Mama continues, were the beans and yams of an expert, at fourteen. "The girl knows how to cook," she concludes. "Just a good girl all around." She pauses. "Eno is no comparison. No comparison at all."

Papa clears his throat. "They're both good girls," he says. He nods at me, smiles, a weak smile. In that brief moment I wonder what he knows. Whether he knows, like I do, that it's only bias, the way Mama feels about Ekaite. Whether he knows, like I do, that the reason for the bias is that Ekaite's face reminds her of the faces she sees on her magazines from abroad. Because, of course, Ekaite's complexion is light and her nose is not as wide and her lips not as thick as mine or Eno's. I look at him and I wonder if he knows, like I do, that Mama doesn't go as far as saying these last bits because, of course, she'd feel a little shame in saying it.

He dips his pounded yam into his soup. Mama does the same.

I don't touch my food. Instead, I stare at the velvet tamarinds, and I remember the first time she came back with boxes of those creams. Esoterica, Movate, Skin Success, Ambi. It was around the time the television commercials started advertising them—the fade creams. And we'd go to the Everyday Emporium, and there'd be stacks of them at the entrance, neat pyramids of creams. It was around the time that the first set of girls in school started to grow lighter. Mama's friends, the darker ones, started to grow lighter, too. Mama did not at first grow light with them. She was cautious. She'd only grow light if she had the best quality of creams, not just the brands they sold at the Everyday Emporium. She wanted first-rate, the kinds she knew America would have. And so she made the trip and returned with boxes of creams.

Movate worked immediately for her. In just a few weeks, her skin had turned that shade of yellow. It worked for her knuckles, for her knees. Yellow all around, uniform yellow, almost as bright as Ekaite's pawpaw skin.

She insisted I use them too. With Movate, patches formed all over my skin, dark and light patches, like shadows on a wall. She insisted I stop. People would know, she said. Those dark knuckles and kneecaps and eyelids. People would surely know. We tried Esoterica next. A six-month regimen. Three times a day. No progress at all. Skin Success was no success. Same with Ambi. "Not to worry," Mama said. "They're always coming up with new products in America. Soon enough we'll find something that works."

We must have been on Ambi the day Ekaite walked in on us— into my bedroom, not thinking that I was there. I should have been at school. She was carrying a pile of my clothes, washed and dried and folded for me.

Ekaite looked at the containers of creams on my bed.

Mama chuckled uncomfortably. "Oya ga-wa," she said. *Well, go ahead.*

Ekaite walked to my dresser. The drawers slid open and closed. Empty-handed now, she walked back toward the door.

Mama chuckled again and said, "Uzoamaka here will soon be fair like you."

Ekaite nodded. "Yes, Ma." There was a confused look on her face, as if she were wondering at the statement.

Mama cleared her throat. "Fair like me too."

Ekaite nodded again. Then she turned to Mama. "Odi kwa mma otu odi." *She's fine the way she is.*

Mama shook her head. "Oya ga-wa! Osiso, osiso." The door clicked closed.

I tell Mama that I'm not feeling well. An upset stomach. I excuse myself from the table before Mama has a chance to respond.

I carry my dishes into the kitchen, where Eno is waiting for me. Ekaite sits on a stool close to the floor. I feel her eyes on me and on Eno.

Inside the bathroom, the air is humid and smells clean, purified, a chemical kind of freshness. There is no lock on the door, but we make sure to close it behind us.

Eno holds the towel and stands back, but I call her to me, because I am again finding myself skeptical of the water and of the bleach. In my imagination, I see Clara's suspicious eyes, and I hear Boma's disbelieving laugh. Fear catches me, and I think perhaps we should not bother, perhaps we should just pour everything out. But then I hear Mama's voice, saying, "Foolish Eno. Dummy Eno." I take the towel from Eno. "You should go first," I say. It is a deceitful reason that I give, but it is also true: "Because you're not supposed to be here. That way you'll be already done by the time anyone comes to chase you out."

Eno nods. She concedes straightaway.

She gets on her knees, bends her body over the wall of the bathtub so that her upper half hangs horizontally above the tub, so that her face is just above the bucket.

"We'll do only the face today," I say. "Dip it in until you feel something like a tingle."

She dips her face into the water. She stays that way for some time, holding her breath. Even if I'm not the one with my face submerged, it is hard for me to breathe. So much anticipation.

Eno lifts up her face. "My back is starting to ache, and I don't feel anything."

"You have to do it for longer," I say. "Stand up, stretch your back. But you have to try to stay longer."

Eno stands up. She lifts her hands above her head in a stretch. She gets back down on her knees, places her face into the bucket again.

"Only get up when you feel the tingling," I say.

Time passes.

"Do you feel it yet?"

The back of Eno's head moves from side to side, a shake with her face still in the water.

More time passes.

"Not yet?"

The back of Eno's head moves again from side to side.

"Okay. Come up."

She lifts her face from the water first. She stands up. The color of her skin seems softer to the eyes, just a little lighter than before. I smile at her. "It's working," I say. "But we need to go full force."

"Okay," she says. "Good." She watches as I pour the liquid from the bucket into the tub. We both watch as the water drains; we listen as it gurgles down the pipe. I take the bucket out of the tub, place it in a corner of the bathroom by the sink. The bath bowl is sitting in the sink. I pick it up, hold it above the tub, pour the bleach straight into it. I get down on my knees, call Eno to my side, tell her to place her face into the bowl. She does. Only a little time passes, and then she screams, and her scream billows in the bathroom, fills up every tiny bit of the room, and I am dizzy with claustrophobia. Then there is the thud and splash of the bowl in the tub, then there is the thud of the door slamming into the wall. Ekaite rushes toward us, sees that it is Eno who is in pain. She reaches her hands out to Eno, holds Eno's face in her palms. Eno screams, twists her face. Her cheeks contort as if she is sucking in air. She screams and screams. I feel the pain in my own face. Ekaite looks as if she feels it too, and for a moment I think I see tears forming in her eyes. Papa looms in the doorway, then enters the bathroom. He looks fiercely at me. He asks, "What did you do to her? What did you do?" In the doorway, I see Mama just watching, her eyes flicking this way and that.

"What did you do?" Papa asks again. I turn to him, pleading, wanting desperately to make my case, but I don't find the words. I turn to Mama. I beg her to explain. She looks blankly at me, a little confusion in her eyes. I stand in the middle of them, frozen with something like fear, something not quite guilt.

By then, even Emmanuel has made his way into the house, abandoning his post at the gate. He stands just behind Mama, and his peering eyes seem to ask me that same question: *What did you do?*

My legs feel weak. I turn to Eno, I smile at her. I think of Mama with her yellow skin, with her creams. "Don't worry," I say. "We'll find something that works." Eno screams.

They leave the bathroom quickly then, all of them, Ekaite and Papa leading Eno. The door crashes closed behind them, their voices becoming increasingly distant, still frenzied. I blink my eyes as if to blink myself awake.

Days later, when the scabs start to form, I imagine peeling them ·off like the hard shell of the velvet tamarind. Eno's flesh underneath the scabs is a pinkish-yellow like the tamarind pulp, only a little like a ripe pawpaw peel. And even if I know that this scabby fairness of hers is born of injury, a temporary fairness of skinless flesh, patchy, and ugly in its patchiness, I think how close she has come to having skin like Onyechi's, and I feel something like envy in me, because what she has wound up with is fairness after all, fairness, if only for a while.

Kristen Iskandrian

The Inheritors

S HE AND I WORKED together in a consignment shop called
Second Chances, which many people thought was a homeless
shelter or a soup kitchen due to the name; the round, convivial
font on the sign; the lack of any qualifying tagline; and the part
of town it was in. Also, the front windows were thickly curtained,
making it necessary to go inside to find out what was inside. In
fact, I had gone there initially to inquire about volunteer work,
but as soon as I entered I felt compelled to pretend that there had
been no mistake, that I was a bona fide thrifter, and when the
owner introduced himself it seemed inevitable that I would either
buy something or ask for a job. The other person in the shop
came over from where she had been doing something with safety
pins; greeted me curtly, one pin in her mouth; and asked the
owner a question about a credenza. Immediately, she reminded
me of someone I couldn't place. For weeks after I started working there, having abandoned my plan to achieve some degree of
insight about my life through unpaid service to others, she irritated me, because she had used the word "credenza," but more
so because she was familiar in a stubbornly untraceable way. I
couldn't look at her without not seeing her and seeing instead a

placeholder, a version of her as she was reflected by my straining memory. Then I realized that it wasn't a person she reminded me of, but a thing, a thing depicting a person, and by then the gradations of recall and association had blended into a kind of folkloric confusion to which she, in my mind, remained bound.

The thing she reminded me of was a painting that used to hang in my parents' living room of a girl waiting for a train that was approaching from the upper-right corner of the canvas. The girl stood with her back to the living room, relieved or frightened, who could know, by the train's imminent arrival, with her wrists poking out from the too-short sleeves of her red jacket, one hand white-knuckling the handle of a weathered suitcase, the other stretching itself, fingers spread and pointing downward, as though trying to pull clean of its arm. Her feet were close together and turned slightly inward, and her legs, thick and a bit misshapen, shone whitely where her gray skirt ended. The painter probably wasn't much of an artist; I think my parents bought it at one of those hotel expos, along with a few smeary watercolors in thick gilt frames that hung in the powder and guest rooms. But I always liked this girl and wished I could see her face, and H. Teale, whoever that was, had done a nice job with her hair, a bob that looked womanly somehow, not the flaxen, glistening hair of children, but dusty and heavy. Sad hair. The hair and the stance of protracted waiting are what brought her to mind when I thought of the painting, and what brought the painting to mind when I saw her.

I don't know what happened to it. After my mother died, a lot of things went into boxes that then disappeared, and for a while I hoped and half believed that it would turn up in the shop, and I imagined that I would have a hard time deciding whether to give it to her or keep it for myself. Most of what's now in my dad's condominium in Florida, save for a few ashtrays and photo albums, is unrecognizable. I don't like going there. It makes me sad, being amid all of that desperate, widower-y newness. It's the sort of sad that makes me angry, a feeling she termed *sangria* during a particularly slow day at work, with not a little bit of pride. She claimed as a pastime the reappropriation of words and was oblivious to how distracting it was in the midst of serious stories. She also greatly enjoyed using certain expressions and figures of speech, however wrongly, such as, for example, *ad nauseam, trump card, au courant,* and countless others. I like being sad, which mystified her; I like it until I reach the nadir where sadness changes, as if chemically, to repulsion and self-loathing, making me wish that I was "capable" of "handling" things instead of turning away from them in disgust until my disgust disgusts me, and my anger at my inadequacy as a human being angers me, and all of that pure, easy, delectable sorrow gets squandered. She refused, cheerfully, to understand this, and it wasn't her refusal that was maddening but her cheer.

But both of us liked old things. She liked them as a lifestyle, a matter of ethics. She clung to old things the way I cling to sadness. And she could be emphatic, which could be tiresome.

"There's just no need for it. This world is choking with stuff, drowning in it. I think there is enough stuff in the world for every single person to have plenty, enough old bikes for every kid in the whole world to have a bike and enough coats for everyone to have a coat. Buying new, it's pretty much criminal," she said. "Everything, and I mean everything, in my apartment is pre-owned."

"Same here," I said, which wasn't completely true. "Except for socks and underwear. That I can't do."

She sniffed. "Oh." She was sorting buttons and had a large red one between her teeth. "That doesn't bother me," she said around the button. "In fact"—she took the button out—"my mom got me a three-pack of underwear for Christmas last year and I never opened it."

"What about your appliances?" I asked. My landlord had put in a new refrigerator that year. I loved it. Its hum was almost melodic, and the freezer made perfect half-moons of ice, automatically.

"Nope," she said. "Old, old, old. My stove takes twenty minutes to heat up and then burns everything." She sounded pleased. "So do you want the underwear?"

I checked to see if she was joking. She was not. "No," I said. "But . . . thank you."

She made a face. "Fine," she said, moving some buttons around on the counter. "It's a shame, though, since you like brand-new underwear and everything."

For a while, I wasn't sure what kind of friends we were, she and I. It appeared at first that we could become close, but I don't tend to make friends like that. My closest friend had been my boyfriend once, but we somehow transitioned seamlessly from having sex to not having sex and were able to meet each other for breakfast and watch movies on the weekends and fall asleep on each other in comfortable and unromantic positions.

Then he moved to Oregon to be with someone he'd known for a week, and my life fell apart a bit, as it would have if we had never stopped dating. I hated Oregon with a hatred that became almost exciting. There were other men, before and after, and other friendships, mostly before, but nothing lasting, nothing remarkable. So I remained confused about relationships, all of them, and she seemed especially hard to place. I couldn't even remember what she looked like when she wasn't around; every time I saw her, her features came as a vague surprise. I wanted to know how she felt about me, if she considered me a person in her life or just a person. If she asked for a ride home, did that mean something? Probably less than it would mean if she borrowed a sweater. I wish that people, eligible friends like her, came with conversion charts. Without mile markers, material guidelines, I feel lost. Mornings, I looked hard at myself in the mirror and practiced making kind, open expressions. But then I would walk around brushing my teeth and return to the mirror and see my face as it normally was—worried and weirdly cavernous, everything pushed back, my cheekbones and eyelids like awnings. Throughout the day

I reminded myself to smile but then would do so at the wrong time—not after a joke or greeting but in the middle of a conversation when it was my turn to speak, when certain words, and not a facial contortion, were appropriate, or else alone in the aisle of a grocery store, grinning at boxes and cans like a demented person. Having a disruptive mien, I felt certain, was not conducive to making friends. This had been my problem throughout school, throughout my life.

"You always look like you're up to something," she said.

"Like what?" I concentrated on looking hapless. I felt hapless, and I wanted my face to look hapless also. That nothing about me happens automatically, without self-consciousness, seems to me significant. Or maybe it is my thinking so that makes it seem that way. In general, I had too many thoughts about my thoughts, a condition that translated into an uncontrollable urge to doodle if pen and paper were at hand. "Hypergraphia," the school nurse had called it.

"No, the 'something' is part of the expression—'up to something,'" she said. She sounded exasperated, like a teacher, or a substitute teacher. "Identifying the 'something' defeats the idiom."

"Oh," I said. "I'm not, I don't think."

She looked at me for a long moment. "At first I was sure you were stealing things. When you drove me home I was going to make an excuse for you to open your trunk."

I laughed. She laughed. "What would you have said?"

"I don't know, I couldn't think of anything. Something about your spare tire." We were laughing hard now, just letting the laughter be the reason for more laughter. I felt something shift, something skeletal and real, like discovering a new vertebra and then walking differently. We were nearly friends now, and for the moment, I wasn't questioning it.

At a bar in the early afternoon, she talked about being adopted. That was the first time she'd ever mentioned it and subsequently it came up a lot, casually and in passing. The owner had told us to close early. It had been a slow day and a slow week; the whole town appeared to be hibernating or shopping in department stores. She took the lack of business personally.

"No one cares about stories anymore, about history," she said as she counted out the register. "The world doesn't want a lampshade that is a lampshade. A lampshade that collects dust and gets dusted every week by a person, maybe an old lady, maybe a divorced man. They want biodynamic lampshades, or lampshades that double as clever hats or wall sconces."

She was probably right. Everything did seem newly invested in multifunctionality. My father had a refrigerator with a television built into it. Unless it was, maybe, a television with a refrigerator built around it. I looked about me and everything in the store looked dingy, primitive.

"Those are pretty," she said. "I'll probably buy one." I was folding a stack of tea towels, softened with age. I imagined the Floridian widowers' variety: self-cleaning, self-folding. I saw them scrubbing out their own stains, embroidered corners curling in like starfish, while maybe simultaneously announcing the time. I wanted to say this to her, wanted her to find me funny, and I also wanted to unravel her, to find a loose thread and pull at it, as though she were the towels I was folding, which felt suddenly twee and self-satisfied.

"Are these called 'tea towels'?" I asked. "Tea towels?" My voice was high, almost hysterical. "It doesn't even sound like English."

She looked at me quizzically.

"It sounds like some old Welsh saying reserved for wedding days," I said. "Wedding days during the rainy season." I don't know why I felt cross. "Tee-tow-wuhl."

"That's silly. Tea. Towel. It makes perfect sense," she said.

"But why are they called that? Are they only supposed to be used for cleaning up tea? For wiping one's fingers if they get tea on them? Aren't they just fancy dishcloths? What is their meaning?" I wanted to stop, but felt unable. And she wasn't cooperating. "Seriously, who has the time for tea towels?"

"What's wrong with you?" she asked.

"I don't know." I didn't know.

"We should drink beer," she said. "Do you want to drink beer?" It was a nick-of-time clemency. It was okay with her that we did not share a sense of humor, that she liked to laugh at real things as they happened and I liked to laugh at imaginary and macabre things that would never happen, that she took most things seriously whereas I did not, and that these characteristics made each of us occasionally lonely and agitated around the other. I felt grateful, humbled by her forgiveness, and I did my best to leave it at that, without further aggravation for unknowingly having needed it.

We turned out the lights and she locked up. I drove. She didn't have a car. She fiddled with the radio, as she usually did when I took her home, then turned it off.

At the bar, I drank my first beer very quickly. She was only about a quarter way through hers. "Two years ago, I started calling adoption agencies and asking if they had my records."

"Why didn't you just ask your parents for them?" I concentrated on saying every word. The beer made me feel pleasantly out of control.

"My parents insist that I'm not adopted. They insist that I am their biological child," she said. "But I know I'm not. I just know it."

"How do you know?" I was intensely curious. The intensity of my curiosity seemed, to me, to be worthy of discussion in itself.

She took a straw from the plastic cube on the bar that also held cocktail napkins. She stuck it in her beer. After a labored sip, she looked at me closely. "I know that I do not, biologically, belong to my parents. Like, if I told you that the bartender was your father, what would you say?"

I never knew how to answer taunting questions like that. I tried never to ask them. I suspect she liked the drama of them. "I'd say, no, he's not."

"But what if I told you I was one hundred percent positive that he was your father, then what would you say?" She took another big sip with the straw and the bartender brought a second beer for me. I kept my head down. I didn't want him to hear us.

I made a noise. "That man is not my father. My father is on a beach in Florida, memorizing the jokes in *Reader's Digest*. You're making an absurd analogy."

She leaned in, and her eyes were the color of every color having quit its dream and taken a straight job. Give-Up Green, I thought. Broken-Down Brown. Bruised-Hopes Blue. "That's exactly my point. It's as absurd to me to think of my 'parents' as my real parents as it is for you to think about that bartender as your dad. They've buried the paperwork really well, but I'll find it."

If she weren't so convincing, I'd have thought she was crazy for sure. Or her convincingness made her a kind of crazy that I envied. What was family, anyway, I mused drunkenly. Skin and cells chafing together, hatching things, and then demanding loyalty? I wished I had something to prove or disprove, something outlandish. We talked about what our mothers looked like, her saying that she dreamed frequently of hers, her "real" mother, who looked like Eva Marie Saint, nothing like her pseudomother, who was small and dark. I said that my mother's ears never aged, never looked sick. She said something about plaster of paris and used "tête-à-tête" incorrectly and then she paid for our beers and we left, me blurrily driving twenty miles an hour and her singing snippets of songs as the radio scanned from station to station.

I was taking nail polish off using nail polish remover and toilet paper when she called. There's still a bleached, grayish spot on the side of the phone where I touched it with damp toilet paper. I put the phone between my cheek and shoulder and continued plucking at my fingers. She was telling me that she'd been bored for a week.

"Even at work. Just . . . bored," she said. "I don't feel bad or anything. But I can't believe how aware I am of each minute. It's like I'm waiting . . ." She paused. "Waiting for the other shoe to drop."

A new one, I noted. The nail polish wasn't coming off all the way. "What's the first shoe that dropped?" The nails on my left hand looked pink and bleary, as if they'd just woken up. I could hear her start to protest.

"Never mind. What will you do today?" I asked. It was a Monday, and the store was closed on Mondays.

"I don't know. I just had sex with someone. I thought it would help, but I feel even more bored now."

I don't know why I felt surprised, and very surprised, but I did. There was something about her that seemed to predate sex, that seemed to live wholly beyond and in spite of it. Maybe it was her pervasive certainty that she'd been adopted, that she had occurred by the regular means but then been removed from her sources. I concentrated on my nails. "Who did you have sex with?" I was making a little progress. My thumbnail was getting whiter.

"This guy. He just left. I met him at the grocery store this morning."

I stopped rubbing, focusing entirely on her. I felt maybe this was a test of some sort. But she kept talking. "Anyway, I got a squash. I'm going to make it. You want to come over?"

I was relieved. "Yes," I said. She told me to come in thirty minutes. We hung up and I resumed work on my nails, not quite calmly.

She lived on the second floor of an old Victorian house. I had never been inside. On the wraparound porch there were plastic chairs and a couple of bikes. "Not mine," she said when she met me at the door. "The downstairs people use this porch a lot. I think they hate me, but they're nice. They sold me their TV for forty bucks, down from fifty."

We went upstairs. Her door was ajar and strong smells wafted onto the landing where we stood. She turned to face me and I had the feeling of being in a crowded elevator. "Sorry," she said. "It's a little bit messy."

We entered the kitchen. There were things on nearly every surface—inches of mail on the table; birdhouses, mason jars, and hats on the counters; three ancient radios in a row on the wide windowsill, partially blocking the light being kept at bay by the smudged glass. On top of the refrigerator was a towering stack of phone books.

"I love old phone books," she said. "Here, sit." She pulled a chair out for me, tossing the articles of clothing that were on it to the floor. When I sat down, something sweatery was underfoot. I pushed it to the side and there was a magazine beneath it. I gave up and sat still, trying not to disturb an environment that felt, despite its clutter, very precise. Unlike Second Chances, this appeared not to be a site of haphazard assemblage, a depository for sad or frustrated purges. It was, actually, quite sophisticated, evoking the air of a laboratory where serious, life-improving science could be undertaken. I felt as though I had walked inside of her, through the unruly glen of her instincts, past the exhausting expanse of her quirkiness, and arrived at some clearing, some place of deep wisdom, where she knew far more than I but would refrain from making me too aware of it. Here, there was a certain restraint emanating, it seemed, from the clocks and jars and papers; it was as if the items themselves owned the apartment.

"I like your place," I said.

"Yes," she said, sounding almost wistful, as though the place were not hers, "me too."

She handed me a chipped yellow plate with cubes of squash on it. They were flecked with bits of green and something that looked like cinnamon. I tasted it. It was not cinnamon, but close. It tasted good. She sat across from me, her own plate red and heaped.

"Thank you," I said. "This is good."

She nodded. "Nutmeg," she said.

For a moment, I felt like crying; a strong tenderness filled me, for her nutmeg and her small bare arms reaching to put more squash on my plate from the bowl between us. We sat quietly, and the feeling passed, and we were just eating.

When we were finished, I started to take the plates to the sink. "Leave them," she said. "Let's watch TV."

I felt glad for this plan. It was nice not knowing what would come next, there in that apartment. And I do enjoy television, although I've never owned one. My father had offered me his old one, but said I'd have to pay to have it shipped, which in my mind ruined the transaction. I told myself that it would cost more to ship it than it would to buy my own television, but I didn't know that for a fact, nor did I try to find out. So the offer kept me suspended between two possible courses of action, buying my own set or paying to ship his, and there, helpless to move beyond the potential of television to its actual ownership, the offer finally dissipated. This still bothers me, with something like regret, but it seems, as so many other things have, too late to do anything about it. I think I am frequently held hostage by my hunches. I think my father gave the television to someone else, someone uncomplicated and close by.

I followed her to an oddly shaped room that had a large television on one side. The room was cold like a cellar. To the left against a recessed wall facing the television was a fold-out sofa bed strewn with sheets and pillows. A blanket hung off the edge. One corner of the thin mattress was visible—a shiny, patterned blue—and curled up slightly where the sheet had sprung off it. I tried not to look at the bed, not to think about the sex that had occurred there, but both bed and sex felt very much alive, filling the drafty spaces between the inert things of the room, between me and her, like a vague electricity.

She sat on the edge of the bed and I sat next to her. She groped around in the muddle of sheets and, finding the remote control, switched on the TV. A talk show host's face filled the screen.

It was a close-up of the host talking. I sat back, leaning on my elbows. I felt the metal beneath the mattress. She changed positions and lay on her stomach. I kept thinking about the sex, which she appeared to be completely oblivious to—it and my thinking about it. She was listening intently to the talk show host, and her engrossment had a soothing effect. All at once I felt comfortable, part of the room, part of the bed, part, even, of the earlier tryst. My body relaxed into the sheets, which smelled faintly like roses and something else I couldn't place.

Now the camera showed that the talk show host was sitting on a sofa next to a woman. The woman was talking animatedly but with a stricken look on her face, and she was using her hands. The talk show host looked stricken, too. I registered all of this before I made sense of the words, and when I forced myself to pay attention to the words it was as though they were coming from the television itself, and not from actual people.

"That is pathological," the talk show host was saying. "Truly pathological."

"I know!" the woman said. "I know. And I couldn't stop. Nothing could stop me."

"It sounds as though you were at the mercy of something greater than yourself," the talk show host said. "More powerful than yourself. It's almost . . . mind-blowing"—she looked at the camera—"how pathological this is." The camera panned across the audience members, the majority of which were nodding their heads or wiping their eyes.

"I know. It really is." The woman was crying now. "I'm so ashamed."

The talk show host touched the woman's shoulder and looked again at the camera. She was wearing purple and her lips were shiny and purplish. "When we come back, a mother reacts to her daughter's shockingly pathological behavior."

A car commercial came on. A man was wearing a cowboy hat and yelling. I looked at her and she was still staring fixedly at the screen. It was too early to be dusk, but outside, through the window opposite and tinted by the gauzy curtains, the sky looked like dusk. I still felt mostly comfortable, but my mind was beginning to move beyond the room. When would I leave? How would I leave? The commercials had disrupted the sense of timelessness, and now I felt a decision pressing to be made, pacing back and forth between us and the television.

She got up and went to the kitchen. When she came back, she had the bowl of squash. She sat down on the bed with the bowl in her lap. Now the earlier part of the visit was here with us, which seemed to signal something. I felt the urgency and anxiety of the previous moment lift. She ate squash with her fingers. I hesitated, then ate some too. It tasted better than it had before, as though it was supposed to have been eaten this way all along, with our fingers, with us slanting into each other on the pullout bed.

We watched a lot of television that day, into the night, and we talked little. I felt strange when I got home. It was after midnight, and my mind was deadened and jittery at the same time, from the television and the odd room and the lack of conversation and the inactivity that all combined to create a bizarre but unquestionable intimacy. I was at a loss as to what to do next. I felt like calling her, but I hadn't had much to say in the last nine hours, and I didn't have anything to say just then. I poured a bowl of cereal and sat eating it, trying to think of something I could call her to talk about. As improbable as it felt, I missed her, the way I missed things when I was younger. I looked at the back of the cereal box for a while, and then at some unopened mail that was on the counter, and then eventually brushed my teeth and went to bed. I dreamed that I was drunk and disorderly at a party, and she was there and drunk and disorderly too, and when it came time to leave it was clear that we were despised by everyone else there, and we couldn't leave fast enough because we were stumbling around, looking for my coat, which was my mother's coat and which I was desperate to find. But drunk-desperate, and therefore filled with conflicting urges, to apologize, and to redeem myself, and to disappear, and to kiss the host, and to explain the importance of my mother's coat. In the end, I did some combination of all of these things, and I awoke feeling mortified, my embarrassment like a hangover. I showered and drank coffee and decided to go to work early, to busy myself and to distance myself from everything of the last three-quarters of the previous day.

By noon, she still hadn't come in. The owner looked displeased when he dropped by to do some paperwork, and he told me to call. "You shouldn't be here all day by yourself," he said. "It's bad for business."

We rarely had more than one customer in the store at a time, and no real business to speak of, but I didn't argue. I called her and she answered on the fifth ring, just as I was about to hang up.

"Hi," she said.

"Hi. Are you sick?"

There was a pause. "A little bit, I think." Her voice got muffled. ". . . chills . . . but"—her voice got muffled again—". . . fine."

"What? I didn't hear everything you just said."

"Oh, nothing. I'm fine."

"Okay," I said. "Are you sure?"

"Yes."

"Do you want me to bring you anything?"

"Nah. No. I'll be in tomorrow. Sorry to leave you in the lurch. I owe you one."

We hung up, and I told the owner that she would be coming in at one, and the owner asked if I would be all right by myself until then, since he really wanted to go to an estate sale and "scavenge."

"I'll be fine," I said. "Don't worry."

I spent the rest of the day in the shop alone, tidying up racks and organizing inventory lists and dealing with two people, one older man who wanted to find a hat for his wife but left with nothing and seemed displeased and one college boy who bought three extra-small T-shirts that he would wear, I could only guess, ironically.

When she didn't come in the next day or the day after, and didn't answer the phone when I called repeatedly, forcing the owner—who by then was so flustered that he plastered the front door and windows with Help Wanted signs and left the curtains wide open, giving the shop an unnatural brightness that made everything look more drab—to work with me, I got begrudging permission to leave on my lunch break and drive to her place. One of her neighbors with the bikes was sitting on the porch.

"You here for your friend's stuff? The landlord's up there now, but go on in."

"Oh," I said, trying not to look as puzzled as I felt. "Okay. Thanks."

I went upstairs. Her door was partially open. A thin, middle-aged man in ripped jeans was looking in the refrigerator. He turned and faced me.

"Broke her lease, just like that. And no forwarding address. Called this morning and left a message saying she'd leave the key and someone would come by for the rest of her things. That's you, I'm assuming? You can tell her that she won't be getting her security deposit back, not a chance."

It looked like most of the phone books were still on top of the fridge. The old radios were gone. "She left all of this?"

"It's all yours, or it's getting trashed." He looked at me and smiled, a little unkindly. "Is she in some kind of trouble? Where'd she go in such a hurry?"

I kept staring at the phone books. "She's not in trouble," I mumbled. I felt sick but also relieved—as though I'd had a fever and it was breaking and I could sit up and drink ginger ale, as though nausea and recuperation were happening in the same moment, the contrast its own kind of balm. "She's—it's her family, I think. Some sort of family . . . emergency, she said." I thought to myself, It doesn't matter what I say, it doesn't make a difference, she's gone, she isn't here, she's no longer here, and it felt almost like joy, but not really.

The landlord told me to lock the place up when I was done and leave the keys with the neighbors. When he left, I wandered into the other room. The furniture was still there, including the television, and it looked expectant, as if I could turn it on and it would tell me something. I sat on the fold-out couch and turned it on and there was a soap opera, one woman facing the camera and pouring amber-colored liquid from an ornate decanter into a glass, and swirling it, and turning around slowly, deliberately, and another woman with her back to the camera, looking out a window and touching the edge of a lace curtain, framed by the window and the camera and the gaze of the other woman and waiting, it seemed, for some cue.

Michael Parker

Deep Eddy

W᷄ᴇ ʜᴀᴅ ᴛᴏ ᴘᴀʀᴋ by the bridge where the black ladies
fished through dusk, ignoring us as they peered into the
murk for the bob of red cork in the water. A quarter-mile walk
along a root-ruptured path to where the river whirlpooled and the
bottom dropped so wildly myth bubbled up from it, a froth of
dead babies crying on moon-shiny nights, suicide pacts of numer-
ous young lovers, an entire stagecoach of painted ladies, midway
from Charleston to Baltimore in pursuit of a regiment of whore-
mongers, sucked under its current. Sorcery, devilment, human
sacrifice: legends spread for decades by teenagers who heard them
from grandmothers trying any old lie to warn them away from a
place known for deflowering. But we went that night and other
nights seeking only the wild circling current. We'd just been to
see a movie where a dingo ate a baby, stole it from a tent in the
night while the parents slept alongside it, and we were talking all
Australian. Bye-bee, she called me, my bye-bee. We went in with
our underwear on, laughing at our awful accents. She'd lost her
flower with the first of a string of boys and she liked me only in
the way girls like those boys who make them forget, temporarily,
some pain I hoped was only temporary. My job was to make her

laugh. So we laughed at babies carted off by dogs on big grainy screens; we mocked the fantastic rumors of that cowlicked spot in the river and dubbed it Jacuzzi, we laughed at the word *Jacuzzi,* hollered it into the dark woods so we could laugh again at the echo. But the word rang in my head until it was frightening, not funny, so I told her something true that I knew she might misinterpret as the first line of a joke. Today I saw part of a snake. If she said, What part? I would swim to shore, pull on my clothes, and leave. If she just said, Which? I would stop fighting the current and allow it to deliver me to her. Everything—then and since— hinged on a single word. There was no answer, just a gurgling in the dark water, laughter from the eternal circle of poor drowned whores, the baby in the dingo den, the short end of the snake.

Maura Stanton
Oh Shenandoah

M Y FIANCÉ—I STILL THOUGHT of him as my fiancé although I was already planning not to marry him—came out of the bathroom with a funny look on his face. I'd heard the noise in there, even in the living room, where I was fussing with a pot of basil sitting out on the window ledge over the canal. I was wondering if it was going to rain or if I should water it.

"What did you break this time?" I asked. Hugo had already dropped the hair dryer, shattering the plastic casing, and knocked the glass shower doors off their rails. These were not good reasons for breaking our engagement, of course. I had other reasons that were going to be hard to explain to him, which is why I kept putting it off.

"The toilet seat cracked." He looked sheepish. "It just fell down. They're not supposed to do that."

I followed him back to the bathroom. Sure enough, the wooden seat had cracked straight across. It was still usable, but the cleaning woman who came in on Saturday was bound to report it to the owner, who'd charge me a fortune.

"We've got to buy a new one," I said. "Pronto."

"In Venice?"

"Venice is full of toilets," I said. "They must sell the seats somewhere."

I was the one who'd rented the apartment, with help from an Italian friend of my aunt, so I felt responsible. I'd told my aunt, and she'd told her friend to tell the landlady, that I was a quiet single asthmatic young woman who was looking for a place to escape the spring pollen that always made her sick. I hadn't said anything about sharing the tiny apartment with my fiancé because I didn't think he'd be able to get away.

I'd met him at the community garden back home. Our plots adjoined, and when we were both there on Saturday afternoons we'd stop work and talk about this and that. He'd been an English major without much of a future. But then he'd been hired by his entrepreneur brother who ran an airport shuttle service. I was going to graduate school in English, living on fellowships, loans, and summer jobs.

I gave Hugo big bunches of basil, my most successful crop, and he gave me red peppers. One July day when it was especially humid he saw me gasping, and took the weed clippers out of my hand and finished the job for me. Then one day in August a wasp got down my T-shirt. I screamed, and Hugo dropped his rake and rushed over. He reached down the neck of my T-shirt and probed with his fingers and crushed the wasp with his fist before it could sting me. I leaned against him. "See if there's another one down there," I whispered. There wasn't, but it took him a while to be sure, and by then we were both shaking and gasping. We went back to his truck, and we drove to his apartment and spent the weekend together. That was last summer.

In March, when I could feel my chest getting tight again, I decided to use my savings plus some help from my parents to spend the month of May, the month that always made me really sick, in a place where I might not need to use my inhaler every day. I'd figured out that Venice had no grass and hardly any trees and was surrounded by water. At first, Hugo seemed fine with the idea. Then, in April, he got wildly nervous about being separated from me. He wanted to marry me. He wanted to marry me right away.

"Let's wait until I get back from Venice. It's only a month."

"What if you meet someone?"

"In Venice? I don't know a soul. I'm just going for my health."

Hugo talked to his brother. His brother was reluctant to lose him for a whole month, but in the end he said it was fine, if Hugo promised to work during Christmas. I knew nothing of all this. When Hugo announced that he was coming with me to Venice, I was flabbergasted.

"You know it's a really small place," I said.

"But you said there's a king-sized bed, right?"

"Right," I said. "I just don't want you to be bored. I have to finish that paper for my incomplete."

"Bored in Venice? Are you crazy? Anyway, I'm never bored. Have you ever seen me bored, Marie?"

Actually, I hadn't. Hugo had more energy and wider interests than anybody I'd ever met, and when the shuttle company was shorthanded on drivers, he loved taking people to the airport and getting their stories. He was constantly calling me or texting me and when he came over to my apartment it was like having a party. He took up the space of three people—not just because he was tall but because he moved around so much. It was like living with a bear, and I didn't think I could live like that for the rest of my life. Take his proposal of marriage. It wasn't so much a proposal as an assumption. I'd assumed it, too, for a couple of months. But now it seemed impossible. Even though I loved him—he was a very loving person—and enjoyed the sex, we were just too different. He liked other people. I liked to be alone. Over my desk I'd thumbtacked a postcard with a quotation from Virginia Woolf: "I have three entire days alone—three pure and rounded pearls."

Hugo had seemed a normal-sized tall man back in the Midwest, but here in Venice he seemed like a giant. He had to duck under doorways, and the beamed ceiling was only an inch from the top of his head. His sloppy can of shaving cream and his razor and dirty comb sat on top of the little washing machine in the bathroom, and his large boots and shoes dwarfed mine in the bedroom wardrobe. The cleaning lady had reported him immediately to the landlady, who was still trying to get me to pay extra for him.

I pulled the phone book out of the desk and rifled through the pages. I found something called Bagno di Camuffo and a couple of places that said accessory WC. I wrote the addresses into my notebook where I usually wrote the addresses of restaurants.

"Let's go," I said. "Grab your umbrella."

"Naw," he said. "It's not going to rain."

"Oh, right," I said, sticking my umbrella into my back pocket.

Hugo was good with maps and had already internalized the maze of Venice. At the end of our narrow street we turned the corner and walked alongside the little canal until we came to an arcade that led to a *campo*. I was immediately lost, but Hugo strode ahead confidently. We passed a palazzo draped with banners, and he led me down a street as narrow as a tunnel that seemed to lead us around the back of a church. But finally I recognized the Fondamenta Nuove, where boats left for the islands. Waves were lapping against the stones. We were hit by a strong sea wind.

"Uh-oh," I said. "Look at the sky. You were wrong."

"There's a storm in the offing. But it's going to stay in the offing."

"What's the offing, anyway?"

"The near future."

"No, what is it really? What does it mean—*offing*? Is it a nautical term?"

"Beats me," Hugo said. He pointed at some dark clouds building on the horizon. "But there it is. The offing."

The offing looked pretty scary.

We had to tuck our heads down against the wind, especially at the top of bridges. Finally we turned down a street away from the sea. We passed a funeral parlor and a florist selling funeral wreaths, and several shops selling Murano glass. Then we stopped in front of a dimly lit shop window.

"Doesn't look promising, does it?" Hugo said.

We stared into the window at two marble sinks. It looked like the showroom for a contractor.

"It's not even open," I said, trying the door.

Hugo looked into the glass shop next door, where the window was filled with glass vases and glass tulips and glass horses' heads.

"Too bad they don't make glass toilet seats."

I felt something cold on my forehead. "That's a drop."

More drops plopped from the sky. I opened my umbrella. Hugo stepped back under an awning.

"Shall we go home?" I asked. Hugo was too tall to walk under my little red umbrella. If he held it, then I'd get soaked.

"Naw, this is just a spit bath. The storm's in the offing, like I said." He reached into his pocket. "Want one?"

His palm was full of cellophane-wrapped candies. I shook my head. He opened a butterscotch and popped it into his mouth.

The rain stopped, but the sky above the funnel-shaped chimneys looked ominous and the air was full of drizzle or mist. I showed Hugo the next address in my notebook, and we walked on, me under my umbrella, Hugo's thick hair glistening with drops. The place we wanted was on a busy shopping street, and its windows were brightly lit and full of towels.

We went inside. The tables were piled high with bath towels and hand towels in all colors and designs. A middle-aged man in a nice suit and a red tie came toward us.

"*Buon giorno,*" Hugo said in a loud voice. "Toilet seat? Have you a toilet seat?"

The shopkeeper looked puzzled. He swept his hand around to show us the towels.

"Toiletto—*bagno?*" Hugo asked.

The man pointed at some terry cloth bathrobes.

"No," Hugo said. "WC."

The man drew himself up. He looked offended. "WC, no!" he said. "Not for tourists." He pointed out the door.

"What?" Hugo said. "No, you don't understand. Toilet seat. WC."

The man's face grew red. "*Eccolo, eccolo,*" he said, still pointing.

"*Signore,*" I said, and then, as if I were playing charades, I made a lifting and falling motion with my hands, the toilet seat going up, coming down. Hugo got the idea right away, but Hugo-like, he took it even further. He squatted down, pointing at me. Then he pointed at himself. He spread his legs apart, and put his fist at his crotch.

The shopkeeper looked aghast, and I didn't blame him. He stepped away from us.

Hugo frowned. "I don't think he gets it. But there must be toilet seats in here."

He walked to the back of the store. The shopkeeper's face turned from red to purple. His hands twitched. He ran after Hugo and pulled at his arm. "*Signore,* no, no. No WC," he shouted.

Then it hit me. "Hugo, he thinks we want to *use* the WC. Let's get out of here. They only sell towels anyway."

We fled to the street. Hugo was laughing. My face was hot with embarrassment.

"He must have thought we were crazy idiots."

"He just thought we were cheap tourists who didn't want to pay to pee." Hugo laughed. "You know it costs almost two bucks to use the public toilets in this town."

"What next?"

"We'll try that hardware store near the Rialto Bridge."

The drizzle had stopped, and the paving stones glistened as we walked along. We stopped for gelato, and I was still licking my cone when we reached a narrow street where an orange plastic fence surrounded a large muddy area of upturned paving stones. We stepped around the fence and came to a gloomy shop window full of tools and implements and electrical cables.

Hugo tried the door and it was open. A naked bulb burned above a wooden counter, but no one was around. I looked at a row of dusty blenders and mixers, models that looked years out of date. Hugo fingered some faucet heads. There were boxes of washers and bolts and clothespins and plugs.

"Shall I ring that bell?" Hugo asked, pointing to the counter. But a bead curtain rustled just then. A bald head poked out. "Hello, there," the bald man said in American English. "I'm sorry, this place is closed. I forgot to lock the door."

"We're looking for a toilet seat," Hugo said.

"A toilet seat?" The man stepped further out, the beads draping his shoulders. He had thick dark eyebrows and was wearing a bright Hawaiian shirt. "I don't think we have any toilet seats. Anyway, this place is closed. Closed forever."

"Forever?" I asked.

The man nodded. "My grandparents owned it. They're dead now. I'm just cleaning things up." He sighed. "But it's going slowly."

"I'm sorry to hear that," Hugo said. "You're from the States, right?"

"Chicago," the man said. "But my pop came from here. And his parents never left. They lived over this shop for sixty-five years. Sixty-five years, the whole of their married life. And they died within five days of each other. She went first, and then he went. It was a real romance."

Hugo whistled. "Sixty-five years! Wow!"

"Yeah, that doesn't happen anymore, does it? You marry someone and then you get bored or you fight over money or you meet someone else and you both go your own way and you start over again. I've been divorced twice, myself. Hey, listen," the man said. "You said you were looking for a toilet seat?"

Hugo nodded. "Our toilet seat broke. We've got to replace it so the landlady doesn't get on our case. We've been looking all over Venice, but now we've run out of ideas."

"Right, got you. Listen, you two look like a nice couple. Well, there's a lot of junk back here. Maybe we can find you a toilet seat, who knows. I'm just throwing most of this stuff away, or giving it to charity. You two married?"

"Not yet." Hugo grinned. "But soon. This is Marie, by the way. I'm Hugo."

"Well, Hugo and Marie, stick together, that's my advice. Keep on loving each other. Stay the nice couple you are. Most couples have an ex in their future. I should know. I'm Tony, by the way. You expected me to be called Tony, didn't you?" He laughed. "Ah, don't listen to me, really. I'm a cynic. Everyone tells me I'm a cynic." He laughed again, heartily, and I could see the pink part of his throat surrounded by his strong-looking teeth. "Hey, I never actually met these famous grandparents of mine. I was too busy making money back home. But now I've made my pile, so when Nonna and Pappy finally bit the dust, I told my pop, who hates to fly, that I'd take care of business." He stepped away from the door, and the last of the beads slithered over his shoulder and tinkled into place. "I must admit, I thought there might be a small real estate fortune over here. I thought I could sell this shop and the apartment upstairs. But it turns out that Nonna and Pappy were renters! Renters for sixty-five years, can you beat that? All they own is this stuff you see." He swept his hands out like an orchestra conductor. "Come on back. There's a lot more in here."

We followed Tony through the bead curtain into a storeroom crammed with what seemed like everything in the world that newlyweds might need to set up house: vacuum cleaners, pole lamps, toasters, seed packages, corkboards, dustpans, floor fans, bottle warmers, egg timers, rakes, plungers, and coffeepots. He began to rummage here and there, tossing out pillows and electrical cords that got in his way. He dug in this box and that box and upturned ironing boards and crates, but although he found a kitchen sink leaning against the wall in one corner, and a glass shower panel and some silver pipes in another, there was no sign of a toilet seat.

"Hey, listen," he said. "I've got an idea. You need a toilet seat, I've got a toilet seat. Come on upstairs. There's a toilet up here that nobody will ever use again. Once I get this junk out of here, the owner plans to renovate this place, make a fortune out of it. They don't want Nonna and Pappy's old toilet seat. You can have it."

"Oh, no," I started to say, "we couldn't do that."

But Hugo was already following him up a staircase. I hurried to catch up. The stairwell was damp, and there was a glass panel door at the top standing half-open that led into a dim room crowded with ancient furniture, overstuffed sofas and chairs with lace doilies on the armrests and bureaus crammed with knick-knacks.

Tony led us into a bathroom that smelled of talcum powder and rot. The mosaic floor tiles were lined with black gunk, and the claw-foot tub was streaked orange and yellow. There were damp stains on the walls. A threadbare bath towel hung on a rack. You could almost see through it. Two toothbrushes with moldy roots were standing upright in a glass. I imagined the old couple leaning over the sink day after day, brushing their teeth, and I tried to think about something else.

"There you go, we can just unscrew it," Tony said.

Hugo and I looked at the toilet seat. It was warped and yellowed with faint cracks in the lacquer. If it wasn't sixty-five years old, then it was at least twenty years old. The idea of sitting on it made me cringe.

"I'll get a screwdriver and some newspaper to wrap it up."

"I don't think—" I started to say, but Hugo nudged me.

"Great," he said, lifting the seat. "This shouldn't be hard to get off."

"I'll wait downstairs," I said. I went down and paced around in the gloom. I picked up a yellow gardening glove and tried it on. I was going to have to tell Hugo soon, very soon, that we weren't going to be getting married. The longer I waited the worse it would be.

I heard them coming down. Tony had found a ball of string. He tied the bundle neatly and handed it to Hugo. "There you go. All set. You want those gloves, Marie?"

"What? Oh, I forgot I had this on. No, I don't." I flung off the glove. "But thanks."

"Yes, thanks a lot," Hugo said. "We really appreciate your giving us this."

"No problem. Glad to be of service." Tony shook hands with both of us. "I'm glad I can pass on something useful from Nonna and Pappy."

We waved good-bye to Tony. Once we turned the corner I looked at Hugo. "We can't put this piece of crap on the toilet!"

"Hold on tight, Marie. I know that," he said. "It's the wrong shape, for one thing. This is a round one and we need an oval one. But I didn't want to hurt the guy's feelings."

"Well, now we're back to zero." I shrugged.

"Look, Marie, I'm going to get you a toilet seat, I swear. At least I know the word in Italian now, Tony says it's either *il sedile del WC* or *WC sede*. Why don't we get a cappuccino somewhere and rest up a bit?"

We spotted a café and sat down outside, near the door and under the awning. Hugo put the newspaper bundle containing the toilet seat on an extra chair, and we ordered cappuccino. He went in to use the toilet.

He was grinning when he came back. "Boy, I wish I had Tony's screwdriver. There's a perfect seat in there, brand new, just the right size."

"We can't steal a toilet seat!"

"Hang on, Marie. I was just joking."

"Maybe you were joking, maybe you weren't. What about that bottle of steak sauce?"

"Oh, that." He blushed. "I'd never seen that brand before."

The waiter brought our cappuccino. Hugo sucked the foam off the top of his and acquired a white mustache. The café was filling up. Two older American couples were trying to settle at the next table, but there were only three chairs.

"Excuse me," one of the men said. "Are you using that chair?"

"Oh, no, sorry," Hugo said, removing the newspaper bundle. "We're not. Please take it."

The older man smiled. He put his hand on the back of the chair and looked at us. "Bet you two are on your honeymoon, aren't you? That's just great." He nodded at one of the women behind him—either the one with the shiny cheeks and brassy hair or the one with gray bangs and a silk scarf; it was hard to tell. "Joyce and I came here on our honeymoon thirty years ago. And here we are now. It's a lucky place, Venice."

Hugo nodded. "It's going to be lucky for us, too."

"Have a great life," the man said as he scraped the chair back to join the others.

Hugo looked at me, grinning. "Hey," he whispered, "what do you call this anyway, being in Venice before your wedding?"

I shrugged. "I don't know."

"Why are you in such a bad mood, Marie?"

"I'm not in a bad mood."

"Marie, Marie, hold on tight."

"I wish you wouldn't quote that all the time."

"You started it. You quoted it to me."

"Well, you can't forget a line of poetry with your own name in it, especially when it's *The Waste Land*." I flipped open my notebook and showed him an address. "Here. We've got one more place to try. A plumbing supply store."

We got up and were halfway across the square when the waiter called us back. We'd forgotten our package wrapped in newspaper. Hugo thanked him, and stuck it under his arm. We crossed the Accademia Bridge. Lots of people were hanging over the side looking at the view where the Grand Canal opens toward the Salute church. Clouds were piled up in the sky, but any storm was still in the offing.

A crowd of huge young men, men even bigger than Hugo, came striding toward us. They were giants with burly chests and seemed to be some kind of team because they were all wearing identical orange T-shirts with blue lanyards. We moved out of their way but one of them thrust a flyer into my hand. An unearthly hum began to rise up. They began to sing "Shenandoah." It was a song that always made my neck prickle, although I had never seen the Shenandoah River or the Shenandoah Valley and had no idea why it should cause me so much emotion. The words of the song rose up loud and strong, filling the street, triggering astonished and joyful looks from passersby as the young men strode along like a company of angels. The crowd parted before them. People applauded. Hugo and I stood there listening until they had crossed the bridge.

"Wow!" Hugo said.

"That was beautiful." I looked at the flyer. "The Indiana Wesleyan Men's Choir. They're singing tonight at seven p.m. at San Giobbe."

"That was amazing, just amazing." Hugo looked yearningly in the direction the young men had gone. "I wish they'd just walk around the streets singing like that all the time. You know, I was in a chorus for two years in high school. Did I ever tell you this? We used to take a bus around the state to these small towns and sing in school auditoriums. Sometimes they put us up overnight in dorms. It was okay, I sort of liked doing it, but it never meant anything much.

"Then I remember one night after a performance I was all het up and restless for some reason and I walked down a path to a little river or maybe it was just a creek and I stood there on the bank feeling really strange like I was full of something that was going to burst in my chest. And for the first time I listened, really listened, to what was out there in the dark.

"First I'd hear the cicadas, then they'd stop, and the tree frogs would start in, and then lightning bugs would dance around as if they were trying to write the tune. And it struck me that when I was standing with the other guys on the bleachers singing—and 'Shenandoah' was one of our songs—that we were just doing the same thing as these bugs and frogs. These creatures were expressing my feelings for me, they were manifestations, you might call it, of my feelings. And me and the other guys onstage, we were expressing the feelings of the people sitting out there on the folding chairs. That's why they always got these happy dreamy expressions on their faces when they listened to us. That's what I felt just now."

Hugo sighed. He looked a little bewildered after his speech.

"So why didn't you pursue a career in music?"

He looked at me oddly. "It has nothing to do with a career."

We heard a rumble of thunder just then.

"Hey, Marie, why don't you go back to the apartment? The store we're looking for is up near the railroad station. That's quite a ways."

"No, I'm coming with you," I said. I knew if I went back I'd just pace around wondering what I should do—tell Hugo I didn't want to get married and get it over with? Or just let things drift for a while, the way they were drifting now?

"Well, let's at least take the boat."

We stood in line at the ticket booth, and Hugo paid for two tickets. Then we got behind the crowd jostling against the chain as the noisy vaporetto bumped against the floating dock. People pressed forward. Hugo touched my shoulder. "Go ahead and get on, Marie," he said. "I forgot the toilet seat. It's over there leaning against that booth."

"Oh, forget it," I said, but Hugo was gone, pushing back-

ward through a group of Chinese tourists in bright rain jackets.
I climbed on board, but although I was shoved this way and that
way I managed to stay near the rail. I spotted Hugo. He had
the newspaper-wrapped package under his arm and was running
back toward the floating dock. But the boatman locked the chain,
and then jumped on board. The boat slid away from the dock.

"Wait, wait," I screamed. "Let him on!"

But the boatman could not possibly have heard me over the
noise. I waved frantically at Hugo. "Where should I get off?" I
screamed.

He waved his free arm and pointed up the Grand Canal and
shouted something but I couldn't hear him. The boat was out in
the middle of the canal now. There was another clap of thunder,
and it began to rain. Everyone on board shrieked and pushed
back from the edge. I glimpsed Hugo ducking away down a street
and then he was gone from my sight. People who'd had their cameras out were wiping the lenses and stowing their gear.

I got off at the railroad station. Hugo had said that the plumbing supply store was near there. I had the address in my notebook,
but I lacked a map. Hugo probably remembered the address,
and was on his way up here. But maybe he didn't remember the
address. Maybe he'd just gone back to the apartment and was
waiting for me. Our cell phones didn't work in Europe so we
hadn't brought them, and there was no way I could call him
unless I bought a phone card and located a phone and called the
apartment.

Luckily I had my little red umbrella. But it was raining hard
and my feet were soaked. Nevertheless, I did my best to get to
where we'd been going. I showed the address of the plumbing supply store to a young woman in a clothing store, and she
pointed to the right. But I couldn't find the street. A waiter in a
café pointed me to the left. Still no luck. Finally I decided to go
back to the apartment. Hugo must have been waiting for me and
I didn't want him to worry.

But when I got back, there were no wet shoes sitting outside the door on the landing, and the sisal mat was dry. There was no damp jacket hanging on the pegboard in the hall. I left my umbrella open on the landing, took off my own soaked shoes and left them on the mat, hung my socks on the bathroom radiator, and made a cup of tea in the kitchen. When I carried the tea to the living room, I saw that the window had blown open in the storm and my pot of basil was on the floor.

I set my tea down and scooped up the dirt and repacked it around the basil roots. I closed the window and swept the floor. Then I sat down with my cup of tea to wait.

Twenty minutes went by, then an hour. I looked at the phone. There were a lot of English books that other renters had left in the apartment over the years, and I picked up a novel and tried to read, but I kept jumping at every noise and couldn't get interested. The outer door banged open downstairs several times, but the footsteps always continued up to other landings.

I was getting worried. I paced into the bedroom and looked at the king-sized bed still unmade from the morning. Hugo's pillow was wadded and dented and the sheets on his side were twisted. A few hard candies with cellophane wrappings glittered on his bedside table. I walked into the bathroom and held the sleeve of his bathrobe hanging on the back of the door.

It was time for dinner, but I wasn't hungry. At eight o'clock I made another cup of tea and ate a handful of chocolate biscotti. I couldn't call the police and report a missing person because I didn't speak Italian. I'd have to go to the police station in person, wherever that was. But surely nothing had happened to Hugo! This was Venice. It was a safe city. There weren't any cars to worry about. And Hugo was a friendly guy. He'd probably just met somebody, maybe in a café, and had forgotten all about me.

I started to feel resentful. Why didn't he call and tell me where he was? Why was he doing this to me? Was this what our married life was going to be like?

But we weren't getting married, were we?

I looked out the dark bedroom windows at the apartment straight across the street, where a woman was doing the dishes. I looked out the kitchen window above the canal, where a man was tinkering with his boat in the twilight. The rain had stopped and clouds were streaming across the sky, leaving dark blue patches. I looked out a corner window in the living room where I could see a little bridge farther down the canal. A man and a woman were standing there, looking up. I looked up, too. The moon was just rising through the clouds.

I went back to the novel. I got up after ten minutes, having understood nothing. I walked into the kitchen and opened a bag of cheese puffs and stuffed some in my mouth. Then I went into the bathroom and sat on the cracked toilet seat. I could feel the crack—the seat wasn't quite even now—but I didn't care. Where was Hugo? In the morning I really would go to the police if he wasn't back.

I picked up an afghan and wrapped it around my shoulders and stretched out on the blue sofa. I remembered years ago when I was a babysitter and used to wait up for parents, trying not to fall asleep. My eyes felt dry and scratchy. Once or twice they fell shut but I always opened them again. Or I thought I did. It was an hour later when I looked at my watch the next time.

I meant to get up, but I didn't. Then I dreamed, or thought I was dreaming. I heard distant singing. Somewhere a bunch of people were singing "Shenandoah" and they were coming closer and closer.

Oh Shenandoah
I long to see you
And hear your rolling river
Oh Shenandoah
I long to see you
Away, we're bound away
Across the wide Missouri

I wasn't dreaming, because I didn't know the words to the song and couldn't have dreamed them so clearly. I sat up. The singing was coming down my street, a street that dead-ended in the canal. Whoever was singing was coming straight in this direction, not just passing by.

I got up and went to the window and pushed back one half of a green shutter that had blown back from the wall. I looked down. Right below me were eight or nine young men in white shirts and blue ties, all of them singing "Shenandoah" at the top of their lungs. All down the street, windows were flung open and sleepy heads were peering out. The singers saw me at the window, and some of them waved, but they all kept singing. And then I saw Hugo.

Hugo was standing in the middle of the group. He was singing, too. And over his head he held up a shiny new toilet seat.

They sang for me—first "Shenandoah" and then "Danny Boy" and then a Shaker hymn. And they caught all that was inside me so exactly that I felt I'd been opened up like a geode. I could feel my face shining as I looked down at Hugo. I didn't know what was going to happen next. Was I really going to hand over the pure and rounded pearls of my lonely life for this? I leaned over the windowsill, confused by such happiness, if that was what it was.

Laura van den Berg

Opa-locka

M Y SISTER WAS THE photographer. From a rooftop deck, nestled between two enormous ferns in clay pots, she photographed our target, Mr. Defonte, entering the adjacent apartment building. He wore a white linen suit, boat shoes, and a straw sun hat with a chin strap that dangled beneath his jaw.

"Only in Florida," Julia said, snapping a photo. "Does he think he's on a safari?"

Mr. Defonte paused outside and stared at his feet. He was only a few steps away from the entrance of the glossy high-rise building. The doors were made of blue glass with silver handles in the shape of leaping fish. Julia took another picture. I was crouched beside my sister and peering through binoculars. I could see his face in profile, his long downward-sloping nose and soft chin. I knew his full legal name, his social, his date of birth, where he lived, where he worked, his favorite lunch spot, and his license plate number. His wife had hired me and Julia to investigate him. Together we made up Winslow & Co., the private detective firm we'd been running for the last year.

"I don't think he's going inside." I lowered the binoculars. It was Boca Raton in June. My throat was slick with sweat, my underarms damp. "I just have a feeling."

"If that motherfucker doesn't walk through that door, I'm going to climb down from this roof and smack him in the face," Julia said. The apples of her cheeks were flushed. Her chestnut hair glistened.

I opened the red cooler we brought on stakeouts and fished out an ice cube. I ran it along the back of Julia's neck and over her cheeks. She sighed in a way that sounded grateful. I kept moving the ice over her skin until it turned into a tiny translucent shard and melted into my fingertips, until it was just my hand on the nape of her neck.

Mr. Defonte opened the door. He hesitated for a moment, then disappeared into the building. Julia snapped three pictures in a row. Now all he had to do was come out. And all we had to do was wait.

What do you want? That was how the conversation with Mrs. Defonte began, how they always began. You don't hire a private investigator unless you want something. In our early twenties, Julia and I hired a detective to track down our father, who vanished in the middle of the night when we were teenagers. I was fifteen, Julia thirteen. We just woke up one Saturday morning and found him gone and our mother in the backyard, staring at the sky. Our detective was expensive and didn't have any luck. We knew what it was like to want something so badly, it burned a hole inside you.

Mrs. Defonte had hired us for the same reason most women hired PIs: she suspected her husband was having an affair. In the last six months, she explained in her living room, his behavior had changed. He took phone calls in the middle of the night. He worked later. Something about his tone of voice was different, his smell, even. He seemed to have trouble looking her in the eye. She had followed him once, waited outside his office and trailed him to a café on Second Street, but then she lost her nerve.

Mrs. Defonte had beautiful black hair that nested on her shoulders and nails painted the color of pink geraniums. She wore a snug black sleeveless dress and a white sweater draped over her shoulders, and sat with her ankles crossed. She was in her fifties, around the same age as my mother, who was several weeks into a six-month cruise around the world; it had started in Fort Lauderdale and would end in Monte Carlo. Julia liked to joke that our mother had been away at sea her whole life. She'd done her best to raise us, but once we were out in the world, the distance that had always been there shifted and hardened, like a building shedding its scaffolding and assuming its final shape. We reminded her of painful times, we understood.

"I want to know what's real," Mrs. Defonte said.

"That's exactly what we do." We had been served iced teas and Julia's long fingers were wrapped around her glass. "We gather facts, evidence. We separate what's true from what isn't."

Mrs. Defonte nodded. "It's all very peculiar," she said, almost to herself.

"It's actually pretty common," I said. Julia stepped on the toe of my sneaker. I had a habit of saying the wrong thing to clients. Each one was supposed to think their predicament was special, in need of our expertise. The Defonte case was a big opportunity for us. We'd been getting most of our work from insurance companies, who often hired private investigators to look into claims, but it was the domestic investigations that really paid.

Mrs. Defonte looked at the ceiling for a moment and sighed. She told us that sometimes she wondered if she was making it up. Once she wrote out a list of all the warning signs, all the things he'd done, but on paper it didn't look that damning. Still she couldn't let go of the feeling that something was wrong. It plagued her day and night.

"Maybe I just have too much time on my hands," she said.

"You leave it to us," Julia said. "Give us a month and we'll know what he's been up to."

On our way out, I noticed a photo in a silver frame. It was Mrs. Defonte standing on a stage, a red velvet curtain hanging behind her. She wore a long bronze gown. Her hands were clasped in front her stomach, her lips parted in song.

"I sing in our community opera," Mrs. Defonte said when she saw me looking. "That was from *The Mask of Orpheus*. I went to Juilliard, you know."

"Really?" I glanced up at her. She was nearly smiling.

"It was a long time ago." She opened the front door and watched us walk to our car, a black Explorer with tinted windows and a portable GPS affixed to the dashboard. It was a rental.

That night, back at our apartment, a minimal amount of digging turned up the name of the community opera and their rehearsal schedule. They staged their rehearsals and performances at an opera house in downtown Boca Raton. My sister and I lived in Opa-locka, ten miles north of Miami. Opa-locka came from the Indian name Opatishawokalocka, which meant "the high land north of the little river on which there is a camping place." It was a rough neighborhood. Every night Julia locked all our equipment—GPS, walkie-talkies, tape recorders, cameras, binoculars, laptops—in a safe in her bedroom closet. She kept the Glock 22 I was licensed for on the bedside table. Just last week our neighbor Mirabella had been robbed at knifepoint. I had tried to talk my sister into moving, citing crime statistics and reasonable rents in other neighborhoods, but she loved the two-story blue stucco building with the concrete balcony and the drained swimming pool half-filled with bottles and empty cigarette packs. For Julia risk was like air. The good news was that we saved a bundle in rent and could afford to run ads in everything from the South Florida *Sun-Sentinel* to the *Boca Beacon,* which was how Mrs. Defonte had found us.

One night, a week into the Defonte case, I told Julia I needed to go for a drive. It took less than an hour to reach the opera house. It was on a brick street lined with palm trees, a circular building with a glass facade, so even from the parking lot, I could see the warm light inside. A crescent-shaped pool curved in front of the entrance; a trio of fountainheads shot white water into the air. After finding the rehearsal stage, I took a seat in the very back. The space was empty save for a handful of people in the front rows. They were in rehearsal for *Don Giovanni*. Mrs. Defonte stood on the right-hand side of the stage. She wore street clothes, black slacks and a crisp pink button-down. A long white veil was clipped to her hair. A man with a black mask over his eyes stood in the center of the stage, singing. I watched Mrs. Defonte watch the man and wondered what she was feeling. Another person came into the theater and walked down the aisle, carrying an armful of fake roses to the stage. I sank lower into my seat.

The veil Mrs. Defonte wore in her hair was not unlike the one I'd worn when I got married. I had moved in with Julia six months ago, after my divorce was finalized, and not long after, I'd started getting strange postcards in the mail. They were part of a set. I'd seen a similar kind of thing in a party store once; if I had all the cards they would fit together like a puzzle. So far I'd received two swatches of sky, a cloud, a dried-out river, and a brown ledge. There was nothing on the back except my name and Julia's address. Everything was typed, the letters large and a little smudged, as though it had been done on an old typewriter. The postmarks were from Arizona, Utah, Nevada. I had never seen my husband use a typewriter, but he had always wanted to travel west. He thought Florida was a miserable swamp. And he knew Julia's would be the first place I'd turn. Once, I spread the cards out on the floor and tried to put them in order. I didn't have enough pieces to make sense of what they were supposed to be.

When Mrs. Defonte began singing, my hands dropped into my lap. My chin rose, as though pulled by a string. Each note was as perfect as the crystal goblets I'd noticed on her dining room table. The other actors onstage gazed at her with the same kind of wonder. When she finished, they all applauded. One person rose from her seat. Mrs. Defonte looked around, startled, like she'd just come out of a trance. A voice like that was a weapon.

By ten o'clock, we'd been on the roof for seven hours. The darkness had brought little relief from the heat. We'd used up all the ice cubes, eaten the bologna sandwiches I'd packed, drunk a beer apiece. Over the last two weeks, we had observed Mr. Defonte entering hotels, high-end places near his office, and exiting after an hour; it was always the same days of the week, the same times. Fifteen minutes after he left, the same blond woman always emerged. From the blonde's photo and license plate number, we located her address and tracked Mr. Defonte to her highrise on Royal Palm Avenue. The first time we followed him to her building, it was observational; this time, we were prepared to document. Catching him going in and out of her residence was significant to our case. The hotel meetings could, with some effort, be explained away. He was a lawyer, after all. He could say he was meeting clients, that the blonde's presence was a coincidence. Spending seven-plus hours in her building, however, would be harder to dismiss.

When it was my turn to watch the door, Julia stretched out on one of the white plastic beach chairs behind me. The chairs had mildew on them, which we hoped meant the roof deck didn't get much use. If anyone discovered us, Julia planned to tell them we were police. Before starting Winslow & Co., we'd enrolled in an online detective school. We learned how to take fingerprints and write reports, how to run credit and background checks, how to do surveillance and skip tracing. I liked the school; it made everything seem official. At the end, there was a certificate. Julia was less interested, so I did most of the work for our classes. One thing we were never supposed to do was impersonate a police officer.

Around midnight, the conversation turned to our father.

"Here's a story," I said to Julia.

Once, my father told me a story about a business trip to Chicago with his friend Bill Keller. At a bar, Bill picked up two prostitutes. They were young, with accents and fake fur coats. They all went back to a hotel, an old grand place called the Iron Horse. My father and Bill disappeared into separate rooms, but instead of doing what one would normally do with a prostitute, of doing what Bill Keller was doing in that very same moment, my father said they lay down on his bed and he read to her.

"Read what?" I'd asked.

"A novel," my father had said.

I was eleven. The story made me feel strange. It seemed to come out of nowhere. We were eating lunch at Bojangles'. The Kingsmen were playing on the radio. I knew what a prostitute was, but I didn't yet understand how unusual it was not to do what one normally does with a prostitute, to read her a novel instead. I didn't understand that my father wanted me to see him as being above temptation and superior to Bill Keller, whom I had never met. I didn't know the right questions to ask. *What kind of novel? What did she smell like? Did she fall asleep on your arm? What was her name?* Now I thought I would like to find that prostitute and get her side of the story.

"So?" Julia said, her voice drowsy from the heat.

"I realized the other day that it couldn't possibly be true. I don't think I ever saw Dad read anything, let alone novels, for starters."

"What *was* true?" Julia said.

Our father was a grifter. He spent our childhood selling fake insurance policies. When he vanished, he left behind a mountain of debt; the house we'd grown up in went to the bank. Our mother moved us to Athens, Georgia, where she was from. She threw away all the photos we had of our father and encouraged us to tell people he was dead. All we were left with was the stories. The prostitute in Chicago. The time he escaped the Vietcong by jumping off a cliff. The time he ran with the bulls in Barcelona and saved his best friend from being gored in the ass. Things only children would believe. All story and no truth.

I liked to tell myself that, unlike our father, we were on the right side of the law, me and Julia, with our firm and its solid-sounding name, but that hadn't always been the case. Two years ago Julia had been arrested for breaking into houses. She'd been at it for a long time, picking places where the owners were away. When she finally got caught, in a mansion on Fisher Island, she did six months in Broward Correctional. The idea for the private detective business was hatched during visitation. We talked about how exciting it would be, how lucrative. My husband, a tax consultant for H&R Block, had always thought Julia was a professional house sitter; he was furious that I had lied to him, that I'd once gone down to Coral Gables to swim in the Olympic-size pool of an estate my sister was robbing, and even more furious that I insisted on visiting her twice a week in jail. *Can't you just write to her?* he'd say. *Do you have to actually go there?* Our mother talked about Julia like she was away on a long trip. So it was just my sister and me, like always.

In Georgia, we had gotten bored with college and dropped out, drifting back to South Florida like homing pigeons. I met my husband while working at a watch store in Pinecrest. He brought a Swiss Army in for repair. He'd had it for a decade; he said he liked to hold on to things. We married a year later, in the Miami courthouse. I loved him, but I didn't always understand how to be honest. Over time, each of us became less sure the other was something we wanted to hold on to. And then there was Julia's arrest and visitation. I saw how small she looked in her gray jumpsuit, how she wanted to ask if our mother was coming but knew better. As I listened to her talk about the PI business—her voice quick and grasping—I realized my thirties were on the horizon and I'd never had a job I found interesting. And that I liked the idea of busting people for doing things they shouldn't be. Since Julia had a record, I'd been the one to apply for our firearm and PI licenses. I told my husband Julia and I were starting a catering company. When he discovered a Winslow & Co. business card in my purse, he bypassed fury and went straight to sadness.

"Do you think Bill Keller was a real person?" my sister asked.

"I don't know." I pulled at the collar of my T-shirt; the fabric was stuck to my skin. "The hotel is a real place, though. The Iron Horse. I looked it up once."

"Any sign of Defonte?" I could tell she was ready to change the subject.

I raised the binoculars and scanned the entrance. The perimeter of the building was brightly lit and still. "Nothing," I said. We were prepared to keep waiting. There were two more beers, a thermos of water, and a bag of Cheetos in the cooler, plus a packet of NoDoz in the back pocket of my shorts.

"Maybe Mrs. Defonte is out of town," Julia said.

"Maybe." I happened to know that was unlikely, since she'd had rehearsal the night before and had it again tomorrow.

We waited through the night, and when the sun rose behind us, it brought a heat that was painful. We put on big sunglasses and baseball caps and draped towels over our shoulders. I'd taken too many NoDoz and my hands were shaky, my mouth dry. All the water was gone. We had not taken our eyes off the building since he went inside, not for one single moment.

Julia searched around with the binoculars. I rested my elbows on the edge of the roof. It was unusual for a target to change the pattern so rapidly, to go from one-hour stretches to all-nighters. Maybe Mrs. Defonte really was out of town. Or maybe he had decided to up and leave her.

"Keep looking," she said, passing me the binoculars. "I'll go get us coffee."

"Water," I said. "I feel like I'm being roasted."

A lot of PI-ing was about waiting. Knowing how to wait, being prepared to wait, not giving up on waiting even when it felt like God was one of those assholey kids who holds a magnifying glass over ants until they explode, only He's using the sun. What we didn't know was that sometimes all the waiting in the world won't give you what you need.

After twenty-four hours, we decided something had to be done. It felt like we had been on the roof for years. We'd been trading off for bathroom breaks. Julia had made two runs to the convenience store down the street for water, Nutri-Grain bars, and coffee (while she was at it, she had checked to make sure Mr. Defonte's car was still parked in the same spot; it was). Still, we couldn't stay up there forever. My stomach gurgled. The back of my neck and my legs were sunburned. My eyes itched. Birds had shit on our camera bag and on Julia's wrist. Mr. Defonte had to come out of there eventually, we figured. It was a Wednesday. He had a wife, a job. But the blazing afternoon stretched on and on until finally it was night again.

"We should call Mrs. Defonte," Julia said. "See if she's heard from him." She tossed me the cell phone and said she was going out for more coffee. She liked to do the talking until we had to tell clients something they might not want to hear.

I kneeled on the roof, facing the building Mr. Defonte had vanished into. I'd never had a conversation with Mrs. Defonte alone.

"Do you have any news?" she asked when I called. I closed my eyes for a moment and imagined what her words would sound like if she was singing them.

"Sort of," I said. "Have you heard from your husband lately?"

She said that she hadn't. He was on a business trip in Memphis.

"That can't be true. We photographed him going into an apartment building on Royal Palm yesterday afternoon."

"And?"

"We haven't seen him since," I said. "We've been watching the building. He hasn't come out yet."

She was silent. I guessed she was considering what her husband had been doing in that building for so long and who he'd been doing it with. I pictured her sitting stiffly on the elegant sofa with the cream-colored cushions and the curved wood legs, a hand resting on her knee.

Mrs. Defonte said she would call me back and did so a few minutes after we hung up. She reported that she had tried her husband's cell, twice, but there was no answer. When my husband left, I had wanted to call him very badly, but had gotten drunk instead; at the time I told myself I was washing the urge out of me. I wondered if another postcard had turned up at Julia's apartment in Opa-locka.

"I guess we're not sure what to do," I said, worried Mrs. Defonte might start losing faith in us. "We've been up here a long time."

"You're the detectives," she said.

When morning came, Julia sucked down a coffee and two jelly doughnuts. She picked up the black nylon messenger bag that contained the Defonte case file, stalked over to the fire escape, and started climbing down.

"Where are you going?" I said. "You just made a breakfast run."

"Fuck this motherfucker," Julia said, her hands gripping the ladder.

I followed her down the fire escape. She didn't check for cars before crossing the street. When I caught up with her, she was looking for the blond woman's name on the row of silver mailboxes in the lobby.

"There she is." Julia pointed at box 703. Belinda Singer. Flecks of icing were stuck to her finger.

"This isn't what we do," I said. Private investigators were watchers, waiters. We waited for people to do whatever it was they were going to do, recorded it, and then handed over the evidence. We didn't jump into the middle of situations. We didn't intervene.

"We went to detective school, am I right?"

"*I* went to detective school," I said. "I did all the work. Everything is in my name."

"Well, we call ourselves detectives, don't we?"

I gave her a little shrug. The lack of sleep had made everything bleary.

"I'm ready to do some detecting." Julia held me in a hard stare. She had bright hazel eyes, more green than brown, and could be very convincing.

We rode the elevator to the seventh floor and knocked on the blond woman's door. She looked older up close, her tanned skin creased lightly around the eyes and forehead, her lips thin and dry. She wore a white sleeveless tennis dress and white sneakers with ankle socks. Her hair was pulled into a high ponytail.

"Are you Belinda Singer?" Julia flipped open her wallet and flashed the heavy brass badge issued to licensed PIs; if you didn't look closely, it could pass for the real thing. "Let us in. We're detectives. Police."

The woman didn't move from the doorway. I peered over her shoulder, but didn't see anyone inside.

"Ms. Singer? Did you hear me?" My sister's voice was forceful. I would have believed anything she said. The blond woman opened the door a little wider. Julia edged into the apartment.

"You're a detective too?" she asked as I entered.

I glared at her in a way I hoped was intimidating.

My sister moved into the blond woman's living room. She stood on a leopard-print rug, next to a glass coffee table piled high with issues of *South Florida Living*. I hung out closer to the front door. The floor was cream tile; large cockleshells, each the color of a sunset, had been arranged on the pale pink walls.

"Where is Peter Defonte?" Julia asked.

The woman cocked her head. "Who is Peter Defonte?"

Julia told the woman that she knew exactly who Peter Defonte was, that he had been in this apartment for the last two nights and was probably still here.

"I wish," the blond woman said.

"Do you think this is a joke, Ms. Singer?" Julia replied.

"No one's been here. Look around."

We checked the two bedrooms, the closets, the bathrooms. We looked under the beds and behind the shower curtains. When we were finished, Julia pulled a headshot of Mr. Defonte from her messenger bag and handed it to the blond woman.

"This man, we know that you know him." Julia's voice was softer. She touched the woman's forearm. "Go on, take a look."

The woman pinched the sides of the photo and frowned. "I don't know him at all." She handed the photo back to Julia and surveyed us for a moment, her nose wrinkling like she'd just smelled something unpleasant, which was entirely possible, seeing as we'd been baking on the roof, unshowered, for two days.

"I think your detecting skills need some work," she told us.

"This is the law you're talking to," Julia said. And then we got out of the apartment as quickly as we could. We went back down to the ground floor and showed the photo to the building manager, the superintendent, and a few maintenance men. If anyone asked, Julia did the badge flash and said we were police. No one recognized Mr. Defonte. The maintenance men showed us the side entrance, which had been visible from the roof. Besides the front door, that was the only way out; there was nothing that went through the back.

"Not unless you're Spider-Man," one of the men said, moving a mop across the floor.

In our time with Mr. Defonte, he had never seemed wily or agile, like some kind of escape artist. To me he had always looked weak, with his sluggish gait and doughy face and ridiculous hat. Outside I sat on the sidewalk and slumped against the building. The heat was as strong as ever. I felt like my skin was melting.

"What the fucking fuck?" Julia paced in front of me.

I pressed my face against my knees and groaned.

Later we had to call Mrs. Defonte and tell her we'd lost her husband. She'd phoned his office in Boca Raton and the firm he was supposed to be meeting in Memphis; no one had seen or heard from him. He had simply vanished. Since it had been forty-eight hours, Mrs. Defonte called 911 and then the real police got involved.

We had *seen* him go into that building. We had *seen* him open the door and walk inside. Our stakeout had just started; we were sharp and rested and hydrated. We had taken photos. Could he have slipped out when we were on the seventh floor, even though no one saw anything? Can buildings eat people? At a certain point that seemed as likely as anything.

We were required to turn our camera and film over to the police. They had examined every inch of the building, impounded his car and searched it for clues, and were as flummoxed as we were. Me and Julia and Mrs. Defonte met with an officer at the Boca Raton police station, a Detective Gregerson. He was an older man dressed in black slacks, sweat-stained shirtsleeves, and orthopedic shoes. He didn't look capable of much, but then neither had Mr. Defonte. He slid the photos we had taken across the metal table and asked Mrs. Defonte if she could identify her husband. She gazed at the photos of him standing on the sidewalk, staring at his feet; reaching for the door; pulling it open and stepping inside. She wore a quarter-sleeve dress patterned with red and pink flowers and leather sandals. Her black hair was pulled into a tight bun. She looked tired and confused, as though she'd just woken up in a place she didn't recognize.

"It's him," she said.

"Are you certain?" Detective Gregerson said.

She nodded and pushed the pictures away.

"What about the blond woman?" I asked.

"Belinda Singer." Julia cracked her knuckles, her go-to move when she was nervous.

"We questioned her," Detective Gregerson said. "She doesn't know anything."

"What about all those pictures of her and Mr. Defonte?"

"Did you ever see them talk to each other? Hold hands?"

"No," Julia and I said.

"Did you ever see them interact in any way? Any contact at all?"

We glanced at each other.

"No," Julia answered for us.

"There you go." He swept his hand to the side, like he'd solved something.

"There you go *what*?" I said. "It's an excessive amount of coincidences."

He sighed. "Fucking PIs."

"What did we do?" Julia slapped her hand against the table.

Detective Gregerson said that, in his experience, if you wanted to go looking for trouble, all you had to do was spend ten minutes with a few PIs.

"It's your aura," he said.

"We never stopped watching that building," I said. We hadn't. Not for a minute, save for when we searched for him inside. That was the one thing I was sure of.

Mrs. Defonte looked at us and then at Detective Gregerson. "I never should have hired them," she said. "I just wanted some answers."

"Don't we all," said the detective.

I didn't think it was fair for Mrs. Defonte to blame us, but at the same time I did feel partly responsible for whatever it was that had happened to her husband, as though our mere presence had set something in motion that might have remained dormant otherwise.

"We tried our best," I said. "We did just what you asked. We were very professional."

"You should have seen the mess they left on the roof," Detective Gregerson said. "Beer cans, food wrappers. Styrofoam cups, which are hell on the environment. And you shouldn't take those caffeine pills." He patted his chest. "Bad for the heart."

Mrs. Defonte folded her hands on the table and sniffed.

When the police found out we'd posed as real detectives, we were charged with impersonating an officer, fined one thousand dollars, and stripped of our private investigator and gun licenses. Winslow & Co. was over. Because Julia had a prior, her probation was extended by five years. The police said that if it weren't for overcrowding, she'd have gone right back to jail. That same week, a man was stabbed to death in the parking lot of our building in Opa-locka. Even after the body was taken away, streaks of dried blood stayed on the asphalt until it rained.

The rest of the Defonte saga unfolded on local TV. *Boca Raton resident vanishes into thin air!* The story got a lot of airtime on Florida stations, but never went national. Still, I developed an addiction to the news. I would stay inside for days, reading and watching everything I could find. I would sleep for hours and wake up tired. Some nights I lay on the sofa and thought as hard as I could about what we'd seen, what it meant. Was his body in that building? Was Belinda Singer some kind of criminal mastermind? Had he faked his own disappearance and made off to South America? What had we missed? I didn't come to a firm conclusion about anything.

Julia had no patience for my brooding. The Defonte case reminded us all too much of our father—not just the vanishing, but the inscrutability of it. My sister threw away our Winslow & Co. business cards and letterhead and started working with a shady, unlicensed PI outfit, whose clients were usually as culpable as the people they wanted investigated—a husband with domestic violence priors looking for his wife, a crooked businessman searching for the equally crooked partner who fleeced him. I brought this up to Julia one night, the morality of it. *Who isn't guilty,* she said, and maybe she had a point. On the nights she didn't come home at all, I would wait up on the sofa, in the glow of the TV, and worry.

New postcards arrived in the mail, another cloud and a rocky slope with scrubby bushes. I gathered all the cards and took them next door to Mirabella, who read tea leaves for a living. She was twenty-one, single, and rarely home. She took me into her bedroom. Her walls were covered with posters of tea leaves in various formations. She flopped down on her bed, spread the cards out in the shape of a rainbow, and examined them.

"This is not in Florida." Mirabella lay on her stomach. She had acne scars on her cheeks. She picked up the river and fanned herself with the card. "I don't know what else to tell you. It's hard to say more without all the pieces."

"Harder than reading tea leaves?"

Mirabella said she wasn't charging me and so I couldn't expect her best work. Besides, she added, pointing at one of the posters with the card, the leaves always told the whole story.

"Like I knew I was going to get robbed before it happened," she said.

"If you knew, why didn't you do something?"

"What could I do?" she said. "Not go home?"

I looked at the poster. The tea was a soggy, dark swirl, like wet dirt in the bottom of a white cup. Maybe I just didn't have a knack for seeing things.

Back at the apartment, I called my husband. If he would tell me what he was sending pieces of and why, I was willing to give him the satisfaction of saying he knew working with my sister would only bring trouble. I tried calling three times, but I couldn't get through; his cell phone had been disconnected. For a while I pretended the beep-beep-beep was my husband trying to reach me. I told myself he was using Morse code, which I had learned about in detective school. *Hello*, I said. *I'm listening*.

One afternoon, when Julia was out on a job, two things happened: another postcard arrived. It looked like part of a gorge, the same shade of brown rock, the words WISH YOU typed across the back. The second thing would have been easy to miss. I was unwrapping a Hot Pocket in the kitchenette when I heard something on the news about a man in Nevada who had been arrested for defrauding senior citizens. I left the frozen Hot Pocket on the counter and went to the TV. According to the reporter, this man's racket had been going on for two years. He had raked in hundreds of thousands. A Nevada DA said he would be punished to the fullest extent of the law. They showed the man being led up the steps of the courthouse. His hands were cuffed behind his back. A police officer gripped his elbow. He wore a gray trench coat. The wind blew his white hair across his face, revealing a toupee. He was much older, of course, but there he was.

"No fucking way," Julia said when I told her what I had discovered. The eleven o'clock news replayed the story and she gasped when she saw him walking up the courthouse steps. I felt relieved that she'd recognized him as immediately as I had. We called the number our mother had left; her boat was docked in the Maldives and she was on an excursion to a fishing village. We told the cruise director to tell our mother it was an emergency.

For a weekend, Julia partook in my addiction to the news. We kept the TV on day and night. The Senate was considering a bill designed to safeguard the personal information of senior citizens, so our father's story was getting national play. We read everything there was to read on the web. Julia let her cell phone ring. When we came across more photos of our father entering the courthouse online, she held on to my arm. In one, he was looking right at the camera, his gray eyebrows raised, his lips parted. Age spots dotted his face; his skin sagged. We made fun of his toupee to keep from crying.

The facts went like this: Our father, posing as a financial consultant, had convinced seventeen elderly Nevadans to give him power of attorney over their finances and then fraudulently cashed checks on their accounts. The victims had lost everything. It was Mrs. Calhoun, a ninety-six-year-old widow, who got him caught. Her daughter got suspicious of our father and called the authorities. An investigation was launched. When our father was arrested, he was getting ready to skip town. I wondered what, if anything, he would have been leaving behind.

On the first night, we printed news articles and cut out the photos of our father. We sat next to each other on the sofa, the TV blaring, and studied them under a magnifying glass. He and Julia shared the same high forehead and sharp cheekbones. I wondered if there was anything of him she saw in me.

"He looks so old," Julia said, rubbing her thumb over the paper.

When we called our mother a second time, the cruise director was able to get her on the phone. We put Julia's cell on speaker and told our mother everything. That we'd found our father in Nevada. That what had happened to him, where he'd been, was no longer a mystery. We were breathless, talking over each other. Once we finished, we leaned toward the phone and waited.

"We're going to Sri Lanka next," our mother said. "We're going to ride elephants."

"Mom?" we said. "Did you hear what we just told you?"

"This wasn't an emergency," she whispered before hanging up.

On the second night, we watched a TV special called *Preying on the Elderly* that featured our father and a con man right here in Florida, who had defrauded a whole retirement home full of seniors last winter. They showed one of our father's victims, a hunched old man named Reginald. He was leaning into a walker, a tiny white dog at his feet. The program offered a list of tips for elders: Don't give out personal information over the phone. Be suspicious if someone says you've won a fabulous prize. Get-rich-quick schemes never make you rich. Do background checks on everyone you meet. Julia pointed out that it sounded like the elderly were in need of private detectives. I nodded. I hoped Reginald was watching the same thing we were.

Later, while Julia was in the shower, I realized that after our father was arrested, the postcards had stopped coming. I decided they hadn't been from my husband after all, and was surprised by my disappointment. I didn't say anything to my sister at first. I stood by the closed bathroom door and listened to the water. I took a beer from the fridge and drank it standing up. When Julia emerged from the shower, I suggested we watch a movie. I picked up the remote and started clicking through the channels. *Beverly Hills Cop* was on. All night, I kept my secret.

On the third night, I couldn't stop myself from telling Julia about my theory. My husband hadn't sent the cards. It had been our father all along.

"It makes sense," I said. "A bunch were postmarked in Nevada."

"I should have known." Julia was on the couch in a long T-shirt and socks. "A typewriter didn't seem like his style. Too romantic."

I sat next to her. The news was on. Julia turned down the volume. The cards were stacked on the coffee table. He knew where we lived. He had kept track of us. Was it out of love, or a calculation, keeping tabs on his family in case he ran out of strangers to con? More questions we couldn't answer. I wondered if he knew about my divorce and Julia's stint in jail, if he had seen Mr. Defonte on the news and knew it had to do with us.

"I think this one goes here." Julia picked up the image of the gorge and placed it in the middle of the table. We put the sky and the clouds above it. The river to the left, the ledge to the right. We played with the positioning of the cards, tried to complete the sentence that began with WISH YOU.

" 'Wish you well'?" I said.

" 'Wish you luck'?"

" 'Wish you were here'?"

Julia looked at me. "If that's what it says, I'm glad we're not."

In the end, the puzzle didn't tell us much. We still didn't have enough pieces to know what it was for sure. We could tell it was a big dusty valley of some kind. Someplace out west, we figured. That part of the country was foreign to us.

"The Grand Canyon?" I suggested.

"Is it rocky enough?" Julia leaned over the coffee table, her head tilted. "What about Death Valley? That's in Nevada, right?"

I remembered hearing about the salt flats in Death Valley on TV. Badwater, they were called. The only animal that could survive there was some kind of snail. "Or the Mojave, in California? Do deserts have riverbeds?"

Julia scooped up the cards and stacked them on the table.

Years ago, when we were kids, we often played in the woods behind our childhood home. Somehow these nights had the same feeling as our games. At a certain point, Julia would always drop whatever we were doing and bolt into the woods. I would chase her, call after her, but she would just run and run. Finally I would climb the oak in our backyard and search for the peak of her head moving through the trees. I hardly ever found her. Usually I had to wait until she was ready to come out. Sometimes that took minutes; other times, hours.

My sister stared at the TV. I heard sirens. At first it sounded like they were right outside, but after a while, they began to fade.

"Here's a story," she said. "About two little girls who tried to make something out of nothing."

By Monday, Julia had reached her limit. That night she muted the TV and lay on the couch, her head in my lap. I nestled my fingers in her hair. It was thick and tangled and smelled like her coconut shampoo.

"I can't stay in this place anymore," she said.

At first I thought she was talking about Opa-locka and felt a wash of relief. "It's about time. Where do you want to go?"

Julia didn't seem to hear me. "Mom was right. From now on, we should just pretend he's dead."

I pulled my fingers out of her hair. "How can we pretend that? He's right there on the news."

"It's like being in a maze," she said. "We're never going to get anywhere."

She was right. Between Mr. Defonte and our father, I could feel myself being consumed by mystery. But that was beside the point. It didn't even feel like a choice, to wade into all of this. I didn't understand how she could decide to stop.

"I have to let it go." She sat up and rubbed her forehead. "I just have to."

A still of our father was on TV. It was from when he had just arrived in Nevada. He wore a yellow polo shirt and was smiling broadly, a neat crest of gray hair arcing over his forehead. It might have been under the worst circumstances possible, but he was back in our lives.

"Look at him, Julia." I leaned toward her and pressed my palm against her cheek. "He's right there."

"I know he is," she said. "And I wish he wasn't."

After that night, she went back to working with the shady private investigators. She started coming home smelling like whiskey and smoke, a gun tucked into the waistband of her jeans, even though we'd lost the firearm license. *Just in case,* she told me. She got a pager and it buzzed constantly. She lost weight. Her hair thinned. The spaces beneath her eyes hollowed out. She looked the same as she did in jail, weary and sad. Once I heard her screaming at someone in our parking lot. By the time I looked out the window, my sister was alone and sitting on the ground, her face in her hands. I went downstairs and crouched in front of her, stepping in a small pool of gasoline. I placed my hands on her knees. *Julia,* I said. *Look at me.* She sighed and tipped her head back and for a moment I thought she was going to break out of whatever it was she'd fallen into. But then she jumped to her feet, went upstairs, and locked herself in her room. A few mornings later, I found her asleep on the couch, fully clothed, the gun on the coffee table. Her brown hair fell over her shoulders; her hands were folded under her chin. Her lips were parted in the exact same way our father's had been in the photo we found online; they even had the same long, slender shape. On the couch, Julia was free of the sadness. She looked innocent and sweet and most people would have no idea what she was capable of. But I knew, because she was my sister. I knew she was keeping things from me.

Here is what I kept from Julia: Twice a month, I would go to Boca Raton for Mrs. Defonte's rehearsals. By late July, they were in final preparations for *Don Giovanni*. They had done the last two rehearsals in full costume; the stage held a pair of elaborate gold balconies connected by a wide staircase. The steps were covered by a plush red rug. A chandelier hung from the ceiling. It was like seeing the opera on opening night, minus the audience. I almost felt bad that I hadn't paid anything.

Mrs. Defonte was playing Donna Anna and the masked man was Don Giovanni. She wore a floor-length gown with lace sleeves and green brocade, the veil still clipped in her black hair. Her voice was as beautiful as ever. I wondered how much she thought about her husband, what she thought about him. I imagined she had theories of her own.

Don Giovanni wore black pants, a white peasant shirt, and a wig. The basic problem in the story was that everyone wanted Don Giovanni to change, but he wouldn't. It also showed how a person's actions come back on them, how the seed of what happens next exists in what's happening now. I had started going to the rehearsals because of Mrs. Defonte, but in the end, Don Giovanni was the one who held my interest.

My favorite scene was set in a graveyard. Don Giovanni and the servant, Leporello, were surrounded by gravestones. Giovanni's laugh summoned the ghost of the Commendatore, whom he'd killed in act 1. Leporello was frightened; Giovanni invited the Commendatore to dinner. He couldn't know, couldn't see, what would happen next.

It was a terrible flaw, our inability to see where our lives were leading us. For instance, in the back row of the theater, I could never have imagined that in late August, while Julia was stopped at a red light in Opa-locka, three blocks from our apartment, a man would walk up to her and shoot her in the head. She died at the scene. Our mother had to fly back from Muscat, her neck heavy with blue topaz, which, she had been told, would shield her from grief. I couldn't have imagined how long I would stay in Julia's apartment, out of a strange sense of loyalty, before I broke down and moved to Coconut Grove and took a job as an administrative assistant in a law firm, perhaps not so unlike the one Mr. Defonte had worked in. I couldn't have imagined that, after my father pled out and was sentenced to fifteen years, I would have flown all the way to Nevada to see him in jail, to tell him that his daughter was dead and our mother might as well be, to tell him that I missed him, that I would never forgive him, that he could fuck his fucking postcards, and not be able to get past the entrance. In fact, I couldn't even get out of the rental car. I sat in the parking lot for hours, blasting the Kingsmen CD I'd brought along, the postcards tucked into the glove compartment, before driving away. For the first ten miles I convinced myself that I was doing preliminary surveillance, that I would be back. I wondered if my husband would be consoled by the fact that the lies I told him were nothing compared to the ones I sometimes told myself. No, none of that seemed possible, as I watched Mrs. Defonte and Don Giovanni sing in a way that made my insides tremble.

The Commendatore came back to Don Giovanni in the form of a statue. The singer was painted silver and wore a helmet and a cape made of chain mail; he reminded me of the Tin Man from *The Wizard of Oz.* Even after I'd seen the whole opera, I kept willing Don Giovanni not to laugh in the graveyard, not to invite the Commendatore to dinner. *Run away,* I would whisper in the back row. *Just run away.* He never did, of course, and it wouldn't have changed anything if he had.

Reading The O. Henry Prize Stories 2014

The Jurors on Their Favorites

Once the twenty O. Henry Prize stories are chosen by the series editor, our jurors read them in a blind manuscript. Each story appears in the same type and format with no attribution of the magazine that published it or the author's name. The jurors don't consult the series editor or one another. Although the jurors write their essays without knowledge of the authors' names, the names are inserted into the essay later for the sake of clarity. —LF

Tash Aw on "The Gun" by Mark Haddon

Two boys and a gun; a tough neighborhood of tower blocks and scrapyards; a traumatic, violent event that will mark the story's protagonist. Stripped down to its bones, the story seems immediately familiar: A coming-of-age story, we might think, a masculine-rites-of-passage narrative. Indeed, the one-dimensional directness of the title seems to offer only one choice to the reader. This is a story about two boys who find a gun, go and play with it, and end up committing a horrific act that will scar them forever.

Except that they are not scarred in the way you imagine, and in some ways, the one who pulls the trigger doesn't even seem particularly shocked by what he has done (though we don't see him thirty years later, as we do the protagonist, so we don't really know for sure). And nothing is quite what it seems: Everything hovers on the edge of possibility, flitting among multiple realities. The physical properties of the story, like its emotional terrain, are a shifting no-man's-land, never fixed to one single truth. The bleakness of the council estate where the protagonist grows up is shot through with tenderness, but it is also socially vague— working-class, certainly, but populated by families who read crime novels and do jigsaw puzzles in their spare time; and it borders a huge ring road, bleeding elsewhere into more aspiring areas where people drive BMWs and have china greyhounds on either side of the fireplace. There are woodlands next to factories and junkyards. Everything is ugly; everything is beautiful.

And this constant juxtaposing continues on the emotional and technical planes of the story. Gentleness nestles snugly next to the violence; joyousness is placed squarely with the grotesque; the serious social portrait of the neighborhood is laced throughout with an exuberant sense of the ridiculous, sometimes the absurd. Above all, present forces its way into the past, and vice versa. The infallibility of memory: Nothing is ever quite what it seems, but everything is exactly what it seems.

That is why the event that lies at the heart of the story never seems quite as unbelievable as it should be, for everything in the universe of the story is already set up to be at once fantastic yet rooted in reality. A cow crashes through a roof into a meeting at an ironworks. A dead woman calls her son on the telephone half an hour after she dies. A large deer bounds out of scrubby woodland on the edge of a busy road and is shot by young boys fooling around with a gun, and is then cut up in an apartment on a council estate and roasted with potatoes. Has the protagonist made all of this up? Is he going mad? These are questions he asks himself but never finds the answers to.

In some ways this is the gritty-but-intimate story you might have imagined at the outset, but it is much more than that. It takes a well-trodden narrative and makes it surreal, ever so gently ironic, sad, and hugely affectionate. It pulls the reader in lots of different directions: You never know exactly how to react, for there's never a comfort zone. The protagonist often feels some-what detached from the goings-on around him, even in the most explosive moments of the story, and at times I felt frustrated by his inability to take charge of the swirl of events and emotions around him. But by the end of the story, his state of nonengage-ment seemed entirely fitting to me, and truthful, too. We think we own our memories, we think we construct the narrative of our lives, but in fact we don't. Things just happen—random events, sometimes boring, sometimes monumental, often just plain weird. We are mere observers to the strangeness of our own lives, this sequence of events that unfolds before us, leaving us bewildered, lost in a blurred landscape, just like the protagonist of "The Gun."

Tash Aw was born in Taipei to Malaysian parents and grew up in Kuala Lumpur, Malaysia. *The Harmony Silk Factory* won the Whitbread and Commonwealth Writers prizes for best first novel, was longlisted for the Booker Prize, and has been translated into twenty-three languages. His third novel is *Five Star Billionaire*. He lives in London.

James Lasdun on "The Inheritors" by Kristen Iskandrian

I was drawn immediately to "The Inheritors" by the nervously probing intelligence of the writing. Many short stories, includ-ing some very great ones, involve a trade-off whereby you give your time and attention to some fairly unremarkable chunks of narrative on the understanding that by the end something will have happened to make them magically resonate with each other and add up to more than the sum of their parts. "The Inheri-tors" is rare in offering both that larger, structural, magic and the detailed pleasure of a super-sensitive mind figuring out an enigma, sentence by sentence, right there on the page.

What is that enigma? It has to do with the sense of connection that arises, occasionally, between two strangers. Like the orphaned bric-a-brac in the thrift store where she works, the unnamed woman encountered by the unnamed narrator is of uncertain origin (or so she claims) and quirkily idiosyncratic character. Her presence in the world seems as tenuous as her grasp of idiom, and as striking: It's easy to understand the narrator's growing fascination with her. *Fascination* does seem the word for this odd, original relationship (original in the sense that although it seems extremely lifelike I don't remember ever seeing it as the subject of a short story). Not quite warmth, not quite annoyance, not quite erotic interest, it seems to partake of all these things, and braid them into something utterly—and wonderfully— mysterious. And of course it is further enriched by the narrator's own singular temperament, her very appealing way of combining the whimsical with the scrupulous as she articulates her complex reactions to the ever-evolving mystery of this new acquaintance of hers. Her trains of thought are as pleasurable to follow as they are unpredictable. Musing on the multifunctionality of objects in our world (TVs that double as refrigerators, et cetera), she looks at the tea towels she's folding in the store and imagines how even these humble items might adapt to modern times: "I saw them scrubbing out their own stains, embroidered corners curling in like starfish, while maybe simultaneously announcing the time." Then, in a series of characteristic swerves, she feeds her reflections right back into the puzzle of attraction and exasperation at the emotional heart of the story: "I wanted to say this to her, wanted her to find me funny, and I also wanted to unravel her, to find a loose thread and pull at it, as though she were the towels I was folding, which felt suddenly twee and self-satisfied."

That idea of multifunctionality also seems to be the key to the larger design of the story. If you stand back from its microscopi- cally focused acts of scrutiny and self-scrutiny, what you see is a whole architecture of substitutions and repurposings. From the first image of the woman as a "placeholder" for someone else in the narrator's memory, nobody is quite who they seem, and every feeling comes with a switch that can turn it magically into its opposite. I haven't seen this before either—this kind of delirious but controlled volatility. I found it—like every other aspect of this story—strange, new, delightful, and curiously moving. It leaves you with a sense of unnavigable waters having been accurately and lovingly charted—if not exactly made safe.

James Lasdun was born in London in 1958. His publications include *The Horned Man,* a novel, and *Landscape with Chainsaw,* a collection of poems. His story "The Siege" was adapted by Bernardo Bertolucci for his film *Besieged.* He cowrote the screenplay for the film *Sunday* (based on another of his stories), which won awards for best feature and best screenplay at Sundance. His story "An Anxious Man" won the UK's inaugural BBC National Short Story Award in 2006. His latest books are a memoir, *Give Me Everything You Have: On Being Stalked,* and a collection of stories, *It's Beginning to Hurt.* Lasdun lives in upstate New York.

Joan Silber on "Opa-locka" by Laura van den Berg

Picking just one story was difficult. As I read, I kept forming new enthusiasms—the masterly "The Women" by William Trevor, the astounding "Fatherland" by Halina Duraj, the wonderfully sharp "Trust" by Dylan Landis. In the end, I chose "Opa-locka" by Laura van den Berg. It's a wild story that manages to be utterly convincing—two sisters, down on their luck, have hired themselves out as private eyes, and are first seen spying on an adulterous husband from a very hot rooftop in Florida. While their vigil features bologna sandwiches, ice cubes, beer, Cheetos, and NoDoz, the hokiness of all this doesn't mean they're not close to danger.

What I loved in this story was the way it kept surprising me. It has a number of layers—the two sisters once hired a detective to try to find their own runaway father, one sister has a prison record and an edgy streak and a bad neighborhood, the worried wife who hires them is rehearsing *Don Giovanni*. While I was watching the sisters make a botch of their genuinely vexing investigation, I had the great pleasure of feeling the story go deeper, as it went down several paths.

It's quite a stunning moment when the story announces what it's about. Watching her ex-client sing Mozart, the narrator thinks, "The basic problem in the story was that everyone wanted Don Giovanni to change, but he wouldn't." This bit of smartness—right in character—was especially satisfying to me because I'm sort of an enemy of the old chestnut that a short story is required to show a character changing. Chekhov, I like to point out, is often interested in characters who won't change—"The Darling" sings a whole tune about this. "Opa-locka" is intent on looking at the mystery—to use one of its favorite words—of why some people (father, husband, sister) are so set on doing what they do, no matter how they are loved.

The story has its own sense of pacing—it isn't afraid to include a crucial death at the last moment—and it lets its final loops tie together all the elements. It's a deceptively skilled story, ambitious in a superbly sneaky way.

Joan Silber was born in New Jersey. She is the author of seven works of fiction, including *Fools* (longlisted for the National Book Award and finalist for the 2014 PEN-Faulkner Prize), *The Size of the World* (finalist for the Los Angeles Times Book Prize in Fiction), *Ideas of Heaven* (finalist for the National Book Award and the Story Prize), and *Household Words* (winner of the PEN/ Hemingway Award). She is the author of *The Art of Time in Fiction*, a critical study. Her stories have been in three O. Henry collections, and she's received a Literature Award from the American Academy of Arts and Letters as well as grants from the Guggenheim Foundation and the National Endowment for the Arts. She teaches at Sarah Lawrence College and lives in New York City.

Writing The O. Henry Prize Stories 2014

The Writers on Their Work

Allison Alsup, "Old Houses"

Most of my fiction is drawn from very different circumstances than mine—other eras, places, and cultures. "Old Houses" is one of the exceptions. I grew up on a street very much like the one in the story, with manicured yards and graceful two-story houses overlooking the San Francisco Bay. It's the kind of street where the neighbors stay for decades and grow to be close friends. My parents still live there; indeed the block does throw an annual party.

However, at some point in my childhood, I learned of a terrible crime, a double murder involving a wife and daughter, that had taken place next door a few years before my parents bought our house. The murders were never solved, though the key suspect, a teenage boy, had lived two doors down on the other side of our home. After the crime the family of the accused moved away, and by the time we moved to the street, a new family lived in the house. I became friends with their youngest daughters, who maintained the house was haunted. We knew, or believed we did, which bedroom the boy had occupied, and noted how he could have looked out his window, across my lawn, and to the victims' house.

It seemed inconceivable that not only had such violence happened on our perfect street, but that one neighbor could have done this to another. It was simply too terrifying to imagine, and we rarely spoke of it. Growing up in the space between these two houses left its impression. My home, and by extension I myself, occupied the middle position. Perhaps because I was never able to reconcile the violence with our otherwise placid street, I felt compelled to write the story in order to discover its potential significance. Writers are negotiators, hashing out ideas until seemingly opposite camps can sit at the same table and come to some sort of understanding.

My instinct told me to start with the central characters and witnesses: the houses themselves. The other major choice, the collective point of view, felt right since the story is less about individuals than about a neighborhood and the elements—class, ritual, and most of all the old houses and their histories, both true and mythic—that bind the residents together.

Allison Alsup grew up in Oakland, California. She teaches writing at Urban League College Track, an after-school program for underserved New Orleans high school students motivated to attend college. Alsup is the coauthor of a narrative bar guide, *The French Quarter Drinking Companion,* and she writes for the tourist site GoNOLA.com. Her stories have won several awards, including a Short Story Award from *New Millennium Writings,* the Marguerite McGlinn Prize for Fiction from *Philadelphia Stories,* as well as the Orlando Prize Story from the A Room of Her Own Foundation. She lives in New Orleans, Louisiana.

Chanelle Benz, "West of the Known"

Like most of my stories, this one started out as a melodramatic epic about something else entirely. Originally, I wanted to write a literary western and have a triangle between a sheriff, an outlaw brother, and his younger sister, who is drawn into the gang. The first thing I imagined was an amazingly awful title: "An Apology to Thomas." (Thomas being the sheriff.) But the first thing

I actually wrote was the paragraph that roughly begins: "My brother dressed me as a boy. It only needed a bandanna . . ." The scene in which Lavenia and Jackson first meet followed. Once Jackson stepped in, he took over. Cy came next, bringing the dogs and the stars and the dark. I knew then that I had blood on the page. That's a saying nobody likes but me, but it best describes when I know a story's come alive and I've got characters who can hurt me with their failings, longings, and loss.

Chanelle Benz was born in London, England, and grew up in Virginia. She has an MFA in creative writing from Syracuse University and a BFA in acting from Boston University. Her work has appeared in *Fence, Staccato,* and *The Cupboard*. Her story "West of the Known" was named by Longreads.com as one of the top ten stories of 2012. She lives in Mississippi.

David Bradley, "You Remember the Pin Mill"

It was '88 or '89. I hadn't written a short story for a dozen years. I wanted to write what I knew: the experience of black Americans. But stereotypes and expectations embedded in American culture kept readers from seeing my characters as I envisioned them. Adding corrective exposition meant the narrative got long . . . or lost. But now a magazine was offering me money—good money—for a story. I explained my dilemma to my agent, Wendy Weil. She said, "Why not write about white people?"

I thought of something else I knew: Western Pennsylvania. A rural, mountainous region, 99 and $^{44}/_{100}$ths percent pure Ivory. So I wrote about a couple of white guys—old buddies, Homer and Marhafka, one Presbyterian, one Catholic, both long in love with the same woman, one married to her but divorcing—in a pickup, drinking the local brew. The magazine ran it with an illustration depicting both as black. Stereotypes and expectations apply to writers too.

I didn't write another story for a dozen years. By then I was teaching in an MFA program. A colleague asked me to give a reading. Short fiction rules in MFA programs; I could hardly admit my inexperience with the form. I thought of other things I knew, or actually, remembered: a roaring dump truck, a driver with gloves like gauntlets, the sound of a factory whistle echoing in a valley, the vision of a boy with eyes as yet uncataracted by stereotypes and expectations.

I drafted that story in three days. Fifteen revisions (and eleven years) later it became "You Remember the Pin Mill."

David Bradley was born and raised in Bedford, in Western Pennsylvania. He is the author of two novels, *South Street* and *The Chaneysville Incident,* which was awarded the 1982 PEN/ Faulkner Award and the Arts and Letters Award from the American Academy of Arts and Letters. Both novels have been released in electronic editions. Since 1985, Bradley has worked primarily in creative nonfiction, publishing in such periodicals as *Esquire, Redbook, The New York Times, The New Yorker, Philadelphia* magazine, *The Pennsylvania Gazette, The Nation,* and *Dissent.* His recent work has also appeared online in *Obit, Narrative,* and *Brevity.* Bradley, who holds a BA in creative writing from the University of Pennsylvania and an MA in United States studies from the University of London, has received fellowships from the John Simon Guggenheim Memorial Foundation and the National Endowment for the Arts. Bradley lives in La Jolla, California.

Olivia Clare, "Pétur"
I lived in Iceland for a little while in 2010, shortly after the eruption of Eyjafjallajökull. I stayed in a cabin in Skorradalur, a small lake dale. Seeing land still covered in ash and living in a cabin in this rural area led me to imagine a preternatural mother venturing out into an eerie scrim of ash. But I imagined her walks were purposeful . . . almost before I realized what was happening, she'd met someone.

Olivia Clare was born in New York in 1982 and spent her childhood in Louisiana. Her stories have appeared in *Kenyon Review Online*, *The Southern Review*, *The Yale Review*, and elsewhere. "Pétur" is her first published story. Her poems have been published in *Poetry*, *The London Magazine*, and other journals. In 2011, she received a Ruth Lilly Fellowship from the Poetry Foundation. She lives in Las Vegas.

Stephen Dixon, "Talk"

For the past three years, on almost any day when it isn't raining or snowing or too hot or too cold to stay outside for very long, I sit, around 5 p.m., after a long walk or short jog, on a bench in front of the Episcopal church across the street from my house. On one particular day about a year and a half ago I'd just finished writing a new short story and photocopying it at a copy center in town, and was already getting anxious about not having anything to write the next day. So, sitting in front of the church, with a copy of *Gilgamesh* I was planning to read on the bench, and not having spoken to anyone since the previous day but my cat Louis and also to myself a little, I got the idea to write the story "Talk." A first line came to me, I wrote it down on the inside of the cover of *Gilgamesh* and knew that the following morning I'd type that line on my manual typewriter and would write the first draft of the story in around half an hour. That's what I did, and it took me two weeks of writing nothing but this story to finish it.

Stephen Dixon was born in New York. "Talk" is his fourth O. Henry Prize story. He has been awarded a Guggenheim Fellowship, as well as the American Academy of Arts and Letters Prize for Literature, and the Pushcart Prize. He taught for many years in the Writing Seminars at Johns Hopkins University. He has published many novels and short-story collections. His latest novel is *His Wife Leaves Him*. He lives in Maryland.

Halina Duraj, "Fatherland"

This story is a distillation of a novel draft. I'd been invited to give a reading, and I knew I wanted to read from the novel I'd been working on. I sat down to choose a section to read, but because of the way I'd written the novel—in many short, fragmented sections that jumped across space and time, organized associatively rather than chronologically—I found it difficult to determine a section that could stand alone. I selected a few sections I knew I wanted to read, and then those determined which other sections would be necessary to provide context and an arc for a stand-alone piece. Those first choices acted as magnets, pulling necessary complements from the entire draft. I ended up culling pieces from various points in the manuscript to create this stand-alone story.

Halina Duraj grew up in Northern California and now teaches at the University of San Diego. Her work has been featured in journals including *The Sun, Harvard Review, Fiction,* and *Witness.* She has an MA in creative writing from the University of California, Davis, and a PhD in literature with an emphasis in creative writing from the University of Utah. She is the author of the story collection *The Family Cannon.*

Louise Erdrich, "Nero"

Thirty years ago, I could not have written this story, because parts of it are true. My grandparents really had a dog named Nero who escaped continually from the backyard. He really did rip the electric wire off the top of the fence. He really did end up in the cage with the cauldron to toss around. The misery of his life contrasted deeply with the characters of my tough but kind grandparents. I never knew what to make of Nero until suddenly, one morning, I was writing this story. I suppose I could say something about the water of experience seeping slowly through bedrock shale into the aquifer, but really, who knows? The python lyceum, as well, was based on a real show. It is my most enthralling memory from grade two at Zimmerman Elementary School in Wahpeton. When my grandfather first came to the Midwest from Germany, he made money by going from town to Iowa farm town wrestling for prize money. When it came to setting up the fight scene in fiction, I called on my friend. He is a tae kwon do third- or fourth-degree black belt and Brazilian jujitsu teacher. He sent me some exciting early YouTube videos of tensile Royce Gracie fighting huge guys. If you like that part, please check them out. In other words, this is a story about existence, inevitability, and time.

Louise Erdrich grew up in North Dakota and is a member of the Turtle Mountain Band of Chippewa. Her most recent book, *The Round House*, won the 2012 National Book Award. Her other books include *The Plague of Doves, The Last Report on the Miracles at Little No Horse,* and *The Master Butchers Singing Club.* She owns Birchbark Books, a small independent bookstore in Minneapolis.

Mark Haddon, "The Gun"

Good stories seem to come from some weird zone it's impossible to access in retrospect. After all, if we knew how they came into being they'd be a damn sight easier to write. I know simply that I'd been haunted for a long time by the image of two boys pushing a pram containing a dead deer across a dual carriageway several miles away from where I live, a road I've driven down many times. Where the image came from I have no idea, only that it had a peculiar charge and that it stuck with me. The story grew around it much as those blue crystals grew around the string you left hanging in a jam jar of saturated copper sulfate at school.

Like many writers I'm always trying to strike out in new directions only to find that I've been traveling in a circle, which is not so bad if the place from which you started out is fertile enough. I can see now that the story contains elements that keep cropping up in my writing. There is a tower-block balcony. I find myself writing over and over about tower-block balconies. An animal is killed, which happens quite often when I'm writing. Most important of all, the story takes place in what the poets Paul Farley and Michael Symmons Roberts call edgelands, those grubby, liminal, unloved places that are neither town nor country, whose ownership is dubious and that are never en route to anywhere. I see them still, from train windows, those rags of dirty scrub between the factories and the canals and the sidings. Little holes in the world. And it comes flooding back, the conviction I remember from childhood that they might just be portals to somewhere else altogether.

Mark Haddon was born in Northampton in 1962. He has written children's books, radio plays, TV scripts, and a collection of poetry, *The Talking Horse and the Sad Girl and the Village Under the Sea*. He is the author of *The Curious Incident of the Dog in the Night-Time* and two other novels, *A Spot of Bother* and *The Red House*. In 2010 his play, *Polar Bears*, was produced at the Donmar Warehouse in London. He is working on a second play. He lives in Oxford.

Tessa Hadley, "Valentine"

"Valentine" is in fact an excerpt from my novel *Clever Girl*. But the whole of that novel was written very deliberately as a series of episodes, and each chapter in my heroine's life was meant to stand by itself and have the feel of a whole short story. As well as being a way of structuring the novel, this corresponds to something I feel about experience in time. We like to think of our experiences as having the overarching shape and drive of a novel, but actually life more usually happens in fragments and stretches—when change comes it's often as if we start off on a completely new narrative track, forgetting our former selves. As for the 1970s world of the story: My heroine Stella is nothing like me, but she is my age exactly and was born in the same city as I was—Bristol, in the west of England. So I knew her ambience very well—I had no difficulty imagining what they wore, what music they liked, what they smoked, the places they went. I remember beautiful boys like Valentine. I don't know why I was so certain from the beginning that Stella's first love had to be a doomed love, impossible to fulfill. But that idea was there from my very first intimations of the novel. . . .

Tessa Hadley was born and raised in Bristol. She's written five novels, including *The Master Bedroom, The London Train,* and *Clever Girl,* and two collections of short stories, as well as a book of criticism, *Henry James and the Imagination of Pleasure.* She publishes stories regularly in *The New Yorker.* She is a professor of creative writing at Bath Spa University in Bath, England, and she reviews regularly for the *Guardian* newspaper and for the *London Review of Books.*

Rebecca Hirsch Garcia, "A Golden Light"

I struggled to write this comment for "A Golden Light," a story perhaps more personal than I would like to admit. It seemed as though with every word I wrote I was revealing both too much and too little, fighting to provide insight without forcing my own impressions on any potential reader and failing at every turn.

For "A Golden Light" is a humble story with many interpretations, each of which is as true as the next, none of which I would want to accidentally favor or discourage with these words.

And so I offer my story up without comment and leave it to the readers to find in it what they will.

Rebecca Hirsch Garcia was born in Ottawa, Ontario, where she currently resides. Her work has been published in *Ottawa Arts Review.*

Kristen Iskandrian, "The Inheritors"
There are a few pet obsessions the story vivisects for me; the most fundamental is the multilayered entity of the female friendship. I wanted to create a situation in which two women started out as strangers and wound up as intimates, brought together not by some adventure or other momentous happening but rather by place, by talk, and by silence. I wanted to hang out in the quiet, fumbling bloom of a relationship and to let that be the story's pulse. For me, this is also a story about agency. The narrator of the story is not, I would argue, the protagonist. She is someone to whom things happen, someone who is acted upon. Her counterpoint, her "she," on the other hand, seeks to author her life at every turn, even going so far as to choose her parents, her very origins. Lastly, I chose a consignment store as the central setting because I find them interesting—the sentimental mess of things disowned and things reclaimed, an orphanage for objects—and once there, these characters and their disparate desires took shape and inscribed one another.

Kristen Iskandrian was born and raised in Philadelphia. She received her BA from the College of the Holy Cross and her MA and PhD from the University of Georgia. Her work has been published in *Gulf Coast, Denver Quarterly, American Letters & Commentary, Memorious, La Petite Zine, Fifty-Two Stories, Pank, Tin House,* and many other places, both in print and online. She lives in Birmingham, Alabama.

Dylan Landis, "Trust"
A teenager sneaking through her father's filing cabinet: a search.
I had that image in my head, and then, there was Rainey Royal digging around, and she spotted her hated middle name on her own birth certificate. It's a fishhook that snags everything she finds unlovable in herself. I already knew she was a molested girl. I had to wrench that flash of self-loathing from my own adoles-

cent past, and it was so painful and private I was tempted to tone it down for publication. The second picture that surfaced was of a gun tucked between file folders. I was as startled as Rainey was. I don't know what generated that idea, either, and I didn't welcome it. Howard Royal, Rainey's father, is a seductive, charismatic jazz pianist, and I wanted to pursue their power struggles, not the distraction of a gun. Chekhov said if you reveal a gun in act 1, it must go off in act 3. I believe that. I also believe that if you root in the basement of the mind and grasp an object in the muck, your subconscious put it there for a reason. So I let Rainey and her best friend, Tina, fool with the gun for a while, discussing men and face-blindness, before going out to play robber girls.

They couldn't go out and rob someone solely because they had a weapon, though. So the gun confounded me. Over many drafts, I came to see it as an instrument, a psychological crowbar with which I could apply a stress fracture to Rainey and Tina's intimacy. What finally drives the robbery is the deeper conflict of the girls testing their faith in each other. And I had no more idea than Rainey did how the robbery would end. With every story I write, I like finding my endings in the muck of the basement too.

Dylan Landis is the author of the forthcoming *Rainey Royal* and of *Normal People Don't Live Like This,* linked story collections that feature the same cast of characters. Her work has appeared in *Bomb, Tin House,* and *Best American Nonrequired Reading.* In 2010 she received a National Endowment for the Arts fellowship in Prose. She lives in New York City.

Colleen Morrissey, "Good Faith"

A few years ago, I watched a BBC documentary called *The Most Hated Family in America* (2007), in which the journalist Louis Theroux spent a great deal of time among the members of the Westboro Baptist Church. Of course, the hateful rhetoric of the Westboro Baptist Church holds a train-wreck type of fascination, but what really struck me was the behavior of some of the younger members of the church, the ones in their late teens and early twenties. They were ready with the church's talking points, but their expressions and body language bespoke a lingering uneasiness with what they were saying. They weren't yet totally gone. By coincidence, shortly after seeing the documentary, I read two pieces about Christian ceremonial snake-handling, and I began thinking about how empowering and yet how self-hating such an act was. With "Good Faith," I wanted to capture that pull between power and surrender, and that time of unrest before we plunge into a belief or way of life.

Colleen Morrissey was born in Omaha, Nebraska, and achieved her BA in English at the University of Iowa and her MA in English literature at the University of Kansas. She is currently working toward her PhD at the Ohio State University. Her fiction and nonfiction have appeared in *Confrontation* and *Monkeybicycle*. Morrissey lives in Columbus, Ohio.

Chinelo Okparanta, "Fairness"
This story came to be during a visit to East and Southeast Asia, where I observed, among women of a certain class, a preoccupation with keeping the skin color light. I found myself exploring this issue through my writing. What came out was more a story about loyalty and betrayal across social strata than a story about skin bleaching.

Chinelo Okparanta was born in Port Harcourt, Nigeria, and moved to the United States at the age of ten. She is the author of *Happiness, Like Water*, which was longlisted for the 2013 Frank O'Connor International Short Story Award. In addition to being nominated for a United States Artists fellowship in Literature and shortlisted for the Caine Prize for African Writing, she has served as Provost's Postgraduate Visiting Writer in Fiction at the Iowa

Writers' Workshop, Olive B. O'Connor Fellow in Creative Writing at Colgate University, and John Gardner Fellow in Fiction at the Bread Loaf Writers' Conference, and as visiting assistant professor of fiction at Purdue University. Her stories and essays have appeared in *Granta, Tin House, The Kenyon Review, AGNI, Subtropics,* and *Conjunctions,* among others.

Michael Parker, "Deep Eddy"

I had never written "short shorts" or "flash fiction" in my life until two summers ago, when I wrote twenty-odd of what I called my little tiny pieces. "Deep Eddy" was one of the earliest tiny pieces I wrote, and the title came first. Deep Eddy is a real place, a spring-fed swimming pool in a town where I sometimes live, and even though the water is such a perfect temperature and color I have to restrain myself from drinking it, it was the music of those two words—*Deep Eddy*—that spawned the story. I had no intention of writing a story about a pool where I love to swim, so I set the story in the rural South where I was born and raised. The delicious water of the pool became a brackish backwoods river tainted by rural legend. These places—sacred to teenagers because they were off-limits, said to be haunted or cursed or dangerous—existed in the place and time in which I grew up, and after I had that place darkly in mind, and after I made my way through the woods to that seemingly bottomless swirl that gave the story its title, and dropped a boy and a girl into its circling, I had only to locate the rest of the images necessary to convey what every story I know worth reading is, on some level, about: the sweet, desperate, and inevitable currents of desire.

Michael Parker was born and raised in North Carolina. He is the author of two story collections and six novels, including, most recently, *All I Have in This World.* He is a professor in the MFA writing program at the University of North Carolina Greensboro. He lives in North Carolina and Texas.

Robert Anthony Siegel, "The Right Imaginary Person"

I was asked to read at a benefit hosted by a local bookstore and had nothing short enough to fit the time limit, so I pulled out a section from the novel I was working on—really just a couple of pages of dialogue between a man and a woman that had no clear place in the overall plot of the book and would probably have to be cut. I was just looking for something amusing to get me through the reading.

But in the audience at the bookstore that night sat a husband and wife in their sixties who happened to both be blind. They listened with great attention as I read, and when they laughed it was as if they were laughing at the foolishness of real people they actually knew. Toward the end, one of my characters said something self-serving and totally manipulative to the other character, and the husband turned to his wife and said, rather loudly, "Yeah, right." It was then that I decided to put the novel aside for a little bit and write a story about these characters, to write it just as if I were telling it to the blind couple at the reading.

Born and raised in New York, Robert Anthony Siegel studied Japanese literature at Harvard and the University of Tokyo. In 2013 he was a Fulbright Scholar in Taiwan. Siegel is the author of two novels, *All the Money in the World* and *All Will Be Revealed*. His short work has appeared in *Tin House, Ploughshares, The Oxford American, Tablet, The New York Times*'s "Draft" column, the online edition of the *Los Angeles Times*, the *Los Angeles Review of Books, Bookforum*, and other magazines. Siegel lives in Wilmington, North Carolina.

Maura Stanton, "Oh Shenandoah"

This story started with a true incident. One May in Venice, where I'd gone to escape the spring pollen, I broke the toilet seat in the apartment I was renting. I was afraid the landlady would charge me a fortune, so I decided to replace it myself. I wandered around Venice, with some addresses copied from the phone book, but I had no luck at all. It was an absurd quest in a city full of glass and lace and masks and marbled paper. Eventually I gave up, and paid the landlady thirty euros.

But I was writing stories about Venice, and the quest for the toilet seat seemed like something that might be interesting to write about—the unromantic side of Venice. But I didn't really have a story, just an anecdote, for a long time. Then Marie appeared. As I struggled to get the story going, I glanced up at a postcard from a neighbor pinned to my bulletin board, and I gave it to Marie. That's how Virginia Woolf's quote got into the story and contributed to the theme. Then Hugo appeared. Once my characters took over, the story started to breathe and grow. Marie had a decision to make about her relationship with Hugo. Who was Hugo? I recalled being thrilled a few years ago on another trip to Venice by a chorus of college students singing "Shenandoah" on the Strada Nova—so I put them into the story and Hugo came into focus. And once my invented world got untethered from the real world, and started obeying its own laws, I was finally able to find that toilet seat.

Maura Stanton was born in Evanston, Illinois, and grew up in Chicago, Peoria, and Minneapolis. She has published a novel, *Molly Companion,* and three books of short stories, *The Country I Come From; Do Not Forsake Me, Oh My Darling;* and *Cities in the Sea,* as well as six books of poetry, including *Snow on Snow,* which won the Yale Series of Younger Poets award. She is the recipient of two fellowships from the National Endowment for the Arts, and her stories have won the Nelson Algren Award from the *Chicago Tribune,* the Lawrence Foundation Prize from the *Michigan Quarterly Review,* and the Michigan Literary Fiction Award. She lives in Bloomington, Indiana.

William Trevor, "The Women"
William Trevor was born in 1928 at Mitchelstown, County Cork, and spent his childhood in provincial Ireland. His novels include *Fools of Fortune, Felicia's Journey,* and *The Story of Lucy Gault.* He is a renowned short-story writer and has published fifteen story collections, from *The Day We Got Drunk on Cake* to his most recent, *Selected Stories.* Trevor lives in Devon, England.

Kirstin Valdez Quade, "Nemecia"
When I was a child, the best items in my dress-up box had once belonged to my godmother: chiffon gowns, fur stoles, heeled satin slippers with pink feathers on the toes. In the thirties and forties, my godmother had been a successful competitive ballroom dancer in Hollywood. When I knew her, she was already in her eighties, but she was still blond and made-up. She was generous and expansive and always laughing. I adored her.

Only after her death did I learn details she'd never spoken of: She'd grown up not in Los Angeles, but in the same dusty little New Mexico town my relatives came from. Her first language was Spanish and she wasn't a natural blonde. I learned that when she was five years old, my godmother had watched as her father brutally beat her mother and murdered her grandfather.

The story I heard was just an outline, and Nemecia isn't my godmother. I reshaped these events and peopled them with fictional characters who brought their own agendas and needs to the story. As I wrote I was thinking about the complicated effects of trauma: the way it can elevate and debase, connect and isolate. Trauma can make us more resilient, yes, more empathetic, maybe, yet it can also make us small and ugly and self-protective. Sometimes trauma does all these things at once.

Kirstin Valdez Quade was born in Albuquerque, New Mexico, and lived all over the Southwest as a child. She was a Wallace Stegner and a Truman Capote Fellow at Stanford University, and her fiction has appeared in *The New Yorker, The Best American Short Stories 2013, Narrative, Guernica, Best of the West 2010,* and elsewhere. She won a 2013 Rona Jaffe Foundation Writers' Award and has received fellowships and grants from Yaddo, the MacDowell Colony, and the Elizabeth George Foundation. Her story collection and novel are forthcoming. She lives in the Bay Area.

Laura van den Berg, "Opa-locka"
In the spring of 2011, I was a writer in residence at the Gilman School, an all-boys school in Baltimore. I started "Opa-locka" in my office at Gilman; I liked the energy there. I was thinking a lot about sisters and also about Florida, where I'm from, and at my desk, with the sound of teenage boys roaming the halls in the background, I wrote the first paragraph, then got stuck for a while. I knew I wanted a mystery to surround Mr. Defonte, but I couldn't figure out what I wanted the outcome of the mystery to be, the overall trajectory of the story. When I realized that this story was not about solving a mystery but rather about the unsolvability of so many of our personal mysteries, about what being consumed by mystery can do to a person over time, I got unstuck in a hurry.

Laura van den Berg is the author of the story collections *The Isle of Youth* and *What the World Will Look Like When All the Water Leaves Us,* which was a Barnes & Noble "Discover Great New Writers" selection and shortlisted for the Frank O'Connor International Short Story Award. Her first novel, *Find Me,* is forthcoming in 2015. A Florida native, she lives in the Boston area.

Publications Submitted

Stories published in American and Canadian magazines are eligible for consideration for inclusion in *The O. Henry Prize Stories*. Stories must be written originally in the English language. No translations are considered. Sections of novels are not considered. Editors are asked not to nominate individual stories. Stories may not be submitted by agents or writers.

Editors are invited to submit online fiction for consideration, but such submissions must be sent to the address on the next page in the form of a legible hard copy. The publication's contact information and the date of the story's publication must accompany the submissions.

Because of production deadlines for the 2015 collection, it is essential that stories reach the series editor by July 1, 2014. If a finished magazine is unavailable before the deadline, magazine editors are welcome to submit scheduled stories in proof or manuscript. Publications received after July 1, 2014, will automatically be considered for *The O. Henry Prize Stories 2016*.

Please see our Web site, www.ohenryprizestories.com, for more information about submission to *The O. Henry Prize Stories*.

The address for submission is:

Laura Furman, Series Editor, The O. Henry Prize Stories
The University of Texas at Austin
English Department, B5000
1 University Station
Austin, TX 78712

The information listed below was up-to-date when *The O. Henry Prize Stories 2014* went to press. Inclusion in this listing does not constitute endorsement or recommendation by *The O. Henry Prize Stories* or Anchor Books.

A Public Space
323 Dean Street
Brooklyn, NY 11217
Brigid Hughes, editor
general@apublicspace.org
apublicspace.org
quarterly

AGNI Magazine
Boston University
236 Bay State Road
Boston, MA 02215
agni@bu.edu
bu.edu/agni
semiannual

Alaska Quarterly Review
University of Alaska Anchorage
3211 Providence Drive
Anchorage, AK 99508
Ronald Spatz, editor
aqr@uaa.alaska.edu
uaa.alaska.edu/aqr
semiannual

Alligator Juniper
Prescott College
220 Grove Avenue
Prescott, AZ 86301
Skye Anicca, editor
alligatorjuniper@prescott.edu
prescott.edu/alligator_juniper
annual

American Athenaeum
Hunter Liguore, editor
editor@swordandsagapress.com
swordandsagapress.com/
American-Athenaeum.php
quarterly

American Letters & Commentary
Department of English
University of Texas at San Antonio
One UTSA Circle
San Antonio, TX 78249
David Ray Vance and Catherine
Kasper, editors
AmerLetters@satx.rr.com
amletters.org
annual

American Literary Review
PO Box 311307
University of North Texas
Denton, TX 76203-1307
Ann McCutchan, editor
americanliteraryreview@gmail.com
engl.unt.edu/alr
semiannual

American Short Fiction
PO Box 4152
Austin, TX 78765
Rebecca Markovits and Adeena
    Reitberger, editors
editors@americanshortfiction.org
americanshortfiction.org
triannual

Apalachee Review
PO Box 10469
Tallahassee, FL 32302
Michael Trammell and Jenn
    Bronson, editors
mtrammell@cob.fsu.edu
apalacheereview.org
semiannual

Arkansas Review
PO Box 1890
Arkansas State University
State University, AR 72467
Janelle Collins, editor
arkansasreview@astate.edu
altweb.astate.edu/arkreview
triannual

Armchair/Shotgun
377 Flatbush Avenue
Brooklyn, NY 11238-4393
Aaron Reuben, editor
info@armchairshotgun.com
armchairshotgun.wordpress.com
semiannual

Arroyo Literary Review
Department of English, MB 2579
California State University, East
    Bay
25800 Carlos Bee Boulevard
Hayward, CA 94542
Christopher Morgan, editor
arroyoliteraryreview@gmail.com
arroyoliteraryreview.com
annual

Baltimore Review
Barbara Westwood Diehl and
    Kathleen Hellen, editors
editor@baltimorereview.org
baltimorereview.org
quarterly

Bellevue Literary Review
NYU Langone Medical Center
Department of Medicine
550 First Avenue, OBV-A612
New York, NY 10016
Ronna Wineberg, JD, editor
info@BLReview.org
BLReview.org
semiannual

Black Clock
California Institute of the Arts
24700 McBean Parkway
Valencia, CA 91355
Steve Erickson, editor
info@blackclock.org
blackclock.org
semiannual

Black Warrior Review
Office of Student Media
The University of Alabama
PO Box 870170
Tuscaloosa, AL 35487
Kirby Johnson, editor
blackwarriorreview@gmail.com
bwr.ua.edu
semiannual

Bodega
Emily Pan, editor
editor@bodegamag.com
bodegamag.com
monthly

BOMB Magazine
80 Hanson Place
Suite 703
Brooklyn, NY 11217
Betsy Sussler, editor
generalinquiries@bombsite.com
bombsite.com
quarterly

bosque (the magazine)
Lynn C. Miller and Lisa Lenard-
   Cook, editors
admin@abqwriterscoop.com
abqwriterscoop.com/bosque.html
annual

Boulevard Magazine
6614 Clayton Road
Box 325
Richmond Heights, MO 63117
Richard Burgin, editor
richardburgin@att.net
boulevardmagazine.org
triannual

Brain, Child
Publishing Office
341 Newtown Turnpike
Wilton, CT 06897
Marcelle Soviero, editor
editorial@brainchildmag.com
brainchildmag.com
quarterly

Calyx
PO Box B
Corvallis, OR 97339
editorial collective
info@calyxpress.org
calyxpress.org
semiannual

Camera Obscura
c/o Sfumato Press
PO Box 2356
Addison, TX 75001
M. E. Parker, editor
editor@obscurajournal.com
obscurajournal.com
semiannual

Carve Magazine
PO Box 701510
Dallas, TX 75370
Matthew Limpede, editor
managingeditor@carvezine.com
carvezine.com
quarterly

Chicago Review
Taft House
935 East 60th Street
Chicago, IL 60637
Joel Calahan and Chalcey Wilding,
    editors
chicago-review@uchicago.edu
humanities.uchicago.edu/orgs
    /review
triannual

Cimarron Review
Oklahoma State University
English Department
205 Morrill Hall
Stillwater, OK 74078
Toni Graham, editor
cimarronreview@okstate.edu
cimarronreview.com
quarterly

Colorado Review
9105 Campus Delivery
Department of English
Colorado State University
Fort Collins, CO 80523-9105
Stephanie G'Schwind, editor
creview@colostate.edu
coloradoreview.colostate.edu
triannual

Confrontation Magazine
720 Northern Boulevard
Brookville, NY 11548
Jonna G. Semeiks, editor
confrontationmag@gmail.com
confrontationmagazine.org
semiannual

Conjunctions
21 East 10th Street, #3E
New York, NY 10003
Bradford Morrow, editor
conjunctions@bard.edu
conjunctions.com
semiannual

Consequence Magazine
PO Box 323
Cohasset, MA 02025
George Kovach, editor
consequencemagazine.org
annual

Crab Orchard Review
Department of English
Faner Hall 2380
Mail Code 4503
Southern Illinois University,
    Carbondale
1000 Faner Drive
Carbondale, IL 62901
Allison Joseph, editor
craborchardreview.siu.edu
semiannual

Crazyhorse
Department of English
College of Charleston
66 George Street
Charleston, SC 29424
Jonathan Bohr Heinen, editor
crazyhorse@cofc.edu
crazyhorse.cofc.edu
semiannual

cream city review
Department of English
University of Wisconsin–Milwaukee
PO Box 413
Milwaukee, WI 53201
Ching-In Chen, editor
info@creamcityreview.org
creamcityreview.org
semiannual

CutBank
University of Montana
English Department, LA 133
Missoula, MT 59812
Rachel Mindell, editor
editor.cutbank@gmail.com
cutbankonline.org
semiannual

Cutthroat
Raven's Word Writers Center
PO Box 2414
Durango, CO 81302
Pamela Uschuk, editor
cutthroatmag@gmail.com
cutthroatmag.com
annual

Dappled Things
Meredith Wise, editor
dappledthings.editor@gmail.com
dappledthings.org
quarterly

Denver Quarterly
University of Denver
Department of English
2000 East Asbury
Denver, CO 80208
Laird Hunt, editor
denverquarterly.com
quarterly

descant
c/o TCU Department of English
Box 29727014
2850 South University Drive
Fort Worth, TX 76129
Dave Kuhne, editor
descant@tcu.edu
descant.tcu.edu
annual

Ecotone
Department of Creative Writing
University of North Carolina,
    Wilmington
601 South College Road
Wilmington, NC 28403-5938
Anna Lena Phillips, editor
info@ecotonejournal.com
ecotonejournal.com
semiannual

Electric Literature's
    Recommended Reading
147 Prince Street
Brooklyn, NY 11201
Halimah Marcus and Benjamin
    Samuel, editors
http://recommendedreading
    .tumblr.com
weekly (digital)

Epoch
Cornell University
251 Goldwin Smith Hall
Ithaca, NY 14853-3201
Michael Koch, editor
english.arts.cornell.edu
    /publications/epoch
triannual

Event
PO Box 2503
New Westminster, BC V3L 5B2
Canada
Elizabeth Bachinsky, editor
event@douglascollege.ca
eventmags.com
triannual

Fantasy & Science Fiction
PO Box 3447
Hoboken, NJ 07030
Gordon Van Gelder, editor
fsfmag@fandsf.com
sfsite.com/fsf
bimonthly

Fence
Science Library 320
University at Albany
1400 Washington Avenue
Albany, NY 12222
Rebecca Wolff, editor
rebecca.fence@gmail.com
fenceportal.org
semiannual

Fiction
Department of English
The City College of New York
138th Street and Convent Avenue
New York, NY 10031
Mark Jay Mirsky, editor
fictionmagazine@yahoo.com
fictioninc.com
semiannual

Fifth Wednesday Journal
PO Box 4033
Lisle, IL 60532-9033
Vern Miller, editor
editors@fifthwednesdayjournal.org
fifthwednesdayjournal.org
semiannual

Five Points
Georgia State University
PO Box 3999
Atlanta, GA 30302-3999
Megan Sexton, editor
fivepoints@gsu.edu
fivepoints.gsu.edu
triannual

Fjords Review
2932 B Langhorne Road
Lynchburg, VA 24501
John Gosslee, editor
editors@fjordsreview.com
fjordsreview.com
semiannual

Flyway
Michelle Donahue, editor
flywayjournal@gmail.com
flyway.org
published every six weeks

Fourteen Hills
Department of Creative Writing
San Francisco State University
1600 Holloway Avenue
San Francisco, CA 94132
Ari Moskowitz and Monique Mero,
    editors
14hills.net
semiannual

Gargoyle
3819 North 13th Street
Arlington, VA 22201
Richard Peabody and Lucinda
    Ebersole, editors
rchrdpeabody9@gmail.com
gargoylemagazine.com
annual

Glimmer Train
4763 SW Maplewood Road
PO Box 80430
Portland, OR 97280-1430
Susan Burmeister-Brown and Linda
    B. Swanson-Davies, editors
editors@glimmertrain.org
glimmertrain.org
quarterly

Gold Man Review
Heather Cuthbertson, editor
goldmanreview.org
annual

Grain Magazine
PO Box 67
Saskatoon, SK S7K 3K1
Canada
Rilla Friesen, editor
grainmag@sasktel.net
grainmagazine.ca
quarterly

Granta
12 Addison Avenue
London W11 4QR
United Kingdom
Yuka Igarashi, editor
editorial@granta.com
granta.com
quarterly

Grey Sparrow Journal
PO Box 211664
St. Paul, MN 55121
Diane Smith, editor
dsdianefuller@gmail.com
greysparrowpress.sharepoint.com
quarterly

Gulf Coast
Department of English
University of Houston
Houston, TX 77204-3013
Nick Flynn, editor
editors@gulfcoastmag.org
gulfcoastmag.org
semiannual

Harvard Review
Lamont Library
Harvard University
Cambridge, MA 02138
Christina Thompson, editor
info@harvardreview.org
harvardreview.fas.harvard.edu
semiannual

Hayden's Ferry Review
c/o Virginia G. Piper Center for
  Creative Writing
Arizona State University
PO Box 875002
Tempe, AZ 85287-5002
Beth Staples, editor
hfr@asu.edu
haydensferryreview.org
semiannual

Hobart
Aaron Burch, editor
aaron@hobartpulp.com
hobartpulp.com
published three times every
  two years

Indiana Review
Indiana University
Ballantine Hall 465
1020 East Kirkwood Avenue
Bloomington, IN 47405-7103
Katie Moulton, editor
inreview@indiana.edu
indianareview.org
semiannual

Iron Horse Literary Review
Texas Tech University
English Department
Mail Stop 43091
Lubbock, TX 79409-3091
Leslie Jill Patterson, editor
ihlr.mail@gmail.com
ironhorsereview.com
published six times a year

J Journal
Department of English
John Jay College of Criminal Justice
524 West 59th Street, 7th Floor
New York, NY 10019
Adam Berlin and Jeffrey Heiman,
  editors
jjournal@jjay.cuny.edu
johnjay.jjay.cuny.edu/jjournal
semiannual

Jabberwock Review
Department of English
Mississippi State University
Drawer E
Mississippi State, MS 39762
Becky Hagenston, editor
jabberwockreview@english
.msstate.edu
jabberwock.org.msstate.edu
semiannual

**Lady Churchill's Rosebud
Wristlet**
150 Pleasant Street, #306
Easthampton, MA 01027
Gavin J. Grant and Kelly Link,
editors
info@smallbeerpress.com
smallbeerpress.com/lcrw
semiannual

Literary Imagination
Archie Burnett and Saskia
Hamilton, editors
litimag.oxfordjournals.org
triannual

MAKE
2822 West Dickens #3
Chicago, IL 60647
Sarah Dodson, editor
info@makemag.com
makemag.com
semiannual

MĀNOA
Department of English
University of Hawai'i
1733 Donaghho Road
Honolulu, HI 96822
Frank Stewart, editor
mjournal-l@lists.hawaii.edu
hawaii.edu/mjournal
semiannual

**Timothy McSweeney's Quarterly
Concern**
849 Valencia Street
San Francisco, CA 94110
Dave Eggers, editor
printsubmissions@mcsweeneys.net
mcsweeneys.net/books
quarterly

Meridian
University of Virginia
PO Box 400145
Charlottesville, VA 22904-4145
Jocelyn Sears, editor
meridianuva@gmail.com
readmeridian.org
semiannual

Michigan Quarterly Review
University of Michigan
0576 Rackham Building
915 East Washington Street
Ann Arbor, MI 48109-1070
Jonathan Freedman, editor
mqr@umich.edu
michiganquarterlyreview.com
quarterly

n+1
68 Jay Street, Suite 45
Brooklyn, NY 11201
Carla Blumencranz, Keith Gessen,
    and Nikil Saval, editors
editors@nplusonemag.com
nplusonemag.com
triannual

Narrative
Carol Edgarian and Tom Jenks,
    editors
narrativemagazine.com
annual

Natural Bridge
Department of English
University of Missouri–St. Louis
One University Boulevard
St. Louis, MO 63121
Mary Troy, editor
natural@umsl.edu
blogs.umsl.edu/naturalbridge
semiannual

New England Review
Middlebury College
Middlebury, VT 05753
Stephen Donadio, editor
nereview@middlebury.edu
nereview.com
quarterly

New Letters
University of Missouri–Kansas City
University House
5101 Rockhill Road
Kansas City, MO 64110-2499
Robert Stewart, editor
newletters@umkc.edu
newletters.org
quarterly

New Orleans Review
Box 195
Loyola University
New Orleans, LA 70118
Mark Yakich, editor
noreview@loyno.edu
neworleansreview.org
semiannual

Nimrod International Journal
800 South Tucker Drive
Tulsa, Oklahoma 74104-3189
Eilis O'Neal, editor
nimrod@utulsa.edu
utulsa.edu/nimrod
semiannual

Ninth Letter
Department of English
University of Illinois, Urbana-
    Champaign
608 South Wright Street
Urbana, IL 61801
Jodee Stanley, editor
editor@ninthletter.com
ninthletter.com
semiannual

Noon
1324 Lexington Avenue
PMB 298
New York, NY 10128
Diane Williams, editor
noonannual.com
annual

North Carolina Literary Review
Department of English
East Carolina University
Mailstop 555 English
Greenville, NC 27858-4353
Margaret D. Bauer, editor
BauerM@ecu.edu
www.nclr.ecu.edu
annual

North Dakota Quarterly
276 Centennial Drive Stop 7209
Merrifield Hall Room 15
Grand Forks, ND 58202-7209
Kate Sweney, editor
und.ndq@email.und.edu
arts-sciences.und.edu/north-
    dakota-quarterly
quarterly

Northern New England Review
Franklin Pierce University
Humanities Department
40 University Drive
Rindge, NH 03461
NNER@franklinpierce.edu
annual

Notre Dame Review
University of Notre Dame
840 Flanner Hall
Notre Dame, IN 46556
William O'Rourke, editor
english.ndreview.1@nd.edu
ndreview.nd.edu
semiannual

One Story
232 3rd Street, #A108
Brooklyn, NY 11215
Hannah Tinti, editor
one-story.com
published every three weeks

Orion
187 Main Street
Great Barrington, MA 01230
H. Emerson Blake, editor
orionmagazine.org
bimonthly

Overtime
PO Box 250382
Plano, TX 75025-0382
David LaBounty, editor
info@workerswritejournal.com
workerswritejournal.com/index.htm
bimonthly

Oyster Boy Review
PO Box 1483
Pacifica, CA 94044
Damon Sauve, editor
email_2014@oysterboyreview.org
oysterboyreview.org
published erratically

Pakn Treger
The Yiddish Book Center
Harry and Jeanette Weinberg
    Building
1021 West Street
Amherst, MA 01002
yiddish@bikher.org
yiddishbookcenter.org
triannual

Passages North
Northern Michigan University
1401 Presque Isle Avenue
Marquette, MI 49855
Jennifer A. Howard, editor
passages@nmu.edu
passagesnorth.com
annual

Pilot Pocket Book
PO Box 161, Station B
119 Spadina Avenue
Toronto, ON M5T 2T3
Canada
editor@thepilotproject.ca
thepilotproject.ca
annual

Ploughshares
Emerson College
120 Boylston Street
Boston, MA 02116
Ladette Randolph, editor
pshares@pshares.org
pshares.org/index.cfm
triannual

PMS poemmemoirstory
HB 217
1530 3rd Avenue South
Birmingham, AL 35294-1260
Kerry Madden, editor
poemmemoirstory@gmail.com
pms-journal.org
annual

Potomac Review
Montgomery College
51 Mannakee Street, MT/212
Rockville, MD 20850
Julie Wakeman-Linn, editor
PotomacReviewEditor@
    montgomerycollege.edu
cms.montgomerycollege.edu
    /EDU/Alt.aspx?id=18937
semiannual

Post Road Magazine
PO Box 600721
Newton, MA 02460
Jaime Clarke and David Ryan,
    editors
info@postroadmag.com
postroadmag.com
semiannual

Prairie Fire
423-100 Arthur Street
Winnipeg, Manitoba R3B 1H3
Canada
Andris Taskans, editor
prfire@prairiefire.ca
prairiefire.ca
quarterly

Prairie Schooner
123 Andrews Hall
University of Nebraska–Lincoln
Lincoln, NE 68588-0334
Kwame Dawes, editor
prairieschooner@unl.edu
prairieschooner.unl.edu
quarterly

PRISM international
Creative Writing Program
University of British Columbia
Buchanan E462
1866 Main Mall
Vancouver, BC, V6T 1Z1
Canada
Jane Campbell, editor
prismprose@gmail.com
prismmagazine.ca
quarterly

Raritan
31 Mine Street
New Brunswick, NJ 08901
Jackson Lears, editor
rqr@rci.rutgers.edu
raritanquarterly.rutgers.edu
quarterly

Redivider
Department of Writing, Literature
and Publishing
Emerson College
120 Boylston Street
Boston, MA 02116
Lauren Kay Halloran, editor
fiction@redividerjournal.org
redividerjournal.org
semiannual

Red Rock Review
English Department, J2A
College of Southern Nevada
3200 East Cheyenne Avenue
North Las Vegas, NV 89030
Todd Moffett, editor
RedRockReview@csn.edu
sites.csn.edu/english
   /redrockreview/index.htm
semiannual

River Styx
3547 Olive Street
Suite 107
St. Louis, MO 63103
Richard Newman, editor
BigRiver@riverstyx.org
riverstyx.org
triannual

Roanoke Review
Roanoke College
Salem, VA 24153
Paul Hanstedt, editor
review@roanoke.edu
roanokereview.wordpress.com
annual

Salamander
Suffolk University
English Department
41 Temple Street
Boston, MA 02114
Jennifer Barber, editor
salamandermag.org
semiannual

Salmagundi Magazine
Skidmore College
Attn: Salmagundi Journal
815 North Broadway
Saratoga Springs, NY 12866
Robert Boyers, editor
salmagun@skidmore.edu
cms.skidmore.edu/salmagundi
quarterly

Santa Monica Review
Santa Monica College
1900 Pico Boulevard
Santa Monica, CA 90405
Andrew Tonkovich, editor
www2.smc.edu/sm_review
    /default.htm
semiannual

The Saranac Review
The Department of English
Champlain Valley Hall
101 Broad Street
Plattsburgh, NY 12901
J. L. Torres, editor
saranacreview@plattsburgh.edu
research.plattsburgh.edu
    /saranacreview
annual

So to Speak
George Mason University
4400 University Drive, MSN 2C5
Fairfax, VA 22030-4444
Michele Johnson, editor
sotospeakjournal.org
triannual

Southern Humanities Review
Department of English
Auburn University
9088 Haley Center
Auburn University, AL 36849-
    5202
Chantel Acevedo, editor
shrengl@auburn.edu
cla.auburn.edu/shr
quarterly

Southern Indiana Review
Orr Center, #2009
University of Southern Indiana
8600 University Boulevard
Evansville, IN 47712
Ron Mitchell, editor
usi.edu/sir
semiannual

Southwest Review
Southern Methodist University
PO Box 750374
Dallas, TX 75275-0374
Willard Spiegelman, editor
swr@smu.edu
smu.edu/southwestreview
quarterly

subTerrain
PO Box 3008, MPO
Vancouver, BC V6B 3X5
Canada
Brian Kaufman, editor
subter@portal.ca
subterrain.ca
triannual

Subtropics
Department of English
University of Florida
PO Box 112075
4008 Turlington Hall
Gainesville, FL 32611-2075
David Leavitt, editor
subtropics@english.ufl.edu
english.ufl.edu/subtropics
triannual

Swink
Darcy Cosper, editor
swinkmag.com
monthly

Tampa Review
The University of Tampa
401 West Kennedy Boulevard
Tampa, FL 33606-1490
Richard Mathews, editor
utpress@ut.edu
ut.edu/tampareview
semiannual

The American Scholar
1606 New Hampshire Avenue NW
Washington, DC 20009
Robert Wilson, editor
scholar@pbk.org
theamericanscholar.org
quarterly

The Antioch Review
PO Box 148
Yellow Springs, OH 45387
Robert S. Fogarty, editor
mkeyes@antiochreview.org
review.antiochcollege.org/antioch
_review
quarterly

The Atlantic Monthly
600 New Hampshire Avenue, NW
Washington, DC 20037
C. Michael Curtis, editor
theatlantic.com/magazine
monthly

The Briar Cliff Review
3303 Rebecca Street
Sioux City, IA 5114-2100
Tricia Currans-Sheehan, editor
Tricia.Currans-Sheehan@briarcliff
.edu
old.briarcliff.edu/campus/bc
_review/bcreview_new/about
.aspx
annual

The Carolina Quarterly
510 Greenlaw Hall
CB# 3520
The University of North Carolina
at Chapel Hill
Chapel Hill, NC 27599-3520
Matthew Hotham, editor
carolina.quarterly@gmail.com
thecarolinaquarterly.com
triannual

The Cincinnati Review
PO Box 210069
Cincinnati, OH 45221-0069
editors@cincinnatireview.com
cincinnatireview.com
semiannual

The Fiddlehead
Campus House
11 Garland Court
PO Box 4400
University of New Brunswick
Fredericton, NB E3B 5A3
Canada
Ross Leckie, editor
fiddlehd@unb.ca
thefiddlehead.ca/index.html
quarterly

The Florida Review
Department of English
University of Central Florida
PO Box 161346
Orlando, FL 32816-1346
Jocelyn Bartkevicius, editor
flreview@mail.ucf.edu
floridareview.cah.ucf.edu
semiannual

The Georgia Review
706A Main Library
320 South Jackson Street
The University of Georgia
Athens, GA 30602-9009
Stephen Corey, editor
garev@uga.edu
garev.uga.edu
quarterly

The Hudson Review
684 Park Avenue
New York, NY 10065
Paula Deitz, editor
info@hudsonreview.com
hudsonreview.com
quarterly

The Idaho Review
Department of English
Boise State University
1910 University Drive
Boise, ID 83725-1525
Mitch Wieland, editor
idahoreview@boisestate.edu
idahoreview.org
annual

The Iowa Review
The University of Iowa
308 English-Philosophy Building
Iowa City, IA 52242
Harilaos Stecopoulos, editor
iowa-review@uiowa.edu
iowareview.uiowa.edu
triannual

The Kenyon Review
Finn House
102 West Wiggin Street
Kenyon College
Gambier, OH 43022-9623
David H. Lynn, editor
kenyonreview@kenyon.edu
kenyonreview.org
quarterly

The Literary Review
Fairleigh Dickinson University
285 Madison Avenue
Madison, NJ 07940
Minna Proctor, editor
info@theliteraryreview.org
theliteraryreview.org/index.php
quarterly

The Long Story
18 Eaton Street
Lawrence, MA 01843
R. P. Burnham, editor
rpburnham@mac.com
longstorylitmag.com
annual

The Louisville Review
Spalding University
851 South Fourth Street
Louisville, KY 40203
Sena Jeter Naslund, editor
louisvillereview@spalding.edu
louisvillereview.org
semiannual

The Malahat Review
University of Victoria
PO Box 1700
Stn CSC
Victoria, BC V8W 2Y2
Canada
John Barton, editor
info@magazinescanada.ca
web.uvic.ca/malahat
quarterly

The Missouri Review
357 McReynolds Hall
University of Missouri
Columbia, MO 65211
Speer Morgan, editor
question@moreview.com
missourireview.com
quarterly

The New Yorker
4 Times Square
New York, NY 10036
Deborah Treisman, editor
fiction@newyorker.com
newyorker.com
weekly

The Oxford American
201 Donaghey Avenue
Conway, AR 72035
Roger D. Hodge, editor
editors@oxfordamerican.org
oxfordamerican.org
quarterly

The Paris Review
544 West 27th Street
New York, NY 10001
Lorin Stein, editor
queries@theparisreview.org
theparisreview.org
quarterly

The Pinch
English Department
University of Memphis
Memphis, TN 38152
Kristen Iversen, editor
editor@thepinchjournal.com
thepinchjournal.com
semiannual

The Saturday Evening Post
1100 Waterway Boulevard
Indianapolis, IN 46202
editor@saturdayeveningpost.com
saturdayeveningpost.com
published six times a year

The Sewanee Review
The University of the South
735 University Avenue
Sewanee, TN 37383
George Core, editor
sewanee.edu/sewanee_review
quarterly

The Southeast Review
Department of English
Florida State University
Tallahassee, FL 32306
Brandi Lee George, editor
southeastreview@gmail.com
southeastreview.org
semiannual

The Southern Review
3990 West Lakeshore Drive
Louisiana State University
Baton Rouge, LA 70808
Jessica Faust and Emily Nemens,
   editors
southernreview@lsu.edu
thesouthernreview.org
quarterly

The Thomas Wolfe Review
4778 Westside Drive
La Verne, CA 91750-1862
Paula G. Eckard, editor
arzahlan@eiu.edu
thomaswolfereview.org
annual

The Threepenny Review
PO Box 9131
Berkeley, CA 94709
Wendy Lesser, editor
wlesser@threepennyreview.com
threepennyreview.com
quarterly

The Westchester Review
PO Box 246H
Scarsdale, NY 10583
Naomi L. Lipman, editor
westchesterreview@gmail.com
westchesterreview.com
annual

The Worcester Review
1 Ekman Street
Worcester, MA 01607
Diane Vanaskie Mulligan, editor
twr.diane@gmail.com
www.theworcesterreview.org
annual

Third Coast
Western Michigan University
English Department
1903 West Michigan Avenue
Kalamazoo, MI 49008-5331
Laurie Ann Cedilnik, editor
editors@thirdcoastmagazine.com
thirdcoastmagazine.com
semiannual

Tin House
PO Box 10500
Portland, OR 97210
Rob Spillman, editor
info@tinhouse.com
tinhouse.com
quarterly

Weber: The Contemporary West
Weber State University
1214 University Circle
Ogden, UT 84408-1214
Michael Wutz, editor
weberjournal@weber.edu
weber.edu/weberjournal
semiannual

Western Humanities Review
University of Utah
English Department
255 South Central Campus Drive
LNCO 3500
Salt Lake City, UT 84112-0494
Barry Weller, editor
whr@mail.hum.utah.edu
ourworld.info/whrweb
triannual

Willow Springs
501 North Riverpoint Boulevard
Suite 425
Spokane, WA 99202
Samuel Ligon, editor
willowspringsewu@gmail.com
willowsprings.ewu.edu
semiannual

Witness Magazine
Black Mountain Institute
University of Nevada, Las Vegas
Box 455085
Las Vegas, NV 89154-5085
Maile Chapman, editor
witness@unlv.edu
witness.blackmountaininstitute.org
annual print, semiannual online

WLA: War, Literature & the Arts
Department of English and Fine
  Arts
2354 Fairchild Drive
Suite 6D-149
United States Air Force Academy
Colorado Springs, CO 80840-
  6242
Donald Anderson, editor
donald.anderson@usafa.edu
wlajournal.com
annual

Workers Write!
PO Box 250382
Plano, TX 75025-0382
David LaBounty, editor
info@workerswritejournal.com
workerswritejournal.com
annual

Zoetrope: All-Story
916 Kearny Street
San Francisco, CA 94133
Michael Ray, editor
info@all-story.com
www.all-story.com
quarterly

Zone 3
Austin Peay State University
Box 4565
Clarksville, TN 37044
Barry Kitterman, editor
zone3@apsu.edu
apsu.edu/zone3
semiannual

ZYZZYVA
466 Geary Street
Suite 401
San Francisco, CA 94102
Laura Cogan, editor
editor@zyzzyva.org
zyzzyva.org
quarterly

Permissions